TIS THE SEASON TO FALL IN LOVE

Were you naughty or nice this year? Will Santa be bringing you love for the holidays . . . or will that guy in the Santa suit turn out to *be* your true love? Anything can happen when that holiday magic is in the air—hearts can be lost, hearts can be won, and you never know *who* you'll meet under the mistletoe.

So raise a cup of holiday cheer in a toast to romance, and enjoy six heartwarming stories by Stacey Dennis, Marjorie Eatock, Martha Gross, Helen Playfair, Peggy Roberts, and Joan Shapiro. Love is grand any time of year. But at Christmas, the chance to love again is a very special gift.

WATCH AS THESE WOMEN LEARN
TO LOVE AGAIN

HELLO LOVE (4094, $4.50/$5.50)
by Joan Shapiro

Family tragedy leaves Barbara Sinclair alone with her success. The fight to gain custody of her young granddaughter brings a confrontation with the determined rancher Sam Douglass. Also widowed, Sam has been caring for Emily alone, guided by his own ideas of childrearing. Barbara challenges his ideas. And that's not all she challenges . . . Long-buried desires surface, then gentle affection. Sam and Barbara cannot ignore the chance to love again.

THE BEST MEDICINE (4220, $4.50/$5.50)
by Janet Lane Walters

Her late husband's expenses push Maggie Carr back to nursing, the career she left almost thirty years ago. The night shift is difficult, but it's harder still to ignore the way handsome Dr. Jason Knight soothes his patients. When she lends a hand to help his daughter, Jason and Maggie grow closer than simply doctor and nurse. Obstacles to romance seem insurmountable, but Maggie knows that love is always the best medicine.

AND BE MY LOVE (4291, $4.50/$5.50)
by Joyce C. Ware

Selflessly catering first to husband, then children, grandchildren, and her aging, though imperious mother, leaves Beth Volmar little time for her own adventures or passions. Then, the handsome archaeologist Karim Donovan arrives and campaigns to widen the boundaries of her narrow life. Beth finds new freedom when Karim insists that she accompany him to Turkey on an archaeological dig . . . and a journey towards loving again.

OVER THE RAINBOW (4032, $4.50/$5.50)
by Marjorie Eatock

Fifty-something, divorced for years, courted by more than one attractive man, and thoroughly enjoying her job with a large insurance company, Marian's sudden restlessness confuses her. She welcomes the chance to travel on business to a small Mississippi town. Full of good humor and words of love, Don Worth makes her feel needed, and not just to assess property damage. Marian takes the risk.

A KISS AT SUNRISE (4260, $4.50/$5.50)
by Charlotte Sherman

Beginning widowhood and retirement, Ruth Nichols has her first taste of freedom. Against the advice of her mother and daughter, Ruth heads for an adventure in the motor home that has sat unused since her husband's death. Long days and lonely campgrounds start to dampen the excitement of traveling alone. That is, until a dapper widower named Jack parks next door and invites her for dinner. On the road, Ruth and Jack find the chance to love again.

Available wherever paperbacks are sold, or order direct from the Publisher. Send cover price plus 50¢ per copy for mailing and handling to Zebra Books, Dept. 4379, 475 Park Avenue South, New York, N.Y. 10016. Residents of New York and Tennessee must include sales tax. DO NOT SEND CASH. For a free Zebra/Pinnacle catalog please write to the above address.

MERRY CHRISTMAS, MY LOVE

Stacey Dennis　　　　Helen Playfair
Marjorie Eatock　　　Peggy Roberts
Martha Gross　　　　Joan Shapiro

ZEBRA BOOKS
KENSINGTON PUBLISHING CORP.

CONTENTS

An Affair with Santa

by

Stacey Dennis

"Come on, Katherine, it'll be fun," Iris Johnson said, leaning against Katherine Dumont's makeshift desk. The Hillsburg Rehabilitation Center was dedicated to helping each and every patient who came through the doors. It had the very latest in modern technology and hired only the best, most highly qualified therapists. But Hillsburg had no room for unnecessary frills, hence Katherine's tiny desk that had been hastily crammed into a spare corner when she'd complained that she had no place to write her reports.

Katherine finished writing and laid the folder on top of a growing stack of patient's charts. "The mall, on the last Friday before Christmas?" Her dark brows rose, and she grinned. "Surely you jest." It sounded like pure madness—and just what Katherine needed to lift her out of the doldrums.

At that exact moment Pat Henshaw arrived at

"Katherine's corner," as the other therapists had dubbed the makeshift office. "She's right, Katherine. We'll have fun, and just think of the joy of not having to go home and cook. Doesn't a nice, juicy, cholesterol-laden burger sound great?"

"You know how to hurt a gal," Katherine said, stacking the last of her folders on the pile and standing up. "All right. Why not? I'm sure there must be something I forgot to buy for the holidays." But the holidays were going to be nonexistent this year.

"We'll get our coats and meet you out front," Iris said. "We'll take my car."

Katherine went to sign out and collect her coat and purse, shaking her head in amusement. She'd worked with Iris and Pat for seventeen years. They had seen her through two divorces, the latest becoming final two days before Thanksgiving. Pat had teased her about that, saying that getting rid of Tom was definitely something to be thankful for. In turn, Katherine had stood by Iris when a malignant lump was discovered in her breast, and she'd been there for Pat when Toby, Pat's youngest child, was diagnosed with leukemia three years before. And through it all, the three of them had always found something to laugh about. They liked to say that they were survivors.

We're closer than most sisters, Katherine thought

as she walked outside to meet the others. It was nice to know she could rely on them, especially after she'd learned that neither of her children would be coming home for the holidays. But she wasn't going to barge in on either of their families. She might as well get used to spending holidays alone.

Waiting for Iris to retrieve her car from the employees' lot and bring it around, Katherine remembered the day her daughter, Caitlyn, had called to talk about the ski trip one of her college professors was sponsoring.

"Naturally I told the gang I couldn't go," Caitlyn had said, probably not aware of the wistful note that had crept into her voice. "I told Professor Adams our family always celebrates the holidays together."

Katherine didn't even hesitate. She'd known when Caitlyn went away to college that her mothering days were about over, and she was well aware that, for both her own and Caitlyn's sake, she had to let go.

"Oh honey, I wish you hadn't done that," she said. "I was just thinking it would be really nice to get away from all that holiday baking and cooking this year. We've been terribly busy at the center and I think I'm feeling my age these days." She sighed. "It would have been nice to just kick back and eat a TV dinner and read one of the books I never have time for."

"You mean you don't want me to come home for Christmas?" Caitlyn asked, sounding incredulous. "Mom, is there something you're not telling me? You're not sick, are you? Or worse yet, has that skunk, Tom, come crawling back?"

Katherine had laughed heartily. "Tom's in Tahiti or Timbuktu, or someplace with his latest sweety, hon, and no, I'm not sick. I just feel that I could relish a little peace and quiet." She made her voice smooth and persuasive. "And besides, you really want to go on the ski trip, don't you?"

"Well, sure, I'd like to go, but not if it means leaving you all alone on Christmas. It would be different if you were having Tim and Ellie."

Katherine winced. She wasn't a very good liar, but she knew if she told Caitlyn how disappointed she was that Tim and his young wife weren't coming home either, there'd be no keeping her daughter away, and the more she thought about it, a quiet, no-fuss holiday sounded nice . . . different anyway.

"Please go, hon," Katherine said. "I really want you to. How many chances like this will you have? And it's not that expensive, is it?"

"Not the way Professor Adams is setting it up. Mom, are you absolutely, positively sure you don't mind? I could probably get home for a long weekend in February."

"That would be wonderful," Katherine said.

"Now go dig out your ski outfit and have a fantastic time. I'll be fine."

"Mom, you are the best," Caitlyn said. "One of the girls in my English lit class was complaining about her mother the other day. Judy said she wished her mom would get a life. I'm sure glad you're not a clinging vine like that."

The phrase clinging vine was running through Katherine's mind as Iris pulled up outside the front door. She climbed in the back, letting Pat sit up front with Iris. She certainly didn't want to be a clinging vine, not with Caitlyn or her friends. She'd always prided herself on being independent, and now that she was really living alone, it was no time to wimp out.

"So, what are you going to do with yourself over the holidays, Katherine?" Pat asked. "Would you like to spend them with me and Ed and the kids? We'd be glad to have you."

Katherine shook her head. "Thanks, but I'm planning to have a totally different Christmas this year. For as long as I can remember I've fussed and fumed my way through the holidays—cooking, baking, cleaning . . . wearing myself to a frazzle, and running myself into debt. This year it's going to be different. I'm going to eat what I want, when I want. I may stay in my robe all weekend, and I'm finally going to finish that new mystery novel I bought weeks ago."

Iris sighed. "Sounds good, Katherine, but you

13

have only yourself to please. Pete and the kids would never let me slack off like that."

"Ever hear of putting your foot down?" Pat teased.

"Ever hear of a woman with a death wish?" Iris batted back. "Oh, it's okay. I always complain, but underneath it all I love the hustle and bustle. Well, most of it anyway. If you change your mind about being alone, you can always come to my place, Katherine. It gets a little crazy at times, but we have fun."

Katherine laughed. "I know you do," she said. "I've been to your house at Easter, remember?"

"Speaking of Easter, did either of you hear that little Ginny Simmonds is going to be the poster child this year? She's such a sweetheart, but it kills me to work with her, knowing how limited her progress is," Pat said.

Leaning forward, Katherine shook her head. "Don't feel sorry for Ginny. She has a better outlook on life than most so-called 'normal' adults I know. She'll do fine."

"Sure she will," Iris agreed. "She is one great kid." They talked about some of their patients then, the ones they genuinely looked forward to working with and the ones they sometimes wished they could avoid. And Katherine thought about how much she had learned from her patients over the years. About courage and determination in the face of overwhelming odds. About fate and the way life sometimes dumps more than a fair share of pain on good people, and about the unselfishness and the giving natures of her co-workers, present company included. And then Iris was pulling into the crowded mall parking lot and there was no more time for introspection.

"Look at all those cars!" Pat said. "We'll be lucky if we can get waited on at the food court."

Iris gave them both a cocky grin. "See these?" she asked, making a muscle under her heavy quilted coat. "I've gotten pretty strong lifting patients in and out of wheelchairs. Trust me. We will get served!"

Laughing, Katherine followed her two friends into the noisy, brightly lit mall.

Over burgers and greasy French fries that were guaranteed to clog the healthiest arteries, the girls unwound from the work week. "When Pete told me not to hurry home from work tonight, I took him at his word," Iris said. "I think he and the kids are wrapping my Christmas presents and wanted me out of the way."

"The same with Ed," Pat said. "Hey, do you think the guys have been comparing notes? Seems funny they both turned us loose at the same time."

The three women laughed. "I'm not questioning it," Iris said. "It's nice to have a night out, even if it is in a mall crammed from floor to ceiling with kids."

"Well, we sure know the reason for that, don't we?" Pat said, pointing to a spot in the center of the mall where a gilt throne reposed, with a suitably fat and jolly red-suited man seated on it. "Say, isn't that . . . Ouch! Why'd you . . . ?"

"Hey, I've got a great idea," Iris said, her gray eyes sparkling like a mischievous child's. "Let's go tell Santa what we want for Christmas. Why should the kids have all the fun?"

Katherine turned away from the long line of children waiting to see Santa and shook her head. "No way," she said. "Aren't we just a teensy bit too large to perch on the poor gent's knee?"

"We don't have to sit on his lap," Pat argued. "Come on, Katherine. Loosen up and live a little. What can it hurt? This is a once-in-a-lifetime opportunity."

Without actually knowing how it happened, Katherine found herself herded into the line of giggling, anxious youngsters.

"I feel like a fool," she whispered to Pat. "Maybe we should reconsider. Everyone must be staring at us."

"If we wimp out we won't get anything for Christmas," Iris said sternly. "Santa doesn't come to the homes of people who no longer believe in him."

"She's definitely lost it," Katherine told Pat,

making a circular motion with her finger and pointing at her head.

Then it was Iris' turn, and she boldly stated that she "wanted it all." Furs, jewels, fancy cars. "But if you can't manage that I'll settle for a cleaning woman once a week," she said, to the amusement of the onlookers. After greedily snatching the candy cane Santa handed her, Iris stepped down from the platform and pushed Katherine toward the beckoning Santa.

"Oh Lord!" Katherine murmured in embarrassment. "How did I ever get talked into this?"

"Don't you believe in Santa, young lady?" Santa asked sternly, his moustache twitching. Up close Katherine could see that Santa's face had some wrinkles, and his voice had the ring of maturity. Before she realized what was happening, Santa had pulled her down onto his knee, all five foot eight, one hundred forty-five pounds of her. "Now wait just a . . ." she sputtered, breaking off when Santa gave her a little pinch.

"Chill out," he whispered. "That is what the kids say, isn't it?"

"I—"

"There's a long line of kiddies waiting to get where you are, so we'll have to cut this short," Santa whispered. Then his voice boomed out for all the world to hear. "And what is your name, young lady?"

Her face flaming, Katherine managed to stammer out her name. Then she realized that more than her face was hot. This was no harmless, jolly old elf at all! Even the thick fleece suit Santa wore couldn't completely conceal the hard, masculine contours underneath. Good Lord! She was definitely losing it. Getting excited about Santa Claus!

"And what would you like for Christmas, little girl?" Santa asked softly, his voice only slightly seductive.

Katherine was so rattled she said the first thing that came to mind. "I'd like a puppy," she blurted.

The onlookers roared with laughter, and Katherine wished she could drop right through the floor. This had to be the most humiliating moment of her life. Just wait till she got her hands on Pat and Iris!

"Meet me after for coffee," Santa whispered, his breath warm and decidedly friendly against her ear. "The coffee shop stays open after the rest of the stores close."

Then he winked and handed her a candy cane and Pat was taking her place.

Laughing, Iris pulled Katherine aside. "Are my antennae receiving the wrong signals or was Santa flirting with you? Come on, Katherine, 'fess up. Did he try to—"

"Oh for heaven's sake, Iris! What's in that head

of yours anyway, cottage cheese? He was . . . well, just having some fun the same as we were."

"Right. No harm in that," Iris agreed.

Katherine could see that her former friend was having a hard time keeping a straight face. The urge to strangle Iris was slowly dwindling. What the hell! Everyone made a spectacle of themselves at least once in a lifetime. Tonight just happened to be her turn. And even though she'd been mortally embarrassed it was better than staring at the boob tube and eating a grilled cheese sandwich.

"He asked me to meet him at the coffee shop," she said, shaking her head. "Can you imagine? Santa putting the make on me?"

"Actually he looked pretty good to me, underneath all that padding, I mean."

A grim suspicion was nagging at Katherine. "Iris Johnson, did you deliberately set me up? You did, didn't you? Oh, I should have known! You know that man, don't you?"

"All right, I confess. He used to work with Pete at the post office. He retired last spring. Honest, Katherine, he's a really nice man, and a very young sixty-two. I think you'd like him if you gave him a chance."

"Read my lips, Iris. I'm not interested in a man. I told you and Pat that a dozen times. Why don't you believe me?"

"Because we know you don't mean it," Pat said, coming up behind them and triumphantly waving her candy cane. "You like men, Katherine, and you'd make a lousy nun. Admit it. So, are you going to have a cup of coffee with the poor guy or not?"

Katherine stared into the window of a clothing store. All the holiday glitz and glitter stared back at her, but this year she had no need for a fancy dress or dangly earrings. She made a sudden, impulsive decision. "Why not?" she asked, for the second time that night. "What have I got to lose?"

"Don't worry about waiting for me," she told the girls. "I'll take a taxi back to the center to get my car."

"Okay," Pat and Iris chorused, looking well pleased. "Have a nice time, Katherine, and keep an open mind, okay?"

She felt terribly foolish standing outside the coffee shop waiting for a man she didn't even know and wondering what on earth Iris had told him about her. That she was a lonely, grieving divorcée? That her grown children wouldn't be home for the holidays . . . that she needed cheering up?

I *am* going to kill Iris one of these days, Katherine thought. This time I really think she went too far.

"Katherine?" The deep, resonant voice startled

her and she jumped. "Easy, it's just Santa," he said with a soft laugh. "You're not afraid of Santa, are you?"

Katherine found herself looking into a pair of dark brown eyes and one of the nicest faces she'd seen in a long time.

"I think we were set up," she said, wondering if she should apologize. After all, Iris and Pat were her friends.

"I don't mind. Do you? By the way, my name is Ron Harold. I know you're Katherine. Iris has said some very nice things about you."

Katherine allowed Ron to lead her to an empty table, groaning all the way. It was even worse than she'd thought. Iris was definitely in her match-making mode.

"Iris gets a little carried away," she said, when they were seated and the waitress had taken their order for coffee and apple pie à la mode. "I told her she was as good as dead this time." She wondered if her nose was shiny, and if Ron would think she was a frustrated divorcée who would be grateful for any crumbs of masculine attention. "You'd think she would have enough to do taking care of her own family." Katherine cleared her throat. "Look, I really didn't have any idea what was going on when I agreed to come here tonight. I don't want you to think that I . . ."

Ron laughed, a hearty sound that made Katherine smile against her will. "Iris is a pistol, all right," he said, "but for once she scored in the top ten. I'm really glad to have the chance to meet you, Katherine. I suppose Iris told you that I recently retired. I've been at loose ends lately." He paused and smiled. "That's why I'm playing Santa. I was going stir crazy in that big, empty house of mine."

"You're alone?"

Ron nodded. "I lost my wife ten years ago, and the kids are all scattered across the country. None of them can make the trip home this year."

Katherine nodded understandingly. "That's my situation too. My daughter is a senior in college and one of her professors was organizing a ski trip. She really wanted to go, but she felt bad about leaving me alone, so I convinced her that I'd actually enjoy a quiet, peaceful holiday for a change." Her smile deepened. "My son Tim and his wife are expecting their first child. Ellie had a little scare in the beginning, so the doctor doesn't want her to travel until after the baby comes. They live in Atlanta."

"A new baby," Ron said. "That's nice to look forward to, isn't it?"

Katherine sipped her coffee and nodded. "Yes. I think I'm going to enjoy being a grandmother. My only regret is that I won't see the baby as often as I'd like." She smiled again. "But then maybe the distance between us will keep me from being an interfering grandma."

"I can't imagine that," Ron said, "but kids have to go where they can make a living. That's why mine are all scattered. Ron, Jr., is in Anchorage, Alaska. Betsy and her family live in Spokane, Washington, and the baby, Sandy, is in Baltimore. She's the closest one, but even at that I hardly see her. She's the supervisor of nurses at a big hospital in Baltimore."

"It gets lonely, I know," Katherine said. "I suppose that's why I enjoy my job so much. I'm with other people all day, so at night I don't mind so much going home to an empty house."

"That reminds me," Ron said. "Did you mean what you said about wanting a puppy for Christmas?"

Katherine felt herself redden. "Oh that! I'm not sure why I blurted that out. When I was nine I asked Santa to bring me a puppy, but my parents thought I was too young for the responsibility of a pet."

"So you didn't get the puppy?"

Katherine shook her head. "Then I grew up and got married and my first husband was allergic to animal hair. The only pets we ever had were goldfish."

"What about husband number two?" Ron asked.

"Tom? Well, my marriage to Tom didn't last long enough for me to find out whether or not he liked animals." Ducking her head, Katherine picked at her pie. "I married Tom on the rebound. I was devastated when my first marriage broke up, and he was there."

Suddenly realizing how much she'd revealed about herself in just a few minutes, Katherine thanked Ron for the coffee and stood up. "I really should go. My car is still back at the center, and I have a ton of things to do tomorrow."

"I'll take you there," he said.

Katherine shook her head. "That's not necessary. I can take a taxi."

"Don't be silly," Ron said. "Why should you pay for a taxi when I can drive you?"

Katherine sighed. She knew who Ron was, so it wasn't like she was accepting a ride from a stranger, and suddenly she was very tired. It would be nice not to have to wait for a taxi.

"All right," she said. "Thanks."

Ron didn't mention getting together again when they said good night, and Katherine wasn't sure whether she should be relieved or insulted. When she went to bed that night she had a hard time getting to sleep. Ron had seemed very pleasant, and if she could be certain he wouldn't get any ideas she wouldn't mind seeing him occasionally. He'd been incredibly easy to talk to. Good Lord! He'd gotten more information out of her in a few minutes than most people did after weeks of acquaintance.

* * *

Driving home after making sure Katherine got her car started all right, Ron tried to remember everything Iris had told him about her co-worker. He knew Katherine was fifty-three, that her son was twenty-seven, and her daughter twenty-two. That she was a warm, giving woman, and that her recent divorce had left a bitter taste in her mouth. Well, he'd never experienced a divorce, but he could well imagine that it would do a number on your self-esteem. But Katherine hadn't seemed bitter, just wary, which was why he'd refrained from asking her out to dinner. He would, though. Ron Harold had never been a quitter.

"So what happened? Did he ask you out? Are you going to see him again?" Iris asked the next morning. She'd called just as Katherine was finishing her breakfast.

"Nothing happened," Katherine said. "I told you and Pat that I was finished with men. Why can't you believe that? I don't need a man. I have my work and a few good friends, although they are rapidly dwindling," she said threateningly.

"Don't be mad," Iris said. "We only want to see you happy. You've been moping around these

25

last few weeks, and that's not like you. Do you miss Tom that much?"

"Miss Tom? You've got to be kidding," Katherine said. "No, Tom and I were headed for disaster before the ink was dry on the marriage license. The whole thing was a big mistake. No, I don't miss Tom, and I don't miss Frank anymore either. It's just . . . well, maybe it's just too late for all this romance nonsense, you know? After all, in a few months I'll be a grandmother."

Iris laughed. "Like Pat and I always say, you'd make a lousy nun, Katherine, and where is it written that grandmothers plop themselves down in rocking chairs and learn to crochet? That may have been true once, but no more. Why, look at Liz Taylor! Now there's a role model for you!"

Katherine groaned. "Heaven forbid! I'd never have the stamina."

Iris laughed. "Have a good weekend," she said. "I'll see you on Monday."

After showering and dressing in softly faded jeans and a peach-colored sweatshirt, Katherine climbed the pull-down stairs to her attic and got down the artificial Christmas tree she'd bought a few months earlier. The discount store where she frequently shopped had had a sale, and she'd decided that an artificial tree would be easier than a real one. Besides, shopping for a real Christmas tree and loading it into her trunk, not to mention dragging it into the house and setting it up, was really a chore without anyone to help.

Actually, once the tree was all put together it didn't look too bad, and she knew that once she got the ornaments she'd collected over the years strategically placed, it would be beautiful.

Every year she thought the tree was the best ever, and she was pretty sure this year would be no exception, even though it would be the first time she'd ever decorated it alone. Last year Tom had been around, and before that there were Frank and the kids. Katherine paused, her hand raised to place a string of minilights, as her mind went spinning backward to another time when her whole life had stretched ahead of her, a long road of unknowns. When she and Frank got married they weren't sure they could have children. Frank had caught mumps as a child, and they weren't sure he could be a father. But they were lucky, and Timothy James Dumont was born a few weeks after their first anniversary. Then Caitlyn came along five years later, and they decided their little family was complete. Frank had a vasectomy and Katherine settled down to be the best wife and mother possible.

"And I was," Katherine told herself firmly, winding the string of lights through the branches of the tree. She had baked tons of cookies and had sewn dozens of "designer original" Halloween costumes. She had kept a clean house and had made sure Frank's dinner was on the table exactly ten minutes after he got home from work, the way he liked it.

After Caitlyn started school, Katherine decided it was time to do something for herself. She went back to school and got her degree in physical therapy.

As she unwrapped some of her favorite crystal ornaments, Katherine remembered how glad she'd been that she had her career when Frank asked for a divorce. Oh, she'd seen it coming. A woman would have to have been blind and deaf not to see the signs. For months Frank had been quiet and withdrawn. There were frequent, unexplained absences, times when he snapped at her or the kids for no apparent reason, and then, finally, the day when he came right out and said it. He was tired of being married. He would always love her and the children, but he felt stifled, and he needed some "space."

Katherine had wanted to explode. To scream and rant and rave and throw things. But Caitlyn and Tim were depending on her. They were stunned by their father's desertion, even though they were adults themselves. So she had to be strong. She had to keep herself together for her son and daughter.

"And gradually the awful, raw pain eased," Katherine murmured, draping a string of cream-colored pearls over the branches. "And now I'm fine," she told herself. "I don't need any more men in my life, and it's perfectly normal for a woman to talk to herself while she trims her Christmas tree."

She could handle just about anything that came along . . . except Christmas tree lights that didn't light.

"Damn! Wouldn't you know it?" Well, the lights were old. She couldn't expect them to last forever, and new ones wouldn't be that expensive. It was just that she didn't feel like getting dressed and going to the store.

But she had to, or else postpone the tree trimming until another time, and she didn't want to do that. She always liked to finish what she started.

"What the heck," she said, running a comb through her short, light brown hair. She wouldn't be the first woman to visit the mall in jeans and a sweatshirt and wearing no makeup. It would take less than an hour to drive there and back. She could finish trimming the tree before dinner, then spend a quiet, pleasant evening reading and enjoying the tree lights.

"Katherine! We meet again."

Santa Claus came out of the coffee shop at the exact moment Katherine went to turn in at the tree-trimming shop next door.

"Hello," she said, smiling at the sight of Ron swaddled in red fleece and fluffy white fur. "Are you taking a break?"

Ron nodded. "Even Santa has his limits," he said. "I wish you'd gotten here a few minutes earlier. You could have joined me." Ron had never cared much for women who loaded their faces with paint, and now, seeing Katherine in jeans and a sweatshirt, her face scrubbed clean, made him more eager than ever to get to know her better.

Katherine laughed. "I'm really not dressed for a day at the mall," she said. "I was trimming my tree when I discovered that all my lights are dead. I just ran in to get some replacements."

"You're trimming a tree just for yourself?" Ron asked, sounding a little wistful. "I haven't bothered with a tree for years. Without the family around it didn't seem worth the bother."

"It isn't Christmas without a tree," Katherine said. She couldn't imagine not putting up a tree, even if she was the only one who ever saw it. Then, mentally unbalanced by the soft sound of Christmas carols playing in the background and the sight of fake snow and glittery tinsel, not to mention the deprived look of the man in front of her, she weakened and issued an invitation. "Would you like to come by and see my tree when you finish work?" she asked.

"I'd love that," Ron said quickly, almost as if he were afraid she'd change her mind.

"You know where I live?"

Ron grinned behind his fluffy beard. "Iris told me."

Katherine groaned. "Good old Iris."

"You can say that again," Ron said, laughing.

All the way home Katherine berated herself. Inviting Ron to her home had been a stupid thing to do. For that matter inviting any man to her home would be stupid. She was off men for life, and there was no sense in starting something she didn't intend to finish.

Besides, Ron is needy, she thought, as she maneuvered her little car through the afternoon traffic. She had seen it in his eyes last night, that lost, almost helpless little-boy look she knew so well.

Well, letting the man enjoy her Christmas tree for a couple of hours wasn't going to kill either one of them, she decided. After all, it was Christmas, the season to share. She'd make hot chocolate and put out some of her famous coconut snickerdoodles, and maybe slice some fruitcake and . . .

Katherine laughed at herself, realizing that she was actually looking forward to entertaining, even if it was just a one-time thing with a man she hardly knew. It was Christmas, for pete's sake, the time to be jolly and spread cheer, so why not?

Just as she finished putting the angel on the top of the tree, Katherine's phone rang.

It was Pat.

"Katherine? It's Toby. He . . . he's had a relapse, and Ed and I are going to have to take him to Baltimore to the Children's Cancer Center there. I hate to bother you, but . . . well, could you come over here and just kind of keep an eye on things until my parents get here tomorrow? You know how Amy is. She thinks she's too old for a babysitter, but I can't handle the idea of leaving her and Sheila alone in the house overnight."

"Of course not. I wouldn't let you. Just let me throw a couple of things into a bag and I'll be there, and hang loose, okay? Toby's a strong kid. He'll get through this."

"Yeah. That's what I keep telling myself. It's just that it was so sudden. One day he was fine and now . . ."

"He'll be fine again," Katherine said firmly. "Keep the faith, Pat."

But when she hung up, Katherine felt like crying. Toby was such a neat kid and he'd already gone through so much. To have this happen now, right before Christmas . . . it just wasn't fair.

Life rarely was fair, Katherine thought, throwing a nightgown and a change of clothes into a bag. She thought about her patients. They ranged from children with birth defects to elderly stroke patients, and every day she was awed by their courage.

Toby will be fine, she told herself. With any luck the doctors in Baltimore will fix him up and send him home before Christmas.

She almost left without leaving Ron a note of explanation. She was all the way out to her car before she remembered him.

Hastily she scribbled a note, telling him where she'd gone and why. She apologized and suggested that maybe he could see her tree another time.

Amy and Sheila were trying very hard to be brave and grown up. At fifteen and thirteen, they were right at the age when tears were never far below the surface.

Quickly assessing the situation, Katherine took in the half-trimmed tree, the general state of disorder in the normally immaculate house, and the dread in the girls' eyes.

"Okay, let's get this situation under control," she said. "Amy, how about helping me straighten up around here, while Sheila sorts the tree trimmings? As soon as we get things neatened up, we'll tackle the tree. When your parents bring Toby home they'll be surprised at what a good job we did."

"Gramps and Nana Foster are coming tomorrow," Sheila said, wrinkling her nose. "I love them, but . . . well, sometimes they just don't understand stuff."

"That's because they're old, stupid!" Amy snapped. "They're not used to kids anymore."

"I'm sure it won't be for long," Katherine said. "I'll bet your parents will be bringing Toby home before you know it."

"Sometimes I think it would be better if he just died and got it over with," Amy said quietly, her dark eyes filled with misery. "Things go along good for a while, and then something like this happens and it ruins everything!" The tears she'd been holding back started to overflow, and Amy clutched Katherine's arm in desperation. "Do you think I'm terrible, Katherine? Are you going to tell my mother what I said?"

"Of course not," Katherine promised, "and you have every right to be angry. Both of you do," she added. "People, even parents, sometimes forget that everyone in the family suffers when there's a sick child. Tell you what, instead of cleaning right now, how about going out for pizza? We'll take care of all this later."

"Can we have pepperoni on the pizza?" Sheila asked eagerly.

"I like mushrooms," Amy said, wiping her eyes.

"Then we'll have both," Katherine said, grinning.

And after they stuffed themselves with pizza, they talked. Katherine started the ball rolling by

34

telling Amy and Sheila how angry she'd gotten at her sister, Judith, when Judith fell and broke her leg.

"Everyone made such a fuss over her, and they forgot all about me. It was like I didn't even exist. And Judith loved all the attention she got. She could be whiny or fresh but no one ever yelled at her, at least not until after her cast came off. Then they forgot all about her accident and treated her just like the rest of us."

Amy and Sheila laughed. "Are you friends with your sister now?" Amy asked, gnawing on the last bit of pizza crust.

Katherine nodded. "Judith and I get together every chance we get. But she lives several hundred miles from here, so we write each other long letters every week, and I know if I needed her she'd be here in a heartbeat."

"That's sort of how we feel about Toby. I mean, he's just a kid now, but someday, when we're all grown up, I know he'll be our friend as well as our brother. It's just right now that's hard. Everyone worries about him all the time, and sometimes it's like they forget all about us. It's like we're invisible or something."

"I know it seems that way, but did you ever think of how hard it must be for your mom and dad to divide themselves up between the three of you? Boy, I wouldn't want to be in their shoes!"

Neither girl replied to that, but Katherine knew

35

she'd given them something to think about, a new perspective from which to view their situation.

Pat's elderly parents arrived the next afternoon, and by that time the house was presentable and the tree was trimmed. Both girls were able to smile as they greeted their grandparents.

Katherine drove home thoughtfully. Pat had called from the hospital to report that the doctor had put Toby on a new medication and they were hoping it would put him back into remission, but it didn't look as though any of them would be home for Christmas.

She spotted the note as soon as she pulled into her driveway. It was written on bright red paper, and it stood out against her white door like a flag.

Smiling, she took out the thumb tack and started to read.

" 'Sorry about Pat's boy. Also sorry I didn't get to see your tree. I'll call this afternoon to see about rescheduling. Ron.' "

Rescheduling indeed! Katherine smiled all the way into the house.

When the phone rang at three-thirty, she jumped, hoping it was Pat with good news.

"Katherine?"

It was Ron, and for some crazy reason Katherine realized she was glad to hear from him.

"Hello," she said. "Are you on break again?"

"Sure am, and I just finished the worst cup of coffee I ever had. I'm certain it was left over from the breakfast crowd."

Katherine laughed. "You poor thing, and all those kiddies to smile at and be nice to."

"Actually I'm enjoying it," he said. "How are things with Pat's son?"

"We're hopeful," Katherine said, repeating what Pat had told her, "but it looks like Pat and Ed may have to stay in the city with Toby through the holidays. It's going to be a pretty bleak Christmas for their two girls."

"Mmm, it does sound that way," Ron said, "but who knows what will turn up by then? It pays to be optimistic, doesn't it?"

"Absolutely."

"Well, may I cash in my raincheck tonight? I get off at nine, and I can probably be at your place by nine-twenty. Is that too late?"

"Not at all," Katherine said. She decided she was actually looking forward to Ron's visit. She didn't feel like spending the evening watching television, and for some reason she was having a hard time getting into the new book she'd bought.

It was nine-twenty-three when Ron arrived. Katherine knew because she'd been anxiously staring at her watch.

Then she heard a car door slam and looked

out her front window to see Ron coming up the walk.

"Come in," she said, holding the door open. "It's freezing out there, isn't it?"

"Close," Ron said, pulling his scarf from around his neck.

He had a nice neck, Katherine thought, studying him objectively, and he didn't look his age. He looked closer to fifty than sixty, and there was a lively, animated twinkle in his eyes that fascinated her.

"Come on into the living room," she invited. "I made some hot chocolate, and I thought maybe you'd like to sample some of my homemade cookies."

"Sounds great," Ron said. Then, when he saw the tree he stopped short. "It's breathtaking," he said. "You're an artist, Katherine."

"Not really," Katherine replied. "It just takes me a long time to do my tree. I have to make sure each ornament is in exactly the right spot, and I don't just throw the tinsel on. I hang it, strand by strand."

Ron nodded. "My wife was the same way. Edna loved Christmas."

It could have been a sad moment, and yet it wasn't. They were two people, who were alone, sharing a precious time. It made Katherine smile, and she was glad to see that Ron was smiling too.

"Well, tell me about all those handmade orna-ments," Ron invited, settling himself in a com-fortable lounge chair. "I'm sure there is a story in each one of them."

"Settle back and sit a spell," Katherine said, rolling her eyes heavenward. "Truer words were never spoken."

They didn't make it through all the ornaments. There were just too many, and besides, Katherine decided it would be nice to save something for another time. But after the ornaments were dis-cussed and discarded, they talked about them-selves. Ron told Katherine about his thirty-year marriage to his high-school sweetheart. Katherine told him about Frank deciding he needed space after twenty-eight years of marriage. Ron con-fessed that he hated anchovies and loved pickled artichoke hearts. Katherine admitted that she simply could not abide rocky-road ice cream, but that she went gaga over marshmallows dipped in chocolate.

"And I've always been so glad I went back to school," she said, as she finished telling Ron about becoming a physical therapist. "If I hadn't had my work, I'm not sure how I would have survived my divorce from Frank."

"Do you still have feelings for him?" Ron asked.

"Frank? Good heavens, no! At least not in the way you mean. I suppose I'll always have some fond memories. After all, he is the father of my children, but I don't even know where he is, nor do I care."

"Good," Ron said. "I'm not sure I'm up for that kind of competition."

It took a few minutes for the meaning of his words to sink in, and when they did, Katherine's eyes darkened. "Ron, I don't . . . well, I don't plan on ever getting involved with a man again. I struck out twice. I'm not planning to try for a third strike. I'm satisfied with my life just the way it is."

Ron smiled. It was a gentle, non-threatening smile, and yet it was filled with confidence and just a hint of smug male complacency. "Never is a long time," he said, the twinkle in his eyes deepening. Then he laughed. "Don't worry, Katherine. I'm not into whirlwind romances or sweeping a woman off her feet, even one as lovely and desirable as you, but I would like to get to know you better. You don't have anything against friendship, do you?"

"Of course not, but . . ."

"No buts," Ron said firmly, laying his hand over hers and lightly squeezing her fingers. "I'm lonely, and I think you are too. What's the harm in our getting together once in a while and doing away with that loneliness?"

"None, I suppose," Katherine said slowly. She could feel herself weakening, succumbing to

Ron's open friendliness, his honesty and good nature. What the heck, she thought, why not?

As Ron drove home from Katherine's house he chuckled softly. Iris had told the truth. Katherine was a lovely woman. She had a warm gentleness that reminded him of Edna. But that wasn't why he was so eager to strike up a friendship. No sir! He wasn't looking for a replacement for his late wife. He and Edna had shared love and passion. Together they'd rode their youth right into middle age. They'd built a warm, comfortable home and raised a family. That kind of relationship was a once-in-a-lifetime thing. If he had a relationship with another woman, it would be different. He was older now, mellowed out, as his kids liked to say. And there were some memories in his heart that he would share with no one. Memories of precious, intimate moments with Edna, memories that belonged only to them. So any relationship he had now would be different, but there was no reason why it couldn't be just as sweet and satisfying. At least that's how he saw it, Ron thought as he pulled into his driveway. Whether or not Katherine could see it that way was another story. She reminded him of a wounded bird. She insisted she had no feelings for her ex-husbands, but he was sure that wasn't quite true. Every now and then the hurt and sense of abandonment peeked out from her lovely dark blue eyes, showed in the shape of her lips when she smiled . . . in her body language when Ron had touched her. Maybe she didn't miss the second guy, because by her own admission that had been a mistake from the very beginning, a rebound romance that was doomed from day one. But Frank, the partner from her youth, the father of her children, no, that was another kettle of chowder!

Well, even if nothing came of it, it would be interesting to dig under Katherine's protective shell and find out what was underneath. As he pocketed his car key and opened his front door, Ron smiled into the darkness. A light flurry of snowflakes swirled around him, and he looked up at the sky. "She's a beauty, Edna," he said. "I think the two of you would have liked one another."

For the very first time since his retirement, Ron slept well.

"He came over to see my Christmas tree," Katherine told Iris on Monday morning when the two women got together for a coffee break. "We had hot chocolate and ate homemade cookies. Now, does that sound like a hot date to you, nosey?"

Iris laughed. "Maybe it wouldn't have twenty

years ago, but now . . . well, actually it sounds kind of nice."

"It was nice, and that's all. I told Ron I wasn't interested in a relationship."

"So the subject did come up?" Iris persisted, her lips curving in a self-satisfied smile. "I wonder what else could come up if you were just the least bit encouraging?"

Katherine had to laugh. Iris could be totally outrageous. "Nothing is coming up," she said firmly, "except my next appointment. It's a new patient, a teenage girl who broke her leg in four places in an auto accident."

Iris groaned. "Teenagers! They're usually the worst patients. Give me a little kid, or even a senior citizen, anytime. Good luck, pal."

Katherine buttoned her white coat and peered into the mirror to make sure her hair was neat. Then she headed for the treatment room.

"Well, Ashley, how are you today? Since this is our first session I'll tell you a little about myself. My name is Katherine and I—"

"Stuff the small talk," Ashley said, her face twisted in anger and resentment. "Can we just do what we have to and get this shit over with?"

Katherine nodded okay. This was going to be one of those deals. Well, it was Monday—and she was well rested. She could handle it.

"Do you want to get well, Ashley?" she asked.

43

She looked straight at the girl, refusing to let Ashley glance away.

"Of course I do! What do you think I'm here for . . . to count the strands of gray in your hair?"

Katherine laughed. "If you can do that you're a better woman than I am! All right, Ashley, let's get down to the nitty-gritty here." Her eyes competently scanned the young woman's chart.

"You were in a bad accident. You broke your left leg in four places. Right now that leg is weak and virtually useless, but together we can change that—only it's going to mean a lot of hard work. It will be painful, especially at first. Are you up for it, or would you rather spend the rest of your life limping around and moaning about your bad luck?"

"I can take pain," Ashley said, but she didn't meet Katherine's eyes and her chin was trembling.

"Good," Katherine said. "That's a great first step. Now, what are you afraid of, Ashley?"

The girl started to shake her head; then her pretty gray eyes filled with tears and her bravado crumpled. "I'm a runner, or at least I was before the accident. The doctor who took care of me and set my leg said I'd probably never run again. Is that true? I . . . was hoping to go to college on an athletic scholarship. My high-school track coach said I was one of his best runners."

Katherine weighed her words carefully. Ashley's

accident had done a real number on her leg. She was confident that with the proper therapy, and at least a minimum of cooperation from the patient, Ashley could eventually walk without a noticeable limp, but run? She wasn't sure, yet she didn't want to take away Ashley's dreams if there was even the slightest possibility of her realizing them.

Finally, taking the girl's hand in hers, she spoke. "Ashley, I can't give you any guarantees. I wish I could. I know that you can walk again. Maybe you won't even have a limp, but about the running, I'm just not sure. All I can promise is that we'll give it our best shot."

Ashley scrubbed at the tears on her cheeks. "That's what I thought you'd say, and I know it's not your fault, but what am I going to do if I can't run anymore?" The girl's eyes were huge. "What's going to happen to my life?"

Katherine discussed Ashley's case with one of the doctors at the center before she got ready to go home.

"Is it even remotely possible for her to run again?" she asked.

"I wish I knew," Ted Andrews said, "but you know how these things go, Katherine. It could go either way. The leg was badly injured. Some of the major bones were shattered. If you want my best guess I'd have to say that it isn't likely."

Katherine nodded. "That's what I thought too, but I didn't want to take away all Ashley's hope. Right now she's pretty precariously balanced. She's trying to be brave, but I get the feeling she's on the verge of a deep, debilitating depression. I want to avoid that if I can."

"Then let her hang on to her hope, at least for a while, until we see how it goes. She's a pretty girl, isn't she?"

"Very, but I get the feeling she's not the kind of kid who relies on that. There's a lot more to her than a cute face and a shapely body."

Ted nodded. "Then she'll do okay, either way. The human spirit is an amazing thing, Katherine. It can withstand a lot of hard blows."

She caught up with Iris before she left, and each promised to let the other know if any news about Toby was received.

"What a miserable Christmas for the girls," Iris said. "Pat's parents are dears, but they're really kind of old and frail to be looking after two active, intelligent teens."

"I know," Katherine said. "I was thinking maybe I should go over there and spend Christmas with them and try to liven things up a little."

"Oh, that would be great, and you could all come to my place for dinner if you don't feel like cooking."

"Thanks, but I really enjoy cooking holiday dinners. It's just that this year, I didn't think there would be any reason to do it."

"Uh, what about Ron? Are you planning to include him in your plans?"

Katherine thought for a moment. Should she? It hadn't occurred to her before, but he probably missed seeing his children and grandchildren. Maybe he'd enjoy spending the holidays with Amy and Sheila. But would she enjoy spending the holiday with him, or would she be better off leaving things as they were?

"I'll have to think about that," Katherine said, frowning. "Some of your ideas aren't all that bad, Iris, but I'm not sure about this one."

"I love you too, Katherine," Iris said, grinning. "See you tomorrow."

For the next couple of days Katherine and Iris were super busy at the center. And while some of her patients were in a heightened state of excitement, others were deeply depressed.

"Not everyone looks forward to the holidays," she remarked to Iris at break one afternoon. "I felt so sorry for old Mrs. Peters this morning, I had all I could do not to break down and cry."

Iris nodded grimly. "She's totally alone. Her husband is dead, and her children are on the other side of the country. I think she's planning to spend Christmas day at the senior citizen's center."

"Thank goodness for that center," Katherine said.

Three days before Christmas, Katherine got a phone call from Pat.

The minute she heard her friend's voice Katherine knew the news was good. "Is Toby better?" she asked.

"The doctors are cautiously optimistic," Pat said, "but you know how doctors are. The thing is he's responding to the treatment. His blood count is better, and he's not as tired and weak as he was. You don't know how scared Ed and I were, Katherine. We were afraid this was it." Pat paused, and Katherine heard a heavy sigh. "The bad news is, we're going to have to stay here through the holidays. The doctors said the earliest Toby could possibly be released is the first or second of January. We just can't leave him alone. This relapse really scared him. Katherine, I hate to impose on you, but do you think you could look in on my folks and the girls? Mom and Dad are sweethearts, but they aren't used to young people anymore. This will be the first Christmas we've ever been away from the girls, and lately, well, I think they've been feeling neglected. We try not to push them aside, but it's hard."

"Don't worry about a thing," Katherine said. "I'd already decided to cook Christmas dinner at your place, and if your parents don't mind I'll move in for a couple of days. I finished wrapping all your gifts; then last night I went over and helped the girls bake some cookies."

"Oh, Katherine, how can I ever repay you? You are a real, true friend."

"It's no problem," Katherine assured Pat. "I really wasn't looking forward to eating a frozen TV dinner. This way I have the perfect excuse to cook and fuss in the kitchen. Now give Toby a kiss from me, and don't worry about any of us. We'll be fine."

When she hung up, Katherine sat thinking. A few days earlier she'd been wondering how she could possibly fill all the empty hours until Christmas was over and it was time to go back to work. She'd even been looking forward to her next session with Mr. Grimes, a notoriously difficult stroke patient. Funny how quickly things changed, she mused. Now she wasn't sure there was enough time left to do all she wanted to do. There were pies to bake, her special eggnog to mix, more gifts to wrap, and, most importantly, a family to cook for and fuss over. Now all she had to decide was whether or not she wanted to include Ron.

If she didn't include him, she was pretty sure he'd be spending the holiday alone, and she knew she'd feel guilty, even though his happiness certainly wasn't her responsibility. "Oh shoot, Katherine, you know you want to invite him, so do it and get it over with! Stop fiddle-faddling around!" She quickly changed clothes and drove to the mall. It was only a little after eight, and she was sure she could still catch Ron.

She smiled as she watched him lift a chubby, blond toddler onto his lap. His smile was genuine as he spoke softly to the wide-eyed child, and when he put her down and handed her a candy cane, he spotted Katherine and waved.

She nodded to indicate that she would wait until he was done for the night. And there was the danger, she told herself. Ron made her want to smile. He had a knack of making her laugh at herself, and he was too nice. It would be too easy to like him.

But observing Ron with the children was a pleasant pastime, and before Katherine knew it, the mall security guards were starting to lock up and Ron was walking toward her.

"Did you want to see me?" he asked, his eyes hopeful. "I called the other evening, but there was no answer."

"I was with Pat's daughters," Katherine explained. "We were baking cookies."

"Oh, and how is the boy?" Ron asked.

"So far Toby's doing well," Katherine reported, "but Pat called earlier to tell me that she and Ed will have to stay there with him until the first of the year. I'm going to spend Christmas with the girls and try to cheer them up. Would you like to help?"

"Me? You really want me?" Ron asked, his eyes lighting up.

Katherine nodded. "I could use the moral support, and how are you at grating cabbage for coleslaw and loading a dishwasher?"

"I can grate with the best of them," Ron boasted. "I've never met a cabbage I couldn't tame."

"Then it's a deal," Katherine said. "Compensation for your cheery smile and willing hands will be a feast fit for a king, if I do say so myself. I do a mean turkey, and my sausage stuffing is to die for."

"I can hardly wait," Ron said. "When can I meet Pat's girls? I suppose it's too late tonight?"

Katherine nodded. "Pat's parents go to bed early. Are you working Christmas Eve?"

"Only until two in the afternoon."

"Good. I'm moving over to Pat's house tomorrow. We'll expect to see you sometime after two on Christmas Eve. Bring your appetite and plenty of corny jokes. Those girls are going to need some cheering up."

"I'll be there," Ron said. Then he did something Katherine wasn't expecting. Right there at the entrance of the mall, with people milling all around them, he bent his head and kissed her. It wasn't a hotly passionate kiss, nor was it offensive. It was just nice. Warm and pleasant. But as Katherine pulled away, touching her lips where

Ron's polyester beard had tickled her, she knew that the kiss had held a promise of more, if she wanted it. And a part of her did. That was what made the situation so scary.

"Hey, way to go, Santa!" a young man shouted, grinning.

"Atta boy, oldtimer," an elderly man cackled. "Just because there's snow on the roof doesn't mean there's no fire in the furnace, eh?"

"If there were any children watching, they may never recover," Katherine said sternly. "Santa Claus making out at the mall!"

"I couldn't help it," Ron insisted, pointing above Katherine's head. Only then did she see the huge spray of mistletoe hanging over them.

The next day when she got off work, Katherine went straight to Pat's house. She'd loaded her car the night before, and when she arrived Amy and Sheila hurried outside to help her carry things in.

"Thanks for coming, Katherine," Amy said. "Christmas will be much nicer with you here. Gramps and Nana are dears, but Nana's just too old and tired to do all the holiday stuff Mom usually does."

"Well, I can't guarantee that this Christmas will be exactly like the ones you've shared with your parents and your brother, but I'll do my best, and if we all remember to count our blessings, I think we'll do fine."

"I've invited a friend to join us for Christmas Eve and Christmas dinner," Katherine said after greeting Pat's parents, Rose and Jim. "I think you'll all like him. He's a retired postal employee who's been working as Santa at the mall."

Sheila giggled. "You mean Santa is really coming to this house on Christmas Eve?"

"You don't mind, do you?"

Rose smiled. "The more the merrier I always say. What's Christmas without a crowd?"

Everyone got to work after that, except Jim, who firmly declared that he was officially retired and had earned the right to supervise and give orders.

The girls put tapes of Christmas carols on the stereo, and Katherine mixed her special eggnog, nonalcoholic for Rose and Jim and the girls. To a separate pitcher she planned to add brandy for herself and Ron. Soon the house was filled with the scent of fragrant apple pies, and as she mixed the pumpkin and poured it into pie shells, Katherine realized she was humming.

"You're a lot like Mom," Amy said shyly. "She likes to mess in the kitchen too."

"Guilty as charged," Katherine admitted. "You girls saved me from a fate worse than death this year."

"How come?" Sheila asked, decorating a tray of sugar cookies under Katherine's watchful eye.

"Well, my own children couldn't make it home.

My daughter-in-law is expecting a baby and Caitlyn went skiing."

"Snow skiing?" Amy's eyes went all dreamy. "Like in a real ski lodge?"

"The same," Katherine said, thinking of Caitlyn and hoping she was having a wonderful time. "It sounds lovely, doesn't it?"

"Oh yes," both girls chorused. "Mom said maybe someday, when Toby is better, we can all go."

"Only Toby never seems to get better," Amy said, the light going out of her eyes. "Or he does for a while, and then something happens, like now."

Rose caught Katherine's eye and shrugged helplessly. What can I say to that? she seemed to be asking.

"I know it's hard," Katherine agreed, giving Amy a quick hug, "and it's especially hard on your parents, because they're trying to do the best they can for your brother—and for you guys too."

"Amy said she thinks they care more about Toby than either of us, but I don't believe that," Sheila said.

"Oh, Amy, no!" Katherine said. She stopped chopping apples and went to the refrigerator where she'd placed a pitcher of fruit punch. "Let's have some punch," she said, "and take a little break, okay? I don't know about you guys, but I'm winding down."

So they all sat at the kitchen table and drank punch and ate cookies, and once again they talked about Toby and how unfair it was that he had leukemia. They wondered if he would ever really be cured, or if he'd be sick for the rest of his life until one day he just got too tired to fight anymore. And they even touched on the subject of what it would be like if Toby died. Amy and Sheila said they would miss him, and that their family wouldn't be the same without him.

And they talked about parents who were torn between healthy and sick children. Katherine didn't have answers for Amy and Sheila, but she sensed that they needed to get their feelings out in the open, that they needed to talk about the fears and doubts troubling them. She also sensed that it was easier for them to say these things to her than to their mother.

Finally, when Amy left the room to get a tissue, Katherine got up and went back to chopping apples. Sheila joined her. "You're a neat lady, Katherine," she said. "I'm glad you're our friend."

"Me too," Katherine said.

That evening they had a simple supper of broiled hamburgers and baked beans. "No fancy stuff tonight," Katherine said, as the girls set the big round table in the kitchen.

"This is fine with me," Jim said happily, cutting into his burger. "I haven't had a hamburger in months. Rose watches my diet like a hawk."

"Who would, if I didn't?" Rose retorted. "Isn't Gramps just about the stubbornest man you've ever seen, girls?"

"And Toby is going to be just like him when he grows up," Sheila said; then a stricken look washed all the color out of her face.

"Hey, don't do that," Katherine said. "You're absolutely right. Toby is a stubborn little beast, and I pity the poor girl he marries. She'll have her hands full all right!"

"Yeah!"

"You can say that again," Rose said dryly. "Pat is going to have her work cut out for her when that young man reaches puberty."

"Maybe that's what's wrong with me," Jim teased. "Could I be having a delayed puberty?"

"Silly old man!" Rose said, but she was smiling. They were all smiling, and Katherine couldn't remember when she'd felt more content.

The girls went to bed early that night, worn out by their participation in the holiday preparations, and their emotional outpourings, and after Katherine had said a private good night to each of them she went downstairs.

Jim was reading the newspaper, and Rose was comfortably ensconced in a lounge chair, her feet elevated. She smiled when Katherine entered the living room.

"Thank you for sharing yourself with us so generously, Katherine," she said. "I have to tell you that I was dreading the holiday until you arrived. When you walked through the door the whole atmosphere of this house changed." She looked a little wistful. "I guess I'm just too old to be much use anymore."

"Not at all," Katherine said quickly. "The girls love both of you dearly. It's just that I have a daughter only a few years older than Amy and Sheila. I remember how emotional girls can be at that age, and especially in a tough situation like this. It's difficult for everyone."

"What do you really think Toby's chances are?" Jim asked, folding his paper neatly and laying it on the floor. "Is our boy going to make it?"

"I don't know," Katherine said honestly. "Pat seems to think he's responding well to the new treatment, but there aren't any guarantees. I guess all we can do is stand by them and keep hoping."

"I'm looking forward to meeting your friend," Jim said. "What did you say his name was?"

"Ron Harold. He's alone this year, and I thought it would be nice to include him."

"No one should be alone at Christmas," Rose said. "My heart bleeds for Pat and Ed."

Katherine nodded. "But they're not alone," she reminded Rose. "They have Toby and each other."

After watching the ten o'clock news on television, Katherine could see that Rose and Jim were getting tired, so she excused herself and went to the small guest room off the family room.

It was strange not to be in her own bed in her own home, but she was glad she'd made the commitment to help Pat's family through this difficult holiday. Smiling as she brushed her teeth in the adjoining bathroom, Katherine wondered just who was really helping who? She'd thought she was resigned to doing without all the fun and fuss of Christmas this year, and now she knew she'd been wrong. Having Pat's daughters to worry about and fuss over was like a gift. She smiled ruefully. Why hadn't anyone ever told her that motherhood was a terminal condition?

They were busy all day Christmas Eve. Jim made several trips out into the yard to bring in small loads of wood for the fireplace, and Katherine managed to keep the girls hopping doing all sorts of last-minute chores. And then, at two o'clock, knowing Ron would be arriving shortly, Katherine went to shower and change from jeans and a sweatshirt to the soft velour pantsuit she'd picked to wear on Christmas Eve. It was deep sapphire blue, a color she'd always liked, and she thought it was a pretty contrast to her light, gold-brown hair and brought out the color in her eyes.

But of course it wasn't because of Ron that she was dressing up. She'd always believed that bright, pretty colors made people feel cheerful, and although Amy and Sheila had perked up quite a bit since she'd arrived yesterday, she was sure there would still be some tough moments ahead, like this evening when it was time for midnight mass and the girls had to go without their parents, and tomorrow morning when it was time to open presents.

Hopefully, Ron's presence would be a distraction. He was someone new and different, someone for the girls to practice their budding feminine wiles on, and as Rose had said, what was a holiday without a crowd? And what an unlikely group they were! Two temporarily orphaned girls, elderly parents, a lonely retiree, and Katherine. She laughed as she stepped into the shower.

Ron arrived at three-thirty, looking like the jolly old elf himself as he got out of his car laden with brightly wrapped packages.

Amy and Sheila raced each other to the door, acting more like preschoolers than teenagers, giggling about "Santa" coming right to their front door!

"Ho, ho, ho!" Ron did his best Santa imitation as the girls flung open the door. "I heard there were some good little girls living at this house."

"Two of the best," Amy said, flirting outrageously as she batted her big blue eyes at Ron and tried not to laugh.

"The kids at school will never believe this!" Sheila said, shaking her head as her sister shamelessly tugged Ron into the living room where her grandparents waited by the tree.

"Gramps, Nana, look who's here? Santa!" Then the two girls exploded in giggles, hugging each other as Ron shifted the padding at his belly.

"I didn't expect you to come in uniform," Katherine said. "You took me literally when I said you'd work for your dinner, didn't you? Rose, Jim, this is my friend Ron. You can come out from under all that fuzz now, Ron. You're officially off duty until next year."

Ron shook hands with Jim, greeted Rose, then enlisted Katherine's help to divest himself of fleece and fuzz.

Katherine had seen him out of his Santa suit before, of course, and she knew that under the velvety suit Ron was fully dressed, but somehow, helping him out of his jacket and watching as he unstrapped the huge lumps of padding seemed terribly intimate. Or maybe she was just overreacting. After all, she'd already sampled the eggnog and Christmas carols and brightly trimmed trees always had a strong effect on her. Whatever the cause, when he finally stood before them in his street clothes, Katherine was struck again by what a handsome man he was. And it wasn't just his physical looks. There was a deep, genuine warmth about him that was like a beacon, drawing them all into his good humor.

Luckily, Ron didn't seem to notice Katherine's scrutiny. As soon as he stepped out of his Santa pants, he went off in a huddle with the two girls. Katherine watched with interest as Amy and Sheila looked back at her and giggled, then nodded their heads solemnly in response to whatever it was Ron was telling them.

"Katherine, would you please put my suit out of the way somewhere?" Ron asked, giving her an innocent, little-boy smile. "There's something the girls and I have to do outside for a few minutes."

"But it's freezing out there," Katherine protested, "and Amy just got over a bad cold."

"I'll bundle up good, Katherine," Amy promised, already struggling into her down jacket, "and we won't stay long, but this is very important." She glanced at Ron and burst out laughing.

"What is going on?" Katherine demanded, her hands on her hips. "What in the world are you up to, Ron?"

Rose moved to Katherine's side and put a hand on her arm.

"Leave them be, Katherine. Have you forgotten

that this is what Christmas is all about, secrets and giggles and furtive looks?"

"Oh, so you're on his side too, are you? And what about you, Jim? Where do you stand?"

Jim leaned back in his chair and chuckled happily. "I'm just an interested bystander, ladies. I wouldn't dream of taking sides."

Katherine tried to lift the curtains at the front window to peek out, but Rose wouldn't let her. All she could do was pace around the room trying to figure out what Ron was up to until he and the girls came back in.

They were carrying a cardboard box and handling it as though whatever was inside was made of pure gold. Katherine started toward them, but Ron held up his hand. "It's a surprise," he said, "for later." Then the three of them disappeared into the utility room behind the kitchen.

A few minutes later they joined Katherine, Rose, and Jim around the tree.

"I'd give anything for a glass of eggnog," Ron hinted. "There must have been thousands of kids in the mall today, all wanting to have one last-minute chat with Santa. I thought two o'clock would never come."

"You're a better man than I am," Jim said, laughing. "I'm not sure I could have handled being Santa, even in my younger days."

"I enjoyed it," Ron said, taking the glass Katherine offered. "Thanks."

His eyes said more, and Katherine was suddenly glad there were other people in the room. There was something building between herself and Ron. She wasn't sure exactly what it was. She passed the nonalcoholic eggnog to Pat's parents and the girls, and sent Amy to the kitchen for a tray of cookies.

"So, what is that huge pot simmering on the stove?" Ron asked. "Did I mention that I was hungry as well as thirsty?" He winked, and both Rose and Katherine laughed.

"Rose gave me a wonderful recipe for oyster stew. It's a tradition in her family to have oyster stew for dinner on Christmas Eve."

"Homemade oyster stew? I haven't had that in years," Ron said. "What a treat this will be."

Amy came back with the cookies. Before she passed them around she whispered something in Ron's ear.

"Good," Katherine heard Ron say. "That's good. This is going to work out fine."

Before Katherine could inquire as to what was going to work out, Jim proposed a toast. He wished everyone in the room a merry Christmas, and he asked that they all say a little prayer for Toby's recovery.

"Amen," they all said in unison. "Amen."

After dinner Pat and Ed called to wish them

a happy Christmas. The girls spoke to their parents first, then Pat asked to speak to Katherine and instructed her to switch the telephone on to speaker.

"Hi, everybody." Toby's voice filled the room, and everyone gasped. The tree lights were suddenly brighter, the Christmas carols playing on the stereo were more beautiful. "I'm feeling better," Toby said, "but I sure miss my sisters, and you too, Gramps and Nana. The doctors said I'll be able to come home soon if I keep on improving."

"Hi, Toby," they all yelled back. "We love you!"

"Now that is what Christmas is really about," Ron said softly, leading Katherine to a quiet corner of the room. "Love. You could actually hear it in the girls' voices."

Katherine nodded, her eyes damp with unshed tears. She tried hard but couldn't remember when she'd had a busier, happier Christmas. Sure she missed her own son and daughter, but they were all well and happy and she knew she'd see them soon. And meanwhile she was with people who needed her. She looked with pride at the tree she'd helped the family decorate, at the garlands of fragrant pine and holly draping the doors and windows. And she thought of her own little house, with the frozen turkey TV dinner reposing in the freezer. Impulsively, she laughed out loud as Ron pulled her close for a hug. "I'm glad you're here," she said. "I'm glad we're all here."

By ten-thirty that night they knew they wouldn't be able to make it to midnight mass. It had started to snow and the roads were slick and icy. They all decided that they could honor the spiritual side of Christmas right in their own home. Actually, the girls didn't seem as disappointed as Katherine had expected them to be. Throughout the afternoon and evening one or both of them was constantly disappearing into the utility room, then giving whispered reports to Ron. It was making Katherine crazy because she couldn't imagine what they were all up to.

Finally, her curiosity got the best of her. "What in the world are you girls doing out there in the utility room?" she asked finally. "What have you got hidden out there?"

Amy and Sheila exchanged a furtive glance with Ron and tried not to laugh. "Is it time?" Amy asked excitedly. "Can we bring it out, Ron?"

Ron smiled and shrugged. "Sure. Be careful carrying the box, okay?"

"I demand to know what is going on," Katherine said. "The three of you have been acting like government spies all evening. What have you hidden out there?"

"You're going to find out very soon," Ron said mysteriously. "Maybe you'd better sit down. It's a special present I got for you, Katherine. I hope you like it."

"If she doesn't, I do," Sheila said, helping her sister carry the box into the room.

Rose and Jim watched the proceedings with bright-eyed interest. "My goodness," Jim said, "this is almost as exciting as 'The Price Is Right'!"

"Gramps!"

"Open it, Katherine," Amy prodded. "Hurry!"

"Well, I . . . good heavens, this box has holes in it! What is going on here?"

"Just open it," Ron urged.

So she did. First she just stared, her eyes as big as dinner plates, then a soft gasp of wonder slipped past her lips and Katherine reached down into the box and lifted out a tiny ball of black and white fluff. "A puppy!"

"You said that's what you wanted," Ron said softly. "Remember?"

"Oh, Jim look! It reminds me of Buttons!" Rose reached out and rubbed the tiny pup's head. "Isn't it precious?"

"Humph! Didn't you get enough of piddling pups when we were younger, woman?" Jim asked, but he, too, couldn't resist patting the pup's tiny head.

Amy and Sheila were dancing with excitement. "We had a dog like that once," Amy said. "But we had to give it away when Toby got sick. He

66

developed an allergy to animal fur. Do you think we could come and visit your puppy once in a while, Katherine? Maybe we could dog-sit for you when you go out."

All eyes were on Katherine and her tiny new friend, but neither of them seemed to mind. Katherine was in a trance of joy and disbelief. Once, long ago, a puppy had been her fondest wish. She hadn't thought of that in years, but now she could remember the sharp, painful disappointment. Over time she'd pushed the memory aside, other things in her life had taken priority, but now she knew that childhood hurt had never really gone away until now, when the tiny ball of fur licked her cheek and cuddled trustingly against her. "He's really for me?" she asked, her eyes shining as she looked up at Ron.

"She," Ron corrected. "Yes, she's really yours, if you want her."

"Want her? Oh yes, I want her!" Katherine hadn't even realized it, but there had been a hole deep down inside, and now, because of a perceptive man and a cuddly ball of fluff, it was filled.

Katherine's eyes suddenly widened as she felt a warm dampness against her lap, where the pup was cuddled. "Oh no!"

Everyone started to laugh, and if anyone noticed Katherine's tears of happiness they were too polite to say so.

When the others had all gone to bed, Kather-

67

ine and Ron sat before the dying fire and talked. The puppy she'd named Pepper was curled in a ball on Katherine's lap.

"Just stroking her makes me feel content," Katherine said.

"A pet is worth its weight in gold," Ron said. "Do you know that petting a dog or cat can actually lower your blood pressure?"

"I heard that, but I wasn't sure it was true."

"It is," Ron said. "I don't know what I'd have done after Edna's death if it hadn't been for my dog, Charlie."

"Do you still have him?" Katherine asked.

Ron shook his head. "Charlie died of old age about eight months ago. I'm going to get another dog one of these days, but I had to give myself a proper mourning period for Charlie. We were buddies for a long time."

"Have you always been this sensitive?" Katherine asked. "Or is that one of the benefits of maturity?"

"Don't make me blush," Ron said, laughing. "I'm nothing special, Katherine. I just try to feel what other people are feeling and act accordingly. Actually, I have a bad temper, and when something really gets me riled . . . well, you wouldn't want to be within shouting distance, believe me."

Katherine smiled and gave a sigh of relief. "Thank goodness! You've got a flaw. I was getting worried!"

Then their laughter faded as the reflection of the tree lights played across Katherine's face.

"This has been the nicest Christmas I've had in a long, long time," Ron said. "I'm a little surprised you decided to include me."

"I almost didn't, and this is why," Katherine said, as somewhere deep inside her a trembling started. She took Ron's hand and laid it over her heart so he could feel the rapid *thump-thump*. "See what you're doing to me? I was perfectly content with my life as it was. I had my job, my friends, my family . . . and now . . ."

"You'll still have all those things if you let me into your life, Katherine," Ron said quietly, making no move to take advantage of the position of his hand. He was touching her, but there was no pressure, only a calm acceptance that, for the moment at least, Katherine was in charge.

"What will you do now that your Santa job is finished?" Katherine asked, taking Ron's hand and moving it to the space between them on the sofa. "Do you have any plans?"

"Several," Ron said. "Playing Santa was great fun. I'm really glad I did it, but it made me realize something. No matter what the US government thinks, I'm too damn young to be retired! I've got a lot to offer, Katherine. Why should I waste it puttering on a golf course or learning to weave baskets. Time enough for that when I'm old, right?"

When Katherine's eyelids began to droop, Ron settled the puppy in its cardboard box and insisted that she go to bed. It had been decided earlier that he would spend the night. The weather was too treacherous for anyone to be driving.

Before she went to the guest room, Katherine fixed the sofa for Ron. "Are you sure you'll be comfortable here?"

"Pepper and I will be fine," Ron said, and then, before Katherine could protest, he drew her into his arms. He kissed her quite thoroughly, leaving no doubt in Katherine's mind that there was indeed plenty of fire inside Ron's furnace.

Although they all felt Toby's absence on Christmas morning, Katherine's frisky new friend helped brighten the day for everyone. They all tore into unwrapping their gifts with high spirits. Ron carved a permanent place for himself in the girls' hearts by giving Amy a beautiful makeup kit, and Sheila a complete manicure set. The girls spent hours in the bathroom experimenting with Amy's paints and powders.

When they sat down to dinner that afternoon and joined hands to give thanks, they all agreed that it had been a wonderful Christmas. "And you weren't pulling my leg, Katherine," Ron said, helping himself to a hearty serving of sausage stuffing. "This is the best I've ever tasted."

When it was time to decide between Katherine's pumpkin pie and Rose's apple-cranberry tarts, Ron endeared himself to both women by asking for a small serving of each.

"I never knew Santa was such a diplomat," Katherine whispered in Ron's ear.

"There's a lot you don't know yet," Ron declared, with a devilish wink. "Stick with me, kid, and you're in for a lot of surprises."

When the kitchen was clean and all the leftovers had been wrapped and stored in the refrigerator, Katherine gathered her things and said good-bye. The girls hugged her and Ron, and Rose and Jim extended their thanks to them.

Ron carried the pup out to his car and insisted that he'd follow Katherine home and help her get it settled before he went on his way.

As Katherine drove, savoring the wonderful memories of the past days, she thought of Ron, of his kindness and sensitivity. How many men would have realized how badly she'd wanted a puppy as a child? How many would have cared enough to see that her wish was finally fulfilled? A little thing? Maybe to some people, but not to Katherine. In her book Ron was a very special Santa.

He helped her carry everything into her house, and then they stood staring at one another. She is one good-looking lady, Ron thought. With her in his life he knew each day would be a little brighter.

He is definitely a handsome male animal, Katherine thought. Too bad I'm not interested in men.

"Well, Christmas is officially over," Ron said, clearing his throat. "I guess it's time to put away the Santa suit and get back to reality."

"I guess so," Katherine said. "Uh, I think you made a great Santa."

"Thanks. It was fun."

"Ron . . ."

"Katherine, I . . . You first," Ron said, with a little laugh. "What did you want to say?"

"I wanted to say that I'd really like to get to know you better, Ron, without all the fleece and fluff. I can't make any promises, but I could use a friend like you, and maybe you'd like to stick around and see how Pepper turns out." She glanced toward the pup who was systematically chewing its way out of the box.

Ron grinned, closing the door behind him as he shrugged out of his overcoat. "Friendship is good," he said. "Now how about some of that great hot chocolate before you send me home?"

Epilogue

"So, can we count on you and Ron to join us for Christmas dinner?" Pat asked, her cheeks flushed with happiness and excitement. "This is truly going to be the best Christmas ever."

"I guess so," Katherine said. "Toby's checkup was that good, eh?"

"So good I'm still pinching myself," Pat said. "When I remember last year . . . how frightened we all were . . . well, I still can't believe we'll all be off to Disney World on the twenty-sixth."

"You'll have a fantastic time," Katherine said, "and you all deserve it, after everything you've been through. I almost wish I could go with you."

Pat laughed and hugged her friend. "No you don't, you faker. You'll have plenty to do here getting ready for the wedding. And don't worry, Ed and I will be back in plenty of time to weep with the best of them. Is Ron still balking at wearing a tuxedo?"

"He's gotten used to the idea," Katherine said, rolling her eyes, "although for a while it was touch and go. Can you really believe my baby daughter is marrying her college professor, and that she actually asked Ron to walk her down the aisle?"

"It's a beautiful compliment," Iris said, coming up behind the two women. "Say, Katherine, did you know that Ted is giving Ashley permission to start running soon?"

Katherine shoved her hands down in the pockets of her white smock. "I did, and I'm almost as thrilled as Ashley is. She is one determined young woman. I'm proud of her."

That evening when Katherine went home, Ron was waiting for her. Pepper, full grown now and every bit as beautiful as Katherine had known she would be, danced around until her mistress bent to pet her.

"Dinner's almost ready," Ron said. "I'm trying another new recipe."

Katherine groaned silently. In the past year Ron had taken a gourmet-cooking class, and now he delighted in trying his new creations out on Katherine. Fortunately he only cooked on the days he wasn't working at his new business, a mail packaging service. Katherine's hips were already starting to spread, hence the new home exercise equipment Ron had bought her for Christmas.

As she lifted her lips for Ron's welcome-home

kiss, Katherine decided that even with her increasing girth, she liked her life just the way it was. She and Ron had a wonderfully warm and satisfying relationship, and because of his enthusiastic involvement in his new business, he seemed content to let Katherine have her space when she needed it. They maintained their own homes, enjoying togetherness when it was mutually convenient and desirable. They put no pressure on one another, and there was no talk of marriage. Maybe there never would be, and Katherine was content. She was also very glad she'd decided to give her feelings for Ron a chance. And she knew that as long as she lived she'd believe in Santa Claus!

Stacey Dennis is the author of two TO LOVE AGAIN romances—*REMEMBER LOVE* and *SEALED WITH A KISS*. She lives in Key West, Florida.

Over the River and Through the Woods

by

Marjorie Eatock

It was a bright, sunny winter morning ten days before Christmas, and Norma June Bailey was outward bound for a glorious holiday with her family three states north when, on the edge of town, her car died. Dead. Kaput. Not even any funny *chuff-chuffs* or whines or jerks to show it was even trying to go on. Just silence.

Saying a word not generally attributed to sixth-grade teachers, she coasted to the curb, waited a moment, and tried to start it again. Zip. Gloved hands tapped the wheel. Then releasing an enormous sigh, she popped the hood up and got out.

There was no point in diddling around. What she knew about a car was how to start it, how to stop it, and how to steer. What else she knew, thanking God for small towns, was her locale: Jefferson Avenue, which was also the highway, and that was Martha Bogel's house right over there, with the bare strings of ivy hugging aged brick.

Someone must be home because an elderly Chevy sat in the drive, the inquisitive nose of a cocker spaniel pressed against a side window.

Remembering Martha fifteen years ago when she'd been Martha Mason with a cute ponytail and a total inability to comprehend decimals, Norma buttoned her tweed coat against the December chill and hurried up the porch steps.

There was a bell. She punched it. Behind her, the cocker barked accusingly; over his bark she heard interior chimes and the welcome sound of feet.

The door opened. And it certainly wasn't Norma June Bailey's day, because standing there was the last person she wanted to see—ever. Her principal, Ted Dunkel. A little late she remembered that Mr. Dunkel, being new in town, and single, had taken an apartment in Martha's house.

He'd been zipping himself into the heavy, padded jacket he wore over faded jeans. It made him look even more like a barrel, she thought, the fleeting comment unkind for the man was "broad-shouldered" to his knees from his stocky Germanic ancestry, not dissipation.

He said in surprise, "Well . . . hello!" in the meantime glancing over her shoulder to the street.

Forestalling any comment that might be forthcoming, she said, "May I use the telephone?"

"Of course."

He stepped aside, still not leaving much room in the small boxy foyer, and pointed around the corner. "Right in there. I gather you have a problem. May I help?"

"No." In case that had been too brusque to be other than rude, she amended over her shoulder, "Thank you, but I'll call Bill Durr's garage. He's just two blocks up. He'll come. He knows my car."

Bill said, indeed, that he'd come immediately, and as Norma hurried back through the foyer, she drew a soft breath of annoyance. Mr. Dunkel had gone on down the steps and was peering into the depths of her engine. But as she approached, he held up both big gloved hands and grinned.

"No touch, ma'am, no touch!" he said in that dry but almost melodic voice she'd grown to know too well in one semester. "I admit to having the mechanical aptitude of a seal in wool mittens. Did you get Bill?"

"Yes. He's coming."

"Fine. A good man." Then the dark eyes in that broad, strong-jawed face caught the heap of bright Christmas packages stacked on her back seat. "Oh, hell. And you're trying to leave town, aren't you? I remember Miss Long said you always went to . . . to Wisconsin, isn't it? Janesville?"

And why had Hilda Long felt impelled to discuss her co-worker with this man, their boss though he might be?

"Near there," she answered, and let it go at that. "You needn't wait, Mr. Dunkel. I'll be fine."

"No problem. I was just taking Martha's dog to the vet's to be boarded. They're in Springfield for a few days. Do you know Madison?"

"Madison?"

"Wisconsin. I lived there a few years."

"Oh. No, I don't. My daughter and her husband have a dairy farm and rather avoid the cities. They prefer country living, especially while raising children." Now why had she volunteered that—except just now her four-year-old granddaughter's round face was very much in her mind, as was the sweet whispery voice on the phone saying, "Oh, Grammy—please come for my birthday!"

That event was just four days away! And her daughter had said later, "Please come if you can, Mom. It would mean so much to Jill. She has the lowest self-esteem of any child we've adopted."

Ted Dunkel interrupted her thoughts, saying cheerfully, "Here he is now! That was a fast trip, Bill!"

Swinging from the cab of his tow truck, the mechanic grinned. "When Mrs. Bailey commands," he said, "you snap! I learned that in sixth grade twenty years ago. What's the problem?"

Norma June shrugged. "It just . . . quit," she said.

"Okay! We'll have a look-see."

The "look-see" was not rewarding. It ended, in fact, with Norma's car hitched to the wrecker, and Ted Dunkel helping her up into the high seat beside Bill Durr.

"Happy holidays," she said, almost automatically, and was glad to lurch into motion, leaving the wide, bundled man on the curb, wind ruffling the gray hair across his forehead and a cocker spaniel barking persistently behind him.

"That is sure one neat guy," said Bill cheerfully, rounding the corner and heading back toward town. "My boys think he's just tops. A better basketball coach than Mr. Wamsley, Johnny says. And he spends a lot of time with kids—you know, Scouts and a church group and stuff. No family, I guess?"

"I don't believe so." Norma did *not* want to talk about Ted Dunkel, no matter how philanthropic he was. In her own job situation he was the pits. "Is my car serious, Bill?"

"I'm afraid it is."

And he was right. After an hour of greasy delving and myriad telephone calls, he came to where she sat in his junky office, wiping blackened hands on a piece of dirty rag and shaking his head.

Her heart sank at his long face. "No good?"

"No good. The earliest I can get that part will be Tuesday."

Tuesday! Jill's birthday was Tuesday!

He had turned, filled a chipped mug with coffee the color of ink, and was handing it to her. "I'm awful sorry. How about the airlines?"

She accepted the coffee, took a cautious sip, and discovered even caution was not sufficient. The stuff was liquid acid. She put it down on a corner of his metal desk and said, "I'll try. I've a credit card. May I use your phone?"

He gestured at the dusty instrument buried in work sheets, said, "Sure. Call me if you find anything," and went back out into the garage.

In truth, she already knew the answer. And she was right. These were the holidays. Even if someone would haul her from this small town to the nearest airline hub seventy miles away, there was nothing left but stand-by. Ditto Amtrak—which was also forty miles in the opposite direction. And ditto rental cars and loaners from car agencies—unless she meant to buy a new one. But Bill said her car would be fine. When he got the new part. Tuesday.

It looked like, in the parlance of a rude world far far away from the social mores she tried to instill in her sixth-grade students, she was screwed.

No waking up to the sound of happy chatter, the *whish* of ten-year-old Russell sliding down the bannister to breakfast, her door cracking open and a ball cap sailing inside, accompanied by fourteen-year-old Jimmy's voice saying, "C'mon, Grandma, stir your stumps! Dad says it's milkin' time!" They always threatened her with hand milking, saying the power was off, the cows must be "stripped," and she had to help! Last summer little Jill, still too new to the family to understand, had thrown her small arms protectively around Norma June, protesting in that shrill, angry voice, "You let my grandma alone, you guys! She no have to do nothin'!"

Bless her little heart, Norma thought sadly. The boys were great, and she loved them dearly. But the thin, undernourished child with the enormous brown eyes had gone straight to her innermost feelings and locked in there. What her previous life had been, Norma had never asked. It didn't matter. She was home now, with Deanna and Will and the boys.

She wrenched her mind away from the faraway child with the funny double part in her dark, silky hair—hair for which "Grandma" had wrapped two emerald green velvet bows in Christmas paper—and ran a desperate hand through her own brisk, soft frost-tipped black locks.

What was she to do? Must she give up?

The pathetic and desperate imaginings of a fifty-six-year-old grade-school teacher, bags and holiday packages piled at her feet, standing by the highway with her thumb in the air was interrupted suddenly.

Bill had reappeared. But he wasn't talking to Norma; he was saying over his shoulder, "Yeah, she's here."

And Ted Dunkel stepped into the untidy little office.

Damn! She had to deal with his new policies and his structural changes and his idiotic scholastic theories every day in the classroom. Must she also countenance his presence during her Christmas vacation?

"Hi," he said. He still wore the padded jacket and the jeans, which were a far cry from the suit and the tie that generally got loosened about ten o'clock and stayed that way until dismissal, when it came off entirely. And he suddenly wore a purposeful look on that broad-jawed face, an expression she'd become familiar with and automatically braced for, because it meant something was coming.

"Hi." At least she could say that.

"Bill says the car is definitely a no-go."

"Yes."

Bill Durr corroborated this, shrugging his shoulders. And suddenly, with no rationale whatsoever, Norma realized that even though Bill, at almost six foot, was a good three inches taller, beside the mass of Ted Dunkel he looked like a skinny Christmas elf. "Tuesday," Bill was saying again. "At the earliest."

"You've not come up with anything else?" Dunkel was asking Norma.

"No. It's the holidays. There isn't anything." If she sounded a little peevish, surely circumstances would dictate forgiveness.

"Then ride with me."

For a moment she didn't assimilate what she'd heard. Or—perhaps—didn't want to assimilate it.

She almost quavered: "What?"

"Ride with me. I said I was going to Madison."

What he'd *said* was that he used to *live* in Madison, but at that moment she had been so stunned by the wrecking of her plans she had hardly remembered her name.

"You . . . you are?"

"Yeah. I've some business there. And you're welcome. Let us load your gear, and we can be off in ten minutes."

Norma June Bailey was suddenly confronted with one of the toughest decisions she'd made since her husband, Dean, died in 1980 and she'd had to sell the beloved family home. A three-day trip, alone, in the same car with Ted Dunkel—the "Captain Change" of North Elementary. A nonstop listen to his justifications of all the unnecessary revamping he'd done in her grade-school world!

Also, if fifth-level Hilda Long got hold of it . . . the amused eyebrows and the sneaky innuendoes when she got back—assuming either she or Dunkel survived. Hilda was an old friend, a true friend, but she'd been intimating for weeks that the principal had more than a professional interest in Norma June.

That had to be put against not seeing her family in Wisconsin and spending a quiet, boring ten days here, with all her friends otherwise involved and nothing to do that really mattered. She wasn't a shopper, she wasn't a card player, and going to the movies alone had all the appeal of a root canal.

Was his offer worth it?

Yes. Damn it, yes! Her family was worth it— whatever the cost.

And she heard herself saying, "All right. Thank you."

"No problem. I'll be glad of your company."

And I'll be stuck with yours. But she didn't say that, of course. Instead, ignoring the grin on Bill Durr's face—it disappeared instantly when she looked at him—she got up, gathering her gloves, handbag, and the old Rex Stout mystery she'd taken from her luggage to read while Bill fixed her car. She made herself smile.

"Then let's do it."

Ted Dunkel held the swinging half-door open for her. "I like a woman of action."

"You got one," Bill said cheerfully, following them out. "Finished with your coffee, Mrs. Bailey?"

Norma almost laughed. "Yes, thank you, Bill."

"Too strong, huh?"

"A bit."

"Can't imagine why. It's only yesterday's. Yes . . . may I help you?" This to a skinny man in a dark overcoat standing by Norma's car.

"Looking for Darryl. Not here today?"

"Oh, you're the guy who sells him those computer games he peddles. Sorry—Darryl's in the hospital. Springfield, I think. He won't be back here, anyway. I had to can him. Mr. Dunkel, why don't you drive your car in alongside of Mrs. Bailey's? That will make it easier to load."

The man in the overcoat was persisting. "Excuse me. But did he leave any of my stuff behind?"

"Not a thing. Sorry."

Then, as the man walked away, Bill added in a lower voice, "The kid did work for me. But he got a real drug problem, and I had to let him go. Now I hear he overdosed. A shame. Real good boy with carburetors."

Norma was unlocking her trunk. She said, "Darryl . . . Darryl . . . I had a Darryl Jackson—"

"Not him. He went to the university for a couple

of years and ended up selling insurance some-where. This kid came here from the city—St. Louis, I think. He lived over the drugstore, sold computer games in the little towns along the interstate and worked for me weekends. This guy was his supplier, I guess. Sort of a smarmy fellow, I always thought. Hey, Mrs. Bailey, before Mr. Dunkel gets his car in here, I didn't mean to—to railroad you."

"Into going with Mr. Dunkel?"

"Yeah. I mean . . . he is a pretty nice guy—and I'd sure hate to see your Christmas ruined. I know how much Deanna and her family look forward to having you."

Norma June smiled, and patted the muscular young back. "I'm not . . . railroaded, Bill. I do want to get there. It'll be fine."

He flashed that pixie smile again. "But you'd better take the backstreets out of town."

"Bill Durr! I'm almost a hundred. Anyone looking for gossip would be better off eyeing that blond filly in the superintendent's office."

"Okay. I get the message. What do you have in these suitcases—bricks?" He was grunting as he heaved them from her trunk.

"You never know about Wisconsin. It could be twenty below tomorrow. Don't miss the sleeping bag."

"You're planning to sleep by the roadside?"

"No, Bill. It's for my grandson. He's into camping."

She stepped aside as Ted Dunkel backed his Chevy neatly into the slot by her car, swung out big booted feet, and opened the trunk. He had, she noted, only *one* suitcase with a piece of shirt sticking from a crack. Probably as good a packer as he was a principal.

The two men stowed. Bill asked, "What about the Christmas stuff?"

"Back seat," Ted Dunkel said, and opened the door. He blinked a little at the enormous stack of red and silver gifts, but wisely made no comment.

"Nice Chevy."

That was the computer games man again, sipping on a soda can. He added, "An eighty?"

"Seventy-nine."

"Runs good?"

"Excellent." Ted shut the door, said to Norma cheerfully, "Hop in."

"Oh!" Pink suffused Norma's cheeks. "I'm sorry . . . I wasn't thinking. I'd better . . . go. Bill, you do have a rest room?"

"Right over there. Past the muffler rack."

The facility was adequate, although Norma decided if she scuffled her feet she might rediscover dinosaur bones. She dried her hands on a paper towel, looked in the mirror with chipped edges and scowled. Her lipstick was shot, and for driving two hundred or so miles by herself she hadn't bothered with eye makeup. She fixed the lipstick with her tube of soft pink (at fifty-six one didn't wear flashing scarlet any more) and let it go at that. If Ted Dunkel wanted a beauty queen, he'd have to find one in Madison.

So why was she glaring at herself in discontent?

Her dark hair swept in a frosted dip over nicely arched brows and eyes as dark as sable. Beneath the open tweed coat were a dark red heavy sweater and well-tailored slacks. She didn't wear scarves because her neck was too short and her shoulders were too wide, but the ornate silver chain Dean had given her just before he died looked fine. And she wasn't fat. Well, perhaps she'd picked up a *little* weight—Hilda Long *would* bring those yummy cookies to the teachers' lounge—but her clothes weren't tight. Snug, maybe. She looked fine. No one should be embarrassed to have her as a traveling companion!

And—damn it!—in those awful jeans, Ted Dunkel was no fashion plate.

With that last conclusion, she unlocked the door and emerged into bright sunlight streaming across greasy cement, shoulders erect and feeling somehow like a Crusader.

The stranger was still sipping soda and standing with Bill and Ted. As she approached, she heard him say, "You're going to Wisconsin?"

"Madison," Norma answered briskly, aware that

the other two men were only making polite conversation while they waited for her. "Okay. I'll leave my car in your hands, Bill."

"She'll be fine." He was holding open the passenger door of the dark blue Chevy. "Have a good trip. See you after the holidays. Take care of her, Mr. Dunkel—I've got a kid in sixth next year."

Ted slid in on his side, starting the engine. He grinned at Bill. "No problem. All clear?"

"All clear."

Bill stepped back and waved them on. The other man was already at the sidewalk, getting himself into a black car with Missouri license plates. He waved as they pulled around and headed east. Norma waved back. It was a conditioned response. Then she buckled her belt and looked at her wristwatch. Nine-thirty. Already an hour and a half late.

"On a schedule?"

He wasn't laughing, but he was almost. Irritated, she tried to answer politely, "No—I just usually get going by eight."

Her black slacks were picking up dog hairs. Apparently the cocker spaniel hadn't always stayed in the back.

"Sorry about that," he said, noticing her frown. "Fluffy was all over the place. Martha doesn't discipline him very well."

Remembering Martha, she could understand.

But suddenly she was distracted by something else. "You missed the turn!"

"What?"

"You missed the turn!"

"The interstate's two blocks up!"

"But I don't go interstate!"

"What? Why not?"

Because interstate traffic scares me spitless!

But she couldn't say that—not to this man! A little embarrassed, she did say, "The old way is much more scenic. Along the river. You know. But . . . you're driving. Do what you like."

He muttered something she instinctively knew had been "Shit!" But he also did a wheelie in the middle of the street and headed back toward the turn to Highway 51.

"I guess I'm not in a hurry if you're not."

"I . . . I just need to be there Tuesday. For my granddaughter's birthday."

"Oh. Sure. How old is she?"

"Four. She'll be five."

"I have a granddaughter turning five." He added under his breath, "Somewhere!" But she didn't hear that. She was too caught by the fact that a granddaughter meant a daughter and a daughter meant a wife—at some point in this man's existence if not currently.

"In Madison?"

"In the area."

He was reaching a long, heavy arm past her

and scrabbling in the glove department. His fingers found a small travel atlas, dropped it in her lap. "You navigate, okay?"

"I'd be glad to help drive."

"That, too. Right now I'm more interested in a good place to have lunch."

At nine-thirty! Then a suspicion hit her. "Did you eat breakfast?"

A sheepish grin tucked up one broad, neatly shaven cheek. "Well . . . not really. I was going to eat after I delivered Fluffy, then I got sidetracked."

"I'm sorry." And she really was. "Look, about two miles on up there's a nice little roadside cafe. Let's stop. Okay?"

"Okay."

She was surprised at how fast the two miles were covered. He said, "This is a nice way to go. The bluffs are beautiful." And she answered, "You should see them in the spring." Then he asked, "Are you local? You seem to know the country."

"We moved here about twenty years ago. Dean was superintendent at the grain elevator. Then when Deanna started school I got back into teaching—and I've been there ever since. Oh, look! Eagles!"

They were crossing the broad, half-frozen Illinois River. On each side at the foot of the bluffs, shattered, dry reeds moved in the light wind like crumpled spaghetti. High above, two enormous birds soared on silent wings, intent on anything that might move.

Ted Dunkel hit the steering wheel lightly with a massive, closed fist. "Isn't that great?" he said. "I tell you, lady, they can have the cities. This is what I like. Thank you."

Puzzled, she asked, "For what?"

"For taking me off the interstate. You know, sometimes we're all in such a hurry we . . . we forget. This can be a nice trip. Maybe—maybe we'll get to know each other."

He said the last part very quietly, not even looking at her. She felt her body tighten, though. Whoa, mister! Is that it? Do you think maybe this is your chance to win me over to some of your far-out ideas on how to educate a ten-year-old?

Well, don't hold your breath, buster!

But she didn't say those things. She only smiled—albeit a little tightly—and answered, ignoring that last part, "Sometimes change is good for us."

"Click."

"What?"

"Click. My jaw. Surely you heard it."

"Why should I hear it?"

"Because of what you said. That sometimes change is good. Ye gods and little fishes, woman, what have I been trying to put across to you for a whole damned semester?"

Fortunately he was laughing at the same time he passed a pickup truck towing a load of hay bales. So he didn't see her face. If looks could kill he would have been dead as the classic mackerel.

But the whole thing came back to her—the pure shock of walking into August Grade Conference to meet the new principal and finding that instead of instructing one class all day long as she'd done for years she was now only teaching history and reading to a departmentalized group of three classes, which she'd have twice a day!

That wasn't change. That was revolution!

He was adding, "And you have done so well! I have the semester state test scores in my briefcase. Lady, you've pulled your history-class kids up ten points!"

Butter time. Well, spread it on your own toast, buddy. I *know* I'm a good teacher. Do you *know* you're a good principal? Or is all this nonsense just to shore up your own sense of achievement?

Aloud, she said shortly, "Thank you."

"I'll show them to you tonight. Or tomorrow. No hurry."

Then the secondary shock hit: *Tonight.* Or *tomorrow.*

Very quietly, she asked, "Do you have motel reservations?"

"No. Never thought of it. Do you?"

"Yes."

97

"Then I'll find something close to where you are. No problem."

She said grimly to herself, You want to bet? This is holiday time! But that melodic, cheerful voice went on.

"This country is amazing! You drive through miles of bluffs and cedar scrub and scraggly walls of rock, then bingo! Suddenly it all changes, and there's nothing but level farmland as far as you can see. Hey—there's a water tower up there. Is that where we'll find the cafe?"

"Yes. About a half mile ahead. On the left. See the Christmas lights?"

"Right on. And about time, too. I'm spittin' cotton."

He pulled across into the parking lot, and stopped between two pickup trucks. Over their heads flashing red lights read GERTRUDES, and below in black letters, Special Today—All You Can Eat! Everything was ornamented by plastic holly and green ribbon.

He was climbing out his side, and she did the same with the sudden bemused realization that if she took her turn at driving she'd have to move the seat so far forward he'd have to ride in the back.

"Brrr!" he said, turning up his jacket collar. "Hustle. I think it's getting colder. Lock your door."

"Okay." Absurd! People didn't lock doors around here. However, it was his car.

But the parking lot did seem chilled; she was glad for the warmth of the little dining room. There were quite a few people sitting on the mismatched chairs at the shabby tables, many of them farmers, denim jackets over chair backs, shoveling pie. They all nodded, smiled incuriously, and went on shoveling. A chubby little lady in a calico apron bustled over, saying, "Hi there, Miz Bailey. Who's your friend?"

"My boss."

"Oh, wow. Do I curtsey?"

Bemused, Norma June shrugged and answered, "A simple bow will do. How's the coffee supply?"

"Just made a pot." Behind thick glasses, her eyes went from Norma to Ted Dunkel. "Anything else? How about a fresh cinnamon bun? Judy took some out a minute ago."

Norma settled for that. Ted settled for that plus eggs, sausage, sausage gravy on biscuits, and a large orange juice. Then he unzipped his jacket, leaned back, and smiled at her.

"This is my kind of place. I may never drive interstates again. Hey . . ."

"What?" Norma was accepting a steaming mug of coffee and waving off the sugar and cream. The sound of his voice made her look up, follow his gaze.

99

Levelly, he said, "Isn't that guy at the counter the one in Bill's?"

It was, indeed. He was paying his check, gave them a general, all-purpose wave, and went on out the door.

Ted said, "Good. I didn't want him sitting with us. For some reason I don't like the fellow."

"He likes your car."

"Why do you say that?"

"He's standing by it just looking. And patting the top. There. He's going on, now."

Ted had swung around, but there was no longer anyone to see.

He muttered, "Good" again and resettled himself. With his jacket unzipped, she saw he was wearing a black and white pullover sweater of a size to fit an aircraft carrier. She slipped her own coat off, and draped it over the back of her chair. Her own sweater, she mused, would only cover a landing boat. Deanna always had bought overlarge clothes for her mom—unless she was trying to make a point.

Surely not. She'd only gone up one size in ten years! That wasn't too bad. Besides, students didn't care if Mrs. Bailey was skinny or not as long as she passed them on to seventh grade. . . .

A long arm came over her shoulder and the hand grasped Ted Dunkel's, shaking it enthusiastically. "Good job last night, Dunkel! You're the best we've had."

100

Ted Dunkel said, "I think the kids were pleased."

"They had a ball. Who's this—Mrs. Dunkel?"

Smoothly, Ted answered, "No, no—one of my co-workers. Mrs. Bailey—John Schmutz."

"Oh, sure . . . you had my brother's boy in sixth."

Now Norma's hand was enveloped, and the shaker moved around to show himself, a jolly, round-cheeked gentleman in orange hunting gear. "Lady," he went on, "you should have seen this guy last night. The finest Santa Claus we've had in years!"

Well, Norma June could believe that. A white beard and Ted Dunkel could probably out ho-ho the old saint himself. They exchanged a few more words in which Norma divined that last night had been the annual Lions' Club Christmas party; then with a resounding shoulder pat that would have crumpled lesser men Mr. Schmutz moved on, and Ted tied into the eggs and sausage. The biscuits and gravy were on the side.

Norma watched, amused in spite of herself. He was eating as though breaking a fast. Through the chomping, he muttered, "Help yourself. The biscuits are great."

"No, thanks. I'm fine." She sipped coffee, enjoying the fact that it did not taste like battery acid. "So you're a Lion."

"Have been for years."

"A Kiwanian?"

"No. They're pretty much younger guys. Please, eat a biscuit. I feel like an awful pig."

"If you'll eat a cinnamon roll."

"Cimmamon roll."

"What?"

"Cimmamon roll. That's what my little girl used to say."

Norma laughed, thinking of her own small granddaughter. "I think all kids do that."

"I suppose. It's a deal on it, anyway. They look great."

"We'll not eat any dinner!"

Then fully surprised, she noticed she'd said "we"! But he was laughing—she was noticing also that his laughter was pleasant—and saying with a twinkle in those dark eyes, "Speak for yourself!"

He paid the check, grinning as she protested, "Come on—it makes me feel macho! We'll set up a pay rota later. Okay?"

"Okay."

And it was colder outside—definitely colder, with the sun eclipsed in a gray sky. He started the engine, and let it run a moment. Norma June noticed that their waitress was waving good-bye through the tinsel-draped cafe window, and she waved back. Then she had a wry thought: Half the people she knew ate at Gertrude's. How long before everyone in town heard she'd gone on vacation in Mr. Dunkel's car?

He had twisted about, his big arm resting across the back of her seat, and was backing out. His face in profile was calm, businesslike.

All right, damn it! Let them talk. Since the local pharmacist had finally selected his fifth wife they needed something new, anyway.

And she did want to get to Deanna's!

Suddenly he was mumbling something. She asked, "What?"

"Oh, it's my fault. I forgot to tell you this is an old car. All the doors have to be locked manually. When we loaded up your Christmas stuff Bill forgot to relock the one behind you. Nothing missing?"

She craned her neck to look at her stacks of packages, and forbore laughing. As if at Gertrude's anyone would swipe anything in the parking lot! Get real, Dunkel. But all she said was, "No, not that I can see. But I will remember. How long have you had this car?"

It had seemed a fairly safe topic of conversation. But she knew she was wrong when she saw the brief look of pain on his face.

He answered, "Fifteen years. Almost. My—my wife had died, and I thought I could entice my daughter to come live with me."

"With a new car?"

"We . . . we'd been divorced for quite some time. Edna had brought Jackie up with some pretty materialistic values. But she'd just turned

103

seventeen and had her mother's bad opinion of me . . . so it was a no-go."

Norma June hadn't meant to open a can of worms, but the pain in his voice was so real she had to put some sort of salve on it. And she had, after all, seen his gentle touch with kids. She said, "Your daughter missed a good bet. She's still saying 'no'?"

"She's dead, too."

"Oh. I'm sorry. It's not my affair—I didn't mean to rattle cages."

"You're not. Sometimes it even helps to say it out loud: *Jackie's dead*. Turn the page, Dunkel!" He gave Norma June a wry, sidewise smile. "Now find her little girl."

"She had a child?"

"So they tell me."

His eyes were fastened on the highway ahead, a straight shaft of concrete between shorn cornfields. "Jackie got in with a pretty wild"—he was hesitating, groping for words—"far-out crowd. A cult."

"Religious?"

"Pseudoreligious. They proved their faith by doing their leader's bidding. Jackie's task was to help steal a jade statue from a museum. The outfit insisted it belonged to them. But when she lifted the thing another statue fell on her. She died instantly. And the rest of them just . . . faded into the woodwork."

104

"With her little girl?"

"With her little girl."

"But she has to be somewhere!"

"That's what I keep telling my lawyer!"

Now he was half-smiling. And Norma, thinking of her own precious granddaughter, said, "Don't give up."

"No way. However, I have a pretty good collection of dead ends already. It's been almost three years. Hang on."

Since he'd stomped down on the gas pedal and was in the process of passing three large grain trucks in a row, she obeyed. She also shut her eyes.

But no tire screeches came, or jouncing or indignant horn blats. She felt him whip back into the right-hand lane again, resuming normal speed, and she opened her eyes.

Things were fine. The trucks were far behind, and he was glancing at her in surprise.

"Scare you? I'm sorry!"

"I'd forgotten men did that. Dean used to give them the finger when he passed. Did you?"

He grinned. "Never mind the details. Now, you've heard my sob story. Give me yours."

"With sobs?"

"Lord, I don't care. We have three days."

"I hate to be redundant. What do you know?"

"Your husband is dead, you have one daughter, married, with two kids—"

"Three."

"Okay. Three. You got your degree from Drake University in Iowa, you've always taught sixth grade, your students both love and respect you, and you don't like carrots."

Aha! Only Hilda knew that.

A bit acidly, she asked, "What else did Miss Long tell you?"

"You don't really want to know. It would show my hand."

He was laughing. She wasn't certain she was.

"I see I shall have to speak to Hilda."

"Do that. And while you're at it, see if you can get her off that Williams kid's back. He's dyslexic, not dumb, damn it! I keep telling her!"

For a brief moment Norma June longed for the ancient days when dyslexia had been as unknown as Asian flu. "You mean Joey? Don Williams' little brother?"

"Yes, Joey. You'll get him next year. Perhaps I'll have better luck with you. Hang on again."

This time it was just a tractor pulling a wagon load of fire wood. The young, bundled-up farmer, the tips of his ears red with cold, chugged his equipage off on the shoulder and waved as they went by. Ted tapped his horn in thanks.

"There's an intersection up ahead. Which way?"

"Straight on. That will take us up the east side

of Springfield and north again. Is that snow on the windshield?"

"Just a little. But it is getting colder. I've cranked up the heat twice in twenty minutes. How far do you usually go in a day?"

She put her finger on the atlas map. "Just to here. It's a little bitty town, but the motel is all right." She'd slept there regularly for six years, but he didn't need to know that.

"That is—as my dad used to say—a 'fur piece.' "

"All I usually stop for is gas and a drive-in."

"Fine by me."

He glanced at his wristwatch, reached over, and turned on the radio. Through a fading miasma of Christmas music, a well-known commentator's voice came on and Norma June made a wry face. Don laughed.

"You don't like this guy?"

"I hate him. He's rude and a boor. He tackles the most sacred of my cows, and sometimes he's right—then I really can't stand him."

"What an honest lady. Then read your book for half an hour. He's tackling the state legislature today, and I want to hear it."

She reached for her Rex Stout, found her place, read ten pages—and went to sleep. The school Christmas program and the parents' tea and closing her department for the holidays had taken more out of her than she'd realized.

She woke up with a feeling of both panic and

embarrassment. The car was parked, it was getting dark, in the gloom Ted was smiling at her, and she needed a bathroom.

"Fast food," he said. "Tell me what you want, and I'll order. The temperature is really dropping, and we've got fifty miles to go."

When she emerged from the rest room he was standing at the condiments bar, loading up on catsup. They found a table behind a nodding Santa Claus and as far away as possible from the speaker booming out something vaguely identifiable as "Jingle Bells."

Tackling the first of his roast beef sandwiches, lathered with half a cup of horseradish, he asked, "Whatever happened to Bing Crosby singing 'White Christmas'?"

"I think it went out with baggy ski pants."

"And white gloves?"

"That, too."

"We're dating ourselves. Do you still own a hat?"

Norma thought of the broad-brimmed straw with the flowers on the top shelf of her closet. "Yes. Do you?"

"And how. Creased crown, snapped brim, ribbon band. I thought I looked like Humphrey Bogart. Probably it was more like a small lid on a large cookie jar, but one has one's illusions." He was smiling, but she caught an infinitesimal hurt and knew that he, too, had suffered in childhood the slings and arrows of skinny peers. He was adding, "I've always been big. My mother had to make my clothes."

"*Make* your clothes?"

"I was brought up Amish. Hadn't I said that? Black Bumper Amish. We had a community van, but no chrome on it."

"You're not now?"

"I wanted to see the world. So I joined the navy, and sort of . . . never looked back. Most of my family are dead now, just an uncle or so left—and I'm welcome. They are fine folks. But I'm in a different world. You're not eating your fries."

"I'm done. Help yourself."

He did. And she understood one reason why he was "big." This man *looked* at food and it disappeared.

What he was really looking at was his watch. "Do you mind taking your sandwich and coffee to the car? We'd better go."

She didn't mind. She climbed in and sipped as he brushed the light coating of snow from the windows, noting that on a flashing jeweler's clock next door the temperature said barely zero. That was more than a twenty-degree drop!

"Brrr!" He climbed in, bringing cold and fresh air, filling up his side of the car as he buckled the safety belt over his padded girth. "You didn't see that funny guy from Bill's?"

"No."

"I thought I did. Probably not. Ready to roll?"

"Ready."

They rolled.

The dark came on fast, augmented by gray, sullen clouds, but the snow stayed light, blowing off the sides of the old blue car. They drove in silence, both with their thoughts far away.

Norma June had one sudden, silent, but almost guilty thought: Dean *always* talked when he was driving; he said it kept him awake, and sometimes I got so bored hearing about docking for weeds in a load of grain, or breaking loose a stopped-up auger, or bins caking up with wet grain . . . I didn't care. It wasn't my thing. And he didn't care about the two sixth graders in the back of the room rolling marbles with their feet during math class. That wasn't *his* thing . . .

It *would* be Ted Dunkel's thing . . .

But Dean was my husband. A good provider. A companion . . .

Yet . . . he *is* gone. . . .

That last, poignant thought made her blink blurred eyes in the gloom of the car, glance hastily sideways at Ted Dunkel, and hope that in the dark he hadn't noticed.

He hadn't. His heavy-jawed profile was briefly clear against an intersection light, and the short glimpse she had was of eyes set straight ahead, shoulders unmoving, life only in the hands on the steering wheel.

Where was his mind when she'd been thinking about Dean? With that nebulous ex-wife? His daughter? His sad search for her child? Or on another woman, somewhere up ahead—perhaps in Madison . . .

She abruptly remembered something else Hilda had said—Hilda the happily single, easygoing, fifth-grade teacher whose friendship she'd valued for years. Hilda had interrupted a tirade against Ted Dunkel, a spate of angry words at which she ordinarily laughed because she knew Norma June spoke them to no one else.

"Norma J," she'd said, "cool it! Give the man a chance!"

Well, she had. Hadn't she? A whole semester of chance!

Or . . . had Hilda meant something else. A different sort of chance . . .

"Is that it?"

She jumped, so deep was she in her musings. "What?"

"That motel up there on the left. I can see a sign."

"Oh! Yes. That's it. Pull in by that dumpster; the office is right next door. I'll run in and see if they can find you a room."

"Don't worry about it." He was sliding the old Chevy alongside a trash-heap trailer. "I have to go get some gas anyway—we're down to a quarter-tank. I'll find something."

111

The warmth of the office was almost as palpable as a shower's. The skinny, balding man behind the desk glanced up from a hand-held, bleeping video game and said, "Yes? We're filled up."

"I have a reservation. Where's Mr. Arthur?"

"Oh. They sold out. Last May. Went to Phoenix. Name, please."

Vaguely upset, she gave it. He ran a finger down his book, said, "Oh, yeah. Bailey. Number fifteen, right to your left. Here's the key."

"There's nothing else vacant here?"

"No, ma'am. Not since this morning."

Morning! Why hadn't they thought of it this morning?

Chagrined, she took the key. "Is there another motel in town?"

"Oh . . . there's a crumby one down a block. You got someone coming in?"

"Yes." That would do.

"Lots of luck," he said, and went back to his video game.

Wind greeted her, biting her face as she went back out. Ted Dunkel, shoulders hunched, was standing at the dumpster and picking up a large box that had previously held toilet paper.

"Let's put your Christmas packages in this," he said. "It will make carrying them in and out a lot easier. No rooms?"

She always left the gifts right there in the back

of the car, but she didn't mention that. She was worried by something else. "No. Nothing. He says there's another motel a block down."

"Okay. I'll give it a shot. What's your number?"

"Fifteen. Right there."

"Good. I won't even have to move the car. Unlock, and I'll tote this stuff in." He was loading the box with gifts. "How many suitcases?"

"Just the one. The brown one by the sleeping bag."

"Leave the bag; I may have to use it." He chuckled, and followed her through the bars of light from the office windows to the first unit on the left.

She opened the door, pushed it hard across the too-high worn carpet laid over worn carpet and snapped on a lamp. As usual, there was the standard double bed, a bureau with mirror, one chair, a ten-inch TV, a clothes rack, and a bathroom.

"Home sweet home," he murmured, hardly finding room for his girth as he put her suitcase on the bureau and the awkward box of presents on the floor beneath the clothes rack. "Are you hungry?"

"Not at all."

"I'll get a bite then, where I settle in. What time in the morning—three o'clock?"

He was teasing her. She wasn't certain she

liked it, or the reason for it. Surely she wasn't that noticeably inflexible! Or . . . was she?

"Six?"

"Six is fine. Sleep well."

"Call me."

"What?"

"If you get a place to stay."

"I said I'll be fine. Don't worry!"

Through the window of a suddenly large room, she watched him back out and drive away. She felt . . . what? Bereft? Nonsense. Uneasy.

Perhaps the gas station could help him find something . . .

Holding that idea, she turned and discovered he'd hauled in the wrong suitcase.

Oh, well. It was too late now.

But what in the world could she sleep in?

She opened the case, and surveyed its contents. Mostly slacks and tops. One dress for church. A green sweatshirt for Deanna; craft people had made hundreds like it last year. It had a hand-painted animal appropriate to the season on the front—this one was a cute reindeer—and when one punched the animal's nose, it jingled a song also appropriate to the season. This one played "Santa Claus Is Coming to Town."

Well. The sweatshirt was long. Deanna wanted them bulky. With plenty of blankets, it would do. Norma June only caught colds when her throat and shoulders were bare.

She creamed her face, put two rollers in her hair where the bangs looked frizzy, checked the bathroom for soap and towels, and read the standard notice on the wall by the door. The office closed at ten, opened at six, checkout was before eleven. Nothing new there.

One good shove, as usual, would tear the night chain right out of the wall, but she wasn't anticipating anything like that. Her uneasiness was not about anyone breaking and entering. It was about Ted Dunkel.

Well . . . he'd said he'd call.

Hadn't he?

No. He hadn't. He'd just said, "Don't worry."

All right. She wouldn't.

With that noble conclusion, she threw back the covers, crawled in, and opened her book.

Ten minutes later she got up for an antacid tablet and glanced outside.

The snow had stopped. In the yellow light from the office there were his car tracks going out, but not in.

Vaguely reassured, she went back to bed, wrinkled her nose at the odor of mothballs in the top blanket, and returned to Nero Wolfe again.

It was not a success. Wolfe's renowned girth only served to remind her of Ted.

Not Mr. Dunkel. Ted!

She hadn't called him Ted for the entire semester, although everyone else had. She'd wanted that space between them.

Of course it was because of the cavalier way in which he'd totally reorganized her department. Of course!

But he'd also said that her history students had aced up ten points.

That did give her a glow. She loved teaching history. She was, in fact, damned good at it—far better than she'd been teaching decimals. The kids had really put themselves into the era of the Civil War, bringing dulled, old sabers and ancient photographs and canteens and maps to school. All sorts of artifacts had appeared in this area that had paid a considerable price in that conflict. Young Billy Webb had written a very good report on the warships plying the Mississippi. And she had to admit that having two history classes instead of one had sparked some competition. . . .

The last thing she remembered was a fierce gust of wind whining savagely against her window. The book dropped, unread, and she was asleep.

The wind! Gracious, it was really blowing! Blam! Blam! Blam!

Then, finally arousing to consciousness, Norma June realized it was not the wind.

Someone was banging on her door.

First she froze. Then she reached for the telephone. Then she decided to have a look outside.

Telephones in this motel didn't always work. She remembered that from last year. What if something had happened to one of her kids in Wisconsin? They knew where she stayed. Deanna had a complete list of numbers.

She slid from her warm bed, her bare feet hitting the cold floor. Sure. The heat was controlled in the office, and they always turned the thermostat down after ten.

Shivering, she stumbled to the window, dragging a blanket with her, and pushed back the dusty drapes and looked out.

A pathetic sight met her eyes. Ted Dunkel stood there, gloved, stocking-capped, an inadequate sleeping bag clutched about his middle, as he banged with both fists.

He saw her ghostly image and said distinctly, "Let me in!" adding another word of a caliber not acceptable at North Elementary.

She didn't even think. She obeyed, fumbling with the ancient lock-button. He didn't wait for the night chain, but pushed like a demon. It flew out to its fullest extent, then fell, rattling to dangle, and he entered like an animated blob, kicking the door shut behind him, rasping, "God damn! I thought I was going to freeze out there."

"Oh, you poor man! What happened?"

"What happened? I'll tell you what happened!"

He almost fell into the rumpled covers of her bed, pulling them around him, glaring up at her. "There's no place in this town!" He adorned the word "town" with an expletive, and proceeded to use it freely in the next three sentences. "There's no place within forty miles of here. That asshole in the office wouldn't let me sleep there. And I ran out of gas, because they only have one fuel stop and it closed at nine o'clock!"

"You've been sleeping in the car!"

"I have been trying to sleep in the car. But I'll tell you something, lady, when the very snot freezes in your nose it is time to move on. I'm sorry, Norma June"—his angry voice suddenly lowered, and he tried to smile—"but you're stuck with me, kiddo. It's fifteen below. And I am not going back out there."

"Of course you're not!" She wasn't, after all, that kind of idiot. She knelt, trying to undo his heavy boots, and in the struggle her sweatshirt began to play.

He stiffened, glanced at the black television screen, then back to the woman at his feet. "What the hell is that?"

She showed him. He began to laugh. So did she, uncontrollably, until the tears streamed down her creamy cheeks.

"Oh, good Lord," he gasped, mopping at the bristle just beginning to show on his broad face. "Good, ever loving, never failing Lord! What a fortunate thing we'll never have to tell anyone about this, because they'd not believe it! But jeeze, I'm still cold. Is there any place to get coffee?"

At least the water was hot. She fished a packet of instant from her bag, put it in a paper cup, stirred and handed it over. Gratefully he drank, and his shivers began to subside.

She made one for herself, curling her bare feet beneath her in the tatty chair.

He said, "Is it also cold in here, or am I just not warmed up yet?"

"It's a little cool."

"What do they do, turn down the thermostat?"

She nodded, sipping her barely tolerable coffee.

"And no one's in the office."

"No."

"What a dump."

A little defensive, she said, "Ordinarily it's all right."

He shrugged, forbearing any more comment, and tossed the cup into the wastebasket.

"Okay, then. If you think you're going to try to sleep in that idiotic chair because I'm in your bed, lady, you have another think coming."

"But . . ." She hated the sound of her voice, hated knowing her cheeks had pinkened because that was exactly what she *had* been thinking.

"Bull," he said flatly. "Look. We are adults,

119

right? Cold. Bring that blanket because I suspect we'll need it, and climb back in. On that side. This is my side. Okay?" Now he was grunting a little, bending over to pull off his heavy boots, then unzipping his jacket. "Look at me. Fully clad. And staying fully clad. Besides, my dick is frozen. If I did try to come on to you, it would probably break off, and I wouldn't care for that at all! Good night, Norma June. Whatever's left of it. Wake me at six."

He was stretching out beneath the covers, then bringing his massive knees up, saying, "Brrr!" and going onto his side, facing the door. Away from her.

Norma June Bailey was saying to herself, I don't believe this. It can't be happening. Not to me.

But it was.

And she *was* cold.

The springs creaked as he drew his knees tighter to his chest, huddled the blanket over his still-stocking-capped ears.

To her amazement, she found herself dumping the rest of the so-called coffee and climbing in beside him.

She arranged herself on her designated side, drawing her own knees up against the fleeting warmth of her own body heat.

He was motionless. Breathing evenly.

But his bulk was enormous. He might think

she had half the bed, but one third was more like it.

How long had it been since she'd slept with a man . . . or, as a matter of fact, anyone?

Not since last year, when little Jill had crept into her bed, pressing bare feet and those odd double ankle bones against her, cuddling into her encircling arm, murmuring, "Love you, Grammy . . ."

Before that, Dean. For almost thirty years.

Sex? Sometimes. Always when they first went to bed. Dean had a routine for morning, and sex wasn't in it.

At least not with her. His wife. As for that bitch with the dyed hair in the grain office, Norma June didn't care to even think about her anymore. She'd been a passing fancy. He'd had at least four in thirty years that Norma June knew. They'd all passed. He'd come back, every time.

Nothing had ever really changed. Not the essentials. The house. Deanna. Her job.

Of course she'd missed him when he died. They'd been good companions. Friends.

And how cleverly she'd disguised the hurt from his philandering with tolerance. How grateful Dean had been . . .

Had she loved Dean? She'd thought so when she'd dreamed longingly of him every night he was in Viet Nam.

When he came back . . . that was when things changed. Fantasy cannot hold up against reality.

Perhaps it had been so with him, too. She'd never thought of that until now. A little late . . .

One thing she knew, guiltily: she was a lot more comfortable being a widow than a wife.

Beside her, Ted Dunkel stirred in his sleep, flopped over toward her. And, with Ted Dunkel, that move had features of both an earthquake and a landslide.

Almost smooshed, clinging grimly to the very edge of the bed with a deeply sleeping man's breath on her neck, Norma June considered her options, sighed, got up, went around the bed, and slipped in on the other side.

Ah. Space. Much better, she thought, and—surprisingly—went to sleep herself.

She woke up the next time suddenly conscious of daylight through untidy drapes, and this large man leaning on one elbow and looking down at her.

"I thought I was on that side."

"You changed sides."

"Oh. Sorry."

"No problem."

But she was abruptly conscious of her tousled hair, the sweatshirt almost slipping off one white shoulder and the fact that he didn't seem to be breathing at a proper pace—that his breath was quickening.

She wasn't ready for that, at all—nor the sudden flicker of . . . something . . . in his dark eyes.

Instinctively she reached up, touched the painted reindeer's nose. And it began to play.

For ten seconds the man beside her remained suspended. Then he visibly relaxed, laughed, and swung around to put stockinged feet to the floor.

She thought she heard him say to himself, "Round One to the lady." But she wasn't certain. And at the moment, she couldn't handle thinking about it. Instead, she asked, "Do you want the bathroom first?"

He was lacing his boots. Over one sweatered shoulder, he said, "No. You go ahead. I've got to get some stuff out of the car."

In the ensuing twenty minutes she tried to come to grips with some immutable facts. One, this guy was her boss. Two, he was merely getting her to her daughter's as an accommodation. Three, she'd disliked the man for an entire semester. Why should she get all adolescent over him now?

She had seen absolutely *nothing* in his eyes!

Holding that thought, she opened the door and found him delving into what she had predicted to be a jumbled suitcase.

Glancing around as he buttoned another shirt, he pulled the same sweater over his graying head, saying, "Next?"

"Next."

"I'll just shave."

"There's time for a shower." Then she blushed helplessly, thinking *he surely wouldn't suppose I just want to see him naked.*

But he was already going in, turning sink taps.

"No hot water," he said over his shoulder. "I guess everyone is gearing up at the same time."

He was right. The tap ran icy cold. She sighed, rolled up her laundry, poked it into a corner of her own neat suitcase, clicked the lock, and put the suitcase by the door.

The large box of gifts caught her eye.

She *could* try to take them out to the car. She ought to help a bit.

That was when a small package on top with just a little different wrapping paper caught her eye.

That wasn't hers!

Curiously, she picked it up. It was a small box. It didn't rattle. On the bottom a typewritten label read: *To D. with all my love.*

Conscious of a sudden clouding of her day, Norma put the gift back down on top of the other ones.

So he was giving presents too. So big deal! It was, after all, Christmas.

Who the hell was D.?

It's none of your business, she was adjuring herself firmly when the bathroom door opened and he stepped out, filling the room with both his presence and the pungent smell of aftershave.

"Hoo boy!" he said, fanning the air. "That's the new stuff you girls at North Elementary gave me—and I do thank you, but I'm not certain something called Explosion No. 1 is my thing!"

So much for her contribution of a buck fifty to the fund.

He bent, closed his own suitcase, picked up the padded coat. "Ready?"

"Ready," she echoed. As he hoisted the box of gifts she reached out for the door—and it opened almost into her.

The motel manager stood there, frowning, clutching a jacket over thin shoulders against the wind.

He said indignantly. "I thought so! I thought you were in here. You owe me ten more bucks, buddy! Really, Mrs. Bailey, we don't run this sort of place!"

Ted Dunkel's broad face set stonily, and the look on it had the manager backing up.

"What sort of place?"

"Well . . . I mean . . . inviting men in . . . at all hours."

Ted almost roared. "No heat! No hot water! A dinged-up night chain! Listen, whoever you are, I wouldn't stay here if you paid me—and I'll make damn sure this lady doesn't do it again!"

"But . . . but . . ."

"That's what you'd better take out of here before you land on it!"

And the man did, fairly scurrying across the damp walk into his office. Laughing mirthlessly, Ted dropped a ten on the table.

"Scum," he muttered. "Sorry about that, Norma."

"It's okay. Really. This motel is nothing to me."

"Good. Then let's shake it."

They loaded a cold car and Norma slid inside while he fluffed a light dusting of snow off the windows. Stowing himself in by her, he said, "I think I saved enough fuel to get up the street to the station. But I can't let it sit and warm."

"It will warm soon enough. Let's try to go get the gas."

They made it, left the car to idle while they hurried across the street for a fast-food breakfast, and were ready to go in twenty minutes.

Perhaps a good thing. It was starting to snow—this time as though it meant it!

Ted said, "How many miles today, pilot lady?"

"About two hundred."

"Cross your fingers. Also, fish under your seat. Isn't there a thermos shoved back toward the rear?"

There was—accompanied by field glasses, a shabby copy of Tom Clancy's *Hunt for Red October,* three soda cans—empty—and a doggy bone.

Ted said, "Good." He loped back into the fast-food place and filled the ancient thermos. Norma pitched out the soda cans, tossed the Clancy into the back seat on top of the "To D. with all my love" thing, and put the doggy bone in the glove compartment. It didn't look chewed, and if they got into a real Wisconsin snow, she and Dunkel might have to share it.

"Now!" he said, sliding back in and handing her the thermos and some paper cups. "We go for real."

"For real," she echoed, and they nosed out into the street.

In a hesitant voice she asked, "Do you want me to drive?"

He shot her a sideways glance, and she noticed he'd nicked himself shaving. "Do you *want* to drive?"

"No!" But in case she'd answered too fast, she qualified it. "But I will. To help."

"Just now I'm fine."

"Just tell me."

"I shall."

As they left the outskirts of the small town the country began to roll again, rocky bluffs with their tops obscured by the same snow making white stripes on the flat, shorn cornfields below them. The traffic was not heavy but was consistent, leaving wet lines and throwing occasional splats against the sides of the Chevy.

She said, "Shoe factory employees."

He was frowning, bending forward to search the lanes ahead. "What?"

"There's a shoe factory back there. Those guys are probably going to work."

"Or in for coffee." Now he was frowning. "Look at that! Forty-nine cars on-coming, and only one ahead of me—doing twenty-five miles an hour! Blast! If she doesn't like to drive in the snow, why doesn't she stay home?"

Mildly Norma observed, "I'd say she was quite a ways from home. That's a Missouri license plate." She did not say that she didn't like to drive in snow either, and that driver very well might have been her.

Still muttering, he found a long opening between oncoming cars, whipped his Chevy out and around the offending car ahead and then back into the proper lane again. Norma intended to say sarcastically, But it wasn't a "her," it was a "he!" then changed it to "Good heavens! That's the guy from Bill's garage!"

"Again!"

"We're probably just on his route."

"Mmmfh."

He was increasing his speed to what he considered a reasonable minimum, now making virgin tracks on his side of the road.

"There," he said, and took one arm off the wheel to extract it from his jacket sleeve. She helped, pulling the coat loose, and tossing the bundle into the back. Part of the tail caught a package on top of the gift box, cascading it to the floor and under the front seat, but she didn't really care. It was the one that said "To D. with all my love."

That's his problem, she thought, and wondering fleetingly why she was being so nasty.

"How about yours?"

"What? Oh . . . my coat. I can get it."

She did, tossing it back to join his. The car temperature was very comfortable. She pushed up the sleeves on her red sweater—if he didn't change, why should she?—and said, "Look at the black birds!"

An enormous flight of them swooped over the road ahead, did an aerial, swinging turn, and settled down among the snow-topped corn stubble edging a long country lane. The lane entrance was flanked by huge, old evergreens, draped with red Christmas tinsel. Far back from the highway, nestled against the feet of sky-reaching bluffs were farm buildings with five or six silos pointing upward.

Well, she thought, at least we're getting close to Wisconsin. Silos and endless lines of black and white dairy cows would mark the landscape from now on—like that parade of placid, ruminating beasts in the other field, broad backs against the snow, hardly raising their heads as the car drove by.

Following her gaze, Ted said, laughing, "When you've seen one dairy cow, you've seen 'em all."

"Perhaps they think the same of us."

"Perhaps they do. Pour us some coffee."

While she juggled paper cups and the thermos, he asked, "How did your daughter come to settle up here?"

"She met Will in college. When his father died suddenly, he took over the family dairy." She said nothing—nothing!—about the terrible wrench at hearing her only child meant to move miles away. Oh, the private tears and sleepless nights with Dean just dead, and Deanna gone. No one home when she went there, no one to talk to, no one with whom to share either trials or laughter. It had taken a long time to adjust.

Ted was asking, "No other family?"

She shrugged. "Not really. A few cousins, an uncle here and there. No one close."

"Me, too. And under those conditions it's sure not hard to let Christmas mean . . . nothing at all."

She nodded, thinking of the last few days when she'd gone home from a room full of bright-eyed, anticipatory kids to an empty, quiet apartment—where this year she'd not even got out her artificial tree.

"Of course," she said, "I have Deanna."

"What if you didn't?"

The idea was like a dash of cold water.

130

"But I do!"

"What if she called, said, 'Mom, we all have the flu. Don't come this year.' What then?"

Reluctantly, she answered, "I . . . I don't know."

A large brown farm dog on some important mission was trotting right up the center of the road. Ted swerved around him, then went on calmly, "This is hypothetical—for you, anyway. Not for me. I have no Deanna. But as I see it—and I do, I have to—you either fall in a heap and do the martyr bit and everyone avoids you like bubonic plague, or you resign yourself to making the best of it and start looking around for a new world. Does that make sense?"

"Yes. But even as a hypothesis it scares me."

"It scares me. And in my case it isn't a hypothesis."

What was he telling her, that with his old life shattered he was trying to build a new one? Fine. Commendable. But *why* was he telling her? Unless he wanted her to help him build it . . .

Her breath caught; she shot a covert glance at him. His eyes were straight ahead, his voice calm if a little tight. No. No, no—it wasn't that. Norma June Bailey was not the heroine type. He was simply saying that when one's world is shattered, there are always ways to survive. A good, sound philosophy.

So why was her heart beating like a triphammer?

For the first time in five years she desperately wished she could reach out, punch the dash lighter and have a cigarette. Small things like that covered so many social awkwardnesses.

Since a smoke was not an option, she laced her fingers together and said inanely: "There's always something."

And suddenly he grinned. "Did you play that a lot when you were a kid?"

"Play what?"

"Dodge ball."

Then she understood. She protested, "I am not dodging!"

"Horsefeathers! But . . . never mind. We'll pursue it later. At a more propitious time."

She didn't much like that, either. A lot of "propitious times" can occur in two days. She picked up her coffee cup, found the coffee stone cold, drank it anyway. A small sacrifice for changing the subject.

Coward!

The word echoed in the back of her head! Coward! *Scaredy cat—always have been, always will be!* A boy in her junior-high days had taunted her with that, a now faceless boy except for his sneering mouth. He'd wanted her to sneak out into the dark behind the school with him during the Halloween party. She wouldn't. Lorrie Hadley went, and Norma June had never forgotten the pussy-cat smile on her face when they returned.

Suddenly she realized Ted was talking to her. She started, saying, "I'm sorry. I was thinking about something else."

"Well. So much for my hypnotic powers. I said, What's next on the map? This snow is getting worse."

It was indeed. They were now the only car on a white road whose sides were barely distinguishable.

She looked down at her atlas. "Oh, my. Quite a ways. A hundred miles—a hundred and ten, perhaps. Surely they'll get the plows out."

"The plows are on the interstate." But he said it without rancor. "Okay. We'll just plod along. Are there any towns?"

"Oh, yes. None of any size, though."

"I was thinking about gas. We're okay now, but the next chance we get let's fill."

Looking through a house window at soft, silent, floating fairy fluff can be enchanting. Driving through it at barely twenty miles an hour is something entirely different. Norma June didn't think she'd ever been so glad in her life to see looming ahead the snow-draped signs of civilization.

"Bit touchy out there, ain't it?" asked the gas station man, zapping Norma June's credit card through his machine.

"Just a bit." Ted was loading his pockets with

133

candy bars, while the girl at the counter filled his thermos. "How is it up ahead?"

"Th' bread man was in here a while ago. Said it was lighter around Duke City. So you may drive out of it. Thank you, ma'am. You folks have a good trip, now."

"Good" being in the eye of the beholder, they did not "drive out of it." They covered the last ten miles at a virtual crawl, grateful to get behind a solitary road grader, two or three other cars creeping along in their wake.

Ted turned into the motel parking lot between two mountains of fresh-scooped snow. His eyes bleared by the unrelenting silvery glistening, he shut off the engine, leaned back wearily, and said, "This is it, kiddo. End of the line for today."

They both went into the motel office, stomping the snow from their shoes, blinking at the rush of warmth. The frizzy-haired young woman behind the counter said, "Well . . . hi, Mrs. Bailey! I didn't figure you'd make it! Bad out there, I hear."

"Yes, it is. This gentleman needs a room, too, Melba. I hope you have one."

Melba ran a long-nailed finger down a list. "Sure. We're getting cancellations. I'll give him No. 10—at the other end from you. And if worse comes to worse—I mean if they show up after all— we'll fix a cot here in the office."

"You're a good girl," Ted said, signing his name.

Doing Norma's credit card, she pointed over her shoulder. "Coffee around the corner. Fresh. And I made it, not Dad, so it's not too thick to stir."

Ted was picking up both keys. "Maybe later, thanks," he said. "I'll unload, and leave the car up here. Give me about an hour's sack time, then we'll eat somewhere. Okay?"

"Okay."

Watching him go out into the snow, Melba said, "Whooo! You found yourself a big one!"

"Well, he's not mine. He's my principal—but he is big."

Why was she so compelled to explain? Annoyed with herself, Norma want around the counter and poured coffee into a Styrofoam cup. Melba was going on.

"Like a sumo wrestler! He said you want to eat. There's not much open."

"What is?"

"The lights went off at Colonel Cluck's across the street half an hour ago. Maybe Bunnyburger. Check with me when you leave."

Norma nodded and went out, shielding her cup against the snow. Ted was already down the row, unlocking his own door. He waved and disappeared, leaving nothing behind but fast-filling

135

boot tracks. Three other cars were between them, a silent line of white ghosts.

She found her own room bright with light, the box of gifts on the floor and the wrong suitcase—again—on the bed. Well, she hadn't told him it was the wrong one!

Norma shut the door, took off her coat, shook it, and found a hanger. She went to the bathroom, turned on the television, and sat down in the one chair. The place still seemed empty—and overlarge.

She drank the coffee, put unseeing eyes on the evening news, and wrestled with the unsettling sense of something missing. It was ridiculous. Wasn't this exactly what she liked—the same motel room, the same hot coffee, nothing changed? Hadn't that been her security for ten years?

It was very good coffee, but she was hungry. They'd had candy bars for lunch.

An hour, he'd said. Give him an hour's sack time. He was tired. Of course he was. That sort of hazardous driving wore everyone out. An hour. *That would make it six o'clock.*

Before she saw him again? Was that what six o'clock meant? Not eating. Seeing Ted?

"Oh, I don't believe this!" Norma June Bailey said out loud, and she started desperately switching channels, looking for anything—anything—to bring her to her senses.

A panel discussion on PMS would hardly do it.

136

She was past that six years ago. The latest fashion from Paris? When you've seen one stack of bones switching her hips down a runway you've seen them all. The weather? She had enough of that right outside her door. Settling for an ancient rerun of "Gilligan's Island," she slipped off her heavy shoes and rubbed her feet, wincing at the latent arthritic twinge in her left shoulder. It would give her fits some day, no doubt. It had plagued her mother.

She watched the clock.

Damn.

As punishment for her silliness she let five more minutes go by before she called the office and asked for Number 10.

The phone rang a few times before Ted answered, obviously stifling a yawn. "Hi."

"Hi. It's six—ish."

"Okay. I think I'm alive. Be there in a couple of minutes."

She brushed her hair. Fixed her lipstick. Then remembered that this was the night she usually called Deanna.

She was on the telephone explaining, and Deanna was laughing, when there was a thunderous knock on the door. She said, "Wait a minute—I have to let him in."

"My mother with a man in her room? *My mother?*"

"That's enough," said Norma June shortly, not

appreciating misplaced humor in her only child. "Hold on."

"I wouldn't hang up for the world!"

Ignoring that, Norma put down the phone, opened the door.

He came in on a draft of cold air, kicking the door shut behind him, unzipping his jacket, shoving blown gray hair off his forehead. "Wow! It's still snowing! Oh . . . sorry. Didn't know you were on the phone."

"Just my daughter."

But when she picked the receiver up, it wasn't. It was Jill.

"Hi, Grammy! You comin'?"

"As soon as I can, sweetie."

"Who with you?"

"Just a friend. A gentleman."

"I know him?"

"No. Not yet."

"Grammy! You bring me a Grandpa?"

Four-year-old voices carry. Norma turned to Ted, started to apologize. Saw his face. Saw the abject longing, the misery on it, then the attempt at a smile.

She never remembered what she did say to Jill, only that it ended in, "Kiss, kiss, baby. I have to go. See you soon."

By the time she turned back from replacing the telephone he had himself under control. He said, "She sounds real cute."

"She is. Just a doll."

He picked up her coat, held it for her. "Where do we eat?"

"Probably *Bunnyburger.*"

"Fine. Anywhere we can go without tunneling."

It was *Bunnyburger.* The tall bunny cutout by the door had red Christmas balls in his ears and tinsel on his whiskers. The balls matched the nose of the cold Salvation Army man ringing his bell. Ted put something in the pot that didn't clink and hurried Norma June inside.

It was surprisingly busy. Norma gave Ted her order and looked for a vacant table. Two long-legged boys in "letter" jackets arose from one by the Christmas tree, one of them saying, "Here you go, ma'am."

"Why, thank you," Norma said, sitting down, stripping off her gloves and feeling rather elderly. "I'll see you get on Santa's list."

He grinned, showing braces. "Hope it's better than the list I'm on at home," he said to his buddy as they went out the door.

Norma hoped so, too. He seemed like a nice kid.

Ted was coming, carrying a tray and wending his way carefully among the diners. He unloaded two bunnyburgers for him, one for her, an enormous stack of fries, and two pieces of apple pie.

"Coffee's coming," he said, placing the tray behind him on the rack, and sliding the table toward her so he had enough room to sit. "The little girl up there said they've already made enough coffee this evening to float a battleship."

"I'll bet they have."

She took a bite of sandwich, found it good, let her napkin slide to the floor, retrieved it, and found Ted staring perplexed at a couple before him, the woman saying, "It is! It is! It is Teddy Dunkel! I knew it!"

Teddy Dunkel?

But she hadn't time to fully assimilate that. The woman was thirtyish, very, very blond, with huge eyes made up in azure blue, expensive jewelry adorning her slender frame; and she was carrying an enormous fur coat. She tugged at the arm of the elderly gentleman with her. "Sit down, Raymond. Just for a moment. We're not in that much of a hurry. Teddy, how *are* you?"

Ted was saying slowly, "But I'm not—" And she rushed over to him, "Chrissy Manheim. Herman's little sister! Oh, it's been donkey's years!"

She was settling next to Ted, scooting him over, waving her companion to Norma's side. "Oh . . . oh—I'm sorry—this is my husband, Raymond. Raymond Stone."

Norma had glimpsed one click of recognition in Ted's eyes; then they went blank as he said, "Oh. Chrissy. How do you do, sir." She'd hardly had time to absorb the surprising word "hus-

140

band" before those blue, and now very appraising, eyes turned on her.

Their owner said, "And who is this?"

The men had shaken hands briefly, and Raymond Stone was obediently sitting down at Norma's side. She caught a whiff of whiskey and a worse, though more expensive aftershave, than the teachers had given Ted for Christmas, also a small grimace of apology.

Ted said briefly, "Mrs. Bailey, Mrs. . . . Stone, is it?"

"For twelve years. Isn't that right, Ray?" And she was holding out her scarlet-nailed hand, showing an enormous diamond that sprayed iridescence from the Christmas lights overhead. "We were on our way to catch a flight to the Azores when we got stopped by this old snow. I would have gone on, but Raymond's super careful, aren't you, pet? Ted, what is with you these days? I know this isn't Janet!"

"This" was Norma June, and now the blue eyes were more than appraising, they held purpose.

"No, it isn't," replied Ted calmly. "How's Herman?"

"That old stick-in-the-mud! Still on the farm, still in the eighteenth century. Raymond's corporation wanted to buy out the whole colony and put a refinery there, but do you think they'd sell? Not a one of 'em! You and I have been the only

141

two with brains. Go on and eat. I just couldn't resist stopping a minute."

Norma had been eating—if not tasting. Ted resumed. Chrissy chattered. She also started playing with the glittering chains that fell into a collective vee and accentuated her well delineated and opulent breasts.

"Old friends," said the man beside Norma through the chatter. She turned, saw how thin he was inside the expensive chesterfield coat—and how apologetic were his heavy browed and rather rheumy eyes.

She smiled, and let it go at that. Chrissy was saying to her directly, "You two work together? Oh—oh, my—is this a relationship? Are we . . . interrupting something?"

She was laughing, asking it lightly, but now there was definite purpose in her tone.

Frankly, Norma wanted to reach over and slap that made-up artificial face. But she merely smiled and said, "We work together."

"How nice. Is Teddy fun?"

Norma caught Ted's eyes, tried to read them. Nothing. Define fun. "Of course," she answered lightly.

Chrissy had been playing with Ted's fork. She dropped it to the floor, bent and retrieved it with a startling display of mammary amplitude. "I just thought of something. Could I impose?"

Raymond Stone said, "Chrissy, really . . ."

"Now, Ray. I'll bet they won't mind." Her lashes were batting like butterflies, and despite herself, Norma felt more acid dislike than she'd felt for anyone in years. Why? The woman was patently an idiot!

"Well, silly old me—I forgot to pack Ray's heart tablets, and he's run out. Our pharmacist has FAXED the prescription here to a place on the other edge of town, but they aren't delivering. Driving through snow is so hard on my Raymond, and of course, you know, Teddy, I don't drive at all. Could I ask you to take me over there?"

Nailed. Then she had the temerity to pound in another one. "You two can stay right here and chat. The cold air is just awful on Ray's chest. We won't be long."

Ted finished his fries. He said, "Sure. Okay."

He did not look at Norma June.

"Super!"

Chrissy stood up, cuddling herself into her fur coat, and the smile on her face was that of a nice, winsome little girl. "Teddy, you're so sweet to do this!"

"Teddy" said nothing, merely stood up and zipped his jacket. They went out together into a blast of cold and snow, his massive frame engulfing all signs of her but high-heeled shoes.

Raymond Stone was slowly pushing himself erect, walking around, sitting back down in Ted's place.

His seamed face wore such a sad expression that in the midst of Norma June's own confusion she knew one thing for certain: she felt sorry for him.

He turned, beckoned one of the bunny-eared waitresses. After she'd poured more coffee and left, he said in a weary voice, "It will be a while. Would you like anything else?"

Why would it be a while? Because of the weather? Or because somewhere along the way Chrissy meant to get Ted in bed for a quick one?

Startled at herself, she took a gulp of coffee, found it blistering, and sputtered.

He pushed a glass of water at her.

She managed to say, "Thank you. No, nothing else. I've eaten all I need."

He leaned back like a tired old man, one hand brushing a neat white moustache. "What is Dunkel? Professionally, I mean."

"A grade-school principal."

"And you?"

"A sixth-grade history teacher."

He sighed. "How innocent that sounds."

He'd obviously never been in a classroom. At least not in this century! Not trying to look outside, not trying to see them driving away, she said lightly, "It's all in your point of view."

"Of course. Forgive me, but . . . you're not lovers."

"No." Was she being propositioned? In a fast-food place?

"Then I feel better. Calling a spade a spade, I mean."

Maybe you feel better, but I don't. Yet, she couldn't say that. She merely waited.

"Chrissy's been my . . . showpiece. My prestige among my peers. Until . . . recently. Now I can give her anything she wants—except sex."

This could not be a conversation at a Bunny-burger!

Seeing her aghast, he half-smiled, waved a thin hand. "Am I embarrassing you?"

"I . . . I'm not sure."

"Then let me soothe my male ego by saying out loud that I know my wife has turned into a tramp."

"If . . . if it makes you feel better."

"Oh, it does. But something else even improves that feeling."

And he leaned forward, smiling a wry smile. "She's going to get a real surprise when I die." Then he put a conspiratorial finger against his thin lips. "Don't tell."

What in the world does a small town, sixth-grade school-teacher answer to that one?

Damned if Norma June Bailey knew! She shrugged, made a face, and a wry inanity: "Whatever turns you on."

He leaned his head against the seat back,

sipped his coffee, made a face, and dumped in two or three packets of sugar substitute. Then, stirring, he asked, "What's it like?"

"What's *what* like?" Considering the previous conversation Norma was being very wary.

But he only continued calmly, "Being a—what was it?—sixth-grade teacher in a small town."

"I like it."

"Why?"

It's the only thing I know. Not a good answer—or an entirely truthful one. Instead she said, "I enjoy the kids. Seeing them learn, seeing them get excited about things that happened years ago." Watching their bright eyes as they hold out old things, saying like Johnny Martin had, "Mrs. Bailey, I found this at the quarry—and my dad says it's a real Indian arrowhead!" But would this old man understand that? With his cynical, lined face, his money, his tone of voice when he talked of his "tramp" wife, who right at this moment was somewhere with Ted Dunkel . . .

Hurriedly she ripped her mind away from *that*, saying instead, "I'm a history teacher, you see."

"So you do the same thing—year after year. What is the satisfaction in it? Security? No need to change?"

"History does not change."

"Then you needn't change, either. And it is security."

She thought of the enormous scholastic spoon

146

with which Ted Dunkel had stirred her yearly regimen this last semester and answered a little dryly, "Oh, no. We have to change. I have to change. Do it—or get fired. Even schools must move with the times, Mr. Stone."

Then she realized what she'd just admitted. *My God! It was I who just said that! I said out loud that perhaps Ted Dunkel is right!*

He was glancing at his watch, which made her own swift look acceptable. "Twenty minutes," he said. "Give them another half-hour. Chrissy acts fast—unless your friend is harder to persuade than I estimated."

"I have no idea." Despite herself the words were stiff. He turned his head, surveyed her closely.

"I'm sorry. I sound callous. And I think perhaps that—that you do care." The wrinkled lids dropped and he took up his coffee cup with a hand that shook. "God help us both. So do I. So do I."

After an awful moment, he went on, talking into his coffee cup. "You should have seen her—when we met. Little. Shy. Cotton dress to her ankles. Bare feet. Big blue eyes that looked up at me full of innocence. And I took her away. I did it. She thought I was God. And I thought she was just another mistress—to be used, and tossed. Well, we were both wrong."

Gently she said, "Perhaps she could try to understand—to sympathize with—your problem. But you have to ask."

"My dear, in the world of high finance there's very little room for sympathy. I'm afraid I've taught her well—by example. 'As ye sow, so shall ye reap.' How proud my Episcopalian mother would be to hear I remember that." Now he was half-smiling. "Also, something about after making one's bed, one has to lie on it. How's your bed, Mrs. Bailey?"

The sudden question came out of left field, as it were, and she almost had to bite her lip to keep from saying, "Empty."

Come on, Norma June. Even if she felt halfway sorry for this weary old man she was not going to confide in him something she'd just begun to realize herself.

What she wanted—desperately—was for Ted Dunkel to walk back in that door.

And he did! Brushing off snow, face totally impassive, eyes searching across the crowded diner to be sure they were still sitting where he'd left them.

"Mission accomplished," he said, towering over them and using a phrase they could interpret any way they pleased. "I left Chrissy in your car, keeping it running, sir. Nice to have met you. Have a good trip to the Azores."

Chrissy's husband stood up stiffly, buttoning his topcoat.

148

"Thank you," he answered in a totally expressionless voice. "Good night, Mrs. Bailey. I enjoyed our . . . chat."

Ted Dunkel slid into the abandoned seat, shoving the table smack into Norma June's midriff again, but she found she didn't care. However, all he said was, "It's still colder than bully hell. Where's the coffee lady?"

He found her, and she came, Christmas balls tinkling on her velvet lop ears. "May I get you anything else, sir?"

"Nope. This will do it. Thank you."

He took what could only be defined as a slurp, made a face, and twisted the paper corners off two packets of cream stuff. "Wow. This batch must be one they made this morning! Well. How was your chat with Mr. Stone?"

"He seemed . . . very nice. Very tired."

"I'll bet. From what I saw of Chrissy, she probably keeps him exhausted."

How much did you see of Chrissy, Mr. Dunkel? Just two bare boobs or the whole package?

But he was stirring, grinning to himself, saying, "However, I got to ride in a Rolls. My first time, and my last, no doubt, but what a classy vehicle."

And what else did you ride, Mr. Dunkel?

If Norma June Bailey hadn't been so upset at her *being* upset, she'd have been further dismayed by her mental language. But he didn't even no-

149

tice. He just sat there drinking coffee with that pussycat smile on his face.

Wasn't that the way men were supposed to be after they'd had sex? Totally relaxed, a soft pile of tomcat fur? Dean had been like that—just a silent, detached heap under the covers. After five minutes, a snore.

Something in her face must have caught his eye. He said suddenly, "Hey. Are you mad at me?"

"No. Why should I be?"

"I have no idea. I helped an old friend's sister. I came back. But you're looking like I cheated on my pop quiz. Am I missing something?"

"No. Of course not." She added, feeling a little silly, "I think I'm just tired."

"I did all the driving."

"I did all the worrying."

But they were smiling at each other. He said, "Okay. Let me finish my coffee and we'll go."

It was still snowing, but lightly now, making a fairy world of white and shadow with twinkling artificial wreaths swinging red and green from the street lamps. Having learned to do so, Norma June stood by his car door while he slid in on his side, leaned over and unlocked the other. She had a sudden memory of his package tumbling off the stack and going beneath the front seat. She caught a glimpse of one corner of it.

If she remembered tomorrow, she'd tell him.

If she didn't . . . it was his car. He'd find it when he wanted it. For "D."

Making a face at her uncharacteristic pettiness, she climbed in next to the mass to which she was becoming so accustomed, and said, to make some sort of amends, "Well, I like your Chevy."

"You have good taste. But I knew that."

They followed a snow plow into the motel parking lot. The No Vacancy sign was now flashing, and the only place left was in front of Norma's unit. A tractor trailer was filling his and the one adjacent. He nosed the Chevy in and said suddenly,

"Hey!"

"What?"

"Did I just see someone fooling around your door?"

"I wasn't looking." Nor was she concerned. At a motel it could have been a maid with towels, or merely some disoriented patron trying to get into the wrong unit.

But he took her key, hopped out, surveyed the mishmosh of tracks in the sidewalk snow, shrugged massive hunched shoulders, and said, "Guess not," as he unlocked the door. He took a swift glance inside and shrugged again. "Come on in; I'll check the bathroom."

Grateful for the warmth that met her, she stomped the light snow from her shoes, waited until he emerged saying, "All clear," and asked ruefully, "May I have my other suitcase? I have some . . . stuff in it I need." For some reason she was reluctant to say "nightie," but that sweatshirt was not the most comfortable sleeping gear. It kept playing that darned tune every time she turned over.

"Sure."

He went to the back of the car, hesitated. Then she distinctly heard him say, "Shit!"

"What? What's wrong?"

"My trunk lock's popped."

"It's what?"

"Popped. Jimmied. So someone could get in the trunk. When the hell did they do that?"

"At Bunnyburger?"

"I guess. Well . . . your suitcase is still here but it's been opened. I hope you didn't have any money in it."

"No. Nothing."

He was scooping up clothes and stuffing them back into the case. "Stay there. It's cold. I'll bring it in."

"But . . . your trunk!"

"It will be okay. I'll wire it shut in the morning, and my insurance will cover a new lock. But—jeeze!—whoever he was, he didn't do an amateur job. He'd popped a few. Times," he went on, brushing past her and plonking the open case on the bed, "must be tough if the pros are hitting small towns like this. You check. I may have missed something."

She knew what she'd had: underclothes—did younger women say "lingerie"?—panty hose, blouses, slacks, cosmetics, and the new nightie Deanna had given her last year, all pink silk and lace.

Naturally because she was trying to draw no attention to it, it slipped from the pile and flowed in a silken heap to the floor.

He picked it up and whistled. "Wow. I'll bet you look great in this!"

She may as well brazen it out. "Of course. Just like . . . like . . ." Good lord! Who were the movies queens of today? "Marilyn Monroe," she ended lamely, dating herself.

"Not my type," he said. "Besides, she's dead. You aren't."

On the last two words, his voice made a half-turn, got curiously deeper. Some primitive instinct told her to go on folding clothes, not look up.

"Look at me, Norma," he told her.

"No." She said it again, doggedly. "No. And if you've suddenly got some half-baked idea of a little free fun time, then go find Chrissy again!"

"Again!"

The word came cranked out, made of iron.

"What do you mean, *again?* Good God, woman, is that the opinion you have of me—that I'm so

153

deprived I'd fall into bed with an old friend's sister who even came on to the damned pharmacist? Thanks a bunch. I sure as hell have shot two days and five hundred miles for nothing."

"Well, I didn't ask you for this trip!"

His voice went calm.

"No," he said. "You didn't. You're quite right. Okay. Good night—for what it's worth. Call me in the morning and we'll shove out."

Bang! went the door, leaving Norma June Bailey staring at it.

First anger surged. *Well, damn it, you big moose, get on the telephone and call "D" who probably thinks she "has all your love." But don't tell her you tend to dilute the product in motels with co-workers. She might not care for that. I wouldn't.*

I went through it with Dean. For years. It hurt. I don't want to do it again . . .

But—oh, dear God—the room was suddenly silent. And empty.

Norma June Bailey sat down on the standard motel-room chair, and for the first time in years took an honest look at herself.

Not in the mirror. Mirrors were to show whether her hemline was straight or three weeks of Thanksgiving goodies had finally gone on the hips or the new face cream was really doing a number on the lines around her eyes like Hilda said it would.

154

Inside. Where she hadn't bothered to look for a long, long time.

And what was she seeing?

Something she suddenly didn't like: a smug, self-satisfied fifty-six-year-old, with the security blanket of family and school pulled so tightly around her that she saw nothing else, nor did she deal with anything else.

That was why she'd resented Ted Dunkel in September. He'd poked a hole in that blanket.

Now there was more than a hole. It was a rip.

Cold light was pouring in.

She shivered, sitting there, and reached for the cover on the bed.

Then she let it go.

She had the sudden, mental picture of a, wet, bedraggled butterfly creeping painfully out of its chrysalis. A sad thing, she used to tell her kids in science class—before Ted Dunkel, when she was allowed to teach science.

But just wait a few hours!

Then she'd show them the film of the butterfly, shaking its wings, drying them, gaining strength and purpose—and finally fluttering away in graceful, iridescent flight, a joy to see.

The fact that its beauty was sometimes only measured in days—or hours—had not been important.

Nor was it important now.

Was this to be Norma June Bailey's butterfly Christmas?

And had she just a few moments ago screwed it up—royally? Wanting just straight lines in her life, tolerating no change, afraid of unscheduled events because sometimes they hurt . . .

When would she have the guts to listen to those simple truths she'd mouthed so glibly to her kids?

Now.

And now she did look at herself in the mirror, saying to that wide-eyed face beneath the frosted swing of tousled hair, "And whoever 'D' is, if he's committed to her, he'll tell me—because he's that kind of man."

She got on the telephone, dialing Room 10.

There was no answer.

It was like cold water in her face.

Numbly she went to the window, shoved aside the drapes. She was just in time to see a lanky man in an ACE TRUCKING jacket climb into her side of Ted's car, Ted back the car around, and nose it left toward town.

The feeling was not unlike smashing into a brick wall.

Numbly she undressed, got back into the reindeer sweatshirt and climbed into bed. Alone.

And she hated it!

At three in the morning she heard car doors slam, the muted sound of male voices, and a few wind-caught bars of a song whose words were fortuitously blurred by distance as they made it to rooms 9 and 10.

Then she slept.

Her phone rang at six, and he didn't even have the decency to sound hung over. "Ready to roll?"

"I'm . . . I'm not even up yet."

"Then get up. Half an hour. Meet you in the lobby; this nice girl here has made coffee."

Figuring he wouldn't really leave her behind, Norma showered, fluff-dried her hair, spent fully fifteen minutes on the violet shadows beneath her eyes, and put on a skirt. Dean had always said she had nice legs. Topping the skirt with a soft blue silk blouse, she snapped shut both suitcases, slid into her coat, and faced a brisk wind through sunshine to the lobby.

She found Ted sitting in it. He was a little hard to miss; the lobby was small. Next to him sat the lanky trucker, swigging coffee from a lidded container that said SLEEP? WHAT'S THAT? on one side.

They both said, "Good morning," Ted, cheerfully, the trucker appraisingly.

Melba, on the phone, pointed to the coffee pot. Norma poured herself a cup. The trucker hooked a chair over to their table with one shabby boot. "Sit down, ma'am. Have a cookie. M' wife makes 'em, 'less I forget what home's like."

She took one. Oatmeal. With raisins. She looked at Ted. "What's the weather?"

157

"Clearing up. My buddy here says our next leg should be a shoo-in. Charlie, Norma June. Norma June, Charlie."

They smiled at each other. Charlie had a space between his front teeth wide enough to spit through and a nice grin.

"You could probably make it into Janesville iffen you wanted to drive late," he said. "Me, I'm headin' south. That's not so good. Plus I get me a load of hogs in the Quad Cities and—phooey—they do smell. Well. Better git. Nice meetin' you, Norma June. Look after this guy. He's prime."

Ted shook the big bony hand. As the trucker left, he said, "It's nice someone thinks so," and looked wryly at Norma June.

She felt herself blushing.

"Ted . . . I owe you an apology."

He waited.

"I should have known better. I had just never met anyone quite like . . . that man. Her husband. He was so sure. So—so matter-of-fact." And I was so devastated! Should she say that?

Ted was picking up the words for her, making it easier, "I never said she didn't try. And I guess I never said I wasn't interested. I suppose I just assumed you knew. Male ego."

Female insecurity. But she didn't say that. What she did say was, "I know, now."

"Thank you. Oh—hey!—I forgot to tell you—we have a passenger. Just to our next stop."

158

"Oh?" She was conscious of enormous disappointment, of having to share the last day of Ted's company with a stranger. What a change from Saturday when she would have welcomed Dracula!

He had leaned back, making the chair creak, and whistled. "C'mere, Rocket."

Into view around the counter trotted the longest basset hound Norma had ever seen, with twelve-inch ears, sad eyes, and paws the size of saucers.

"He's Charlie's," said Ted. "But his truck heater isn't working properly, so I said we'd drop him off at home since we were going that way." He was smoothing the silky head. "He's a good boy, aren't you, Rocket? Likes beer, too."

She had the grace to not ask how Ted knew that item.

"Hi, Rocket."

Rocket offered Norma one of his large paws. She shook it solemnly.

Ted asked, "Like dogs?"

"Oh, yes. Big ones. Not little, yippy ones."

"Those aren't dogs; they're wind-up toys. Okay." He was getting to his feet, bending, snapping on a leash. "You take Rocket, then. I'll load your gear. He can ride in the back."

"The back?"

"Back seat. Next to the box of stuff. Charley

159

gave me his blanket. Thanks for the coffee, Melba. See you on the down trip."

"You're welcome, guys. 'Bye, Rocket."

Rocket did a little dance and then took Norma June to the door. He obviously knew the way.

He sniffed four snow piles, six canopy posts, and a mail box, anointing them all. Then he amiably hoisted his short-legged girth onto the old, fusty blanket next to the box of gifts, sniffed them incuriously, curled into a semicircle and awaited the next move.

Ted filled his side of the car. "Which way?"

"Left to the intersection."

"Away we go."

The roads were plowed, the sun dazzling, the sky an incredible blue. Norma felt like a child anticipating—what? Christmas. Of course.

He said, "I forgot to say you look awfully nice, today."

"Why, thank you." When had she felt such warm delight?

"Of course, you usually do. I liked that pink sweater thing, too, the one you wore when we took the kids on the bus to the museum."

It was in her suitcase. She'd wear it tomorrow.

If there was a tomorrow . . .

She was suddenly aware of his looking sideways at her, brows drawn. Hesitating.

Then he said, "Now we've both apologized and cleared the air, are we friends? Finally?"

"Finally?"

"Come on, Norma June. Help me. Despite our . . . our professional differences." Now he did look levelly at her, and her cheeks went pink.

She conceded. "Yes. I . . . I think we are."

He took his big right hand off the wheel, held it out. She put her left one in it. His warm fingers curled, and he didn't let go. What he did was raise it to his hard cheek, moving his face against it. "Well. That's a start." Then he added, "Wow. Maybe this trip will pay off, after all."

She wasn't quite ready to examine that statement despite the quickening of her heart. She said, "Especially if you can find your little granddaughter."

"Oh, I'll find her. If I'm a hundred and ten, I'll find her. In the meantime . . . do you suppose I could share yours?"

She laughed. "She's ready. You heard her!"

They were behind another load of hay bales. He dropped her hand, passed the load, and since she hadn't moved her hand away, picked it up again. Once more she thought of butterflies, breaking from the old cocoon, spreading their wings to the sun . . .

A fifty-six-year-old butterfly?

Why not? It was a fifty-six-year-old cocoon. She might as well face facts. No one had ever seen the real Norma June inside. Certainly not her parents. From their only child they'd expected strict obedience and more than average grades. High school had been lonely and useful only in developing a callous over wanting to laugh and chatter and wear silly hairdos and stay out late like other girls did. College had been an acceptance of her peers only seeking her company when they needed scholastic help because she seemed to prefer to be alone. And Dean—he'd dated her on a bet—hadn't realized the degree of her naiveté and trust, had gotten her pregnant, then had decided that a wife with a college degree plus an additional paycheck wouldn't be all that negative.

"Norma."

She hadn't realized how deeply she'd been lost. "Oh. What?"

He chuckled. "So much for the magic of my presence. The oatmeal cookies are wearing thin. Is there anywhere to grab a bite around here?"

"Wait a minute." She looked at her map, trying to find where in the world she was—besides Oz. "There's another little town up here on the left, if you don't mind getting off the highway. I know there's a place to eat—I've seen the sign—but I've never tried it."

"Shall we give it a shot?"

"Why not?"

"Atta girl! Adventurous, all the way! Flexible. I've seen that in you with your classes and really admired it. Remember the day I was sitting in

162

with the county superintendent? You were scheduled to talk about General Washington's spring
campaign against the British. But when one kid
asked a question on Valley Forge you got off on
a discussion of the hardships the troops suffered
that winter that did more academic good than
listing twenty battles. It was great. You know your
onions, lady."

Norma's jaw dropped. She said, "But I was so
embarrassed, I didn't know what to do. I knew
what my lesson plans said, and what you'd expected."

Yet she'd said to herself, Hey, this is more important. And she'd let the discussion have its
head. Dean had always called that placing priori-
ties. He *had* contributed some good to her life.

"Shoot. It was the most spontaneous discussion
I'd heard in years. Mr. MacGrew was so impressed he still talks about it. Is this the place?"

She nodded, and he turned off the highway,
driving between rows of lumber companies, im-
plement dealerships, car lots and farm stores until he came to a tall sign—a red rooster wearing
a bib.

He turned into the parking lot, nosing against
an enormous dirty snowdrift. "The car's warm
and we won't be long. Rocket can stay here, can't
you, boy?"

Rocket, who'd sat up, lay back down again and
closed his sad eyes.

"Trucker's dog," Ted said, sliding out his side. "Oh, shit!"

Norma, who had delayed reaching back to lock the second door, not caring to remember how many times she'd *forgotten* to do it, locked her own and buttoned her coat. "What?"

Then she turned almost smack into the man they'd met in Bill's garage. Startled, she said, "Oh . . . excuse me. I didn't see you there!"

"It's okay. We meet again. Nice dog."

"He's a friend's. We're delivering." She almost ran to keep up with Ted, who'd taken her arm and was hustling her toward the cafe door. The man followed, reached around, and opened it for them. In the warm entry, Norma, as usual, turned toward the rest rooms. As she went, she heard the man ask, "Almost to the end of your trip?" and Ted answer shortly, "Yeah."

When she emerged, the guy was gone. Ted beckoned to her from a booth by the window. As she slid across the plastic seat with its worn frieze of parading roosters, she glimpsed the man again, in the parking lot, talking to two other men who towered over him.

"Gee, he talks to everyone," she said, picking up a hot fry. "I guess I was hungry."

"Mmph," said Ted, munching scrambled eggs and sausage on a bun. They both watched while the man drove away, leaving the other two just standing there. Then he swallowed, said, "So do you. I sort of wish you wouldn't, hon."

"Wouldn't what?" The words so surprised her she missed the "hon."

"Talk to everybody. Especially him. I mean—now don't get mad—he's strange. You didn't need to tell him we were going to Madison."

Puzzled, she rejoined, "Who'd care? That's just conversation." Then light broke. "You think he's been following us? Why in the world would he do that?"

"I've no idea. But we've certainly run into him a lot."

"Bill says he delivers. Maybe we're on his route."

He shrugged massive shoulders, shoveled in sausage. "Oh, well. He's gone. I wonder who the other guys were."

"It doesn't matter. They're gone, too."

"In a car?"

"Yes."

"His direction?"

"I can't see. The UPS truck's in the way. Oh—one guy's left. He's coming in here."

He was, in fact, bound for their booth. A pleasant-faced man in a suit and tie beneath a tan car coat, he said, "Hi." He was also quietly showing an ID card that made Ted blink. "May I sit a minute?"

"Sure."

The man turned, beckoned a waitress. Norma June, whose nearsighted eyes hadn't caught the ID mouthed "What?" at Ted. He mouthed back, "Narcotics."

"Jim Benson." The guy was holding out his hand. Ted shook it, introduced himself and Norma June. They waited.

Jim Benson got his coffee, took a sip. Intent gray eyes swept them both. "We're on an investigation. How did you meet that guy in the parking lot?"

Norma June opened her mouth, pressure from Ted's hand silenced her, and Ted said, "At a garage. At home."

He explained, concisely and simply—much better, Norma June admitted to herself, than she would have done. Deanna said her mother's explanations always overran because of her penchant for adjectives and side-issues.

Benson nodded. "Okay. That jibes."

"Jibes?" Ted's gray brows were up.

Benson grinned. "We check out everyone, Mr. Dunkel."

Norma June had to say it: "What's he done?"

"He's a drug dealer, Mrs. Bailey. A little fish, but eventually they lead us to big fish. Thanks. Enjoy your breakfast. And—if you see him again—here's my card. And a phone number."

Norma swallowed. "You . . . you think we might?"

Benson shrugged. "He's certainly been interested in you. Hasn't he?" And his calm eyes swept them both. "No idea why?"

Ted shrugged, puzzled. "Not a clue. Since you know about us, you know we're the last people to—to make a buy."

"So it would seem. Okay. Enjoy your breakfast." He suddenly grinned. "If you can. He didn't know we were anywhere in the area; I think we made him nervous this morning. You may not ever see him again. Anyway, just watch it. Simple precautions. Lock your car—which you did. Nice dog."

This time Norma June did *not* say, "He's not ours." She didn't say anything. She was too astounded.

Ted said, "We always do."

"Good idea. And your room doors. And most of all, don't open to strangers. Other than that, guys, have a nice Christmas."

He left.

Ted's dark eyes met Norma June's. She swallowed. She said, "Are there movie cameras around? Were we on TV? I . . . I can't believe what he said!"

His big warm hand found hers. "Let's believe," he said. "And do exactly what he said. Suddenly my Christmas is looking up, and I sure as hell don't want anything to happen to it."

She found she didn't want the rest of her sandwich. She took her napkin, wrapped it up.

Ted asked, "A snack?"

"For Rocket."

"That's *people* food!"

"He's a *people* dog!"

"If we ever have a dog, sweetie, you won't feed him that junk!"

"You want to bet?"

He rolled up his eyes, then grinned. Suddenly she felt okay. Calm. Unafraid. "Eat the rest of your fries."

"You don't want them, too?"

"I don't feed dogs fries. Potatoes aren't good for them." She was standing, buttoning her coat. "Want some coffee to go?"

"Sure."

He met her at the exit, took his go-cup. "Ready?"

"Ready."

"For whatever comes?"

"The look in his steady eyes couldn't be avoided. She met them with her own.

"For whatever comes."

"I can't kiss you, here. But God, lady, I want to!"

"It's okay. Just don't wait forever."

He waited until they were in the car; he had it started, and Rocket was happily munching sausage in the back. Then he reached over, pulled her as close as he could with two heavy, padded coats between them in the front seat of a car, kissed each closed, fluttering eyelid, then her mouth . . . tenderly, gently.

"Preface for beginners," he said in her ear, then let her go and put the car into reverse. "But it's a start."

Traffic had picked up enormously. The roads were cleared, it was three days closer to Christmas, and people were on the move. Even though the highway had gone four-lane, Ted had to keep his hands on the wheel and his mind on the road.

That was all right with Norma June. She had things to think about. Amazing things.

Was she falling in love with Ted Dunkel? Could a fifty-six-year-old widow "fall in love"? Or was it just a delayed action from her emotionally deprived youth when she'd so envied the girls around her? And what would Deanna say? Or Hilda? Or the entire faculty of North Elementary School?

Then a cold idea hit her. A shock. A real-world jarring of her senses. Whoa. She was thinking commitment.

What was Ted Dunkel thinking?

What if his idea of this was a fantasy trip to Paradise that was pseudo—a trip that, when it ended back home, would find him saying pleasantly, "Thanks. Bye-bye."

"You're quiet."

His deep voice caught her unawares. She started. Hesitated. Said, at last, "You're busy."

"Not that busy. You looked a thousand miles away. Where were you? Back home?"

Bingo. She sighed, nodded.

"Worried?"

To put it mildly. "Yes."

"Don't. I'll handle it."

Handle what?

Unfortunately, she had no opportunity to ask, nor he to answer. A car cut sharply into the lane in front of them, Ted hit the brakes, they skewed with a screech of tires, a cascade of gifts got Norma in the back of the neck, and a large basset hound came halfway into the front seat, his ears outspread like the flying nun's habit.

Ted got the car straightened out, back in the right lane, and at a proper speed. The guilty vehicle was already far out of sight. Wondering if she had noticed the sucker had been black with a Missouri license, he turned, said, "Wow. You okay?"

She had her arms around a teetering basset. She nodded. He saw a wayside park up ahead, said, "Hang on," and made for it.

The space was open. No clustered trees, no buildings, just a picnic table, a map board and a telephone on a pole. Fine. Just now he didn't want anything anyone could hide behind. To say he wasn't comfortable was putting it mildly.

By the time he'd stopped the car Rocket had scrabbled over into Norma's arms. From safe harbor, the dog eyed him accusingly.

He said, "Hey, man, that wasn't my fault!"

"No, it wasn't," Norma agreed. She found the dog's leash, snapped it to his choke chain. Rocket then soothed his spirit by watering the posts of the map board and badmouthing a bluejay who squawked back. Ted used the phone and rejoined them, shrugging his shoulders.

"Charlie's wife left a message on her answering machine. She won't be back until morning. The town's just up there a piece. Why don't we check, and if no one *is* home, we can stay over. Charlie said just to dump him in his kennel, but I hate to do that—it's so cold. It would just make us get to your daughter's a little later tomorrow. What do you say?"

Very, very conscious that what she did say would probably effect the rest of her life, if not his, Norma June Bailey answered without hesitation, "Okay."

Her first reward was his smile.

Her second was a quick hug and a kiss on her cold mouth.

At their feet Rocket burfed.

Ted said, "I don't kiss dogs," and opened the car door to straighten the gift boxes, replacing

171

the cascade from the front seat. "All right. Hop in. Not you, buster. You go in the back again."

Another small town, another row of farm implements, car lots and agricultural stores. And a motel.

He pulled into the motel parking first, got out, spent five minutes, and emerged smiling.

"How's that for good timing?" he said. "They only had two rooms left. Let's unload, then go find Charlie's house."

The last was easy. Rocket announced it by placing his big paws on the window ledge while his long tail thudded against the seat back. But there wasn't a soul around.

"I guess it's fate," said Ted, and headed back for the motel. Norma June asked hesitantly, "But . . . Rocket? Motels don't generally care for dogs."

"Oh, they've got heated kennels. But they know Rocket. If everything's full he can sleep in the office. How's it feel to be popular, old boy?"

The dog, responding to his tone of voice, indicated that was fine.

"Also," Ted went on, in a somewhat different tone to which Norma June responded with quickening heart, "the motel lady said there's a nice restaurant down the street. Real food. Shall we have our first date and . . . take it from there?"

"I—I'd like that."

"Me, too."

He parked before her unit. "You go—what is it girls do—freshen up? I'll deliver four-on-the-floor, here."

He bent over to fasten Rocket's leash. Norma June, hardly aware of positive motion, unlocked her motel door, opened it.

Then she said, "Oh!"

He straightened like a shot. "What?"

"My . . . my gifts. They're all over the floor. Any my suitcases are open."

He was behind her in three gigantic leaps, looking. He cursed. "Don't go in there!"

She wouldn't have! She was frozen, surveying the mess. All her patiently wrapped packages, torn and spewed; Jill's teddy bear with its seam split, the boys' new soccer balls ripped open.

He put Rocket's leash in her hand. "Come on. I have to call that guy—Benson."

"You don't think—"

"I do think. I think it's a damned strong possibility."

She sat in a lobby chair, Rocket's chin on her lap, his eyes shut as she stroked his silken ears and tried to slow her whirling mind. Things like this just didn't happen to small-town grade-school teachers!

What in the world did the man want?

Ted loomed over her. He looked calmer. He sounded calmer.

"Okay. I got him. Or them."

"What—what do we have to do?"

"Nothing. Not a damned thing. They'll handle it. Only, is there anything you absolutely must have from that room?"

She shuddered. "Not . . . not now. I'll have to rewrap the presents. What's left of them."

"Tomorrow. No sweat. I'll help. And relax. They're going to have guys watching the motel, the car, the works. Come on, doll. Let's turn over the dog and go to my room. It's okay. We checked."

The worried-looking motel clerk said, "Hi, Rocket! Oh, Mr. Dunkel, I'm so sorry. This has never happened before."

"It's under control. Don't worry. I'm taking Mrs. Bailey down to my room. Okay?"

"Okay."

They left a concerned girl staring after them while behind her a patently insouciant basset had hoisted himself up on a lobby chair and was drinking placidly from the fish tank.

The sudden cold air brought Norma back to her senses. "Wow," she said. "I can't believe this."

"Don't worry. They've found his car parked. They're watching it. They'll get him for breaking and entering then go from there. Here we go."

He'd led her down the cement walkway like a Boy Scout guiding an old lady across the street. She didn't much care for that image.

She straightened up, took a deep breath, and made herself laugh. "Well," she said, "I always wondered what an adventure was like."

"Do you feel like Lois in Superman?"

"I feel like Lois can have Superman. I think I want my life a little milder."

"How about the happy ending?"

"Has she ever had one?"

"I'm not certain." His big hand was beneath her elbow, as he said, "But you want one."

"Doesn't everybody?"

"Then let's give it a shot," he murmured, and pushed open the door.

It was a standard motel room. Nothing new. A double bed, two chairs, a desk, a place to hang clothes, and a bathroom. And one thing more: a folded cot.

Despite herself, she caught her breath. He turned from hanging coats, caught her eyes, and said levelly, "I asked for it. I am not going to leave you alone tonight, hon—but neither am I going to come on to you like gang busters if . . . if things aren't right. Okay?"

"Okay." It was a very soft answer.

He caught his own breath. "However," he said, "that does not preclude holding you in my arms as I've been wanting to do since at least October. If I may. Your choice."

There was no choice, and she knew it. She went toward him, felt those big warm arms close around her, and heard his deep voice say against the top of her head, "Oh, thank you, God . . ."

When was the last time Norma June Bailey had been held with love? Had she ever been? Dean's approach was always very direct, but she really hadn't experienced any others.

She knew one thing for certain, though: this was different. His hands moved slowly, caressing her back; his mouth slid from hers to the warmth of her throat. She couldn't encompass his girth with her arms, but she could cradle his tousled gray head as he lifted her, sat down in a chair that creaked, and moved his seeking lips inside the obediently opening blouse to the round, satin opulence there. Then she knew another thing: never in her life had she felt the breathless ecstasy that suffused her entire body as one gentle hand freed her breasts, stroking the velvet balls as lips touched them with soft, fleeting kisses before gently taking one round, burgeoning tip and then the other.

She began to move against him in a primitive rhythm of desire, not even realizing the motion.

He did. He caught his breath, moved his face away, pushed it into the hollow of her shoulder. His voice came muffled. "Whoa. Whoa, sweetheart."

"Why? Why? Am I doing something wrong?"

"Good God, girl, no! It's all right. It's too right—I can hardly stand it. Are you sure? Are you absolutely sure? Because if we go on, Norma June Bailey, it's total commitment to no one else in this blue-eyed world but me—capital 'D' for Dunkel—and are you ready for that?"

It was the capital "D" that did it, that brought her into a sudden horrible reality. "D"! "With all my love"! And he hadn't mentioned committing himself, just then. Only her!

He felt her go rigid. He went very still.

She was frozen. But her voice was not. She said through gritted teeth, "Sure. Me. Not you. Do I stand in line after 'D' or before her? And don't lie to me! Dean always lied to me!"

"What?"

"You heard me! *D!* The one you got that gift for—in the car. That card 'with all my love.' What do I get—the leftovers?"

She didn't have to struggle loose. He dumped her. In the chair. Towered above her with black eyes blazing. Said in monumental fury, *"What the hell are you talking about?"*

"I told you! That gift from you. In the car. It slid beneath the front seat, but I know it's there."

She was glaring up, torn with self-loathing, with anger at him, with unmitigated fury at a fifty-six-year-old body that had almost betrayed her.

Then she saw something genuinely go *click* in those dark eyes. He said, "There's another package. Under the car seat? Right now?"

"Yes! Yes, damn it! Where are you going?"

"To find the thing!" Only he added the crude adjective often used by sixth graders among their peers.

"Well, it's there!"

"I hope so!"

Totally confused, she watched him wrench at the chain, then disappear, leaving only late afternoon sunshine falling in cold bars across the worn carpet of the room.

She heard a car door open. The sound of grunting as an overlarge man fished about in an area too small for his girth. A voice said, "Eureka!" The door banged again, and he came plunging back in through the motel-room door, slamming it to with his heel.

Carrying the package. Ripping at it. Saying, "See! See? That's it!"

Clutching her open blouse against the cold, she could only stare.

Bright Christmas paper fluttered in shreds to the floor. In his hands was a plastic bag. Full of white stuff.

He whistled. "My God! There must be a fortune here!"

"What?" It was a mere whisper. She could hardly make her lips move.

"Dope, sweetheart! Don't you see?"

No. But she understood the word "dope." She said faintly, "Oh, my God."

"He thought we'd transport it to Madison for him. God knows when he put it in with the other presents, thinking we'd never notice one more, that he could filch it back when he wanted. But you said it slid under the seat."

"Yes . . . yes."

"So to him it was gone. That's why he popped the trunk. And every night we took the box into the motel room. Then when it was on the seat, Rocket was there! Poor guy—we must have driven him nuts!"

He'd turned, was dialing a number on the telephone. She asked faintly, "But . . . but who was 'D'?"

He shrugged those massive shoulders. "I don't know—Darryl, maybe. Wasn't that the kid Bill said he canned? Hi, this is Ted Dunkel in Number Three. I think we have something interesting to show you. Sure. I'll watch."

Then he hung up, and turned around, smiling—his look warming her heart.

"I don't know any 'D,' Mrs. Bailey. But I do want to know a certain Norma June. Feel better?" Then he added, "And button up. We don't want to cause talk."

She blushed. And buttoned. Tidied her hair. Straightened her skirt.

He added, "Did I say nice legs? Wow! Here he comes, already! You can't say the government isn't prompt when it wants something."

What one could say was that Mr. Benson was pleased.

"Got him!" he said softly, handing the bag to his companion, who tasted with one wet fingertip and said, "Whoo boy!"

Ted asked, "How? He's not in possession? We are."

"No problem. He hasn't picked up his car, yet. When he does, we'll get them both, and—what do you know?—there'll be dope in the trunk! Thanks a lot, guys. We really appreciate your co-operation."

The door closed gently behind them.

Norma June stayed in the chair. Ted Dunkel sat down hard on the side of the bed. They looked at each other.

After a long, poignant moment, he said gently, "That was a hell of an interruption. But maybe it was also a good thing. We don't *need* to be in a hurry. Do we?"

"No." And she was stretching out her arms, like a butterfly, joyous in the light and air, in the future.

"Okay. Then I'll tell you what. I'm going to take a shower. Cold, I might add. And solo. Next I'll put on my last clean shirt, and maybe even a tie—if I brought one. I packed in kind of a hurry. Then, as previously indicated, I am going to take my girl out to dine—and see what develops."

He stood, grinning down at her. "And you, my dear?"

"I think I'll call Deanna. To say we'll be late." And something else, but he didn't need to know about that. Yet.

He scrabbled in his suitcase, went to the bathroom, shut the door. She heard him whistling, heard the shower go on. Such a friendly, homey sound!

It was a brief conversation with her daughter but an interesting one. Norma June hung up and leaned back into the chair, hardly daring to breathe.

At around two years old, Jill had been left, sedated, on the steps of a convent. The only word she could say was "Jackie," which was why they'd named her Jill.

It was too good, too pat to be true. She'd never tell Ted herself. She'd never even mentioned Jill was adopted. And she was not going to break his heart with false hopes.

She didn't even say anything when he came out of the bathroom, a white tee shirt stretched across that enormous chest, bare legs like tree trunks beneath striped boxer shorts, and wet gray hair falling into his eyes from two odd parts above his brows.

He was frowning. "Got any salve? Or cream?"

"I think so. Why?"

"I've got these funny double ankle bones. My

dad had 'em. Jackie, too. And sometimes when you wear boots too long they rub."

He sat down on the side of the bed again, the mattress groaning. "That's fine. Thanks. It just takes a little." And then he was smiling up at her, not noticing how joyously she was suddenly smiling down at him. *Two hair parts—and double ankle bones! Oh, Merry Christmas, Ted Dunkel! Have I ever got a gift for you!*

He was saying, "You never realized. Did you?"

"Realized what?" she asked, letting it go at that.

Because as she'd decided earlier—about Jill—if things were right, they'd happen.

"That I never had to go to Madison."

"You . . . what?"

"I didn't have to go. Hell, I can talk to my lawyer on the telephone. I had no idea what I was going to do for Christmas. Then your car went poop, and I saw my chance to spend it with you."

She said slowly, "Bill knew."

"He may have guessed."

"So has the whole town. By now."

"Fine. When we get back, we'll really give them something to guess about. And do you know what else, Norma June Bailey? Most of them will be glad. As I hope your family will."

"Jill will love it." Then she added, "And the boys. Everyone."

"Good. Merry Christmas . . . Grandma."

"Merry Christmas . . . Grandpa."

"I think," he said, "I'd better get my clothes on. Then we'll go eat. After that . . . who knows?"

He was grinning at her. How could she *ever* have thought his grin was snide!

She had, of course. But that had been back in her chrysalis days.

Norma June the butterfly bent swiftly and kissed the top of his wet head.

"Who knows, indeed!" she said, and she escaped to the bathroom to fix her face.

Or meant to escape . . .

Whatever.

Marjorie Eatock was one of the two "launch" authors for TO LOVE AGAIN books with her first novel, *THE TIME OF HER LIFE*. A second TO LOVE AGAIN romance, *OVER THE RAINBOW*, was published in January of this year. She lives in Pittsfield, Illinois.

Callie's Christmas

by

Martha Gross

It felt like one of those provocative soap episodes—the last few moments, rife with double meanings, before the big love scene exploded. Ned, striding easily down the beach in his ragged jeans, looking, in the fading light, like a man who belonged to the sea. Callie, in heels and a proper Ann Taylor suit, scrambling after him and gasping, half from passion and half because she could barely keep up. She could almost hear the background music playing faster and faster as the sexual tension mounted. In a moment, he would stop, turn to her, sweep her into those sinewy arms, kiss her with unrestrained ardor, and carry her off into one of the clumps of sea grapes they were hurrying past. And there, while the music faded to a soft harp and cello, he would fall on her with a hunger that matched hers. . . .

She stumbled over a soda can and almost fell. End of scene.

Damn! Why had she agreed to this walk along the ocean? Especially at dusk. The beach might look a little tacky in the sunshine, but as the light faded into the dusty pinks of sunset, a romantic aura softened the view, producing in Callie a feeling best described as a kind of longing.

There were other places on this planet that did that to her. Western North Carolina, with those sweeping mountains guarding the inviting valleys below—she had edited some travel shoots for Warwick Cable up there—and the shoreline below San Francisco, its trees bent and shaped by the wind—she had attended her son Chuck's graduation there.

Right now, despite being starved for oxygen, she was in a mushy mood. She could almost feel Ned's arms crushing her. He was going to kiss her, for sure. And despite her resolve, oh, how she wanted him to. Even though that was the *last* can of worms she should open now, when she was zeroing in on Jack. So successfully that south Florida's tycoon of the year thought he was zeroing in on her. What did she need Ned for? Ohhh, her chest ached. Didn't the man have any slower gaits?

"Am I moving too fast for you?" he asked, suddenly stopping and looking back to see her struggling to keep up. Striding back, he reached for her hand to help her over a tangle of seaweed. Not letting go, he led her at a far slower pace.

His hand, so much bigger than hers, made her feel small. Protected. Oh gosh, she wanted to stroke his palm and hear his breath come faster, too.

"Your stride *is* a little longer," she said. Ned was over six feet. She was five feet two. What did he expect?

He grinned down at her, that small lopsided grin she wished she could catch on camera. What audience appeal he'd have if he could just get past his stiffness. But he didn't show this relaxed side of himself on the tube. Not a hint.

"I wanted to get you alone for a few minutes," he said. "We never get to talk. We always get interrupted. I've really enjoyed it this past month when we've worked or gotten a bite together. But you're always so busy there."

"There" was Covent Cable Company where Callie had become the executive program coordinator five weeks ago. Covent's new owner, Jack Brandenhurst, had lured her from Warwick Cablevision in Jacksonville by almost doubling her salary, to do what she had done for Warwick and—for Status Productions in Orlando—to put some zip in the shows that needed it, including Ned's.

"Let's park here," he said, pointing to a patch of sea grapes ahead. "It's the only bench on this stretch." The sea grapes formed a kind of shelter, hiding it from view from up or down the beach. They sat. He was still holding her hand. "Are you afraid I'll run away." She laughed, looking up at him with a suggestive smirk.

"I'm not taking any chances." He wrapped his other hand around her wrist. His face was so close she could feel his warm breath. And see on that taut, muscular neck, a couple of gray whiskers he had missed that morning. He looked like a Scottish warrier. A Viking. And this chemistry! *Change the subject, Callie. And change this conversation's direction. Now!*

"If you dragged me out here to thank me for working with you, that's totally unnecessary," she said briskly, groping at her hair as the ocean breeze swept a few blond tendrils into her face.

"Leave it that way," he said. "It's pretty. So soft."

She stopped, slowly pulled her hand back and let her fine hair blow around her face, then forced herself to look away, out to where the gray-blue sky was dissolving hazily into the darker gray-blue edge of the sea. The water slid languidly up onto the beach, each wave pulled by a fragile ribbon of silky foam. The lights of a far-out cargo ship glowed dimly in the distance. And two sailboats tacked gracefully toward the channel.

Oh, dear! If she moved over just a few inches, she would melt into his arms. "I know we've only known each other for a month," he was saying.

"And we've hardly had a minute alone. If I'm wrong, tell me. But I feel something between us. Like I've known you before, so nothing you say or do surprises me. I'm comfortable with you. But kind of charged, too. Is it just me?"

Callie sighed. Now why did he have to ask that? But she heard herself answer, "No. It's not. I get a feeling, too. But that may just mean we have a rapport. That we'd make good friends."

"I want to know you better—to spend time with you." The hand on her wrist slid around, caressing her lower arm. "I've been so busy the last ten years, going back to college. Getting a master's. Then trying to figure out what to do, once I got it. I wanted to use it in some way that mattered. I kind of tripped over this consumer idea. But it grabbed me and wouldn't let go. The last thing I ever thought of doing was TV. You see I'm not good at it."

"You'll do better," Callie promised. "I'll help you. That's what I'm there for. Yours isn't the only show that needs help."

He tore a twig from the seagrape, and began tracing lines in the sand. "I haven't exactly lived like a monk for those ten years. But for most of them, I was kind of afraid to get involved in anything that might keep me from that degree. But now something's missing. Someone. I haven't felt like this in a long, long time."

"Oh, Ned," Callie began, fully intending to tell

him she was sorry but there was nothing between them, he was imagining things. But when those smokey eyes locked on hers, the words wouldn't come. He leaned closer, and their vision was swallowed up in a distorted blur of huge irises and corneas until their eyes closed as their lips melted into the tenderest of kisses. God, it was sweet. And when he finally eased away she lunged forward to plant her lips back on his, with a passion that made him grip her hard and groan as he kissed her again. He began kissing her face, planting kisses all over her cheeks and forehead, mumbling wordless endearments which Callie returned with anguished whimpers until she somehow managed to wrench herself free.

She leaped to her feet, crying. "No, no! Ned, please! We don't know—we don't— Oh, my God, we can't do this."

He leaped up, too, and reached for her, but this time he didn't pull her close. "Callie, why not? You feel everything I feel. What's the matter? Please. Talk to me."

"I—I don't know. I feel like I'm caught in rapids."

"Tell me about it," he said, with that funny little grin. "We don't have to crash into anything tonight, Callie. We can go slowly. Get to know each other."

"I—yes, we have to go slowly. I—I'm seeing

someone. I can't just flip a switch. I don't know what to do."

"You set the pace, honey. I just want us to take a good look and see what's here. What's almost in our hands, if I'm right."

"Maybe after . . . a good look, we'll both decide we're . . . we're being ridiculous. That nothing is possible," she said.

"Then at least we'll know. But I think we should take that look. And get to know each other, don't you?"

"Yes, well, I guess," Callie said quickly. "Maybe. Anyway, we're definitely going to see more of each other. I'm going to start working with you seriously tomorrow on your show."

Ned groaned again. "Oh, yeah, that. Listen, Callie, I'm not Bryant Gumble. I'm not Ed McMahon. What I'm telling people is useful. Important to them. Isn't that enough?"

"Never!" Callie shook her head. "The audience won't listen because your advice is good. They listen if they like you. If you're fun. If you want to help them, you have to charm the pants off them first. So they'll tune you in even if you're just reading cracker box labels." She stood up. "Sorry, Ned, but I—I have to run. My kids always call me on Monday nights."

They walked back to the hi-rise condo where Ned had parked his car, the Beekman House. He walked slowly, at her pace, said nothing, and held her hand tightly the whole way.

A soap would have had a better ending, she thought. With them admitting their love and kissing passionately on the beach, while the squawking gulls swooped around them.

In the car on the way home, Callie mulled over the situation. When she had first met Ned about a month ago she'd thought he was dullsville personified. But what an incredible body! He moved like a tiger, except on camera. Smart. Surprisingly literate for someone whose résumé said his academic degrees were preceded by employment as a gymnastic choreographer, an acrobatic trainer and consultant. But his stiff manner and that monotone of his had put her off until that day after taping when he and his producer Mac Master, Mac's assistant Astrid, and Callie had all run out to Wendy's for a quick bite. When Callie had ordered a plain baked potato and had then hit the salad bar, Mac and Astrid had teased her about her Spartan tastes. "Have some French fries. Have some cheese in that potato. Live a little," Mac had teased.

And Astrid had sniffed, "I don't trust anyone who won't put butter on a potato!"

But Ned, surprisingly, had stuck up for her. And had chosen the same things. At the salad bar, neither of them took chopped eggs, items with mayonnaise, or dressings. A suddenly animated Ned gave her three cheers. "I've done that all my life. Now they call it Pritikin or a heart-healthy diet," he said. "But I was brought up on it."

"Your parents were ahead of their time. I've only been eating this way for five years," Callie admitted. "I firmly believe in it. I'm ten pounds thinner than I was before, and I feel so much better. Lots of energy."

"Tell me exactly what your guidelines are," Ned prodded, and while gobbling their potatoes with gusto, they traded details on their fat-free regimens. This was a different Ned, smiling, eager.

Back at Covent, she saw him don his reserve again, like a cloak. The only person there he ever seemed relaxed with was Mary, Jack Brandenhurst's dear but wacky secretary. Ned was two different people. And the one with his guard down had caught Callie with *her* guard down. She liked that Ned a lot.

Callie popped a whole mixing bowl full of popcorn, put it on her desk, and got to work on the Christmas shows. One of the fringe benefits of living alone was not having to bother with meals. She had become a chronic snacker.

Just as she reached for the first handful, at exactly eight P.M., Jean called from Jacksonville. "Sorry, honey," Callie told her. "I can't make it up for Thanksgiving. Probably not Christmas, either."

"The children will miss you," wailed her daughter. "And we were counting on you to baby-sit for us that night."

"Hire a sitter. I'll pay for it," said Callie and bid her daughter an abrupt good night. Jean simply could not understand her mother's commitment to the career she had worked so hard to hatch. After being poor as a churchmouse for twenty years, struggling to raise Chuck and Jean alone, working any job that fit their school hours, and taking one night-school course at a time, Callie could finally do work she loved. She had a career. Life was sweet. She wasn't about to give that up, not for anyone. She had a need to accomplish something—to see how far she could go. She had done right by the kids. Now she was doing right by herself.

The phone pealed again ten minutes later. It was Chuck. He took the news better. He always understood. "Don't sweat, Mom. That's how it is. The job says spit, we spit. We'll miss you, though."

They talked eagerly for five minutes, exchanging the week's news. And then Callie got back to her outline. But her mind kept slipping off to

Ned, to the way he moved—that almost feline ease—the warm appeal behind that terrible reserve. Don't think of him, she told herself. Think of Jack. But her mind wouldn't listen.

Callie flew into the convent, the employees' nickname for Covent Cable, at 8:30 the next morning, grabbed the stack of tapes and program folders she needed, and hurried to Jack's office, where his secretary Mary Blickter looked up and grinned conspiratorially. "Room two," she said. "Coffee and stuff's in there already. He'll be in in a sec." Leonard Passeter's secretary before he sold the company to Jack Brandenhurst, Mary had been ready to retire at that time. She had agreed to stay on a few months during the transition.

Callie had liked her from the start. Mary was a zany, incurable matchmaker—a giggling voyeur of romance. It was she who had put the bee in Callie's bonnet about trying to land Jack Brandenhurst. "He's just divorced again," Mary had confided, after that first week. "And you *know* he'll get tied up again. He's a chaser. So nothing's perfect. If you're going to have something that's not perfect anyway, why not have all that money, too? Heeheeheehee! And you could do it, Callie." She had tittered.

Letting those brown, beadlike eyes dart around

first as if to see who might be listening, she had whispered, "Two of his wives were his secretaries first, and one was the vice-president of his sports stores. He gets very dependent on women that work for him. I see how he does with me. And the way he looks at you?" She squealed. "Something's going on in his head, Callie. Or his groin. Heeheehee. You kinda take over as a personal helper before I go, and you're in! Hoohoohooheehee." She stomped her feet with glee.

"But how could I do that?"

"You're almost there! You're his right hand. You have final say on all those programs. Make suggestions. Arrange things for him. Take care of details— you know. Then get an assistant to do all the little crap I do. You'll be his wife in six months." She chortled and rubbed her hands together.

Callie had digested Mary's words slowly. But she'd paid a lot more attention to Jack Brandenhurst after that. He *did* give her looks. He was affable, not bad looking, dynamic. Think of never having to worry about money. Of having lovely clothes, a fancy car, a big diamond—after all those years of scrimping and doing without. Maybe it was worth a shot. Jack only came in three or four times a week. He had other businesses to oversee. But Callie had decided to feel out the possibilities. Could it be that Mary was right?

* * *

In the second conference room, she dumped her tapes and files on the table and turned on two VCRs. She was just pouring their coffee when the door opened and Jack strode in.

"Hey, Callie, sorry I'm late. I got a killer schedule today. And I got a Help the Kids luncheon. We donate sports equipment to all those kids' causes. I gotta sit through an hour of women's gab, when I'd really rather go over your proposals. What do we absolutely have to get done today?"

"I've got four tapes to play. Before and after for two shows. About twenty minutes. Too bad I can't come to the luncheon. While they gab, we could be going over all this instead of wasting time."

"Yeah, too bad you can't." He did a double take. "Hey, why not? Great idea. Wait a sec. Could you bear two charades in one day? I've got a chamber thing tonight. I've got two tickets. . . ."

Callie couldn't believe her ears. If she'd written the script herself, she couldn't have plotted it better. "What time?" she asked, faking a nonchalance she didn't feel.

"I think it starts at six-thirty. Black tie. Be here about then?"

"Yes, I can make it home, change, and be back in time. And by then I'll have had a session with Ned Marshall, so I might have more to tell you about what we can do about him."

"Yeah. We wanna keep him if we can. Consumerism is hot. It's a lousy presentation, but he's got good data and he doesn't pull any punches. We get someone else, they may talk great and not have any meat to what they're saying."

"I agree, one hundred percent," said Callie quickly.

"OK, so what do you have to show me now?"

Callie put the first set of tapes on the two VCRs. "This is Bo Amory, your weather man." The first tape flashed on the screen. "See, he always uses that same gesture with his hands. Better none at all than the same one over and over like that. And his smile would be more effective if he didn't keep it pasted so desperately on his face all the time, if he used it more like punctuation. You'll see in the other tape. And here, see. . . ."

Twenty minutes later, Brandenhurst poked his head into his own office, where Mary was just putting a phone message on his desk. "Whoozit from, Mary?" he asked.

"A Mrs. Dellavan. About a dinner tomorrow night?"

"Some of these broads never give up. Call and tell her I'm busy. I gotta get out of here. I'm taking Callie with me to that lunch today and that dinner tonight. I'll pick her up here around eleven-thirty. We'll be back about two." And he was gone.

Mary quickly called Ardis Dellavan. "Mr. Brandenhurst is sorry, but he's busy tomorrow night," she said. And then she hurried down the hall to Callie's office, burst in without knocking, and almost ran into Callie.

"I was just coming out to talk to you, Mary," Callie grinned.

"He just left. He told me he's taking you to the lunch today and the dinner tonight. Attaway! How'd you do it?"

"I suggested the luncheon. The dinner was his idea."

"It's black tie. Got a knockout gown?"

"Just one. Very knockout. I've never worn it. I bought it on a hunch two months ago. Listen, I'll talk to you more later. I have to work with Marshall now, and I don't want to be late for lunch."

"Oh, I'm so excited," Mary squealed. "My pulse is racing. The minute you get back, Callie—the very second—come and tell me *everything!* I knew it! Oh, I can't wait!" She hurried out, her fingers on her pulse, looking ecstatic.

She had to watch the cooking show first. Chef Stella might know a lot about cooking, but you couldn't prove it by her show. "Today we're making a tim-a-mir . . . a tir-emir— No wait. . . ."

201

She pulled the card out and peered at it through her glasses. "A tiramisu!" she said finally, reading a bit more and mouthing the words. "It's an Italian dessert. All layers, and—you know—delicious."

Callie groaned. Stella set out some eggs and a package of some kind of cheese, and without explaining why, she opened the cheese and sliced it. She began reading the recipe aloud, haltingly, as it flashed on the screen. Callie cringed. How bad could it get? Chef Stella began explanations she never finished and performed little chores in deathly silence. When she did talk, her nasal whine grated. Even after heavy editing, she was hopeless. Callie led director Tony Dispacio out of the studio. Sometimes you had to bite the bullet.

"Get rid of her," she said tersely. "I'm sorry. But you can't make something out of nothing. She has nothing to work with."

"You're telling me?" said Dispacio.

"Why did they even hire her? Does she own a lot of stock?"

The director nodded. "Same difference. She's related to Passeter, the guy who used to own this place. And she had some kind of contract. It's up for renewal next month, anyway."

"Pay her off. Find someone lively, with a voice that won't make you wince. Call Larry Maturi, the head of the maître d's organization. He'll know someone. And let's somehow add a little suspense." She glanced at her watch. "Oops! Time for Marshall. Gotta go."

Ned was waiting in her office. Sitting in front of the screens, his long legs stretched out in front of him, he was poring over a file of papers while chewing on a pencil. Strange that someone with a body like that, so fluid and almost feline in real life, could be stiff as plywood in front of a camera. Or that his deep, deliberate voice, so sexy when they were alone, could flatten out so. Why did this man get to her? Grabbing the remote, she sank into the chair next to him, frowning.

He looked up. "Well, whatever it is, it can't be that bad." He grinned. "Somebody die?"

She shook her head. "I've got to fire someone. I hate to do that. But she's impossible. You couldn't give her show away."

Ned laughed. "The cooking show?"

She was surprised. "How'd you know?"

"Well, they shoot it right before me," he said. "And she always runs late, so I've seen it a few times. It's painful. You gonna get rid of me? Mine's kinda painful, too, I'm afraid."

Callie shook her head. "You have useful, important information. Your presentation's ghastly. You're not a performer. So we have to make a performer out of you."

"I'm not a performer?" he repeated, a curious expression on his face. "Don't be so sure."

"But you can become one," Callie continued. "Just learn to play to the camera instead of resenting it as if it were an intruder. I can help you, if you'll let me."

That broad, high forehead wrinkled up. "Yeah, you're right. I'm not much of a performer at this. But I want to do it. And I guess if you can teach me how to do it better, I'll owe you."

"OK. First, let's play five minutes of your show, and then five minutes of Bob Soper. You tell me what's different."

Ned nodded and she clicked on the first tape—five minutes from his last program. It showed him standing stiffly in one place, talking in a flat voice about food-package labels. "One of the most misleading label phrases of all," he said, "is 'No Cholesterol.' Many viewers assume 'No Cholesterol' means it's a healthy food. Even heart-healthy. Wrong. It may still be loaded with fat and sodium. You must read the whole label."

He went on explaining about the new, no-fat mayonnaise and cheese. And warned that there were no real low-fat potato chips or fried cheese puffs yet. His announcer, Tommy Grant, then came on camera, and Callie clicked the tape off. She clicked on the adjacent screen, and there was Bob Soper, relaxed, chatty, explaining the day's probable weather patterns. "Don't you feel like he's sitting across the table from you?" she asked.

After a few minutes she clicked Soper off and said, "Well?"

He nodded. "Yep. But Bob's like that in real life. I'm not."

"To me, right now, you are. You weren't the first week. I've watched you. You're very reserved with most people. The wall only comes down with friends. Your show is the best of the consumer things I've seen, as far as useful content goes. But the dullest. Useful won't cut it. If you want to stay on the air, you've got to let that warmth show. Change your style."

Ned shrugged. "You're right. I'm very reserved. I was brought up that way. For most of my life, reserve was a necessity."

Callie looked at him, puzzled. "But why, Ned? In your work, why did you need reserve?"

"I've done other things for which it just was the way to go."

"Like what?"

He frowned slightly. "I'll probably tell you sometime, Callie. But not yet. I haven't quite figured you out yet, either. Although you know I like what I see. Today let's concentrate on you teaching me how to make my show better."

"OK," said Callie, a bit miffed. "Here's what I think. You like people, you want to help them, but you don't want too many to get up close." Ned nodded. "Well, you don't have to worry about them getting close, Ned. There are only a camera and a tape in the studio. Be relaxed and easy on camera, as if you want to make friends with each and every viewer. Convey that and they'll listen. Let the camera catch the way you look when you're talking to me alone. You have so much gut appeal—if you'd just let it show."

Ned sighed. "I hear what you're saying, Callie. But I wouldn't know how to start."

"Well, I do. Let me work with you. I'll show you how to point up certain words. How to use pauses. How to relax. Will you try?"

He laughed. "Hell, honey, if it'll get us a little more time together to get to know each other better, and it'll give my program a chance, you can turn me into Johnny Carson."

Callie laughed, too. "Let's not set our sights *too* high," she said. "OK. Let's find an empty studio."

Inside Studio B, she got down to specifics. "I don't want you standing so stiffly, with your arms frozen to your sides. I want the camera to catch you sitting—or leaning on the end of your desk. You've done that when we were talking. It's natural for you. One hand in your pocket, maybe. Try it on that desk in the corner."

He unfolded from his chair and ambled over to lean on the edge of her desk, then looked over at her. "What now?"

"Relax," she said. "Your walk over was perfect. I don't know if I've ever met a man who moves as gracefully as you do—in real life, I mean. Move like that on camera and women will be sending you naughty letters."

Ned chuckled. He felt comfortable leaning against the desk this way. "You mean that's all there is to it?" he asked.

"Almost. Now, if you have to point out a label, I think from here on, we'll use blowups of the labels next to you and you'll point to various parts of them as you talk about them—fat content, sodium, and so on. OK, pretend that schedule board has a blowup of a label on it. Explain it to me. I'm right here behind the camera."

Ned slipped off the desk, walked easily over to the schedule board and made a few comments about an imaginary label, pointing as he talked. "Find where it says nutrition information or nutritional information," he instructed. Callie watched intently. A remarkable difference. He walked back to the desk and half sat on it, then asked her, "Well, madame coordinator, how's that?"

"I'm amazed," Callie sputtered. "You just talked as easily as Soper. Like when you're talking to me alone. Why the hell haven't you been doing that on your program all this time?"

"I don't know. I'm not used to being easy with people I don't know. And who knows if I can do it with a camera watching. That's a lot different than talking to you alone."

"Don't even *think* that you might not be able to do it. You will. I've got an idea. I'm coming to your next couple of tapings. I'll stand right behind the camera and you'll talk to me. Meanwhile, go home and practice talking to a mirror the same way. Pretend I'm there. Talk about the subject for your next program. You're going to make a U-turn here, Ned. You've got so much good stuff that people should know. Now, you'll get them to listen."

Callie was waiting at the front entrance at 11:30, her makeup fresh, a touch of Bijan on her neck. Jack pulled up two minutes later in a blue 500 SEL Mercedes and jumped out to help her in. "We'll be sitting with several businessmen who donate stuff to kids' causes like Big Brothers and Big Sisters. We can talk there or run out to the lobby for fifteen minutes."

"Want me to start now?" asked Callie.

"No, I have to concentrate on driving," he said, laughing. "My last wife was urging me from the day we got married to get a driver. I get so into whatever I'm talking about or thinking about, I forget all about traffic. I go through stop signs. I'm lucky I don't drive up on a curb." He switched on the radio. "Easy listening stuff. That's as much distraction as I can handle."

"Oh, then I guess I'd better not take my clothes off and dance on the fender," said Callie.

"You what?" Jack roared. "Jeeze, are you crazy! If I end up climbing a stop sign here, miss, it's your fault."

"Want me to drive?" asked Callie.

"I'd rather have you dance on the fenders. What's a little accident?"

They bantered thus all the way to Pier 66. He was fun, Callie decided. A hustler. Very basic. A bit crude. Not particularly literate or cultured. But kind. He might do nicely as a husband. She could make him a good wife. If she was sure that was what she wanted, then she mustn't let anyone else get in the way.

Inside Pier 66's Crystal Ballroom almost three hundred women and perhaps twenty-five men, mostly businessmen and contributors, sat at tables around a narrow runway. Jack and Callie shared a table with the Bentwoods—Ira Bentwood owned Tri-County Limo and a helicopter delivery service—the Nestroms—Rick Nestrom was a real-estate developer—the Flahertys—inherited money, generous philanthropists—and the Greenwalds—Ivan leased vehicles, from Rollses to trucks.

Jack had barely made the introductions when

the lights dimmed, spots beamed on the runway, and the music began pounding as the fashion show began. "We'll never be able to hear ourselves think in here," Jack shouted. "Let's hit the lobby." Out near the elevators, she briefed him quickly on the firing of Chef Stella and on her plans, including many more remotes, for the morning news show.

"The consumer show is going to improve dramatically, too. He won't sound like he's reading someone's will anymore. He'll sound like he's talking to a neighbor over the back fence. Women will swoon. He can be very sexy. I think we've lit a fire under him. We'll know in two weeks or so."

"If you fix that show, you can do anything," said Jack.

She smiled sweetly. "I try, boss. I try."

Jack nodded. "You know, Callie, I think the smartest thing I did after buying this company was to hire you to shape it up."

"I thank you, sir. I have tapes for you to watch. And I'll have a sheet on costs and such this week. I've got several other shows to change, one by one. Those that need immediate attention first."

"Then I guess we'd better get back inside," Jack said. "We can leave soon. Five minutes after they serve the main course. Unless it's something we can't resist." He gave her a sly, sideways smirk. "I'm not good at walking away from things I can't resist."

"Oh, then I won't get to dance on the tables here, either." She faked a pout.

He roared again. "What is all this about dancing on tables and fenders." He laughed.

"Just trying to be sure I've got your attention."

"You got it the minute you walked into my office that first day, babe. You dance on any tables around me, it's going to be a private performance." Standing up, he pulled Callie to her feet and put an arm around her shoulder to give her an awkward hug. "Callie Cameron, I can't wait to get to know you better."

Callie laughed but said nothing. She wouldn't touch that line with a ten-foot pole. And a little suspense might be provocative to this man who, if Mary was right, was accustomed to women throwing themselves at him. It would be nice to have a man in her life again, someone she could count on. Would she be able to count on Jack? Someone to be best friends with and be close to. But what if he ever cheated on her? Could they still be best friends?

As they hurried back into the ballroom and to their table, Callie wondered why she felt so peculiar? Almost guilty. Why was Ned's face hovering in a corner of her mind. What was wrong with her trying to stir up Jack a little? How else was she supposed to get him thinking about her? She blinked her eyes. But the image of Ned leaning on that desk wouldn't quite go away.

Before two o'clock, Jack dropped her back at the convent. "Pick you up here about seven?" he asked. "It starts at seven, but it'll only take ten or fifteen minutes to get there. It's at Bahia Mar."

"Fine. Mary said it's black tie. I'll wear my long gown."

"Something cut down to your navel." He chuckled. "So you'll be dressed appropriately in case you decide to dance on the tables."

By two, she was back in a studio with Ned. "OK, now you're going to talk about the lunch-meats and such that say 'ninety-five percent fat free' on their labels, and explain how that's deceiving," said Callie. "Tell it to me. Suppose my arteries are clogging, so I should cut all fat from my diet." She stood behind the camera. Ned nodded over at her, grinned, and began. He hadn't lost the morning's more intimate, friendly style. He looked right at Callie and talked to her. "Let's inspect a few of these labels," he said, and began analyzing those of a well-known company. She'd have to teach him how to stress key words. But otherwise he was much better.

With Callie standing so close to the camera, on tape it would look like he was peering right into the viewer's eyes. He was still a little awkward with his blowups. But he'd get better. This new tack was going to work.

After the taping, Callie had the cameraman re-run it. By and large it was one hundred percent better than Ned's former stiff delivery. If he polished this approach a bit, his show could be a winner. There was something so sincere, so down to earth about those laugh wrinkles and that wide, high brow. People would trust him. And like him. How strange that he presented such a reserved front to most of the people at the station. He said he was brought up that way. But why?

"Another thing. Enough of this week-to-week business. We want to keep four weeks' stuff in the can. Timeless subjects, so we have leeway on when we run them. Let's start on that right away."

He nodded. "OK, Teach."

"Figure on working some extra days. Can you come in Saturday?"

"I guess so. But listen, Callie. I want to take you to the Swap Shop one day, too. You know, the big flea market?" Callie nodded. "Have you seen the circus there?"

"No, but I've heard it's very good."

"I know the producers. The Hannefords. I'll introduce you."

"Well, it sounds like fun, but we'll have to wait until next week. We've got a lot of work to do on your show."

"Next week it is. Pick the day."

Callie leafed through her calendar to check her schedule for next week. "Ummm . . . Wednesday," she said.

"OK, done deal. Wednesday. Two P.M.?"

She nodded, then picked up her notebooks and yawned. "Time to run. I've got to change into a ravishing gown for that ball tonight."

"With Brandenhurst?"

She nodded. He grimaced. "Well, just keep your distance and you'll be OK. I hear he's quite a girl chaser." The smokey eyes looked troubled. "Listen, have you time for a quick cup of coffee first? It won't take long. To talk about my show."

Callie sighed. "OK, if we go right now. Just twenty minutes, no more. I've got to do my nails and my hair and get dressed."

"Your hair and nails look fine," he said as they headed for the entrance.

At the nearby Wendy's they ordered coffee, and sat in comfortable silence, stirring it. "You're very good at what you do, Callie," he said. "And you're right. It's the way to go. I'm going to practice, like you said. I'll get it right."

She nodded.

"I'm really enjoying working with you."

She nodded again and then looked away. She was reading too much in his eyes. He touched her hand, and a warmth flooded her. She squeezed his hand back and then made herself pull hers away.

Sometimes, life was so confusing.

She waited inside the doorway, peeking nervously through the windows flanking it until the dark blue Mercedes pulled into the entrance drive and Jack, wearing a tux, climbed out. She draped the silvery stole—Second Chance Thrift Shop—over her arm, stepped through the door, and paused a moment at the top of the steps. Jack looked up and saw the silver-studded, clinging red gown and the silver stole, whistled, and charged up the steps, singing " 'The lady in red . . .' " Then he added, ". . . will dance with me."

She laughed at him. "Do you promise? Can we actually put aside business long enough for a turn around the floor?"

"I promise," he said. "Look like that and I'll promise you anything, honey. Except to keep my hands off you." He led her down the steps and helped her into the car, chortling, "Oh boy, if the gang could only see me now."

"Flattery will get you nowhere," said Callie. "And you'd better keep your hands to yourself, even if we dance a little, boss. This is business tonight. Remember?"

"We'll call it whatever you say." He hurried around to his side, climbed in, and closed the door. "Whatever you say," he repeated, easing out of the drive. "God, how am I gonna get us to the center in one piece when you're distracting me so?"

"Should I drive," Callie offered, "or go sit in the back seat?"

"Jesus, don't do that! I'd hop back there too, and we'd never even get out of the driveway."

He pulled out onto Andrews, and as he did so, on the second floor, Ned turned away from the window overlooking the entrance and rubbed his jaw. Nothing he could do about it right now. He turned back to the stack of tapes Callie had left him, all made by various talk-show hosts and anchors. She was right. Watching them over and over gave him a feel for what he should do on camera. It wasn't going to be as difficult as he'd thought. But what could he do about Brandenhurst and Callie? He didn't have a clue. He put another tape on the VCR.

* * *

They spent the cocktail hour with executives from Sport Cache, Jack's chain of sporting goods stores, and from Fit and Proper, his chain of health clubs. When he asked what she'd like to drink, she shrugged. "White wine I guess. I'm not much of a drinker."

"One white wine and one double vodka martini—Absolut," he ordered, and then turned back to Callie, "how could you get through one of these without a few drinks? I get itchy. They take too long."

They stood a little apart as Jack pointed out his employees and gave her a quick rundown on each. While he analyzed them, she analyzed him. Perceptive sometimes. Fairly considerate. Generous—he bought raffle tickets from every hostess that approached him. But by the time they went in to dinner, he was halfway through his third double martini. Was he a lush?

Three or four times since she'd gotten the kids raised and started living her own life, Callie had met men of substance who had been interested in her, and she had considered marriage. But there had always been something wrong. The architect had a nasty temper. The news anchor couldn't take a tactful suggestion, let alone criticism. So good-looking, though, that women fell all over him. The inventor was a pig, who made crude sexual allusions. And poor Syd Exler. Sweet, but with no idea how to kiss.

And now, here was Jack. Not perfect. But who in the real world got someone perfect? Liz Taylor, maybe?

The convention center's third-floor ballroom was done in soft pinks and dusty roses. And almost everything else was black. Even the table napery and chair covers, an elegant touch. Black panels framed in pink twinkle lights held large pink and rose watercolors by students at the Art Institute. And from a black arbor overhead, rosy pink paper flowers dangled.

Once they were seated—Jack's companies had taken two whole tables for twelve—and the music was playing, he said, "Come on, let's dance." There wasn't much room to maneuver, but he managed pretty well, and at one point he pulled her close to sway body-to-body for several moments until he swung her out again. What fun it was to dance with someone like him, Callie thought.

The night flew by in a kaleidoscope of laughing and animated conversation. Three different women came over to hug Jack, and eyed her warily as he introduced them. Were these women he was involved with? Or who wanted to be involved with him? Why else would they look at her that way?

After dinner the band played "The Lady in

Red," and Jack hurried her onto the floor to dance body-to-body again. "That song is about you, Lady in Red," he murmured into her ear as it ended. "You're something else."

They left at ten P.M. "Gotta work tomorrow," he told their tablemates. "I'm flying to Tampa at seven A.M."

But on the way out, on the second floor near the escalators, where no one could see them, he stopped. "Sorry, babe; I gotta do this," he said, and abruptly pulled her close, wrapped her in a crushing hug and kissed her soundly. She kissed him back, letting his tongue probe a little. When he finally let her go, he said, "That was just like I knew it'd be. We're a good pair. I didn't think I'd ever want to be locked to anyone again. But now I'm not so sure." He didn't say much on the way back. He just hummed "The Lady in Red" over and over. And drove all over the road.

At the office he handed her a card with his home number on it. He waited until she got her car; then, scratching his head, he watched her drive off. Upstairs, behind one of the second-floor windows, Ned Marshall watched, too. He hurried downstairs, got into his own car, and headed after her. He caught up to her at the second light, but didn't try to let her know he was driving behind her. He simply followed her

219

home, watched her turn safely into her gate, and then headed back toward the beach and his own apartment.

Callie had no sooner entered her office Wednesday morning than Mary scurried in, closed the door, and twirled around twice. "I want a full report," she cried, her black eyes glittering. "I can't wait. I know he called you three times from Tampa after that ball Thursday night. I know about the tea and Sunday and Tuesday nights. Mercy, I booked them. I even know when he takes out someone else, heehee! But he hasn't since Thursday. We haven't had a minute to talk. So tell me *everything*. It's so exciting!" She giggled, dancing on tiptoe around a chair. "You going steady yet?"

"Wait a sec, Mary. Before I tell you anything—this goes nowhere. Right? Swear in blood."

"You mean I can't give it to Todd for the evening news?" Mary tittered, faking Lily Tomlin surprise. "OK. Anything you say, kid. Just *tell* me. I can't stand it."

"Well, we had a marvelous time Thursday night, as I said."

"Yeah, you talked to me for two whole minutes Friday. But how marvelous? Did he come on to you or anything?"

"Sort of. We danced, and he complimented me

220

a lot. And he . . . well, he kissed me. On the second floor, where no one could see."

"Hot diggity! I knew it! How'd he kiss?"

Callie shrugged. "Come on, Mary. I can't tell you everything."

"Why not. I engineered this, didn't I?"

"Well, anyway, he let me know he's—you know—interested."

"I *knew* it!"

"But these aren't dates exactly, Mary. They're business."

"Horse shit! That's what he says so he won't look dumb if nothing works out. These tycoon movers can't bear to have it look like they couldn't measure up in the romance department."

"Sunday night at the collectors' car show he drank too much. I wouldn't let him drive back. I drove. Tuesday night it was a Miami City Ballet rehearsal at Bailey Hall. And dinner. He kissed me good night again. He wants to get more involved. I'm stalling."

"Stalling? You idiot, you'll lose him!"

"I won't be just another number in his little black book, Mary. Lots of women want him. They come up and look daggers at me."

"But you're the one he's getting to count on. You help with his social obligations. Anything he wants help with, do it. He runs his empire, but he needs a wife, secretary, and mother—all in one—to run the rest. Oh, this is so exciting!" she gushed. "I love it!"

"Well, Ned Marshall seems interested, too. And he's so nice."

"Ned? The consumer program?"

"Yes. I kind of like him. Did you see his show this week?"

"Yeah. My God, what a change! I mean he's been such a bomb. And suddenly he's Mr. Like-able. We got fifty calls. How'd you do that? He's kinda starchy with everyone. Not with me—we're pals. But with most people, he is. The gang here call him Mr. Stick behind his back."

"Well, there's another person underneath all that reserve."

"Oh, I know. And he looks good," shrugged Mary. "He's just a sweetie pie, when you know him. But so what? He's about fifty, fifty-five. And what's he done with his life? A two-bit show for a little cable company? Big deal. Why waste time on a loser, however nice, when a winner like Jack Brandenhurst is sniffing around? The way Jack looks at you?" She tittered wildly. "You got his juices going, kid. Forget Marshall, honey. You got a live one hot on your trail."

Callie nodded. She didn't mention that Jack had also told her she was going to be "officially" attending many more social functions, for Covent. Or how he had called her the Lady in Red. Mary would go up in smoke at that.

After Mary left, Callie thought about what she'd said. Why fool around with a loser when she almost had a winner in her grasp? She had agreed to have lunch with Ned at the Swap Shop today. Why had she said yes? They had enjoyed working with each other more than ever this past week. Too much so. She longed to feel his arms around her again. And he seemed to really care. When they had worked very late Monday night, he had followed her home, to be sure she got there safely.

Too late to back out today. But after this, no more playing with fire. She would forget Ned. Concentrate on Jack. Nothing was going to mess up her plans. She'd go with Ned today. But that was it.

Ned drove right by the first Swap Shop entrance. "I have a special pass," he explained. "I can park close to the building." He pulled in at the next entry, flashed a blue card at a guard, turned in behind the produce stands, and parked near the carousel. He helped her out and then led her inside a building where crowds thronged amid a carny setting—a raucous video arcade, food stalls, clowns, vendors hawking cotton candy and popcorn. From the circus ring a pair of clowns and two dancers waved at Ned. He waved back. They made their way over to the edge of the ring. "Hi," said the clown in huge floppy shoes and a teeny yellow hat. The one in a balloon-shaped suit and a huge fake nose and ears pointed to two seats front row center. They were ribboned off. "They're yours," he said, "unless you wanna sit upstairs."

"No, this is fine," said Ned, pulling off the ribbons. "Callie, meet Beaner and Apricot." He pointed at the dancers. "And Andrea Davis and Mara Cristiani. Gang, Callie Cameron." He slapped Beaner and then Apricot on the shoulder, and they slapped him back.

"We're workin' on the new opener," said Apricot. "Beaner keeps turning the wrong way during the break."

"Only because Appie here keeps stomping on my foot right before it," said Beaner. "You hear? We're performing on a Boat Parade barge again. With that sway-pole guy, Jay Cochran. You on this week?"

"No. I just wanted Callie to see all this talent. She's redoing a lot of the shows at Covent Cable, including mine."

"I've never met a clown close up before," said Callie.

"Heck, you came in with one," said Beaner, howling and slapping his leg as if he'd said something terribly funny. "But he's more balanced than most, har, har! A bit of a swinger, har, har!"

Callie looked at him blankly as he whooped and stomped his feet.

"Down, boy," chuckled Ned. "She doesn't know about all that."

"OK, our lips are sealed," said Andrea. "But we gotta go. It's time." And the four of them ran off behind the stage curtains.

"What would you like to eat, Callie?" Ned asked. "They have anything here."

Callie sniffed. Corned beef, Italian pasta, Greek salad—she could see them all. "Umm . . . how about sliced turkey and salad on pita. No dressing. And a diet Coke?"

He nodded and headed toward the food concessions. The rows of seats upstairs and down, and the bleachers opposite the ring, she saw, were filled. People were standing five deep behind the seats, and they filled the stairways. This circus sure packed them in.

Ned returned within minutes with a laden tray. He handed Callie her sandwich, drink and napkin, then put the tray on the floor and sat down himself. They hadn't taken a bite yet when the houselights dimmed, bright spots flashed on the ring, and circus music began pouring from the speakers. A ringmaster in red tails strode into the ring, followed by a group of dancers in beautiful, glittering costumes, tapping and kicking. The circus was on.

Callie watched, entranced, forgetting the sandwich in her hand. A half-dozen clowns came out, including Beaner and Apricot, and amused everyone while the ringmaster welcomed the crowd. Two clowns lowered four thick ropes from the rigging above 'til their ends touched the ring's floor. Then at each rope, a clown gave a dancer a boost, and she climbed up, up, up, at least twenty-five feet or more. And way up there, the dancers performed an aerial ballet in sync, hanging by a knee, by a foot. And finally spinning around while hanging by just one hand.

After the aerialists, Callie watched the trained bears, the juggler, the Bengal tiger act, the trampoline act, the trapeze act, the trained dogs, and the dancing elephants.

And Ned watched her.

When the whole cast came out to wave American flags at the end, amid wild applause, several performers winked or waved at Ned. "A lot of them seem to know you," Callie said. She noticed the uneaten sandwich in her hand and took a bite. "Next, you'll tell me you used to be a circus performer."

"Would you believe me if I did?" he asked.

"Oh, sure. And before that, you were an astronaut." She giggled. "Gosh, that was a wonderful show. But I still don't know why you insisted we come here."

"Promise you'll tell no one, and then I'll tell you," he said.

She smirked at him. "Good grief, is it something illegal?"

"Lord, no. And nothing you'll feel compelled to tell anyone."

"Well, OK. Cross my heart."

He took a deep breath and then grasped her hand. "When you said I'd tell you I was a circus performer, you were right. I was."

Nelly stared at him, openmouthed.

"I was called the Black Eagle because I always wore a black mask. And because I did tricks like— well, they'd say I flew like an eagle. My family— my parents and my sister and brother, my uncle—were circus performers, too. I grew up in the circus. My parents were killed in a circus fire when I was eighteen. My sister and brother quit cold and went to live with some cousins. My uncle was working in England then, so I was on my own. But circus folks are kind of like one big family anyway. Our friends looked after me.

"Only I didn't want to be known as the Flying Marshalls' son. The connotations were too grim. So I called myself the Black Eagle and began wearing a mask. It created drama. I did the trapeze and anything aerial. I'd get big publicity.

Big money. Until I started college ten years ago. But I still do occasional gigs, now."

Callie was amazed. "Weren't you—aren't you kind of, well, old to be doing trapeze work?"

"You're never too old, if you keep up. I know two seventy-year-old sisters who don't work anymore but could. I perform here sometimes when they need an act. The Hannefords—they produce this circus—we're friends for thirty-five years. And I keep up. I have my own equipment. I can do anything I did thirty years ago."

Callie shook her head numbly. "I don't know what to say. I would never in a million years have guessed. Even though your body and the way you move—You're like that Bengal tiger we just saw."

He laughed. "But I don't want anyone at Covent to know."

"Why not?"

"I don't want that to distract from what I'm doing now. I think it needs doing. And I really want to do it."

Callie nodded. "But one thing, Ned," she asked. "Why didn't you go to college before if you wanted to so badly?"

He sighed heavily. "Medical bills. Callie, I was married to another trapeze artist. Randa Scarlett. Randa'd been doing it since she was eight. She was absolutely beautiful. An incredible body. Very high strung. A lot more worldly than I was—she was five years older. And this one time between shows she was fooling around with a kid who did a horse act but messed around on the trapeze, too. I told her not to go up with him, and she got mad. They were trying stuff. No nets. He wasn't that good. She took a leap for him, and he missed her. I ran to break her fall, but I was too far away. She slammed into concrete! She never walked again. Never got over being angry about it. Never got past the pain."

He punched one fist with the other. "Turned out she had a bone deterioration problem, too. One operation after another. It was all too much. She died ten years ago."

"It would be too much for anyone," said Callie sympathetically.

"A few weeks after the funeral, I started school. Without all those huge medical bills, I could have gone through pretty fast, but I figured I'd better stash a little away, too. So I kept working all I could. My uncle retired and came back from England, and we lived together. Right after I got my master's, he died. I tried a couple of things before the consumer business occurred to me. I'm telling you all this because I don't want to have any secrets from you, Callie. I'm not ashamed of my past. I was a star. My agent can still get me all the work I want."

He stood up, pulled Callie to her feet, the half-eaten sandwich still in her hand, and kissed her on the cheek. "Let's head back. You need to digest everything. It was a big mouthful."

Callie munched thoughtfully as they walked. Whatever she might have expected from this outing, it was not this. Most new friendships with romantic possibilities, Callie had found, went along much like one TV script or another she had read or worked on. She would feel she was playing a role. She would know what each man would say before he said it. Well, plots came from real life, didn't they? But no one ever wrote a script like this. Because who'd believe it?

"Another thing," Ned said as they passed through the video arcade toward the door, "I'd like you to come see my place. Actually, I have two—an apartment on the beach and a five-story cell in a business building. That's set up with rigging and equipment. It's where I work out. How about Friday?" He tossed a bill to a clown carrying a tray of pink cotton candy, grabbed one, and handed it to her.

"I have to go to one of those things with Brandenhurst Friday."

"Saturday?"

Callie fully intended to refuse. She knew she had to stop this. Now. Before it went too far. Why was Ned such a magnet? It would mess up everything with Jack if he found out she was seeing someone else. But she heard herself say, "I . . . I guess so. What time?"

"If you want to catch a movie first, about three. If you just want to grab a bite and let me show you my digs, about five or six. Whatever works for you. The Chart House OK for dinner? I kind of like that early Fort Lauderdale setting."

Callie nodded. "I guess so. Better make it six."

They returned to his van, near the carousel. "Well, back to the mines. Just one thing more, Callie. Brandenhurst keeps asking you to go with him to social things. Business. But it won't stay business. I see how he looks at you. Be careful. Or at least be sure of what you want to do."

Callie nodded. "I . . . Yes, I'll try." He unlocked the van. And drove a thoroughly confused Callie back to the convent.

Thursday, she planned to discuss the "Moments" show with Jack, but the second she stepped into his office he said, "You gotta get a few more gowns, kid. You can't wear the same one every time."

"It's the only long gown I have," said Callie. His phone rang.

"Wait a sec," he said, grabbing it. "You got him, Mary? Tell him to get his ass in here in ninety minutes. We're talking about his show, and either he's here or it'll be someone else's show." He hung up.

"That red dress is a knockout," he said to Cal-

231

lie. "But we don't want people to think it's a uniform. We're going shopping—on Covent." Two minutes later they were heading for the Galleria. "I said we'd be there in ten minutes and to have everything out."

At Saks, after Callie changed into and out of a string of gowns, they chose three, plus three handbags—a silver, black, and gold—silver pumps, gold pumps, black strap sandals, and a black stole.

It took twenty minutes. "Deliver it all to Covent Cable, and bill us," Jack said. "I think that'll do for now."

"You mean you're not buying me a mink jacket?" asked Callie. "Oh, well, nothing's perfect."

"Play your cards right, you might get mink, too." He smirked.

"No personal connotation to these purchases, of course."

He squinted at her. "No. Nothing. No obligation. When you and I get it on, Miss Callie, it's gonna be 'cuz you want to. Wear that blue one to the Bachelors' Ball tonight."

"Ohmygosh! It's tonight?"

"Yeah. We're going by limo. I had a few credits to use up. Pick you up at seven. Come on, let's get back. I wanna go over that "Moments" business before we meet with Ches."

Back at the convent, Ned was waiting in her office. "Callie, are you still busy with Jack, tonight?"

She nodded. "That Bachelors Ball, remember?"

"But we're on for tomorrow night?"

Callie sighed. She should say no, but she had already told Ned she'd go. And he looked upset. "Tomorrow's fine," she said.

"We'll go right from work. The Chart House first. Then I'll show you my places. And we'll talk."

"OK."

"And you're working with me this afternoon?"

She laughed. "I don't know if you need me anymore. I saw the extras you taped this week. They're even better than last week's."

"I still need you," he said quietly. And he turned and was gone.

As soon as Mary brought Ches De Land into Jack's office, Callie could tell this was going to be a sticky meeting. Jack's jaw had an angry set to it; his eyes were sullen. De Land flopped resignedly into the chair next to Callie's in front of Jack's desk.

We've got some things we want you to change in the show, Ches," Jack began.

"Actually," Callie interrupted, "the show is basically not bad. Fast-paced, catchy music—"

"If you'll wait just a minute and let me say what I have to say, Callie," Jack broke in irritably. "Then it'll be your turn."

Callie felt she'd been slapped. She'd seen Jack snap at workers a few times, but he'd never done it to her before.

"What I was saying is that you know, of course, what Callie's here for. There are several areas of your show that need help. If we want this show, or any show, to become a top draw, we have to zip it up. Callie?"

"As I said, Mr. De Land, you have one of the better shows Covent is doing right now. But that's not saying much. There are three main areas with room for improvement. One, there are too many inaccuracies and too many IDs are left out. On that cruise ship clip last week, you never identified the ship or line. Inexcusable. And that eighty-year old cruising fan. No name. That's just sloppy work."

"That was just one time," De Land began.

"Sorry. On your last ten tapes we found at least one person, place or event unidentified or misidentified. Usually there were several."

"And the other matters?" asked De Land in a voice dripping ice.

"The show needs more variety. It is fairly good, but with a name like 'Moments' you could do so many more *kinds* of events. You're too heavy on luncheons and ribbon cuttings. Try some Navy League events. Visit a ship, a carrier, when it's in port. Get to Skip Barber's racing school, and catch some ordinary guy taking a lesson because he's fascinated with racing cars. Get over to the Swimming Hall of Fame. That sort of thing."

"I see," said De Land in a chillier voice. The veins in his neck stood out. His face grew darker.

"And the third area for change is this: everyone you shoot is a Wasp. You don't reflect the community. Get some minorities on. Do a Filipino Christmas party for your Christmas show. Get up to the Morikami, down to Calle Ocho and Liberty City. Cover the Black debutantes."

"In other words, dump my show and start over," De Land snapped.

"No, I didn't say that," Callie said calmly. What a jerk this man was. Another one that couldn't bear a touch of criticism. "Your show has the right pace, the right style, nice and light. Keep that, but broaden your range of subjects, include minorities, be accurate. An assistant can check facts. But *you* are ultimately responsible. If one worker doesn't do it right, get someone else who will. It's not an option."

"And you agree with all this?" asked De Land, turning to Jack.

"You bet your sweet ass I do," Jack shot back.

"Don't get huffy, Ches. I want Covent shows top-notch. Or they're out. Half-assed won't do. There's fifty wannabes out there would give their left nut for a chance at your show. Got the message? I want Covent to explode. Bigger. Better. Making more money. If we make more money, so will you. Think of that, and don't be so touchy."

De Land stared at his hands for a long minute. Then he turned to Callie. "OK, Mrs. Cameron, you win. We'll give it a try."

"The name is Callie," she said gently.

He hesitated for a moment, then said tightly, "Mine is Ches." He got up, stiffly shook Jack's hand, nodded to Callie, and hurried from the room. She turned coolly toward Jack, still smarting over his tone and said, "See you at seven." Then she slipped out the door.

Back in her office, she slapped a file down on her desk. He had snapped at her! In front of Ches! Sure, he'd backed her up later, but still . . . Jack was mostly easygoing, but he clearly did not care to be interrupted.

She added this item to her mental file on him. What if he was serious about her? If they got married, would she have to remember never to interrupt him for the rest of her life? But she was always interrupting people. She was basically impatient. Always in a hurry. For twenty years she'd always had too much to do and too little time to do it.

* * *

"Well, what do you think of it?"

Callie stared in amazement at the cavernous room. Up above were complex rigging, massive light racks, four trapezes, thick ropes dangling to the floor. Below, a circus ring with a trampoline, exercise mats, and a small tower. Beyond the ring, a kitchen, a sitting area, four doors, cabinets, a cot, a TV.

"I work out here," Ned explained. "I run over in the morning, do my routines, and then run back to my apartment. It's not far."

"No net," Callie said in a hushed voice.

"Nah. I don't need it. I don't often try anything new."

"It's so high! Did you say five stories? How can that be, here in an office building like this?"

"It was built this way. My uncle owned the land and made a deal. The builder would own whatever he constructed except for this part, which would belong to me. So the whole front side is offices all the way up, and this side is offices on the three floors above me. Come on, I want to show you my apartment, too. It's not far."

He drove her the ten blocks to the plush beachfront condo where he had parked before that first walk. His apartment, on the fifteenth floor, was large, with high ceilings. Two bedrooms, a study, a living room, a dining room converted into a media room with a TV and stereo, a kitchen, breakfast room, and three baths. And chinning bars in two doorways. Ned gave her a quick tour. "It was my uncle's. He lived here until he died, two years ago."

The view was magnificent—the ocean on one side, a view of the city from the terrace.

Ned shrugged. "I wouldn't have bought it for myself. Trappings don't matter to me. But they mattered to my mom, so my dad tried to keep her happy. And Randa was like my mother. Buying was her pleasure. From catalogs mostly. There wasn't much else to pleasure her. Trappings mattered to my uncle, too. I just want you to know," he said with a small grin, "that should trappings matter to you, I'd be willing to rethink my attitude."

Callie digested his words slowly. If this were a sitcom, they would be a tip-off that he was about to propose. Or about to make love to her and then propose.

He led her out onto the terrace. Except for the view, it was more like an old-fashioned veranda. The ocean, an endless swale of dark gray, stretched out below them to the left. To the right, the city's countless lights twinkled like a lavish Milky Way. Callie peered down at the dark clumps on the beach below and realized they were seagrapes. In one of them Ned had kissed her on that walk.

"Tell me, Callie," he said, standing close behind her and gently gripping her shoulders. "What really matters to you?"

As she turned to him his arms slipped around her. What a safe warm place to be, she thought. She had studied these scenes too often in her work not to realize where this one was headed. But she would stop him before they went too far. How hungry she had been these past ten days for a moment like this. She lifted her face for his gentle, tentative kiss. He kissed her cheeks, and his hands rubbed her back, softly at first, then urgently, pressing her to him.

She would break away any second, she told herself. But ohhhh, just a bit more of that touch. She needed to taste that skin. That mouth. She stood on tiptoe, and his arms swept down and picked her up—God, he was so strong—and carried her, as he kissed her neck, back inside and into his bedroom. He laid her gently on the bed and knelt beside her.

I'll stop us in a minute, Callie told herself, melting at his fingers' touch. Oh, God, I've got to stop us. But I don't want to!

He felt too good. It had been too long. Her hands reached to guide his face toward her breast, and he kissed her through her blouse, then quickly scrambled onto the bed with her, whispering urgently, "Callie . . . oohhh, baby . . . I want you so much."

She didn't answer, except to whimper with a need so urgent it was almost painful, and then pressed even closer as he began fumbling with her clothes. And his. Tugging at his belt and pants, lifting her skirt, slipping down her panty hose. Callie helped him, tearing her skirt and blouse completely off, unhooking her bra, pulling his pants from around his knees. They grabbed each other, clinging tightly, savoring the incomparable sensation of flesh on flesh.

She kissed his hand and placed it on her bare breast. Ohhhhh! And they were clutching, tasting, touching all they had been aching to taste and touch all this time. And then they were flying, swinging, soaring higher and higher. Was this what a trapeze was like? A glorious flight, a fusing together—that tight wonderful body hard into hers, harder, tighter . . .

"I want to make you feel so good you'll never let me go," she cried into his ear. "Oh, Ned, my darling, don't stop, don't stop, don't ever stop!" And they flew quickly to the top and hung there, spilling bliss and triumph for a long pulsing moment before they swung down, down . . . back into the world and his bed and his room.

They lay there, panting and hugging, murmuring and hugging again. Spent. Happy. "Is that what a trapeze is like?" she whispered.

"A trapeze should be that good. I'd never come down."

"Oh, you are so wonderful, I wanted to swallow you whole."

"Funny," he murmured into her hair, "that's just what I was trying to do to you."

"Oh, Ned. That was, that was—" She stopped suddenly and sat up. "Oh, my God," she wailed. "What have I done? I didn't do that! Oh, no! I was going to stop us. I just wanted a little more of you. I had to have a little more. I was going to stop. Oh, no!"

She jumped out of bed. Ned was staring at her in shock. "Callie, honey. You didn't want to do that? You seemed to want it as much as I did. Honey, you seemed—"

"I know what I seemed," she cried, scrambling from the bed, snatching her clothes from the floor and holding them in front of her. "Of course, I wanted you. I've wanted you ever since the first day I watched you mess up a perfectly good program concept. I've been fighting it ever since, damn it, and it just keeps driving me crazy. Getting in my way."

"But, Callie, what's wrong with that? If we care about each other, what the hell is wrong?" he cried, leaping from the bed, grabbing his shorts from the floor, and pulling them on angrily.

"I'll tell you what's wrong," she snapped, yanking her skirt on backward, stomping her foot, and then twisting it around the right way. "I've been poor too long, and I'm not having any more of it. Not for anyone. I lived on the edge of poverty when my husband was alive. Then he died, and I had two kids and no money. I worked like a slave for fifteen years. Poor? I bought clothes and everything else at flea markets and garage sales. I rode a bicycle to work. We didn't have two cups that matched. But I did it. I got them educated. They're on their on now. And I've got a career. Only I want more. The pretty clothes, the fur wrap. To be able to afford a face lift when I need one. Jack can give me all that."

Ned slumped onto the bed, stunned. "I've always wanted a pretty diamond ring," Callie howled. "Two carats. Three. I've never even had a chip. I've wanted one for so long. And I'm going to have it."

"Trappings," said Ned sadly.

"Yes, the trappings," she cried, jabbing her arms into her blouse. "I don't care if I'm so crazy about you my heart starts pounding when you stand close. I don't care if I get wet when you touch me. I am *not* giving in! OK, you're not as poor as you look, but sometimes you dress like you live under a bridge. Me—I'm *never* going to be the least bit poor again. I'm going to have a real diamond. It's my turn now." She buttoned her blouse and marched from the room.

Ned followed her, caught her just past the

door, took her by the shoulders, and swung her gently around. "Well, if you don't want to walk through that lobby looking like you've just been up to *something*, you better get your buttons straight," he said. Callie looked down. They were in the wrong holes. He carefully unbuttoned and rebuttoned her blouse.

She pulled away. "Don't come down. I'll take a cab."

"No, I'll take you home." He reached for her hand.

"Don't touch me," she cried. "Please. Being together, loving each other tonight— Well, damn it, I've only got so much willpower." Big tears began rolling down her cheeks. He started to reach over again, then pulled back his hand.

"It's OK, Callie. Please . . . don't cry. I won't touch you. I just want— Oh, shit. Come on, I'll take you home."

When Callie stopped by the office the next morning, she found a long message from Ned on her computer. "I'll be mostly out of town the next four weeks. I have five shows in the can. Right after Christmas, we can do six or eight ahead if you want. I'll call you in a few days. Or leave a message. I'll check my answering machines every day from wherever I am. Happy Thanksgiving."

She rewound the message and played it again. Maybe he thought it would be easier this way for them to forget about each other. Good. She'd concentrate on Jack. She'd try to remember not to interrupt him. That wasn't too much to ask.

After the next party, if he asked her to come up to his place again, she'd go. They had four dressy events booked between now and Christmas. She'd get Ned out of her system.

She just had to take the bull by the horns, let Jack make love to her, and forget Ned forever. She would be Jack's wife. And never again would there be anything she wanted that she couldn't have. She would keep him satisfied. They would build a life. They would live happily ever after—a perfect movie ending.

Then why did she feel so empty?

The limo pulled up to the Marlborough House entrance and the driver hopped out to open the doors. "Wait down here," ordered Jack. "You'll take Mrs. Cameron home later." It was going exactly as she had planned. She had to do this. As Mary said, men didn't propose nowadays until you auditioned. She forced a smile.

The entrance door swung open and they walked in. Jack nodded at the night manager behind the desk. In the elevator, he grabbed her in a bear hug, chuckled throatily, then hugged her again.

At his door, he tried without success to fit a key in the lock, but the door opened anyway, and an elderly, bent man on the other side let them in. "This is Abel, Callie," Jack said in a thick voice. "He runs the place. For twenty-five years. Always stays up till I get in, no matter how late. Abel, Mrs. Cameron. We won't need anything."

Abel nodded and said, "Glad to meet you, Mrs. Cameron. Have a good evening," then headed down a hallway to the left.

"His rooms are at the far end there. He won't bother us," said Jack. "Whatcha want to drink, honey?" His voice was getting thicker by the word. He moved clumsily around to the other side of the bar.

"Whatever you're having," she said, trying to sound sexy and inviting. He poured two glasses of straight vodka, tossed off half of one, topped it, and handed the other to her. "Uh . . . could I have a glass of water, too, please," she asked.

"Anything you want tonight, you get it," he said, pouring a glass of Evian water and spilling a good deal of it on the bar. "Even if it's me." He grinned foolishly, took another long swallow, put the vodka bottle on the bar, and came around from behind it to reach for her and pull her close. "Whatcha wanna do now, honey?" he asked. "Wanna get ta know each other a li'l better?"

Callie nodded and lifted her face. His kiss was ravenous. Was he trying to swallow her tongue? When he let her go, his face was flushed. His breath came in gasps as though he'd just run a mile.

"Le's go to my room," he croaked, topping his vodka once more from the bottle on the bar. He grabbed her arm with his free hand and led her down a hallway to the third door on the left. He pushed it open with his foot, and they entered a huge bedroom with the same glass wall and stunning view as the living room.

He took another gulp from the glass, set it on a night stand next to the king-sized bed, and turned to her, panting heavily. His eyes half-closed, he groped at her shoulders, her breasts.

She recoiled. Her resolve vanished. Damn! This was not the way the scene was supposed to go—the one where they made glorious love together. This was a totally different man from the one she had worked with and danced with. This was a sloppy drunk trying to do something he probably couldn't, groping and panting. A turnoff. Only, good God, now what? How could she get out of here without a ghastly scene? Stall? Yes, stall. Until he passed out.

"No, no, Jack," she cooed seductively. "Let's undress you, and put you to bed first." She began unbuttoning his shirt, very slowly. "Baby," he began, groping at her arms.

"Not until our clothes are off. You first," she said. She pulled his shirt off, tossed it aside, unbuckled and unzipped his pants, dragged back the covers, and whispered, "Sit on the bed."

He sat, stupidly. She pulled his trousers off and tossed them over a chair. He was grinning, but his eyes, by now, were almost closed. She stooped to tug off his shoes and socks. He was flabby compared to Ned. "Look, honey," he said, pulling his shorts down. "Look what I've got for you." He didn't have anything.

Oh, God, let him pass out, prayed Callie. "Lie down now," she ordered. He did, but he reached for her. She stepped back. "Wait until I take my clothes off and . . . put on some perfume." She pulled the covers up and tucked him in. His eyes closed.

Holding her breath, Callie tiptoed over to the bathroom, flicked on the light, and stepped inside. She left the door open just a crack. She heard him mumble, "Hurry up, honey. I'mmmm readyyyy." She waited a minute more; when the heavy breathing grew into a snore, she tiptoed from the bathroom and out of the bedroom.

Quietly, hoping the door wouldn't squeak, she let herself out of the apartment and took the elevator down to the lobby. The driver, sitting next to the night manager, was engrossed in a cross-word puzzle.

"Brogan, wasn't it?" Callie said. "I need a lift home."

He stood up smartly. "Yes, ma'am. You just wait here. I'll bring the car right around." She was shaking. Oh, Lord, was she going to be sick? She fumbled in her purse for her hankie as tears filled her eyes.

Callie, waiting in the conference room, felt Excedrin headache #42—the incurable one—coming on. Jack strode in, all smiles, and gave her a peck on the cheek. "I wish you woulda stayed all night last night, honey. We coulda done it again this morning."

Callie choked mentally, barely managing to keep a straight face. He actually thought they did something last night. Didn't he realize that he had passed out again before anything could happen? She'd taken a cab home this time. At least last night she hadn't needed to go through the charade of undressing him and putting him to bed. This time he had just unzipped his pants and crashed onto his bed, out cold. He hadn't even kissed her.

Mary had warned her not to play hard to get. "He'll get it from someone, Callie. Guys like him never have to do without. Look at Prince Charles.

If you want to snag him, *cooperate!*" But what if Jack was too drunk to know the difference? Besides, sober, he was likeable. Drunk, he was disgusting.

"OK, miss," he said. "What have you to report?"

She opened her file and began. "First off, Tony's got a new chef. Good sense of humor." She told him which pilots were shooting this week. Played tapes of various Christmas shows, some with holes waiting for live coverage segments. "We're interviewing people for embarrassing experiences during Christmases past. We're getting some amusing results."

Jack nodded approval. "Sounds good. I saw De Land's show a couple of times. It's getting there."

"And Ned Marshall's consumer advice program has turned right around. He caught exactly what we wanted—the viewer response has been remarkable. He's four shows ahead. He's away but he'll begin shooting about six ahead as soon as he gets back. I think we'll start scheduling two or three a week. He's getting hot."

"I knew you'd be able to fix our flat tires." Jack grinned. "I'll be in Wednesday. We've got a ribbon-cutting, don't we?" Callie nodded. "And we're busy Saturday, aren't we? Wear one of those new gowns, huh? And we're gonna spend Christmas together."

Callie nodded again, then blurted out, "Oh,

dear, I have to run. Talk to you Wednesday." She slipped out of the conference room before he could say another word.

She wasn't sure exactly how she'd handle Saturday. What if he wanted to make love? Well, she'd cross that bridge then. Darn Ned. She was so mixed up, she didn't know whether to jump into Jack's bed—and life—or run and hide. Twenty-two days since Ned had left. Why couldn't she get him out of her head, damn it, even when she was really trying to get involved with Jack? Or was she trying not to?

She walked down the hall toward Ned's office as she had done every day for three weeks now. It had been closed and dark every time. What a rough three weeks. Dodging Jack without turning him off altogether had kept her tense and uneasy. How could he be so nice during the day and such a nerd at night? And that drinking! He had passed out all three times she had gone to his apartment. But he thought they had made love! Would he ever be any different? Or would the drinking just get worse?

Out on the Windridge yacht last week, with the museum bunch, she had feigned seasickness to avoid going home with him. This toe dancing was so stressful. She wished she had never met Ned. Or Jack.

Ned's office was dark and closed again. She sighed and headed back toward her own. He had called her three times during these three weeks. From Dallas, Los Angeles, and Las Vegas. "Why are you chasing around the country that way," she asked after the third call. "Business," he said. "Wanted to be sure you're OK."

Back in her own office, she sat at her desk, staring at the phone. There was a soft rap on the door. "Come in," she called.

The door opened and there he stood. Callie gulped and stared. He looked tighter and leaner than ever. He moved inside. "I just had to come and see you for a minute," he said.

She nodded, wordlessly. God, he looked good. "How are you?" he asked. His eyes were eating her up.

"Working like mad. I need roller skates. You know how it is right before Christmas. I . . . I wanted to tell you, I think your Christmas show is perfect. All that about holiday discounts. Asking people to write in about misleading labels. Great! I can't believe how much better you are. We'll expand the show after Christmas."

"I just look right to the side of the camera and see you there like you told me," he said. "It works. Are you still seeing Jack?"

Callie hesitated, then nodded. "Yes. He still seems interested, even though I've been a little . . . confused."

"I'm glad you're confused. I missed you like hell, Callie."

She looked down at her hands. But his eyes drew hers like a magnet. "I've missed you, too. I tried not to," she said.

He nodded. "I know. But please, do one thing for me, honey. Spend Christmas Eve or Christmas night with me. Don't see me after that if you don't want to. But I really want to see you then."

"Christmas Eve," Callie said quickly. She was spending Christmas with Jack. They stared at each other, wordlessly, hungrily, for a minute. Callie ached to feel those arms around her. But she didn't dare.

"And one other thing, Callie. That afternoon, would you go to the Swap Shop at four, and watch the circus? I have a reason. I'll have a seat reserved ringside. I'll join you there."

"Yes, I will," Callie said. A satisfied grin touched his face. Then she watched that panther-like gait as he left the room.

The rest of the week was a race against time, getting all the Christmas programs ready. Jack was pleased that she would spend Christmas with him. "It'll be a landmark day, Callie," he kept warning her with a suggestive grin. "I'll bet he's gonna propose," Mary predicted when Callie confided their plans. "I heard him tell that Ardis person on the phone that he was serious about someone so don't call anymore. Maybe he'll give you a ring," she cried, gasping for breath, her eyes glittering with excitement. "Oh, I can hardly stand it. I have a gut feeling. My gut is never wrong. I just can't wait! I think we did it!"

If Mary was right, it would be smooth sailing to a preacher. Wasn't this what she wanted? Then why wasn't she more excited? Why had she agreed to see Ned the day before Christmas?

The Swap Shop was jammed on Christmas Eve. But a special pass had arrived in the mail two days before, so Callie was able to park near the carousel. Inside, she was directed to a pair of rib-boned-off, front-row seats. She made her way over and sat down.

Then, suddenly the houselights dimmed, bright lights over the ring beamed on, and circus music began pouring from speakers. The ringmaster stepped forth, followed by a string of tumbling clowns, and the circus began. But Callie didn't smell the popcorn, or feel the excitement or hear the crowd buzzing. Indeed, she barely heard the music. One corner of her mind was still in conflict. Should she be here at all? Could she be strong enough tonight? Or would it be a repeat of their last wonderful night together? All that had accomplished was to fine-tune her attraction for Ned. And make her critical of Jack, unsure of whether she really wanted her romance with him to succeed. If so, she had to be true to him. If not she should just drop the whole thing.

The aerial ballet, with the four girls climbing and then performing in sync, was over. Where was Ned right now? Why had he asked her to come here? Where had he been the last few weeks?

A loud flourish of trumpets blew such thoughts out of her mind. Two trapezes were quickly lowered from the rigging, as were two thick, black, spangled ropes. And Callie noted some other curious bars and ropes, way up high. "Now, folks," the ringmaster cried, "our special Christmas treat, one of the most consummate trapeze talents of all time—the Black Eagle!"

And in a flash, terrified, Callie knew exactly why she was here. To see her Black Eagle perform.

As the crowd cheered, the ring lights dimmed, and one powerful spot poured onto the side curtain from behind which he sprang—his lean, powerful form in black tights that fit like skin, and a glittering leather openwork vest, his face partially obscured by a black mask. To the music's beat, he leaped into a no-hands cartwheel and a no-hands double flip into the ring. He flew up the nearest sparkling rope, like a cat slithering up to the first trapeze above, almost faster than the eye could see. Without a pause, in perfect timing with the throbbing beat of "Dancing on the Ceiling," he lunged into a fast string of incredible acrobatics almost painful to watch. He swung out on the trapeze, pushing its swing higher and meanwhile performing another set of acrobatic contortions. He stood on his head on the swinging bar, on one hand, on the other. He flipped in a complete circle around the bar as it swung, then simply leaped through the air, catching the other trapeze with his hands!

So fast! Another string of gravity-defying feats. Callie, like the spellbound audience, couldn't tear her eyes away. She was frozen with fear. Now, he leaped from this second trapeze, this time catching the second glittering rope up which he slithered, like a wildcat, into the rafters. And there he walked on an almost invisible rope and a slender bar. He swung down to hang by his ankles! Then swung up again to place a loop in his mouth and hang by his teeth, while performing twirling contortions. Once more he escaped up into the rigging, leaping from one platform to another, leaping back onto a trapeze and swinging on it to fly toward the second, and from there to one of the ropes on which he flipped upside down. Head down, the rope wrapped around his middle, he slid down—no hands—flipping once more at the bottom and landing on his feet in the ring. Another fast string of no-hands flips and balletic leaps toward the back of the stage. And in a wink, he disappeared.

It was all so fast, so incredible, so heart-stopping. The applause was thunderous. The crowd surged to its feet, screaming and cheering and shouting "Bravo!" It took the ringmaster several minutes to get the crowd to sit again and quiet down. "Sorry, folks," he shouted over the melee, "The Black Eagle never does encores. And now—a Touch of Magic!" And he brought on the magicians. But what act could follow the Black Eagle?

Callie was in shock, unable to tear her gaze from the stage. She had no idea he could perform like that—that *anyone* could perform like that. Had he been working here this Christmas week? What about the other weeks? She barely registered the magic act. Or the jugglers that followed. Her mind was churning. That damn fool! He could have killed himself. Oh, God, she'd made the right choice. If she'd picked Ned she'd be a widow before they ever got married.

But still, seeing that body leaping and flying . . . If he were here right now—

And then he was. In blue jeans—no mask, no costume—kneeling next to her seat. She wanted to grab him and hug him to death.

"Callie?" he whispered.

"Oh, N-Ned," her voice caught.

"Let's sneak out of here." She followed him

down the narrow aisle to the back of the circus area, past the grandstand and through the exit. "Where's your car?" She pointed. "It's OK there," he said. "We'll come back for it later."

He led her around the building to his van, helped her in, and drove them to the Beekman House. She groped for his hand. He took hers and held it tightly.

Inside his lobby, as they entered the elevator, she managed to say, "Oh, you take these like everyone else? You don't climb up the side of the building?"

"Not when I have a guest." He grinned.

After letting them into his apartment, he led her to the sofa and sat her down, then parked in the chair next to her.

"Ned, I had no idea! You were incredible. Better than anyone I've ever seen. But at your age—oh, God, I was so terrified. I couldn't believe—"

"I wanted you to see. To know what I've done most of my life. And what I've been doing for these past weeks, Callie. After our . . . our wonderful loving that night."

"But why, Ned? Risking your life like that every day—"

"Sometimes four shows a day. I took a lot of short gigs and emergency fill-ins, all over the country."

"Oh, Ned, please! Don't do it again. Not even once. Ever. Please. I'll do anything . . ." She jumped up from the sofa and threw herself onto his lap and clung to him. The tears flowed as she sobbed into his neck. "Whatever you want. If you w-want me, OK. If y-you don't, OK. But please, stop before you wind up just a heap of mush on s-some circus ring f-f-floor!"

He held her close and patted her back and tried to soothe her. "Callie, nothing will happen. I've done that a million times. I never really quit. I practice every day. Nothing will happen."

"But why, Ned? Why suddenly four weeks solid?"

"Because I guess I . . . I don't know about all this falling in love stuff, this courting business, Callie. It's been a long time. I know I love you. I understand about your not wanting to be poor. I told you, my mother was that way. Randa, too. I'm not rich, honey. But I'm not poor. I never touch capital. I learned that from my dad. I understand your wanting a ring. And you should have one." From his pocket he pulled a small velvet ring box, sprung it open, and handed it to her.

Callie looked down at it and then stared, open-mouthed.

"Merry Christmas, honey. It's four carats," he said. "That's why all the jobs. I told my agent only big-money stuff—Las Vegas, L.A. We booked all I could fit in. It's yours."

Callie stared at the ring Ned was now slipping

on the third finger of her left hand. "OK to put it there?" he asked. She hesitated, then nodded. "You risked your life for this, for me, you idiot?" she cried, and the tears started again.

"I love you, Callie."

"Oh, Ned, heaven help us, I love you, too," she sobbed. "The thing with Jack won't work. It never really got started. I tried. I couldn't. And this is the h-happiest, scariest Christmas of m-my whole life. But there's nothing else I w-want. Honest. Except one. Your show is going to hit big. You'll make all the money you need. So, please, Ned. Don't ever do anything like this again. Ohhhh, I want us to make love right now."

He stood up, still holding her in his arms, and carried her toward his bedroom.

"Oh, maybe, once in a while, honey. I can't quite give it all up. It's part of me." He opened the bedroom door, carried her inside and laid her gently on the bed. "And besides, I might have to. God only knows what you'll ask for next Christmas." As he lay down beside her and took her eagerly into those sinewy arms, he whispered, "Don't cry, Callie. Just love me, honey, and anything you really want, I'll get for you somehow."

Martha Gross is Society Editor for the Fort Lauderdale *SUN-SENTINEL*. She has written two TO LOVE AGAIN romances—*RETURN TO LOVE* and *ONE KISS* (December 1993).

Christmas in Hawaii

by

Helen Playfair

The plane was on time at Hilo and Dorie got off eagerly, searching the crowd for her son and the girl he was about to marry. The rest of the disembarking passengers just shuffled along but Dorie kept bobbing up, trying to see over the people around her and spot Russell. Even in high heels, Dorie was barely five and a half feet.

She didn't see Russell, and as the crowd thinned out, it was plain that he was not there. What could have happened to her little boy?

No, she told herself firmly, he is not a child anymore. He is grown, he is about to marry, he is a doctor, for heaven's sake! But she couldn't help it; she was worrying about her child. Had something happened to him? Had he forgotten?

And then he came running up the causeway, late and laughing and towing with him a girl so pretty, so exotic, so darkly gorgeous that Dorie forgot to walk and the passenger behind her ran into her and thumped her with his carry-on bag.

They both apologized, but Dorie was barely paying attention. She was looking at Russell and his lady. Her boy was tall and handsome, his dark curly hair in disorder and a strand falling over his right eyebrow, as usual. He was not looking at where he was going, or for Dorie, or anywhere at all except adoringly at the girl by his side.

She trotted along on high-heeled sandals that must have been attached to her little feet by magic . . . Well, maybe there was a strap or two. Her loose sundress was ankle length, and her hair fell down her back, past the waist, dark and wavy and beautiful in its disarray. She was giggling and rosy from her run, looking up at Russell.

Of course it would be Lani—who else would Russell bring to meet her? Lani . . . Dorie guessed her age to be sixteen. Well, eighteen maybe. A doctor's wife? What could Russell be thinking of? He was nearly thirty, he had his medical degree and a great future ahead of him, and he was choosing to marry a teenager? Dorie stamped her feet impatiently. She had come all this way for a wedding, was she going to be abetting a disaster?

The skirt of Lani's dress had a long slit in it, and a lot of tanned, perfect leg showed as she ran. There seemed to be not a scrap of underwear and the sweetly curved body moved sensuously under the dress.

Well, even one's son is only human.

Dorie was wearing a suit she regarded as sensible even if it was silk, for it resisted the creases and stresses of travel. It was teal blue, tailored, and perhaps too heavy for Hawaii. She had been comfortable enough on the plane, but it was warmer here in the terminal. However, she was not going to take off her jacket. She was trying to make a good first impression, and this was her best outfit—a soft white blouse, the tight teal skirt, a string of almost-real pearls. Dorie had always loved clothes, and dressing nicely becomes even more important when you are old enough to be the mother of a boy who is nearly thirty.

Dorie kept herself trim. That part was easy; a nurse doesn't need to do aerobics. There may have been some white streaks in her blond hair, some lines at the corners of her eyes; but she knew she looked good. She had a great new haircut, and clothes sense is another of those things that gets better with the years.

She threw open her arms to her son. How good to hug her boy again, her grown-up baby boy! She could have hugged him all day, but unfortunately one had to proceed to the next step. She had to greet Lani.

Dorie smiled her greetings, and Lani offered a gentle little hand to be shaken. She was even prettier close up, with huge dark eyes and a soft little voice one could hardly hear. "We are so glad you came for our wedding," she murmured. "Is this your first trip to Hawaii? I hope you are going to like it."

"What's to not like?" Dorie asked. "It's beautiful here."

Russell laughed. "That's my mom! She's been off the plane about three minutes, but she already has an opinion!"

Dorie laughed too. "Oh, but I know all about Hawaii! I had a layover between planes, didn't you know that? I spent all last night and part of yesterday at Waikiki. In a gorgeous, luxurious hotel overlooking the beautiful beach! How could I help loving this place? I met some perfectly charming people at dinner, and they taught me some Hawaiian words."

Russell actually looked a little alarmed by her enthusiasm. "Yeah? Like what?"

"Aloha, Mele Kalikimaka," Dorie recited.

"Well, Merry Christmas to you, too, but where we're going, it's a little different from Waikiki."

Dorie looked alert. "Oh?"

"Not so crowded," he managed at last.

Russell's car was a jeep, not one of those city jeeps with chromed rollbars, but a serious vehicle, brown and high off the ground. The canvas top was up, and the side flaps were down. These stiff flaps had plastic windows that reminded Dorie of something Russell's grandfather might have had on his car. They created a plastic igloo; muggy, hot.

It took only minutes for them to leave Hilo behind, and from then on, there were fields of sugar cane on both sides of the road. Dorie sweltered in her city suit, and understood why Lani had chosen to make this trip wearing a sundress. She wished she were wearing one. She was about to suggest they open the flaps just a little when it began to rain.

And how it rained! Water sluiced over the car, thundering onto the canvas roof. It was like being inside a drum. The road became a morass. Russell stoically went on driving, and Lani, in the back seat, said exactly nothing, as she had since the drive began.

Dorie clutched at her seat as they plowed through a mudhole. Russell just kept going. "You're so calm!" she said. "You act like this happened every day."

"It does," said Russell.

Through the rain, through the fogged plastic of the windows, she could see fields of sugar cane. They stretched endlessly out on all sides, fading into the rain. The miles went on, and Dorie peeked through the plastic again to see if the scenery had changed. More cane fields.

Then suddenly the rain stopped and the clouds lifted before them, opening up a vista of dripping green fields. Sunshine decorated the gray clouds with shining white edges. Ahead of them, standing in a pool of light from the ragged sky, was a cluster of low buildings, their shallow-pitched roofs nearly touching the ground; and beyond Dorie could make out more houses, a village.

"Here we are," said Russell.

His home was mostly roof, a roof so wide and low the opening that was the front entry cut right into it. There was no door there, just the doorway. No walls or windows. The roof was held up by pillars and the rooms were laid out before them, the sitting room with wicker chairs and brightly printed cushions, the kitchen with a normal stove and refrigerator, all located, as it were, on a veranda with the cane fields behind.

Russell collected her suitcase and ushered her inside and into a bedroom. She was pleased to note that the bedrooms, located in the center of the building, actually had walls and curtains to close off the glassless holes that were their windows. There were mats on the floor and, also pleasing, a real bed, covered with a colorful cotton throw.

Dorie observed, "It's kind of like living on the front porch, isn't it? Aren't you afraid somebody is going to steal something?"

Russell shrugged. "What's to steal? Somebody's hungry and wants to steal the food out of the kitchen, he's welcome. There're a couple closets that can be locked, but I don't keep anything much in them except my medical supplies."

Twenty years of expensive education and my son is living in a hippie pad! Dorie managed to keep that thought to herself, but it was so difficult that she was actually grateful when Lani glided in, holding out a parcel.

With a sweet smile, the young woman said, "I brought something for you. It's a pareu. I thought you might want to wear something cool, now that you are at home."

Dorie thanked her, wondering why she had not thought to bring a personal gift for Lani. There was a wedding present in her luggage, of course, but it would have been thoughtful to bring an extra little something. She did want the child to like her.

She opened the package, wondering what a pareu might be. It was a single piece of brightly printed fabric with two ties attached, and Dorie could see that it was the same type of dress that Lani wore.

Lani took it and demonstrated by wrapping it loosely around Dorie's waist. "There are fourteen different ways to tie it. It can be a skirt or a dress or a light wrap. Take off your suit, and I'll show you."

Dorie took off her coat and was glad to do it, but she wasn't about to strip in front of her son.

It was easy to see how the wraparound worked; Lani's was crossed in front of her body with the ties knotted behind her neck, her back bare.

Dorie said, "It's lovely, dear, and I want to try it, but not right now. Russell is going to show me the clinic."

Russell gamely did not look surprised. "If you'd really like to see it, I was about to go over there."

"I'll come too," Lani said, and they walked together across a central courtyard. Russell explained that the rest of the houses in the little group were the homes of people who worked at the hospital. Dorie counted carefully. There was the clinic, Russell's house, and three others. Not exactly a huge operation.

But it was laid out like a real hospital. The building had walls and windows, and it was much hotter inside than it had been in the breezy house.

She was pleased to encounter a nurse in white, behind a real desk, addressing Dorie's son with proper respect.

She was an older woman, stout and wrinkled, with the brown skin and slanted eyes so often seen in the islands. An old-style starched white cap was pinned to her gray curls. The plastic badge over her registered nurse's pin read Clio Hurle, RN.

She was telling Russell, "I told Millard there

wasn't any clinic today, Doctor, but he wanted to wait anyway."

Obviously she was referring to the one person in the waiting room, an old man wearing tattered jeans. Russell produced a tongue depressor from that magic place where doctors keep them, and stuck it into the old man's mouth. "Say ahh, Millard."

The old man did, and Russell peered studiously into his mouth.

Dorie turned to Clio. "Please call me Dorie," she said. "I'm so glad to see a real nurse here!"

Clio bounced up and leaned over her desk to shake hands. "So you're the *makuahine!* It's good to see you here at last! *Kauka* Russell . . . Dr. Russell's been talking about his wonderful mother ever since he got here."

"I think you're a shameless flatterer," said Dorie. "Boys don't go around praising their mothers."

"Yours does. Are you going to be here for Christmas? Sure you are; it's only a week off. We always have a big party."

"Yes, I'll be here Christmas. I have two weeks," replied Dorie, looking around. "It seems very quiet."

Clio smiled. "It is right now. The only patients are a *keiki*—a baby—who was delivered last night and his mother, and they'll go home as soon as doctor discharges them. There wasn't any clinic today because you were coming, that's why no-body's here. Not everybody got the word, though. Millard didn't."

"Is he a regular patient?"

"Real regular. Russell's too soft with them. He knows Millard comes around because this is the only place on the island where anybody pays him any attention, but Russell looks him over every time anyway."

"Is Millard all alone in the world?"

Clio shrugged massive shoulders. "I guess he's a beachcomber, or he would be, if we were a little closer to the beach."

After a while the old man got up out of his chair and ambled away, out the door into the brilliant sunshine. Russell returned to Dorie, smiling. "Come on, I'll show you around."

They stepped into the next room. "This is the treatment room," Russell continued. "Operating table over there . . ."

"You operate in here?" Dorie demanded, incredulous. "In the treatment room? It's not sterile!"

"Well, we don't exactly do organ transplants. Sloan-Kettering this isn't, you know."

"It could have been." Dorie had promised herself not to criticize Russell or anything he was doing, but it just came pouring out of her; she couldn't stop herself.

"You had an offer from Sloan-Kettering—and

272

half a dozen other places. Good places, prestigious places. You graduated in the top tenth of your class. You have a great future. Why are you throwing yourself away in this primitive shack in the middle of nowhere? You don't really plan to stay, do you?"

She had already said more than she had intended, and she bit off the rest of it. Control . . . She had to get herself in control or she would say the name that was trying to push itself into her mouth.

Lani. It was because of Lani. She didn't really have to ask. She knew Russell was in Hawaii because of Lani.

Russell sat on the edge of one of the tables and crossed his arms, regarding her with serious dark eyes. "I'm kind of surprised at you, Mother. You know why I went into medicine. I want to help people, take care of them. That's why you're a nurse, or so I've always thought. I think we share the same feelings about medicine. I don't need to be a high-powered specialist driving a Cadillac around Shaker Heights; what I need is to be making a difference. I chose this place . . . Well, one reason was because it's Lani's home, but it's starting to seem like home to me, too, because I'm needed here."

Dorie sighed, resigned. "Couldn't you make a difference in Shaker Heights?"

"Don't talk that way, Mother. It isn't like you to say something like that."

"Maybe it isn't, but I'm proud of you and I'm proud of what you have accomplished. Proud motherhood does funny things to people."

"Only female people," he observed, a faint smile twitching his grave lips.

"Don't laugh at me, Russell. If I sound materialistic it's just because I want to see you respected and successful. Taking care of people for wages is okay for me, but I want to see you getting the rewards you've worked so hard to earn."

"The kind of rewards I get here . . . Well, they certainly aren't the sort of thing you're thinking about, but they are the rewards I want. Let me tell you about this place, Mother. There're four or five villages in this area, a couple thousand people, and there isn't another doctor in twenty miles. These people work the cane fields, they have for generations, and there just isn't any proper medical care. What the women got was lower than the bottom of the barrel. I'm running the only obstetrical clinic between here and Kona. Nobody here ever heard of AIDS or yearly Pap smears or mammograms. The older women, once they're past childbearing age, never see a doctor. They have to be educated; the facilities have to be made available to them."

"So you're going to save them all? All by yourself? Just you and Clio?"

He lifted his head, suddenly alert. "Sirens!"

Dorie heard it too, the familiar howl of an ambulance. In the city, one paid no attention, but Russell was the only doctor in twenty miles, so of course they were coming to his clinic.

Russell went to the door and Dorie followed. There were two ambulances boiling up the road. Fortunately there was no traffic, for they traveled abreast, avoiding one another's dust. The rain had scarcely been over an hour, but already plumes of dust followed the two vehicles.

They pulled up in front of the clinic and a paramedic jumped out to talk to Russell. "Car accident on Saddle Road," he reported. "Three hurt."

"Bring the reports in with them, please," Russell said, calm and take-charge, just like always.

Dorie reached into her handbag and took out her name badge. She pinned it on her blouse next to the RN pin she always wore. Then she tucked the handbag behind Clio's desk and she was ready for work.

The gurneys were wheeled inside. One of them left a trail of blood; the patient, cut around the head and neck, was bleeding despite bandages. Dorie and Clio followed Russell to that gurney.

The paramedic asked, "You want him on the table?"

"In a minute." Russell examined the man

briefly, then stepped to the next gurney. "Leg broken," the paramedic reported.

Russell took the patient's blood pressure and spoke reassuringly to the frightened young man on the gurney. He had been the driver, and his accelerator leg was broken in several places.

When they reached the third gurney, Lani was bending over the patient. Her hair had been twisted into a fat braid that dangled down her back. To Dorie's astonishment, she wore a cap like Clio's and an RN badge was pinned to her pareu.

She said in an entirely audible voice. "Head injury. The vital signs are good."

This young man was unconscious, but un-marked. Long dark lashes rested on his brown cheeks.

"Keep him under observation," Russell ordered Lani. "Mom, you come with me."

The victim with the lacerations was hoisted onto the table, and for the next hour Dorie watched her son with deep maternal satisfaction as he stitched the young man back together. The intensity of Russell's concentration, his profes-sionalism, thrilled her. She was proud to work at his side, proud of her own professionalism as she assisted him.

The first patient finished, the team scrubbed and began the long process of setting the broken bones of the second victim. Dorie and Clio assisted; Lani cared for the other patients.

The man with lacerations was coming out of the anesthetic, protesting loudly as he did so, but Russell paid absolutely no attention to his noise, and worked away single-mindedly.

Wondering if self-effacing Lani could handle a combative patient made Dorie nervous, but neither Russell nor Clio seemed worried so she concentrated on her own job and prayed that everything would be okay. After a while the man quieted.

When the leg was finished Russell pulled off his mask and gloves and grinned with satisfaction. They had done a good job. Dorie knew it and barely restrained herself from giving him a high-five for his work. She was proud of her child but afraid that admitting it might not be consistent with the "doctor's" dignity.

She was therefore surprised when he leaned over and kissed her, saying, "Thanks, Mom. That went a lot smoother with the extra help."

Then he turned to the head injury. "How's this one doing?"

"He is still unconscious, but he is stable," Lani reported.

"Just keep observing him. We'll see what happens in the next couple hours."

He spoke to Lacerations, who was quiet now, if not entirely calm, and then he asked Lani,

"What about our other patient? Is Ailiana Smith still here?"

Lani reported, "Her family has come for her, but I told them she was not to leave until you discharge her."

"Okay, I'll go do that right now."

Clio gave Dorie a nudge. "Let's get these guys into the ward." They each took an end of one of the gurneys and steered it into the hall.

As they passed the waiting room, Dorie was astonished by the size of the Smith family. At least a dozen people waited there, all bearing garlands of flowers. One of them also carried two huge pineapples, the spiky leaves poking over his shoulders as he cradled the heavy fruits in his arms.

Behind Clio's desk, a hallway led to the wards. They took their gurney to the right, into the men's ward. On the other side of the hall, Lani was putting Mrs. Smith into a wheelchair and handing her the baby that had come into the world the night before.

When all the patients were in the ward, Dorie returned to the waiting room. She found the crowd even larger. They were greeting one another noisily, and somebody was plunking a uku-lele.

Dorie asked, "Are you all here to take Mrs. Smith home?"

A towering young man, his face as handsome

as a bronze statue's, smiled sunnily and waved vaguely at the group with the pineapples. "Not us; we came to cheer up our cousin Tony. Okay if we go in now?" Before she could say anything he moved past her, into the hallway, as did several young women bearing flowers.

That set off the whole crowd. They followed and in seconds the hallway was filled with visitors, all chattering at once. Mrs. Smith, enthroned in her wheelchair, basked in the admiration of her relatives. The man with the pineapples led his group into the men's ward.

Dorie had not thought of her new patients as people yet. To her they were the Leg, the Head Injury and the Lacerations, but they were people, and people with crowds of friends and relatives.

Tony was apparently the Leg. Now wearing a big white cast and still groggy from the anesthetic, he was blinking and rolling his head on the pillow. His friends covered his bed with flowers and sat around it, chattering. Dorie hoped he would not get the impression, when he fully opened his eyes, that he was at his own wake.

A lovely child in a sundress dropped a lei over Dorie's shoulders and murmured something that was lost in the noise. Lani was serenely pushing Mrs. Smith, in the wheelchair, toward the exit. There were leis draped over her, too, and she smiled and made little jokes with the people around her. The transformation of Lani, from a shy pretty child to a self-confident nurse, seemed to have occurred in a blink, from nothing more than the donning of her starched cap.

Dorie was remembering her own enthusiastic greeting when she had called Clio "a real nurse." Where had Lani been when she had said that? Dorie tried to remember. Could Lani have heard it? What a tactless thing to say, and how could she fix it? Would Lani ever believe that Dorie had not known she also was a nurse? How could it be that Russell had never seen fit to mention it? Dorie could not deny, even to herself, that she had judged Lani, on looks alone, to be an airhead schoolgirl.

Dorie said, "Lani?" and Lani turned to her with a smile. And another youngster came with a lei, to be added to the half-dozen already around the shoulders of Mrs. Smith. It was neither the time nor the place for explanations and apologies.

So Dorie complained. "They're turning this into a party. We can't have all these people in here."

"It's all right," said Lani. "Don't worry. They would be lonely if their cousins didn't come." She meant the patients, Dorie supposed.

She took a look into the waiting room. The crowd there had about doubled, overwhelming the chairs. The visitors didn't mind. Most of them were sitting on the floor, around a large platter full of fruit and big, pink shrimp. There were several ukuleles thrumming at once, a sort of a rhythmic background to the happy chatter.

Joyous cries greeted Mrs. Smith, and everybody rushed to admire her new baby. Dorie turned her back on all of it and went into the hallway. The noise level there was scarcely lower. She would check on Lacerations first.

He was propped up in his bed, his stitched-up head a mass of bandages. What could be seen of his young face was pale, and he was singing. His friends, clustered around the bed, sang too, accompanying themselves with a rhythmic clapping and snapping of fingers.

"Now, we can't have this," Dorie scolded. "He should be resting."

"It's all right," said the patient. "These are my family."

Dorie adjusted the pillows. "Well, they can come back tomorrow and see you. Come on, guys, out of here. Let him get some rest now."

"Oh, can't you let them stay and sing to me?" begged the patient. "Otherwise I'm going to be here all alone."

He was just a kid. Maybe he had never seen the inside of a hospital before, and the experience he had just survived must have been terrifying. Dorie said, "All right, they may sing, but you must lie down and rest. And if they don't sing softly and melodically, I'm going to throw the whole bunch of them out."

"Soft song, men," one of the brown giants ordered his chorus.

"Thanks, cousin!" the patient yelled to her retreating back. She was beginning to get the picture. Around here, everybody was a cousin, except for one's very best friends, who were family.

It was so noisy in the hall that she looked out there and found that dance lines had formed up. Ukuleles were playing backup for a guitar, and the rhythm section carried little clay jugs to beat on. Other musicians had sticks they clacked together and one inventive fellow had turned a waiting-room chair upside down and was beating on the chrome base. It made a tinging sound he seemed to find irresistible.

To this music the little girls were dancing, shaking their slender hips and laughing, long fluffy hair streaming down their backs.

"Now just a minute!" Dorie roared. "This is a hospital! This has to stop at once!"

The strings fell silent and the little girls froze, their hands still gesturing feebly. From somewhere a man rose up, towering over the dancers. He wore nothing but the ubiquitous pareu, a short one, wrapped around his waist, and a necklace of shells that hung down his bare chest. He had been, once, one of the gorgeous bronze young giants she saw all around her, and he still was imposing. His chest was as wide and brown as theirs but he stood somehow straighter, holding aloft his straight nose and a head of magnificent silver hair.

He ordered, "Children, dance."

"Not on my shift, they don't!" Dorie said. "You get your little charges out of here. They can dance someplace else."

"Children, dance," he repeated, and the pot-drums took up their beat again while the little girls straggled back into line and began the dance, watching Dorie apprehensively as they did so, their eyes as big and dark as plums.

"You don't give the orders around here," Dorie told the big man. "Who do you think you are?"

He touched that broad, bare, chest. "Kane." He pronounced it *Kaa-nay*, and she knew she had heard the word before, somewhere, probably on Waikiki, but she couldn't remember.

He repeated helpfully, "Kane. *Kane Ali'i.* Chief."

"Well, Chief, you're in a hospital and . . ."

He ploughed through the dancers toward her and pointed again to his chest. "Kane." He pointed at her.

She made no response to his questioning look, so he bent and took a look at her badge. "Dorie."

So, he could read a little. Dorie tried to say something, anything, but she couldn't seem to. The only thing she seemed able to do was stare at Kane. She didn't see the girls, shaking their way from one end of the hall to the other; she didn't hear the drums. Not with Kane standing so close to her. He had an attraction that was a feral mixture of danger and beauty, ambiguous, powerful, and so mesmerizing that she was uncharacteristically silent.

He said, "Dorie, dance."

That snapped her out of it. Hands on her hips, she demanded, "Who do you think you're giving orders to? I'm in charge here and I'm going to . . ."

What was she going to do? Dorie looked out over the hallway over which she had volunteered to take charge, and quailed. A bunch of young men had joined the dance, waggling their trim butts to the beat of drums.

One of them was a handsome boy with long eyelashes.

Dorie gasped, "Omigod! The Head Injury's dancing!"

Sure enough, it was him, leaping, wagging, shaking with the rest of them.

She hurried to his side and took his arm to get his attention. "You shouldn't be doing this! You must go back to bed at once!"

"Don't worry." He grinned at her. "You the nurse? It's okay. Everything's cool."

"You've had a serious blow to your head. You're under observation. You . . ."

"Don't worry," he repeated. "You know *kanaka*? I'm *kanaka*." He tapped his temple. "Coconut head."

It was then that she saw Russell. The doctor had a wreath on his head and was dancing along with the guys and girls. His stethoscope flapped on his chest; his white coat was stained with blood.

Dorie touched him weakly, and waved to indicate the Head Injury, who was back to his hula.

Russell was laughing. "That's all right, Ma. Let him dance."

He turned serious suddenly and put an arm around her. "I can see this bothers you. It bothered me at first, too, but this is what they always do. They figure anybody in the hospital needs cheering up, so they have a party. There's no way to stop them; so I might as well join in. Why don't you go on back to the house, if you want? You've had a long day; you must be tired."

"Making this many adjustments does wear a person out," Dorie conceded. "I think I will go and unpack."

She made her way through the crowded hallway and the equally crowded waiting room. Mrs. Smith still sat there, surrounded by admiring relatives, including, Dorie was startled to note, Kane.

He stood behind the wheelchair, and when he

saw Dorie he struck his chest proudly with his fist and announced, "My baby!"

So he was Mr. Smith! Dorie flounced to the door and hastened outside, into the blazing sunshine. The father of the new baby! What was an old man doing with a dewy young wife like Mrs. Smith?

The first thing she discovered when she got to the house was the blood—spots of it—on the skirt to her best suit. She had forgotten that she was not wearing her white uniform and had leaned over the bleeding patient on the table. Probably the blouse was done for, too. She put it in the bathroom basin to soak and tried sponging the skirt with cold water. The spots came out, but it was hard to say how the fabric would dry. Probably with puckers.

Dorie unpacked her suitcase and went into the kitchen. There were some vegetables in the refrigerator, and she put them together for soup. It was bubbling and beginning to smell good when Russell came home.

He sniffed and grinned. "Hey, vegetable soup! Remember when you always used to make a real big pot of it on Sunday so we'd have something to eat when neither of us had time to cook?"

"This one's mostly onions and potatoes," Dorie apologized. "That's about all I could find around here."

"There's a woman who's supposed to come in

and cook. Guess she forgot to come today. Come to think of it, she's supposed to cook for the patients, too. Good thing their friends brought all that food."

"I think somebody ought to get your home organized."

He laughed fondly. "That's my mom, always organizing something. Don't sweat it; you'll never get anything organized around here. It just isn't something that happens in Hawaii."

"Do you like that?"

He sat down opposite her, looking serious, and so handsome. "No, not really. Some things ought to be organized. The hospital, especially. How can I care for these people and do it right? They would rather play than work. The Hawaiians look down on the Orientals because they have such a strong work ethic. The Orientals look down on the Hawaiians because they don't, and the whites look down on everybody."

"Really? How can you tell? To me they all look like . . ." Dorie shrugged helplessly "They look like Hawaiians."

"There aren't many full-blooded Hawaiians left, but I'll go along with you, it's hard to tell who's what. Most of the people you see are *hapahaole*, that is, mixed blood."

"So the way you tell a Japanese, for instance, is by his work ethic? I'm glad you straightened that out for me."

Russell laughed. "It's a tangle, all right."

Dorie looked at her watch, which didn't do her much good, for it only told her what time it was back home in Cleveland. "I think I ought to go back to the clinic. God knows what's happening to our poor patients."

"Don't worry." Russell sounded just like a Hawaiian. "It's quieter now. Kane took most of the mob with him when he left, and the orderlies got rid of the rest of them. They started passing out mops so folks could help with the cleaning, and the visitors sort of melted away."

"You've got orderlies? Where were they when Clio and I were wheeling the gurneys around?"

"There's only one who works days, and I gave him today off because there wasn't any clinic. The other two work the night shift because they have day jobs."

"Nothing wrong with their work ethic. Why didn't you tell me Lani is a registered nurse? She must be older than she looks."

Russell looked surprised. "I thought you knew she's an RN. She's a good nurse. She's twenty-four. She probably looks younger to you because you're not used to the way she dresses."

"She does look more ready for the beach than for duty."

"Nobody expected to work today, and this place is sort of one big beach."

"Russell, we have to talk about important

things, like your wedding. When is it going to be? What am I supposed to wear?"

Russell put down his soup spoon and looked serious. "Well, you see, we set it for Christmas day. There's always a big party here on Christmas, and we just thought we'd sort of take advantage of it."

"What? Christmas day?"

"The judge is going to come down to the courthouse special for us. He's sort of a friend of a friend. We didn't want a big wedding or a big fuss."

"No fuss? But fuss is what a wedding is all about."

He chuckled. "Well, maybe it's a little different for Lani and me. We've been together a while, and her family won't be here."

"No family? Doesn't Lani's family live in Hawaii?"

"In Honolulu. You see, they're pretty old-fashioned—straight-laced—and they don't approve of me at all. They've refused to come. That's why it's so important to Lani to have you here. You'll be the only family at the wedding, so we're keeping the whole thing low-key."

Dorie thought about that. No mother to cry as Lani took her vows, no father to walk her down the aisle. Perhaps the children were wise to choose the city-hall wedding.

She said, "Oh, poor Lani! That's so judgmental! Maybe her folks'll loosen up after you've been married a while."

"I hope so. I could do without them forever, after the way they've treated her, but of course Lani would like to get back together with them."

"I guess I can ask her what to wear. No point in talking to you about clothes."

"We could all wear hula skirts for all I care. I just want to make sure I don't lose Lani. She's a fine person, Mom. Her name means 'heavenly.' Isn't she heavenly?"

Dorie said, "Yes, son, of course she is."

They made a supper of the soup and afterward walked over to the clinic to see how Lani was doing. The orderlies were still cleaning up in the treatment room, but the ward was quiet. The Leg and the Lacerations were sleeping quietly in their beds, but Lani reported that Arnie the Head Injury was restless and complaining of a headache.

Russell checked him over and scolded him softly. "You were supposed to stay in bed. You want that head to get better, keep it on the pillow. If you had done that in the first place, like my mother told you to, you wouldn't have this headache."

Arnie opened plum-black eyes. "She's your mama? I didn't know that. If I'd known she was the *makuahine*, I would have done what she said."

"We're going to give you something for the pain, and you try to get a night's sleep."

"Then can I go home tomorrow?"

"I may want you to stay here, under observation, for a couple days. We'll see how you are tomorrow."

Arnie's face crumpled, like a chubby child's. "I'm so lonesome here."

"I'll sit with you," offered Dorie. "Then Lani can go home to dinner."

Lani had the key to the medicine cabinet, and the two women went there together to get the pills Russell had ordered for Arnie.

Lani counted out the capsules into the little paper cup, dark eyelashes covering her eyes as she worked.

"You must be pooped and hungry," Dorie told her.

"Oh, I'm all right. One of the cousins gave me a big dish of pineapple."

"Well, there's some hot soup on the stove at home. You go get some. I'll take care of things here."

"Yes, I will do that. It's so good of you to help us out!"

"I'm a nurse," Dorie explained. "Go home and spend some time with Russell. Come back in the morning."

"Oh, I couldn't do that! Leave you here all night? No, it's too much for you."

"Split the difference," Dorie offered. "Come back at midnight."

"Oh, that would be wonderful! I'd have the whole evening to spend with Russell. But . . ."— her pretty face took on a concerned look—"you want to spend time with him, too. You came all this way—"

"I'll get my chance. You need a break, now go take it. How do you folks handle this when I'm not around?"

"You mean, caring for patients who are hospitalized? It hardly ever happens, you see. When somebody's sick enough to need hospital care, we transport him down to Kona. It's only like this because of the accident. When we have a patient with a new baby, she stays overnight. Clio takes care of her in the day, and I'm on duty at night. Clio only works days, because she has a family."

"We need a schedule. I'll come in the morning and do a shift—"

Lani interrupted. "Let's split the day shift, too. I'll relieve you at lunchtime and then you'll have four to midnight."

"Okay," Dorie agreed. "It's a killer for both of us, but it won't last long."

Arnie got his medication, but it didn't make him sleep. He was frightened, Dorie realized, by his injury, which was not so minor as he had supposed, and by being in a strange place at night.

She sat beside him, and he talked softly so not to disturb his fellow patients. He told her about his family and his job as a mechanic for agricultural machinery. A gentle boy, this Arnie, who loved his family, loved to laugh, loved to dance. And so young. All three of the patients were teenagers, a trio of buddies who had been out for a ride when Tony had somehow wrapped the car around a tree.

Arnie finally went to sleep holding her hand. Lani came at midnight to take her shift, and Dorie went home to bed.

In the morning Russell discharged Tony, and then he and Clio opened up the outpatient clinic. There was a line of people waiting outside.

The orderly carried in breakfasts, and Dorie tried to find something Lacerations would accept. His name was Kamuela. It took her a while to learn how to pronounce it, but she had plenty of time while she coaxed him to eat. Every motion hurt him, even moving his jaws to chew. She finally got him to drink a pineapple milkshake through a straw. The other patients ate heartily; the cook was back in the kitchen, and her output was generous and appreciated.

Tony's whole family came to pick him up. They brought fresh flowers for Arnie and for Kamuela, and of course, they were not content with quietly carrying Tony away; first they held a small musicale in the ward. The young women sat on the floor and waved their arms gracefully to music from a radio they had brought with them. It was a big black ghetto-blaster, but on this island it played sweet Hawaiian steel guitars.

The activities were cheering up Kamuela, who needed it, so Dorie was happy to let them sway away. She was searching for the orderly, to get him to carry out the breakfast dishes, when Kane arrived.

He was dressed as he had been the day before, only a skimpy bit of cloth around his waist, but he had added a sort of cape that hung over one shoulder by a cord. With a wide smile he exclaimed, "Dorie!"

She said, "Good morning, Kane. And how are Mrs. Smith and the baby?"

"Good."

"Is there something we can do for you?"

"No."

"You're a great little conversationalist, aren't you?"

He did not reply, but stalked toward the ward.

Dorie asked, "Are you visiting one of the accident victims?"

"My cousins," he explained. "All my cousins."

Probably they literally were. If he really was the chief, he would be related to every Hawaiian on the island. Or maybe he just saw them as constituents. Dorie went off to continue her search for the orderly.

She found him in the waiting room, flirting with a girl. She sent him after the dirty dishes and then got out the wheelchair for Tony. Tony's friends all helped arrange him in the chair before they wheeled him to the door, calling *"Aloha!"* and throwing flowers around.

Somebody had backed a pickup truck against the door and the cousins lifted Tony into the truckbed and drove away, shouting and laughing as dust boiled up behind the truck and the three autos that accompanied it. The dust even settled over the laughing teenagers in the truckbed, but they didn't seem to mind.

She found Kamuela weeping. He wanted to go home, as Tony had, and he didn't feel very well. She plumped his pillows and straightened the sheets, and the next thing she knew, Kane appeared, stalking around in his Big-Important-Chief cape. All poor Kamuela needs, Dorie thought, a macho bully who'll tell him to stop whining.

She tried to head Kane off by standing in front of him. "Have you talked to Arnie yet?" she asked hopefully.

He brushed her aside and went to Kamuela's bed, saying something in Hawaiian. Kamuela replied in the same language, and then Kane sat down beside him and took the boy's hand. The two of them sat that way for a time, murmuring in their own language. When she dared take a peek at them, tears were rolling down the cheeks of both.

When you thought about it, why shouldn't the kid cry? He was sixteen years old, he hurt, and even though the doctor had sewn him up with great skill, he would have scars forever. He would never again be exactly the same handsome, heedless child he had been only the previous morning when he got into Tony's car.

And Kane, the psychologist in a loincloth, from some primitive wellspring he understood, he knew that the boy needed to grieve. Those two were so close to nature, they could sit together and openly cry.

She checked Arnie's chart. His signs were all stable. Maybe the kid was right, and his head was indestructible as a coconut. He still had a headache and was being very good about keeping his head down, so having breakfast, he had made something of a mess. Time to clean up the patient and change the sheets. Dorie collected the basin and towels and drew the curtain around the bed.

Arnie clutched at his sheet. "Hey, you're not going to wash me, are you?"

"Just until you're able to sit up. After that you'll wash yourself," Dorie promised, soaping up her washcloth.

"Geez, do you have to do that?"

"Think of me as *makuahine*," Dorie advised. "This is how she washed you when you were a *keiki*."

Arnie grinned in spite of himself. "Hey, you're already talking Hawaiian!"

The curtain was swept aside and Kane stalked in. "You wash him good!" he ordered.

Dorie hastily put down the washcloth and tried again to block Kane, and to get him outside the curtain. But he stood there like a rock cliff, his burning eyes on poor Arnie, who clutched again at the sheet.

"You sick?"

"Aw, come on, *Makua Kane*," protested Arnie. "I hurt my head, and the doctor says I have to stay lying down."

"*Kauka* Russell good. You lie down."

"And you get out," Dorie insisted. "Give the man some privacy!"

"Take good care my cousin Arnie." It was an order.

Dorie pulled the curtain closed. There was a large indentation where Kane still stood, but at least he was outside.

When she had finished the bath and changed the sheets, she pulled back the curtain, and he was still standing there. Glaring black eyes followed her every move as she straightened up and tucked Arnie in, fresh and clean.

Dorie ignored Kane and went on to bathe her other patient. She pulled the curtain carefully closed before she began. Kamuela was not exactly cheerful, but he was more relaxed than he had been before. She talked to him as she scrubbed his arms. She couldn't wash his face at all, for the bandages.

"Where do you go to school?"

"Oh, I'm out of school. Work in the fields. I drive the tractor, sometimes."

"Is that what you like, driving the tractor?"

"Oh, that feels so good," he said as she scrubbed at old bloodstains. There had not been an opportunity to bathe him the day before and the stains were everywhere. She was washing away when, to her astonishment, he grabbed her soapy hand and kissed it.

"Don't do that!" exclaimed Dorie, and instantly the curtain was flung aside. Kane again.

Dark eyes ablaze, he gave Kamuela a slap on the nearest spot, which happened to be the soles of his feet. The kid was startled and jumped, which was obviously painful to him, and he fell back onto the pillow, pressing his hand to his neck.

"Mr. Kane, what are you doing?" Dorie roared. "How dare you hit one of my patients? You get out of here immediately! Not just out of the curtain this time, you get clear out of the ward! And don't come back until you can behave yourself!"

Her fury was intimidating, and Kane backed out of the ward. She saw him to the door before she returned to finish Kamuela's bath.

Kamuela apologized. Dorie forgave him.

The patients clean and comfortable, she then went out to the desk to update the charts. Kane left his post at the ward door to follow her and lean over her shoulder.

Although she knew he could read, she thought it unlikely he would understand the medical shorthand used on charts; still, he made her nervous. She fumbled. Suddenly the notations on the chart made no sense to her, either.

He absolutely radiated. You have to be aware of anybody who stands behind your chair, but the air positively hummed around this man. She was aware of his breathing, the heat of his body, of a scent like that of crushed forest leaves. No, it wasn't quite that; it was the smell of a healthy animal. Or maybe sunshine and fresh rain.

Then a large arm came over her shoulder and Kane put his forefinger on the entry she had just made on the chart. "Em el," he said.

More mysterious Hawaiian? She made a brushing motion with her hand. "Go away, Kane. You're bothering me."

"Em el," he repeated. "Not em em. Milliliter, not millimeter."

Dorie leaped to her feet. "Milliliter!" The damn man had the vocabulary of an engineer. "Milliliter! You great big phony rat! Get out of my hospital and don't come back! Out!"

"Dorie mad?"

"Never mind the Tarzan talk, I'm on to you now! Out! Get out!"

He nodded politely. "Tomorrow."

"No, don't come back tomorrow. The patients can get along without your help!"

He turned and walked to the front door, and out. He was no sooner gone than she wondered if she had spoken too hastily. What if Kamuela became depressed again?

She shrugged off her own doubts. The kid was getting better; he'd be all right.

As there had been no clinic the previous day, the crowd of patients was large, and Russell worked right through lunch. Lani brought him a sandwich when she came over to relieve Dorie.

Dorie went back to the house and took a nap. She was weary; it had been many years since she had worked twelve-hour days.

Russell came home in time for an early dinner. The cook had made an Oriental chicken with pineapple and both mother and son ate heartily.

"We really appreciate the way you're pitching in to help out," Russell told her. "But this is supposed to be your vacation. You shouldn't be working all the time. You should go sightseeing, do something that's fun. Lani can handle things. I should be able to send the boys home tomorrow."

"Really? And the wards will be empty?"

Russell squirmed a little in his seat. "Well,

probably not. I just admitted a woman who is in labor, and it's not going very well. She'll take a long time."

"Russell, like you said, we both went into medicine because we want to take care of people. I'd rather be doing that than taking in the sights. How could I go off and have a good time when I knew you and Lani need me?"

"Well, right . . ."

"There is one thing you could do for me. Is there some way to keep that pest Kane out of the hospital?"

"Has he been bothering you? Don't pay any attention to Kane. He's a great tease."

"He acts like he owns the place," Dorie complained.

"He does," said Russell.

"What?"

"We built the clinic on land he donated for the purpose. He owns most of the land around here."

Dorie was astonished. "All that sugar cane?"

"The growers hold the leases, so they're the major employers, but the land belongs to Kane. Some sort of hereditary rights, or something."

"And all the cousins? Does he own them, too?"

Russell's chair scraped back. "I've got to get over to the clinic and see how my OB patient is doing."

"Likes to tease, huh? Em el, huh?" Dorie mut-

301

tered, but Russell was already bounding down the path toward the clinic.

He was scarcely out of sight when Lani came up to the house and it was time for Dorie's shift.

Dorie spent most of it watching television with the OB patient, whose name was Pelika. Dorie was getting curious about the backgrounds of the people she met, so she asked Pelika about hers. Pelika was Hawaiian and German, and her name was the local way to say Freida.

Arnie and Kamuela were so much better they were allowed to get out of bed and walk around, but neither of them came anywhere near the women's ward. The father would not, either. He lurked in the waiting room and smoked cigarettes, refusing all suggestions that he sit with his wife. She was very uncomfortable, and very testy. Understandably, Dorie thought.

When she returned in the morning for her next shift the cousins came for Arnie and Kamuela, and as usual brought their radios and flowers. However, Pelika was getting closer to delivery, and had taken to greeting each contraction with an angry shriek. A couple of those and the spirits of the cousins were severely dampened. They departed with the two boys as quickly as they could arrange it.

Then the hospital was quiet, in between contractions.

Dorie said soothingly, "Everything is going

along just fine, Pelika. It won't be much longer now."

"That's what you've been saying all night!" Pelika complained, not exactly accurately, for it was Lani who had been with her for the midnight-to-morning shift. Dorie was beginning to feel very sorry for her.

Then a deep voice said, *"Aloha, Pelika,"* and in came Kane. He was dressed this morning in a perfectly ordinary shirt and jeans. He even had on shoes.

Pelika scowled at him and turned her head away impatiently. He said something in Hawaiian, and she replied in angry English, "Oh, shut up, Kane. Good wishes from the old *makua* won't do me any good now."

"Your family is worried about you," Kane explained. "They wanted me to see how you are."

"They should be worried!" she shouted. "This is hell! You can tell that no-good husband of mine if he ever comes near me again I'm going to break his head! Damn him for doing this to me! Damn all men! Including you, *Makua* Kane! Get out of here and leave me alone!"

Kane gave Dorie a sheepish grin. "Feisty little thing, isn't she?"

"She's having a hard time," said Dorie, "and she doesn't need some man who will never know what it's like to come in here and tell her she's got nothing to fret about. Why don't you go out

303

and buck up the father? You can even do it in English, you speak it so well now!"

He lifted the gray eyebrows that sat over those slightly slanted dark eyes. "I never said I couldn't speak English."

"Neither did Tarzan. Out!"

Kane left, and Pelika actually laughed to see him go. She said, "Dorie, I like the way you tell 'em off. Really, is it true what you said? Is this going to be over soon?"

"You're close," Dorie assured her.

"Oh, God, you're not putting on a rubber glove again, are you?"

"Just one more time, and if you're as dilated as I think you are, I'll get the doctor in here."

"Hallelujah!" said the patient, and she didn't even howl as she was examined.

Dorie sent for Russell, who dismissed the rest of his clinic patients and delivered the baby. It was a beautiful big boy, and Dorie massaged the mother's stomach while Russell carried the child to the waiting room to be admired by the assembled relatives.

Dorie was heartily annoyed when Kane returned instead of Russell, carrying the tiny, blanket-wrapped bundle that was the baby. Dorie demanded, "What are you doing? Give me that," and took the baby from him.

"His father fainted," Kane explained. "Kauka Russell is taking care of him."

"Give me my baby," said Pelika, and Dorie put her son into her arms.

To Pelika and to Dorie that red, squashed face, still blotched with waxy vernix, was a miracle, and neither had so much as a thought to spare for the man who found it so shocking it made him faint. Pelika asked, "Isn't he beautiful, *Makua Kane*?"

"A fine baby," Kane assured her. "*Pu'ali* for sure."

"*Pu'ali*?" Dorie asked. "What's that?"

"Warrior."

"The world's got enough of those. You want to lay a blessing on him, see him as a future computer programmer. Why do they all call you *makua*? Are you everybody's uncle?"

"Sort of like Uncle Sam," he explained. "*Makua kane* means uncle. *Makua* Kane is me, because *kane* has many meanings; man, people . . ."

"How about macho?" suggested Dorie.

"But this child, Pelika, is truly my niece . . . well, she is the niece of my cousin's wife. We are very closely related."

"Like all the rest of the island. Okay, I'm going to clean up now. You can go. Why don't you find out how the father's doing? I'm sure Pelika is worried about him."

"Sure I am," scoffed Pelika. "He's out there giving the doctor trouble, just like him. Always giving somebody a problem."

When baby and mother were cleaned up and nestled in their beds, Dorie went to check on the father. He was sitting in a chair, smoking a cigarette, and chatting with Russell. Of course the waiting room was crammed with relatives, all demanding to visit Pelika.

The poor woman was exhausted, but she probably would have felt neglected if a mob had not gathered around her bed and loaded it with flowers. Kane, who had already offered his congratulations, remained in the waiting room.

He asked Dorie, "Do you get off at noon?"

"Yes," she answered, too surprised to add anything.

"*Kauka* Russell said you wanted to go sightseeing."

"Sightseeing!" Dorie snorted. "That's an idea he's got in his head that's turning into a fixation. All I want to do right now is take off my shoes and go to bed."

He grinned like the sunny boy he must have been. "I could help you with that."

Dorie folded her arms. "Mr. Kane, I want you to know that I do not appreciate your sense of humor. A hospital is no place for practical jokes and silly masquerades. We are not going sightseeing, we are not going to bed, especially we are not going to bed, and my shift is over and I'm going home."

And she did.

He didn't complain, just stood there and watched her walk to the house and go inside. Dorie was surprised; she had somehow thought he would follow her.

She took off her duty shoes and hung her white uniform in the closet and was surprised to realize that she had wanted him to follow her. Follow and insist.

"Now there's a fine attitude for a grown woman to have," she growled to herself, slipping on the pareu that Lani had given her.

She went out to the dining area and found the cook had her lunch on the table. The smooth mats felt good under her bare feet; a sweet breeze from over the cane cooled the house.

As she sat at the table she could look out over the endless fields, nothing beyond them but a glowing sky. It was beautiful.

She felt disappointed because she wanted to see more of the country, she told herself. It wasn't because she missed the apprehension of never knowing when Kane might appear, or what he was going to say when he did. Who would miss a thing like that?

And it didn't have anything to do with the way he looked. The muscles of his chest under smooth brown skin, those mysteriously slanted eyes, the straight nose with just a slight flare at the end, and that hair, shining silver . . . Dorie wasn't going to think about things like that. It

307

was just that it was a shame to be on this gorgeous island and never see any of it.

At eight the next morning she relieved Lani, who said as she headed out the door, "I'll be back to relieve you at eleven, so you can get away for lunch."

Dorie inquired, "Huh?"

"Pelika will probably be discharged this morning but just in case she isn't, I'll come back early."

"Why?"

"So you can go to lunch with Kane. Don't you remember? He's going to show you the botanical gardens at Turtle Bay."

"Well, I might have remembered, if anybody had told me anything about it."

Lani giggled. "Oh, Dorie! Wear the pareu. It looks so nice on you, and it's going to be a hot day."

"Do they have any other kind around here?"

Again that sweet giggle. "Of course! Sometimes they're hot and rainy."

Russell discharged Pelika and her baby quite early, and then he went to his clinic patients. After Dorie had changed the bed and straightened up in the ward, there wasn't much left for her to do, so she went back to the house. She took a nice, long shower, but when she got out, the air still felt hot and sticky to her, and she couldn't bear the thought of putting on any of her stiff, heavy clothes. She got the pareu and draped it around herself, tying it in front so the strings hung down between her breasts, her shoulders bare. No wonder the Hawaiians loved this cool, comfortable garment.

She was sitting in the living room when Kane drove up in a jeep that was topless and upholstered in leopard print. He honked. He was looking right at her as he did it, so she waved in a friendly manner.

He honked again. Dorie picked up a magazine and pretended to leaf through it.

After a while Kane got out of the jeep. He wore a soft cotton shirt, open at the neck and of a misty green color, and brown trousers. Sports shoes. He said, "Come on, Dorie, aren't you ready?"

At last. The upper hand with Kane. Dorie asked innocently, "Ready for what?"

"We're going to Turtle Bay, to see the gardens there," he answered impatiently.

"Are we? Funny, I don't remember you mentioning it to me."

"*Kauka* Russell said he would tell you."

"Did he? Maybe he forgot." Dorie got up lazily. She even stretched a little. "I prefer to be asked, rather than told."

"Oh, come on, Dorie. You haven't seen anything of the island. I just want to show you a very pretty garden."

Dorie looked up at him appraisingly. "Does this mean the end of your silly games?"

He grinned, those slightly slanted eyes almost shut. "Oh, no, not at all. I have lots more."

"I know I've said this before, but I don't care for games."

He managed to look a little contrite. "Well, maybe I did carry that one too far. It's such a pleasure for me to be here, in my home, kick off my shoes and watch the children dance just because they love dancing . . . I guess I got to acting up."

Dorie smiled. "Well, if the doctor ordered it, and we're both going to be civilized, I suppose I could go and see the gardens."

He ushered her to the car and held the door for her. "It's only a small garden. Just one waterfall. I thought it would be a good place to see today because it isn't big and it isn't far. What time do you have to be back?"

"Four o'clock." She climbed into the seat.

"There aren't any patients in the hospital now. Maybe you could stay longer."

"Around here, I wouldn't take the chance. There seems to be something happening every minute that lands somebody in the hospital."

He got behind the wheel and started the engine. "Okay, four o'clock it is."

As they drove down the dirt road, he took on the tones of a tour guide. "On your right you

310

will see fields of sugar cane, and on your left . . . more sugar cane."

He was clowning and Dorie laughed. "There sure is plenty of it."

"It takes two years for cane to mature. To have a harvest every year, you have to plant twice as much land as you would need for most crops."

"It's a long time to wait. I guess that's why it seems so quiet. Nobody there; there aren't even any birds. Come to think of it, I haven't seen a bird since I got here."

"There used to be lots of them. When I was a boy . . . But now we have the mongoose."

"That little thing like a weasel?"

"You see, in the cane fields there is a big problem with rats. The growth gets very thick, just being there for two years, and it makes a perfect place for rats to hide. Many things have been tried to get rid of them, and one idea was to import mongooses to kill the rats."

"Did they?"

"I guess sometimes, but rats come out at night, and the mongoose hunts in the day. You'd almost think they had a union. In India, where they come from, mongooses eat snakes, but we don't have any snakes, so they eat birds and bird eggs. They've practically wiped out the birds in Hawaii."

"That's tragic!"

"We're trying to get a new custom going, that every tourist, when he leaves, will take a mongoose with him, but neither the tourists nor the mongooses have been very cooperative."

Dorie frowned. "I know you see a lot of tourists, it must seem to you that they come in swarms, but you have to understand that we are people, too. Individuals, believe it."

"Oh, we love our tourists . . . Visitors, that is. Why shouldn't we? They always bring their money with them."

"You can't have it both ways, you know." Dorie thought she was beginning to sound surly, so she added, "Seems like the plural of mongoose ought to be mongeese."

"That sounds even funnier than mongooses."

They were within sight of the sea, on a paved road that wound along the shore, passing pleasant villages. They parked by a shack that sold tickets to the garden and the inevitable souvenirs.

"We have to walk in," Kane explained. "And it's uphill. I'm glad you wore sensible shoes."

Dorie glanced down at her flat sandals. "Is there some other kind?"

The trail overlooked the Turtle Bay, a cozy inlet lined with sharp rocks and ending in a black sand beach. Dorie asked, "Are there really sea turtles out there?"

"Oh, look! There's one now!"

Dorie scowled at the water, broken only by gentle waves. "You're lying. There isn't any turtle there."

"I know. But that's what all the tour guides say. The visitors would feel cheated if nobody saw a turtle."

"Well, you're the perfect tour guide. Don't let any facts get in the way of your spiel."

They hiked through a forest of exotic flowers, of plants from Australia, South America, Japan, and even Hawaii, past perches where imported macaws sat preening in the sunlight. The waterfall splashed prettily among the ferns.

The air was hot and thick with moisture, and then it began to rain.

Kane grabbed her hand. "Quick! Run! The rain shelter is just over there."

Around a bend in the path was the shelter, just a roof held up by four posts, and a couple of logs to sit on. A local businessman had put out orchid plants to sell, turning the crude shed into a bower of colors. The salesman had disappeared; what faith! He knew no one would be so impolite as to carry off his plants or, worse yet, pick the blooms. They were alone in the shelter, the rain so hard it was like four walls hemming them in.

"Did you get wet?" One hand still held hers, with the other he fingered her pareu solicitously.

Well, she certainly didn't want to let him do

that. She stepped away from him, breaking his hold, and lifted her hands to her hair.

"My hair's a little damp, is all." His was not. It looked the same as always, shining like polished pewter, crisp and thick and a little too long. Did he shed water, like a duck?

Rain pounded on the roof and rolled off it to splash onto the ground, so hard there was a mist of spray at ground level. It generated a draft she could feel on her ankles. She moved a little closer to the center of the shelter, and to Kane.

The space in which they stood seemed to be getting smaller and smaller. It was filled with them, with the noise of the rain. Their awareness was in with them; it elbowed them, shoving them together.

She couldn't look at him. She was looking at him, into those mysterious dark eyes. She could hear him breathing, smell the wet-earth scent of the rain. What was he thinking? She couldn't tell; he was only looking at her, with a slight smile, as if the looking gave him pleasure, but somewhere in that expression there was a hint of reproach, a tinge of what? Disappointment?

He was listening, waiting for her to say something, something he was disappointed not to hear. Dorie turned away from him and seated herself on a log. After a short pause, another of those looks, he sat beside her.

Dorie said, "Tell me, Mr. Kane, what is it you

do? Do you take some part in the agriculture on your land?"

He said, "No, I'm a . . ."—he paused, then finished with sort of a verbal shrug—"I'm a politician."

"Oh."

"I served a couple of terms in the state legislature, but I'm not in office now. I find I'm more effective lobbying. Right now is the Christmas break, so I was able to come home, but mostly I'm in Honolulu or Washington while Congress is in session."

"To lobby?" She was having a hard time believing it. She kept getting this mental picture of Kane, in his short pareu and bare feet, stalking up Pennsylvania Avenue. This season of the year, he would be wading in snow.

"It isn't a four-letter word," he pointed out.

"What isn't?"

"Lobby. Five letters. It isn't a dirty word. I lobby for the people of this state, and they need somebody standing up for them. There's so much that needs to be done, but we're out of the loop. It's the location; two thousand miles past the ends of the earth. People on the mainland see us as sort of a big raft, a permanent cruise boat."

"Everybody thinks this is Paradise, and Paradise is already perfect," Dorie said.

"It is a paradise, but it isn't perfect. There's plenty needs fixing. We need to come into the modern world. My people aren't simple Hawaiians anymore. They can't afford to be. They need health care, housing, education, jobs. I want engineers, mathematicians, CPAs and city planners. I've got beach boys and hula girls."

"They can be educated."

"They have to be, or they'll be like slaves. The parents were brought here to cut cane, their children will cut cane and their children's children will cut cane if I can't get them educated."

"Get them all educated, and who will cut the cane?"

"I don't care!" He slapped a palm against his knee. "A machine will do it; they already have one, but I don't care about the cane. I want something better for my people."

"Are the Chinese and the Japanese and the hapa-haoles your people, too?"

"Of course they are. Votes all have the same color. I'm going to build a real hospital. Someday I want a teaching hospital here."

"You dream like a teenager."

"I'm not dreaming! I'm planning! Stay, Dorie, help me build my hospital. You and Kauka Russell are the people I need to run it."

The air was so damp it was hard to breathe it; water flowed along the ground next to their feet. Raindrops fell glittering from the eaves, shining like the pictures he was painting in the air. To accomplish great things, render important service, and finish with something as concrete as a hospital . . . Children could dream of things like that.

Well, children can dream and mature people can accomplish. If a person has experience, knowledge, and a certain amount of clout, and never gives up dreaming, what might be achieved? The last half of life could be richer than the first.

And the man who dreamed . . . Those hot black eyes were boring into her, his big hands clenched on his knees. What a lonely fight he waged, striving to create a new life for people who only knew the old one! To stand by his side, to be part of the struggle . . .

Dorie broke that thought almost before it formed. Maybe for side-standing he needed vigor and freshness, someone like his young wife.

Dorie had a job back in Cleveland, she reminded herself. A life back there, an apartment and friends, a credit rating and a pension plan. When her vacation was over she would go back to Cleveland and leave all this behind. Leave the big dreams on the Big Island.

After a while she observed, "I think the rain has stopped."

"Good. Come with me and I'll show you my Hawaii."

His tour-guide spiel stilled, he drove silently for a long time. Past the gilded beaches where sumptuous hotels rose almost at the water's edge. Down misty valleys where water cascaded into pools for handsome children to swim in and sharp peaks poked up from the misty green jungle. He drove past sugar cane. Miles and miles of sugar cane, until he came back to the village.

"This is where the workers live, the people who tend the cane fields and the pineapples. They've got electricity and sewers and roofs over their heads, but that's about all. The school's inadequate, there's no center for child care, there are no services for anybody. And it's not true that these people, because they are in Hawaii, don't mind living with whole families in one room, don't need mental hospitals, don't need welfare. These are the things I work for, to get these services to my people."

"Speaking of services, it's four o'clock," said Dorie.

"Tomorrow I'll take you to see the surfing."

"Oh, I don't know . . ."

"It's important you see the surfing. You've hardly seen anything that's important on this island, and tomorrow there will be wind. It will be fun to watch, very beautiful."

"Well, okay," said Dorie.

The next day he picked her up on schedule and complained all the way to Hilo because she had not worn a bathing suit.

"Why didn't you bring it along?" he demanded. "I was going to show you how to surf."

"Thank you very much, but I don't think so. Surfing's for strong young people with a good sense of balance."

"It's fun," he pouted. "Why didn't you bring your suit?"

"If you really must know, I don't even own a bathing suit anymore. I have long since passed the age where I want to show my body on the beach."

"What's wrong with it?"

"Nothing spectacular, only it's fifty-one years old. If it was an automobile, it'd be a classic."

He laughed. "That's a good description. You're a classic." He gave her a warm, knowing look that went right through her pretenses, even right through her clothes. He knew Dorie had nothing to be ashamed of in a bathing suit. She just didn't want to be half-naked in the presence of a married man.

Well, this married man.

Dorie was astounded by the size of the waves when they got to the beach. From far, far away they came, forming up farther away than she could see, building into great green walls rolling toward shore, when they would suddenly develop the curl, first the little lip, moving down the crest, faster and faster until it turned into a waterfall, white surf at the bottom.

Kane was smiling as he hauled his board out of the back of the jeep. It was far from pretty, a battered veteran she had assumed was a forgotten discard in the rear of the vehicle.

"You're not going to use that, are you?"

"Especially good waves today," he said.

"Good? A fish would get killed in water like that. Didn't I hear somewhere that these waters are dangerous for swimming in the winter?"

"Don't worry. It's okay if you know what you're doing."

A van pulled up and parked near them, and several teenage boys tumbled out, hurrying to unload their boards. They echoed Dorie's thoughts as they ran toward the water.

"Pretty big waves today!"

"Good surf! Better stay ashore, old-timer!"

"Watch it, grampa, you'll get killed!"

Dorie said, "Oh, Kane . . ."

He hoisted the board over his head, and when he looked at her, he was grinning. "I don't mind them. They're not from our neighborhood, so they don't know me." He ran down the beach.

The boys were already in the water, paddling mightily out to sea. Kane was somewhat behind them, but he paddled briskly until he had reached a position to the left of theirs, and slightly farther out.

They waited, occasionally bobbing over the

forming hump of a wave that had already been rejected as too small.

Then the big wave came. Even Dorie could tell it was a big one. It came straight from the horizon, green and growing, thundering with the vast energy contained in its mass.

The boys jumped to their feet and stood rocking on their boards, watching it come. Kane rose at last, lazily, something in his leashed power answering the potential of the wave.

Then it was breaking, the boys flying high on the crest, riding in joyous speed through the foam. And Kane, Kane was slightly below, she lost sight of him, and then he came shooting out in the center of the curl. Like a jet he flashed down the center of the wave, speeding out of it as it finally lost momentum. Depleted, it pushed him listlessly onto the slope of the beach.

The boys picked up their boards and plunged back into the sea, as did Kane, but now they were together, going back together, like friends.

They stayed out there for hours, treasuring their waves like golden nuggets, a happy bunch enjoying themselves together.

When Kane finally trotted back to the jeep, smiling and happy, Dorie handed him a towel. He rubbed it over his hair, which was dripping. He wasn't a duck after all. He was all man, glowing from his exercise, his chest rising and falling as he breathed deeply.

"I'm sorry we took so long. The waves were good . . ."

"Don't apologize. I've enjoyed watching you. You sure showed up those kids!"

"It's always like that. Kids can't believe that experience counts. Except their experience, of course." He wrapped the towel around himself and jumped into the jeep. "Come on. I'll make it up to you. We'll get dressed up and have dinner at a nice place in Hilo."

Dorie got in beside him. "That's kind of you, but of course I have to go back to work."

"No you don't. No 'of course' about it. There aren't any patients in the hospital right now. You can take the evening off."

"I don't think so. And wouldn't it be better if you spent your evening with your wife and baby?"

Kane said, "Huh?"

"You do remember having a wife, don't you?"

"I remember her very well. We were married for thirty years, and she died eight years ago. Why do you ask?"

"Then you remarried?"

"No."

"You didn't? Then your baby—"

"What baby?"

"When you were taking Ailiana home from the hospital, you said her baby was yours. Do you remember that?"

"Oh, yes, I did say that, didn't I?" He turned a little away, smothering a chuckle. "You know how it is; you're a parent, too. Your child is always your baby, especially when you are proud of her. Ailiana is my daughter."

"The baby is your grandchild?"

"Certainly. I'm too old for infants, now."

Dorie put her hands on her hips and smothered a chuckle of her own. "In that case, let's go and see if they need me at the hospital. If they don't, I think dinner at a nice restaurant in Hilo sounds just fine."

There were no patients that night, but the next day not one but two OB patients came in. It was like every other hospital Dorie had ever worked in; a perfectly normal Christmas Eve.

When she finished her shift at midnight she started walking home across the courtyard. As she passed Clio's house, the nurse was on the front porch. Settled deep into an armchair. Clio wore a vast mu'u-mu'u in a flower print, and she waved at Dorie.

"You there, Nurse! *Mele Kalikimaka!* What are you doing working Christmas Eve? Come on and sit with me. I'll give you a cold beer."

The night was hot and still, and the idea of going inside her walled bedroom to sleep had little appeal. Dorie said, "That sounds like just the right thing."

She went up the steps and took the offered

chair. "What are you doing, sitting up so late on Christmas Eve?"

"Gotta pig down there." Clio gestured toward a patch of earth that was marked by stakes. "Roast pig. For the luau tomorrow."

"You mean it's buried over there? I've heard of that, but I never saw it before. Can you really cook meat like that?"

"It's the only way to cook a pig. The pit is lined with rocks. You build a fire in it for a day, get the rocks really hot, and then you put in a whole pig and bury it for a day and a night. It's so good! When it's cooked just right, the men take it out of the pit and carry it to the table and put it down, and if it's done right, all the meat falls off the bones and you don't have to cut it or anything."

"And you have to watch it all night?"

"My family is in charge of the pig every year. My boys prepared the pit and all that. They've gone down to Hilo for the evening, so I'm watching it until they get back."

"What are you watching for?"

"Mostly to see that nobody digs it up too soon!" Clio waddled to the refrigerator and brought back a beer for Dorie, a fresh one for herself. She grumbled, "You work too hard. This place'll eat you up, if you let it."

"I don't mind. I love taking care of the babies.

Have you seen the little Hong baby? He's so cute!"

"Chinese baby? They're always cuter than the others. You having a good time here?"

Dorie sighed happily. "You bet I am! It was snowing in Cleveland when I left. I wish I could stay in Hawaii until spring."

"Don't like snow, huh?"

"Snow on Christmas morning is pretty. All that picturesque white and the kids playing with snowballs . . . And then there's the next couple months of shoveling, chipping ice off your driveway, scraping it off the front steps so nobody will fall, digging your car out . . ."

"I'd like to see some snow, just once."

"Come visit me in Cleveland and I promise you in a week you'll wish you were back in Hawaii, looking up at the snow on the tops of mountains. That ought to be enough snow for anybody."

Clio's wrinkles arranged themselves into a grin. "Well, if you like it so much here, why don't you stay? You got a boyfriend back in Cleveland or something?"

"Me? Oh, my goodness, no. I'm too old for boyfriends."

Clio's chuckle was almost a wheeze. "There's no such thing as too old."

"Do you have a guy?"

"I've got five kids, so I guess it's pretty obvious I had a guy once, but I don't see much of him anymore. He's okay, but he suffers from Polynesian paralysis."

"Is that a medical condition?"

That wheezy chuckle again. "Very serious, and very common. Hits Hawaiian men whenever they see any work. Anything gets done around here the women do it, or sometimes the Japanese."

"You're pretty much raising the kids by yourself, then?"

"All by myself, and they'll get an education, all of them. I'm not raising any cane-cutters. What happened to Russell's dad?"

The question startled Dorie, but she replied, "I'm not ashamed to tell you. He turned out to be such a rat, I dumped him. I wasn't about to marry a rat, even after I knew about Russell."

"You raised him all by yourself and he's a doctor? How did you do that?"

"Russell made a doctor out of himself. He won scholarships and grants. I helped where I could, but he did it himself."

"He's a good doctor."

"I know, but I love hearing it, so thank you."

"He's also nearly thirty years old. You telling me you haven't had a man in all that time?"

Dorie chuckled a little in her turn. "Well, nobody's perfect."

"Don't you ever fall in love?"

"Oh, sure, but I guess I'm basically a practical person, because as soon as I find out the guy's a rat, I fall right out of love and that's the end of it."

"They're always rats?"

"Always. Maybe there's something about me that attracts the kind of guy who turns out to be a rat." Dorie shrugged, a little uncomfortable. "It isn't like there were all that many. Just a couple rats. Two, maybe three. Make it two and a half rats."

"What about Kane?"

"What about him?"

"Something going on there?"

"Nah." Dorie was silent for a moment. "Maybe. Is he really widowed?"

"Yeah." Clio paused for effect, and a swig of beer. "His wife died . . . Oh, years ago. He finished raising the kids by himself. They all went to school in Honolulu, when he was in the legislature there, and only Ailiana came back here to live."

Dorie decided to change the subject. "We really appreciate your looking after things for us tomorrow."

Another swig. "Nothing to it. Dr. Russell will be discharging the babies and their mothers before he goes to be married, so there won't be anything for me to do. I'll probably spend my time over here with my kids. After you get back from Hilo, we'll all go to the luau."

* * *

In the morning Russell went over to the clinic to take care of the discharges, which was just as well because Lani and Dorie needed the bathroom. Lani was really nervous as she tried to set her yards of hair on hot rollers. Dorie was pressing the silk suit. To her surprise and gratification, the skirt was usable. The couple of places where stains still showed were hidden by her jacket.

When she was dressed, Dorie found Lani still in her robe, untangling hot rollers from her long hair. "I thought you were going to wear it in a French roll," she said.

"I have to, or the hat doesn't look right," Lani replied. "You can't make a French roll unless you put some curls in first, though, for body."

"Your hair already has more body than an aerobics class," Dorie snorted. "The reason you can't get it into a roll is your arms aren't long enough. Give me your brush."

She began brushing out Lani's long, gleaming mass of hair. But Lani couldn't sit quietly. Her hands kept moving as if they were being jerked by invisible strings.

"Relax," Dorie told her. "Don't worry. I'm good at French rolls." Actually, she only had a rough idea of how to go about this, but somebody had to have confidence.

Lani put her hands together and forced them down into her lap. "Dorie, is this the right thing?

I'm so afraid it's not. Nobody wants me to marry Russell!"

"Russell does," Dorie pointed out.

Lani twisted her head around, pulling her hair out of Dorie's hands. "Do you?"

Dorie got hold of her hair again and continued to brush. "I want Russell to be happy, so, yes, I want him to marry you. I'm going to be proud to have you in the family."

Lani began to cry. "Really? Oh, Dorie, I was so afraid you didn't like me!"

Dorie gave her a hug, which was warmly returned. "As soon as I got to know you, I knew you were right for Russell, and I love you for that. I'm glad I got this chance to tell you, because I know I was a little starchy at first."

"Oh, no, Dorie, you've always been so good . . ."

"And I'm good at French rolls, or maybe I said that before. Sit down and hold your head still; we've got a wedding to get ready for!"

After only a couple of tries she was able to get the whole mass of hair rolled smoothly from the ends and pinned into a smooth ebony curve that she tucked against the back of Lani's head. Then Lani put on her little white satin hat with the sensuous curve to the brim and the little fluff of veiling, and it looked exactly right.

When Russell returned she was ready, gleaming in the white satin suit and elegant white satin shoes. The refrigerator was full of flowers, and Russell laid a lei of vivid magenta flowers over her shoulders. She gave him one exactly like it, then put another over Dorie's head. They are beautiful together, Dorie thought, Lani so slender and straight, Russell in his dark suit, the black vest a sharp contrast to his white shirt.

He said, "We'd better go as soon as Kane gets here."

"Kane's going, too?" Dorie asked.

"Yeah, this whole thing was his idea. The judge is some relative of his. We don't want to be late. The judge is giving us his time on Christmas day, and I'm sure he'd rather be with his family."

They waited around, fidgeting, until Dorie suggested, "Let's go over to his place and stir Kane up."

They climbed into Russell's jeep and went to Kane's home. Dorie had not seen it before and was not surprised that it was the most imposing house in the village. Two stories, the lower one completely without walls. You could see through from one side to the other, and there was nobody there. Nor was Kane's jeep anywhere to be seen.

"Maybe he's planning to meet us in Hilo," Russell guessed. "I wish he'd mentioned it."

"We have to go," said Lani.

They kept the curtains on the car closed to keep dust off their finery, and it was stuffy. Dorie couldn't help comparing the ride with the one she had taken the day before, she and Kane with their heads bare to the wind. Sunshine and the smell of the cane. She was glad when they arrived in Hilo.

The courthouse was low and not very imposing, and also very quiet, for everybody was on Christmas holiday. The judge was alone. He personally let them in the door.

There was handshaking all around, and Russell produced his license. Paper was shuffled. The judge looked around and asked, "Where is the other witness? We need two witnesses."

"Kane was supposed to be here," said Lani. "We expected him to meet us."

"Well, we can't do the ceremony without two witnesses."

Lani began to cry. It was sheer nerves; she was shaking. "How can Kane do this to us?"

Dorie put her arms around her, and Lani's head dropped to her shoulder. She said, "Don't worry, Lani. We'll get somebody else. Judge, didn't I see a security guard out there?"

"I'll ask him if he'll do it," Russell said hastily. He rushed to the front of the building and returned with a uniformed guard. Dorie made a show of straightening Lani's hat for her, because she was hoping that Lani would not notice that her new witness was packing a thirty-eight.

"All right," said the judge. "Will you please stand here? And you two, the witnesses—"

"Somebody's making a disturbance," reported the guard. "I've got to go see."

"Very well," said the judge, but he looked at his watch. For him, somebody was probably delaying the start of a turkey dinner and the unwrapping of gifts.

Conversation . . . Dorie smiled desperately and told the judge, "We do appreciate your taking time from your holiday to be here with us . . ."

"Wait for me!" cried a voice that echoed in the hallway, and Kane appeared. His hair was wet and dripping onto his collar, his suit looked crinkled, the jacket not buttoned, but he was there.

Dorie demanded, "Kane, where have you been?"

A look of undiluted guilt crossed his face. He ducked his wet head and admitted, "The surf was up."

Dorie refused to speak to him after that. The judge read the ceremony, everybody signed the papers, the judge produced a few more leis, and then they all went back to their jeeps. Dorie got in with Lani and Russell, and they drove back home.

The luau was beginning. Some young men were stacking fuel for the bonfire that would light the party, others were setting up planks on sawhorses to create long tables. Dorie and Lani quickly changed out of their high heels and tight suits, into comfortable pareus. Russell put on a vivid shirt she had never seen before, and they walked down to the village center. Everybody was already there, and those gathered yelled happily at seeing Russell and Lani. *"Mele Kalikimaka!"*

"Ho'omaika'i!"

And sometimes, "Congratulations!"

The tables were covered with dishes full of fruit, shellfish, and poi. There was fish in peanut sauce and sushi and a dish of *welakaukau*, Hawaiian stew. It sat next to, of all things, a big tureen of gumbo.

The pig was unearthed and carried in a sling to the table. Shouting with glee, the young men swung the pork in an arc and let it crash down onto a big wooden platter. It was perfectly cooked, and all the meat fell neatly away from the bones. Somebody gathered up the skeleton and discarded it, leaving the succulent meat to be sliced up, or just grabbed.

Dorie was filling her plate when an all-too-familiar voice said, "Don't forget the poi."

"Go away, Kane," she responded.

"You aren't going to eat the poi?"

"I don't know that I care for it a lot."

"You probably haven't been fermenting it enough. Don't put it in the refrigerator, leave it on the counter. It has to be at least three days old to have the right flavor . . ."

"Kane, I do not want any poi, and I don't want to talk to you. You're a rat."

"What?"

Dorie put down her plate so she could put her hands on her hips. "The most important day in those two kids' lives—and you had to go surfing. You almost broke Lani's heart."

His eyes rolled and he smiled. "Ah, but you should have seen those waves!"

Dorie took up her plate, then went to sit with the others. She could have gone where Clio was, but Clio would surely have asked her what was wrong, so she sat by some older women. They were all so busy eating, there wasn't much conversation, but Dorie didn't want to talk.

She was waiting for it to happen, and it wasn't. Where was that smooth, automatic click she was used to?

She always fell out of love as soon as she found out the guy was a rat. She had bragged about that. So why wasn't it happening this time? Why wasn't she back to normal, glad to be unattached?

"This isn't my usual pattern," she mumbled to herself, trying to eat a morsel of pork. She was miserable, and the food in her mouth tasted like rubber. What had made her think she was hungry?

Before it was fully dark, the bonfire was lit, and shortly after that somebody started to drum on a hollow log. As the boys finished eating they fetched their drums and joined in, and soon the whole area vibrated with their noise.

A couple of lads fired up torches and tossed them around. They were pretty good at it, but after a while the torches went out and then the girls got up and began to hula. Lani was among them, her hair down her back, her graceful body swaying, slender arms gesturing. Russell joined her, and Dorie wept to see them together, so beautiful, so young and happy.

It's knowing what's ahead that does it, Dorie was thinking. That radiant girl . . . What would her life be? There would be happiness, of course, but every life has hardships and pain. Lani would know long years of hard work, of giving, of loving, and at last, of growing old.

That's why you cry at weddings.

Clio was hauling her to her feet, yelling above the drums, "Come on and dance! Everybody's dancing!"

It did seem that way. The whole village was doing a sort of stomp to the relentless pounding of the drums. Even Clio was rolling and billowing. Dorie joined in.

It was fun. As she warmed up and the beat grew faster she was caught up in it, stamping her feet on the hard-packed ground. Stamping on Lani's blue-nosed relatives. Stamping on all the snobs back in Shaker Heights. And on rats, all rats, including Kane, the surfing rat. Stamp, stamp!

And there was the rat Kane, in his pareu and

necklace. Well, she'd show him she could dance. She could dance as primitively as anybody. It was only a sort of Hawaiian twist.

"Are you going to let me say I'm sorry?" he asked.

"No," said Dorie.

"I didn't know you'd be upset. Most folks around here keep Hawaiian time."

"It's Lani you should apologize to. You made her cry. You owed her better than that, Kane."

"Ah, but it's your good side I want to get on. You do have one, don't you?" He reached out and put his big hands on her waist, and his touch sent a jolt of electricity through her so that her next step was more like a stumble.

She recovered, tossing her head. "You're a rat, Kane *Ali'i*."

He said something, drowned out by drums. Drums and firelight, crazy shadows cast by the dancers all around them. She put her hands on his bare shoulders. His skin was smooth and warm, hard muscles moving underneath as they danced. As drums pounded, they swayed together.

She murmured, "Well, maybe not quite a rat. A mongoose, maybe."

"And you're a tourist. Will you take me home with you when you leave?"

"I might not leave."

He leaned forward until their heads almost

336

touched. They were not really dancing anymore, just swaying and staring into each other's eyes, dazed by the drumming. "Stay with me."

"You and me? That's crazy."

"You and me, that's inevitable."

Dorie shook her head. "Inevitable? Oh, what a word! We don't have to settle our whole future right now, do we?"

"Yes. Don't you know what tonight is? It's our night, the night we find out that we belong together."

"But I can't," Dorie protested. "My pension plan . . ."

"I'll give you a pension plan. Don't you want to marry me?"

"Gee, I don't know. I never got married before. I kind of hate to spoil a perfect record."

He thought about it. "Well, I suppose we shouldn't. After all, I am pure Hawaiian, and you are—What are you, anyway?"

Dorie couldn't help laughing. "Pure American mutt. So what? You don't think, at our ages, we're going to produce a bunch of little *hapa-haoles,* do you?"

He drew back, offended. "Dorie, I don't feel that you are taking me seriously."

"Well, you're not a very serious person, didn't you know that?"

"I seriously love you."

"Well, I love you, too, but you'd better not go surfing when it's our wedding."

"We'll pick a day with no wind," he promised.

Helen Playfair's first TO LOVE AGAIN novel, *A KISS TO REMEMBER,* was published in April of this year; her second will be out in May of 1994. She lives in Canoga Park, California.

A Christmas Tradition

by

Peggy Roberts

"Bah! Humbug!"

Anna Storachenko practiced saying the words. They made her feel better. She had come to hate Christmas! She hated the trees, the lights, the presents, the clutter, the food, the smiling faces. She hated Christmas because it reminded her of how alone she was. She hated it because it was a time when families gathered and hearts were filled with love and a sense of togetherness and belonging.

"I don't belong to anyone anymore," Anna declared and felt dismay that she still hadn't become used to the idea since John had passed away five years ago. Well, some things people didn't get used to. Besides, a part of her fought against this feeling of being disconnected. Her thoughts turned to her children, Nina and Peter. God only knew there'd been no togetherness there over the past few years. Her children considered her nosy and bossy and old-fashioned, so she'd pulled away from them, giving them the "space" they needed. She hoped they understood what a good, progressive mother she was to do such a thing. None of her friends had done that. They still directed married children and their spouses as if they all lived together under one roof.

"Wonder how *they* feel about Christmas," she said out loud. She did that a lot now, talking to the scruffy alley cat she fed on the back porch, talking to her plants when she watered and fertilized them, and lately talking to thin air. "Well, my mind is going," she said, shrugging. Her brown eyes sparkled with humor, her mouth twisted into a wry grin. At fifty-one she hadn't turned into a cranky old woman yet. "Ah, it's coming though," she cautioned herself. "Don't start patting yourself on the back too soon."

She went into her spotless kitchen and put the kettle on for a cup of instant coffee. When the water boiled she made her cup, then settled at the kitchen table with its flowered oilcloth covering, delving into the box of oatmeal cookies she'd bought the last time she did her grocery shopping. Dipping one in her coffee she took a big bite and made a face. These didn't taste like her own cookies, but what was the point of making cookies anymore? She was the only one to eat them. Sighing, she rinsed her cup and put it away and wandered through her quiet, orderly house.

Everything was perfect, from the white doilies on the backs of the chairs in the living room to the braided rug in the back entrance hall. The matching Duncan Phyfe chairs stood like stiff sentinels on either side of the impeccable, starched linen cloth covering the long dining-room table where once they'd all gathered for noisy meals. Every bed was freshly made with stiff white sheets and white bedspreads she'd crocheted herself. There was nothing left for her to do, and it was only ten o'clock in the morning. When Nina and Peter were home, running in and out with their friends, there'd always been work to do. The cookie jar always needed refilling with fresh-baked cookies, the dining-room chairs needed to be realigned, the braided rug to be put back in place, the white doilies straightened, the beds to be made.

"Well, this is fine," Anna said. "I have time now to do whatever I want." But there wasn't anything she really wanted to do. She could call up Olga and offer to work on the new altar cloths for the sisterhood, but she hadn't originally volunteered and thought it was best to leave things as they were.

"I'll make my Christmas list," she decided, and got a pencil and pad out of the neat desk drawer. Sitting in her armchair, her pad resting on the

343

broad surface of the arm, her pencil poised, she hesitated. Thinking of presents for her loved ones used to give her such pleasure, but not anymore. What could she buy a successful lawyer and his wife that they didn't already have? And what could she make for an accountant whose husband took her to Europe, to the best couturiers, right after Christmas?

"Bah! Humbug!" she said, but this time it didn't make her feel better. She thought of Christmases past, of all the richness, all the warmth. They were gone forever. Still she sat with pencil poised and forgotten while she daydreamed of those rich, full days. She remembered her childhood when grandpas and grandmas and aunts and uncles and cousins all gathered in one home to celebrate, to share the traditional Russian Christmas Eve lenten meal and to attend midnight mass and wake the next morning to presents and turkey, an American tradition, but one worthy enough to be adapted to the traditional old country ways, Papa had declared. And so it had been when she and John married and had their own family. They'd continued to celebrate Christmas with joy and laughter, good food, friends and family; and the years had been special.

They'd passed too quickly. Grandparents, aunts, and uncles passed away, cousins moved, John died, and Nina and Peter grew up and went off to the university; one became a lawyer and the other an accountant. They'd married—a young man and woman who were also a lawyer and an accountant. Nina and her husband, Jerry, lived in a modern condo in a rejuvenated and elite area of east side Detroit, and Peter and Susan had abandoned the city for a huge two-story designer house in the western suburbs of Plymouth-Canton.

Anna had never been able to understand why her childless children needed such large dwellings. Who would fill the rooms? Certainly not her grandchildren! Even the mention of such a thing brought shudders to the too-thin, too-pale young women who were her daughter and daughter-in-law. Once Anna had even suggested they see a doctor. They looked so anorexic, she doubted they could even have children.

"Oh, Mama!" Nina had declared.

"Mama, leave Susan alone. She'll know when she's ready to have children," Peter had admonished.

So Anna no longer said anything, only talked aloud to herself about such things when she was alone. It wasn't as if she were the only one. Many of her friends in the sisterhood were in the same situation. Anna often went to church just to meet with them and commiserate over the antics of their children. It made her feel less alone, feel as if, somehow, she still had some small part in her children's life. It didn't help though. None of it did. Her usefulness as a woman, a wife and mother, was over, and her selfish children were denying her her rights as a grandmother.

Sighing she put the pencil and pad back in the desk. There was nothing to plan for Christmas— no menu to go over, no recipes to collect, no toys to hide and wrap and put under the tree, no reason for a tree. No one had called yet to invite her to their home for Christmas, but she knew that would happen. On Christmas Day, Peter and Susan usually picked her up and took her to dinner at a posh restaurant. No steamy kitchen, no leftover turkey and mincemeat pie to snack on later.

"Peter's watching his weight," Susan said when Anna made such an observation once.

They exchanged gifts, spent the afternoon listening to Tchaikovsky on Peter's new CD player, with Susan sneaking surreptitious glances at her slender gold wrist watch until, at last, it was time for Anna to drive back to Dearborn and the little brick house that had housed them all so many years and now sat pristine and untouched by the passing seasons.

No shoes kicked off, no loosened belts, no dozing over a Christmas-day ball game with the television blaring, no dirty dishes, no sense of achievement at the end of the day when to slide into bed beside a warm male body and tuck cold tired feet against warm calves was a great pleasure. Gone, all gone!

Anna was back at the window, staring out at the barren street. This year even the weather wasn't cooperating. Christmas was only days away and still no snow. The trees stood shamelessly barren, their scrawny, naked branches reaching to the skies in insincere supplication. What did they care? Come spring their sap would run again and leaves would sprout. Their seasons repeated themselves. There were no second springs for fifty-one-year-old women.

"You're becoming morbid," Anna snapped. "Cut it out!"

She could offer to have the old traditional Christmas Eve lenten supper. She had before, every year, in fact, but the young people usually had other obligations, Christmas parties and the like with their friends or business associates. She'd offered to have Christmas day dinner before, but the children had vetoed that. She hadn't cooked on Christmas Day in years.

"We remember how hard you used to work, mama. We want you to have a nice relaxed Christmas," they said. So Christmas had become bland, boring, and disappointing and Anna had come to hate it.

Furthermore, the children had taken to playing matchmaker, always introducing her to men. Her own children! Had they forgotten she was married to John Storachenko, their father? She had no need for a man. She was fifty-one years old. She'd had her change. *That* part of her life was over. Thank God!

"Thank God!" she repeated out loud, and the telephone bell pealed as if to accent her words.

"Mama?" It was Nina. Had she won the toss of the coin or lost it as to who took care of Mama for Christmas this year? "Mama, Jerry and I were wondering if you'd want to come over to our house for Christmas this year?"

"Your house? What house? Did you buy a house?" Anna asked.

"No, Mama. I mean the condo," Nina said with that resigned edge to her voice. "Will you come? I thought I'd have the traditional lenten supper on Christmas Eve and do the turkey on Christmas Day the way you used to."

"You want to have a lenten supper on Christmas Eve?" Anna repeated disbelievingly. "Have you asked Jerry?"

"Of course, Mama, and he's all for it. So are Peter and Susan. They would come here this year for Christmas."

"Why don't I make the lenten supper and the Christmas turkey here at the house the way I did when you were a kid?" Anna asked. There was a long pause at the other end.

"I'd really like to do it this year, Mama. I need

to learn how," Nina said, a wistful note to her voice. "I need to know how to start traditions."

"If you hadn't ended them, you wouldn't have to worry about starting them up again," Anna said, then relented. "I'll come if you promise me one thing."

"I'll let you help in the kitchen," Nina said quickly, laughter back in her voice. That hadn't been what Anna was going to demand, but it sounded awfully good to her, so she forgot the rest.

"Mama," Nina's voice came over the wire with that little-girl excitement she used to have. "It's going to be the best Christmas. I have to call Peter and Susan and tell them the time. Jerry will pick you up on Saturday afternoon."

"Early Saturday, if I'm going to help," Anna stipulated and after a final good-bye put down the phone. The sun had decided to shine, she saw. Humming to herself, she went to the back door to put out some food for the scruffy old alley cat. She might even put up a tree after all, that is, if she could get Mr. Repack to set one up for her.

Christmas was three days away. Anna's tree was up and decorated with all the worn and carefully preserved ornaments from previous years. There were the porcelain bells from Germany she'd found when the children were babies, slightly chipped because impatient little hands had often shaken them to make them ring out. And there were the wooden carved ornaments from Peter's years in the Boy Scouts and the Styrofoam balls with tinsel and beads pushed into them which came from Nina's years in the Campfire Girls. Home-crafted, stuffed gingham and lace ornaments hung beside expensive collector decorations from when the kids were older and could afford to buy her something nicer. They were never as treasured as the homemade ones, but she'd never told them that. And there were the shiny glass Christmas balls from John, who'd bought one to celebrate their first year of marriage and one every year that followed. The tree was weighted down with their mementoes and her memories. Anna didn't talk to herself all day. Instead she sang Christmas carols and went to evening vespers so she could drink coffee with her friends afterward and share her plans for Christmas.

"I'm going to Nina's this year," she said to Olga Nicolich. "She's making the lenten supper."

"You're lucky," Olga said. "My daughter-in-law is having a party with eggnog and a buffet."

"That sounds lovely," Anna said graciously.

"Hmmm, what's a mother to do?" asked Olga. "I'll be in the way. I'll probably sit in the back bedroom and read to the grandchildren."

"At least you have grandchildren," Anna reminded Olga, and folding her cape around her slim, erect figure, she walked along the street to her brick house with the blue shutters.

Two days before Christmas, freezing rain fell, coating power lines and tree branches with ice. Bushes bowed, pine branches drooped under the weight of their burden and the sun was hidden beneath layers of gray clouds. The sidewalks and streets glistened with ice, and car motors roared, ineffectually spinning back tires and sending up black plumes of smoke in an effort to break free of the treacherous stuff.

Anna stood at her window and thought how glad she was not to have to go out into the ice and cold. She gave the cat an extra portion of scraps and let him sleep on the closed-in back porch in a box she filled with rags. Then she went to her cold lonely bed and thrashed her feet around until she'd warmed the covers enough to fall asleep.

When she woke in the morning, the world had been transformed into a land from a fairy tale. Snow had fallen, covering the ice and offering traction where there had been none, coating branches and lines and mailboxes and houses with great white dollops. Where yesterday there had been bleakness and ugliness, now there was beauty. It was starting to feel more like Christmas every minute, Anna thought, and she decided to dress up a little bit more than usual this year.

Jerry arrived early and in an uncommonly expansive mood. He grinned a lot and hummed under his breath and didn't seem to mind the traffic or the icy, snow-laden streets. He and Anna chitchatted about inconsequential things and then they were at the broad low expanse of steel, concrete, and glass that housed her daughter. Nina's cheeks were pink, her eyes sparkling, and she'd caught her sleek dark hair back from her face with a ribbon, much as she'd done as a girl.

"Mama! I'm so glad you're here," she cried, coming from the kitchen, an apron covering her dark slacks and pearl-studded sweater. "Isn't it beautiful outside? It's like a real old-fashioned Christmas."

Anna glanced out the wall of windows that overlooked the frozen river and kept her thoughts to herself. Instead she kissed Nina, rubbed a smudge of flour from her cheek, and turned toward the kitchen.

"What do you need me to do?" She took out the apron she'd thoughtfully brought with her and tied it around her waist.

Nina laughed and draped an arm around her shoulders. "Mama, I love you," she said. "You never change."

"Change?" Anna said dismissively, although in

secret she'd liked the hug and the words of love. "Why would I change? Now tell me what you have done and what's left to do?" She lifted the lid of a pot and stirred the contents, then tasted them. "This needs more salt."

"We're trying to cut back on salt, Mama," Nina said, but she reached for the salt box and added a small amount more. "I was just making the pirogui. I have the dough rolled out. Maybe you could help me—" She broke off as Anna picked up the rolling pin and set to work.

"Dough needs to be thinner," Anna said, pushing out the edges of the elastic mixture.

Nina came and stood beside her, a little smile playing around her lips. "This reminds me of when I was a kid, Mama," she said. "I used to come in the kitchen and help you."

"I remember," Anna said. Did Nina think she'd ever forget?

By six o'clock the seven lenten dishes were ready, Peter and Susan had arrived, and the table was set. Susan and Nina went off into the dining room, where Anna heard whispered giggles. But when she joined them, they fell silent, their eyes shining, their expressions conspiratorial.

"I suppose this means you have a spare man coming tonight," Anna said testily.

"As a matter of fact, we do," Nina said sassily.

"He's a lovely man, and he's all alone His wife died three years ago, and he has no one."

"No children?" Anna asked, not because she cared but because it was a negative factor against this unknown and already rejected suitor.

"Three," Nina said triumphantly, "but they were busy tonight."

"Ah," Anna answered, and let it go.

"Anyway, Mama, he's very handsome and he's a gentleman and he's very smart. Papa would have liked him."

"But Papa's not here, so why did you invite him?" Anna snapped.

Nina refused to be deterred. "He's just coming for our lenten supper, Mama. That's all. You don't even have to talk to him if you don't want to."

"I probably won't," Anna declared.

Nina and Susan exchanged glances. "Mama, why don't you take off your apron and go freshen up a bit before supper?"

"I'm fresh enough and so are you," Anna exclaimed. "I'm not going to fix myself up to catch some man I don't even want." The doorbell pealed.

"There he is now," Nina said, taking off her own apron and smoothing her hair. She hesitated. "Mama, he's one of Jerry's clients so if you don't like him, at least try to be courteous."

"What is this?" Anna demanded. "Am I ever

354

discourteous to your friends? Maybe it would be better if I hadn't come tonight."

"Now, Mama, I didn't mean to hurt your feelings," Nina said soothingly. "It's just that . . . sometimes you cut people off before you have a chance to get to know them."

"So I'll be friendly and get to know him," Anna said grudgingly. Nina's bright smile was back in place. Another quick glance at Susan and the two young women ushered Anna into the living room.

Jerry and Peter were talking to a tall man in a business suit. Introductions had already been made, drinks served, and the three men were seated comfortably. The stranger got to his feet when the three women entered.

"Mama, I'd like you to meet Steve Federinko," Jerry said. "Steve, this is my mother-in-law, Anna Storachenko."

"How do you do, Mrs. Storachenko?" His handshake was firm, his blue-eyed gaze direct. He was clean shaven, with high slavic cheekbones. His light brown hair was shot through with silver, and beneath his well-cut suit was a sturdy, lean body with the tiniest hint of a paunch. Anna looked away immediately. She wasn't used to looking at men's bodies.

"I believe everything's ready," she said. "If you'd like to come to the table . . ."

Everyone filed into the dining room with its

garland-draped chandelier and poinsettia-and-candle centerpiece. Nina's best china and crystal sparkled in the candlelight.

"This is lovely," Steve Federinko said. He held out a chair for Anna, but she could see she would be seated next to him.

"Thank you. I believe I'll sit near the door so I can serve," she said, edging around the table.

"Nonsense," Nina said and her voice carried a steel edge to it. "This is my house so I'll do the serving. You sit beside Mr. Federinko."

"Please, everyone, call me Steve," he answered. His sleeve brushed against Anna's arm as he shook out his napkin.

"What do you do, Mr. Federinko?" she asked in the same tone of voice John once used when he interviewed the boys who came to date Nina.

He smiled slightly. His blue eyes really were quite nice. "I'm an engineer," he said quietly. "I have my own company over in River Rouge."

"What kind of company?" Anna demanded.

"We make racks and conveyer belts," he answered. "What do you do, Anna?"

He'd turned the tables on her. She studied her plate, trying to think of a suitable answer. What did she do? She cleaned her house and she fretted over her children. That didn't sound very exciting. Well, who needed to be exciting?

"I tend my home, take care of my cat, and do

356

volunteer work for our church sisterhood," she answered dourly.

"You have a cat?"

"A stray."

"What church do you attend?"

"Saints Peter and Paul on south Madison."

"Ah, Father Michael Saint John is the priest there."

"How do you know him?"

She'd been drawn in deftly. She saw that later. He expressed interest in every aspect of her life, no matter how mundane she tried to make it sound. Nina passed the first course of salt and bread, and the lenten supper with all its symbolism began. Between courses Anna found herself talking about John, life when the children were home, and the loneliness now that they were all gone. He, in turn, told her about his wife who'd passed away, of his three children and five grandchildren, of how life had been when they were all home together, and of how lonely things were now. Then they stopped talking, suddenly aware of how much they'd shared, of how they'd excluded the rest of the table, and uncertain as to just how much further they wanted to go.

Anna had gotten rather used to the lines of his face and the blue eyes which expressed his feelings honestly, without subterfuge. She guessed he was more given to laughter than melancholia, a quality she liked.

But she was not a shallow woman, an incontinent woman. She was the respectable widow of John Storachenko, and she had no intention of taking up with another man, even one chosen by her children, even one of such impeccable manners and simmering sensuality as this Stephen Federinko. She just wasn't interested. Of course, it had been nice that they were seated beside each other and that she'd felt his admiring gaze on her more than once. Nice that she'd worn her new blue dress, which he just happened to admit was his favorite color. She was terribly aware of his hands, good hands, used to hard work. She was glad when the meal ended.

The men went back to the living room, where they sat chatting, and Susan and Anna helped Nina clear away the dishes. By the time all the crystal and china had been hand washed and put away and the pots and pans stacked in the dishwasher, it was time to leave for midnight mass.

"Won't you go with us?" Nina invited Steve Federinko, and he glanced at Anna, a half-smile on his face.

"Perhaps I will," he said, "if I'm not intruding on family tradition."

"We're starting new traditions tonight," Nina said with a mischievous glance at Anna.

"Then I will," he replied. "It will be good to see Father Saint John again."

They all piled into Jerry's Mercedes, all save

Steve who decided to drive his own car and go on home from the church after services. Back on Anna's street, Jerry parked his car and they all climbed out. Steve was right behind them. The snow crunched underfoot as they walked to the church, and their breaths came out in vaporous plumes. The street seemed magically quiet as befitted a night when miracles occurred. Walking along with her children and this tall man who'd fallen into step beside her, Anna felt that same surge of contentment and joy that had always accompanied her to Christmas Eve mass.

Steve stood beside her during mass and sang out the responses and the old Christmas troparian without hesitation. When the mass was over, he followed the line to the front of the church to venerate the cross and greet Father St. John. Immediately, the old priest's face lit up when he saw Steve and he pulled him aside to wait until the line had cleared. Anna hovered at the back of the church watching the two men talk. At last they shook hands, and with a final ablution, Steve turned down the aisle.

"You didn't really say how you came to know Father Saint John so well," she said when he joined her in the vestibule.

"My father was a priest in the Orthodox Catholic Church," Steve revealed. "I was altar boy many times for Father Saint John, and he was a stern task master."

"I can vouch for that," Peter said. "He didn't change much from one generation to the next."

"He wouldn't." Steve laughed.

"Mama, I was thinking, since we have that long trip back across town, maybe Steve could drop you off."

"I'll walk," Anna said. "I do it all the time."

"Oh, not now, Mama, not this late at night."

"I'd be delighted to drop your mother off," Steve said, taking hold of her elbow in such a manner that she swallowed her protestations and followed the others back to the cars. Amid cries of good night the young people got into their autos.

"We'll see you tomorrow for dinner at three o'clock, Steve," Nina called as the car drove away. Anna's lips thinned as she climbed into Steve's Lincoln. He slammed the door and hurried around to the other side.

"I don't want you to get the wrong idea," Anna said as soon as he'd started the motor.

"About what, Anna?" he asked softly. "Because your kids are doing everything they can to throw us together?"

"Well, yes. I'm not interested. I'm perfectly content with my life the way it is."

"You're a lucky woman to be able to say that," he replied. "Frankly, since Helen died, I've been terribly lonely."

Anna was silent for a long moment. "Yes, I've

been lonely too," she admitted. "It's awfully hard to get used to the house being so quiet and no one there to greet you when you return, no one to walk in the door when dusk is falling. I think that's the hardest time of the day."

"For me, it's waking up in the morning and knowing I'm going to spend another day without anyone special in my life, no one to sit over coffee and chat with, no one to ask how my day went."

They were in front of Anna's house now, but both felt a reluctance to have the conversation end. "Look, would you like a cup of coffee?" Steve asked. "We could go somewhere."

"That sounds lovely. There's a bakery down on Oak. It stays open all night, and they make the best nut cakes."

Quickly he turned the car and they moved through the quiet street. Anna sat wondering if she'd made a mistake. Too late now. She'd make the best of it.

The windows of the bakery were steamed over, the light cheerful, the smells divine when they walked in. Steve helped Anna out of her coat and went to the counter to order coffee and rolls for them, while she slid into a booth, fussed with her gloves, scarf, and bag and finally turned her gaze to the handsome man who'd brought her. Was this considered a date? she wondered absently. Was Anna Storachenko out on a date?

"Anything wrong?" Steve said when he brought

361

back cups of steaming black coffee and rich, sticky buns.

"No." Anna shook her head.

Steve took a swig of hot coffee, swore under his breath, bit into a sticky roll and sat contemplating her. "It's kind of scary, isn't it?" he said finally.

"What?" Anna asked, concentrating on stirring her coffee.

"Dating again."

"Is this a date?"

"I'd like to think it is," he said, putting down his roll and licking his fingers. There was such a little-boy quality to him. Anna held on tight to her heart.

"If this were a date," he said, smiling, "then we wouldn't have to go through this awkward stage again. We could go on to our second date."

"Would that be better?"

"I'm not certain," he answered ruefully. "It's been a long time since I dated, but I think it might be."

"Oh," Anna sat, considering his words.

"Of course, if having a date bothers you, we can just consider this something else."

"What?"

He shrugged. "Two new friends having a cup of coffee."

"I think I like that better," she answered, fussing with her gloves and scarf again.

He looked disappointed, but he didn't press it. Instead, he asked about her family, if she'd always lived in Dearborn, what kind of books she read, if she liked concerts. In turn, he told her more about himself. He wasn't a reticent man. He gave honestly of himself. She liked that. Too much, she liked that. She wondered what it must have been like for his wife to be waiting in the evening for him and to have him throw open the door and sweep her into his arms. He'd laugh at her as he was doing now, and he'd tell her a funny story about work or someone he'd met. He would make the house come alive again. He had that quality.

"I'm really glad we met, Anna Storachenko," he said at the door of her house. She thought about asking him in, but the hour was so late and she had her neighbors to think about.

"I am too," she said, giving him her hand in a firm shake. "I guess I'll see you tomorrow, if you're coming to Nina's for dinner."

"Yes. I'm looking forward to it. I wonder . . ." He paused as if uncertain of whether to continue. "I'm supposed to go to my daughter's house afterward. I wonder if you'd like to go with me."

"Oh, I don't think so," Anna said.

"You could meet my grandchildren," he wheedled. "They're terrific kids."

363

"Maybe I will then," she answered, "seeing as I have no grandchildren of my own to visit."

He grinned and leaned down to drop a light kiss on her mouth. His lips were cold and not unpleasant. He'd caught her by surprise.

"I hope you don't mind," he murmured.

"Would it make a difference if I did?" she asked tartly.

"I could take it back," he answered, making her laugh despite herself.

"Good night, Steve. I'll see you tomorrow." She pushed open the door and stepped into the warm darkness of her vestibule. With the door closed firmly behind her, she turned to watch him walk spryly down the steps and get in his car. He moved well for a man in his fifties, very well. He was very energetic. She didn't let that thought go any further.

Anna woke on Christmas morning with that same urgent sense of anticipation she'd had as a child, and like that long-ago child, she lay in her warm bed, hugging the covers to her chin and savoring the moment. Right now, all sorts of wonderful possibilities existed, but once she swung her legs out of bed and began the rush toward the day's completion, she could never stop time and make of the day what she wanted. It would then be given over to other people and what their hopes and aspirations and dreams had been. Now, there were only her dreams, her hopes, her desires. Her dream was to have grandchildren, her hope was to be part of a family again, and her desire . . . Anna blushed and turned on her pillow, because "desire" was a word she hadn't thought to use before, yet there it had appeared in her thoughts, fully fleshed in the person of Stephen Federinko.

"Be honest!" she chided herself aloud. "What do you desire, Anna Storachenko?" She could ask the question out loud, but her heart, timid and new again, couldn't bear a whisper of the truth. To lie in her bed, the bed she'd shared with John Storachenko, and think of Steve Federinko was too disloyal, too unfaithful an undertaking, and Anna had always been faithful and loyal. Sighing, she threw back the stiff white covers and swung her legs over the edge of the bed.

"Poor Steve Federinko," she said, staring down at her bare legs and feet beneath the hem of her prim white gown. "My children have handed you a challenge, indeed, one you'll not likely overcome. It would be better if you were a dragon slayer or a knight of the round table or"—her voice dwindled—"or anything but just a nice ordinary kind of man." Feeling sadly deflated, she rose and remade her bed and straightened her room before showering and dressing. She chose a subdued dress of a rose color that made her slim figure look a little dumpy. No favorite blue today, no gala glittery sweater to enchant or delight the eye of the beholder. She would have to be very straightforward with Stephen Federinko and tell him she . . . what? That she wasn't interested in getting to know him, in having a relationship with him? That wasn't true. Should she tell him she had married John Storachenko for life and thus it would be, for her, forever? Should she tell him she couldn't be disloyal to a man who'd been loyalty itself, that she couldn't put aside the memory of the years they'd spent together?

The phone rang before she was ready with the speech she meant to give Steve Federinko.

"Mama? Merry Christmas, Mama," Nina said, laughter mingling with her soft words. Anna closed her eyes and remembered the Christmas mornings when Nina crept into her parents' room and burrowed against Anna's back, her thin little arms encircling her mother's waist, her childish voice echoing those very words.

"Mama?"

"Merry Christmas, Nina baby," Anna said.

"Are you all ready to come over here?" Nina asked.

"Yes, has Jerry left yet?"

"He isn't coming, Mama. We had a wonderful idea this morning. We called Steve Federinko, and he's going to stop by and pick you up on his way over."

"I thought dinner wasn't until three o'clock."

Nina chuckled. "Well, I'm moving things up. I just can't wait that long, Mama. I have something to tell you."

"What is it?" Anna demanded, feeling her heart stop, then start up again. The last time Nina had had such a surprise, Jerry's company had transferred him to their European office. They had lived in Paris for a year. An exciting experience for Nina, but a lonely year for Anna.

"I'm not telling you what it is until everyone's here and the moment is just right," Nina said. "Now tell me what you think of Steve Federinko."

Anna was quiet for a long moment, unable to jump from one heartrending subject to the next as easily as Nina. "He's a very nice man," she said finally.

"Is that all?" Nina asked. "I tried calling you last night when I got home, but there was no answer."

"Mr. Federinko and I went out for coffee," Anna said flatly. "That was all."

"That's what he said, but it wasn't all that he said."

"What do you mean?" Anna asked, her heart pounding a little bit.

"Well, I think you made quite an impression on Mr. Federinko, quite an impression, indeed."

"Nonsense," Anna scoffed. "We had coffee, we talked a little about our families. That is making an impression?"

"Still, he mentioned how gracious and intelligent you are—and what a wonderful sense of humor you have and how strong you were to carry on after Daddy was gone."

"If I'm going to be ready on time, I'd better go," Anna said abruptly.

"Oh, Mama, don't get all uptight and cold now and turn yourself off from possibilities. I know you've been lonely since Papa died—I don't know how I could bear to go on if something happened to Jerry—and here is a perfectly lovely man who's interested in you."

"I think I hear a car horn," Anna said. "I'll talk to you when I get there."

"Merry Christmas," Nina called gaily and hung up. Anna stood by the mahogany phone table, gazing off into space. There had been no car horn, no need to hurry and dress. She was ready, all except her heart. She had a lot of work to do on that. It seemed to be racing much too quickly, and a silly little smile had curved one corner of her mouth. She caught a glimpse of it in the small mahogany-framed mirror above the phone table.

"Stop this!" she said loudly and sternly, and

instantly the half-smile disappeared. "That's better." It didn't feel better. The day felt kind of gray and without boundaries, as if, if she weren't careful, she might stumble off somewhere in a blue haze and never find her way back to the real Anna Storachenko.

"Your problem," she said to the reflection in the mirror, speaking slowly and distinctly so there would be no chance of being misunderstood, "your problem is that you're lonely and you need grandchildren. You have selfish children who don't want to give up their glossy lives for the plain old down-to-earth, ordinary muck of having children. But that's no reason for you to throw all moral caution to the wind and become involved with another man. Poor John must be rolling over in his grave at this very moment. You were always a good wife to him, and you will continue to be one. Now when you see Mr. Federinko, you will think of him as a . . . a priest, a man but not a man. You will be courteous and friendly, and you will not go to see his children. What good would that do you, since you will never see him again after today? Do you understand?"

The dark eyes that stared back at her were very earnest. Their expression made Anna turn away from the mirror. The doorbell rang and she jumped. Steve Federinko's sleek Lincoln was parked at the curb. She pushed down a flutter of excitement and hurried to open the door.

"Merry Christmas, Anna," he said, stepping inside.

"Merry Christmas, Mr. Federinko," she answered primly. "I'm all ready to go. I'll just get my coat and purse." She turned toward the hall closet. Steve Federinko glanced through the arch to the living room.

"Your Christmas tree is beautiful," he said, moving over to examine some of the ornaments. "It looks the way ours used to when we—my wife and I—put it up for Christmas." He touched one of the roughly carved wooden horses. "My grandchildren used to like to come and look at the ornaments their parents made for us."

Something about his slumped shoulders touched Anna's heart, the same heart she'd been so certain she'd hardened just minutes before his arrival.

"You don't put up a Christmas tree now?" she asked softly.

"I haven't," he said, straightening his shoulders and scuffing at his cheeks with his hands in a gesture not meant to be seen by her. Anna turned to the mirror and fussed with arranging her scarf just so around her neck. When he had recovered, he hurried over and held her coat for her.

"You know, you should put up a Christmas tree

370

every year, regardless," she said. "It gives your spirits more of a lift than you suppose and gets you through the rough times."

"Is that the voice of experience?" he half-teased.

"Very much so," she answered. "It helps."

"Then I'll do it next year," he said. "Maybe I'll even insist the kids bring their families over to my house like they used to."

"Do that," Anna encouraged. "They may not want to—mine don't come anymore—but you need to assert your needs as well. And if you need family around at Christmas time, then you need to tell them so."

"Is that what you've done?"

She looked away. "That's what I'm going to do," she said, taking up her gloves and drawing them on. "I've really tolerated quite a lot from my children, no grandchildren and no old traditions, although they've decided now to bring them back." She picked up her handbag and smiled at him. "I'm ready to go."

"You look lovely, Anna. That rose is—"

"Don't say it's your favorite color too," she exclaimed.

He laughed. "Maybe the fact that you're wearing it has something to do with my fickleness. Anyway, it makes your cheeks all flushed and pink like a little girl's."

He leaned forward and kissed her then, so

naturally that she never once thought to push him away. And when the kiss endured for more than the brief moment she'd expected, she found herself kissing him back. His lips were warm and smooth against her own. The kiss was very pleasant and when he stepped back, she met his gaze unwaveringly.

"Thank you, Anna Storachenko," he said softly.

"For what?" she asked, slightly bemused by this big tall man who could cry and kiss a woman with equal ease.

"For sharing your holiday with me."

"Oh, we'd best get under way," she exclaimed, letting her own emotions get lost in the flurry of leaving. He carried out her sack of presents and helped her into his car. Olga Nicolich was on the sidewalk, just returning from church. In the past few years, she'd taken to attending the Christmas morning mass rather than the midnight services, so she hadn't seen Steve Federinko yet. Now she stood on the sidewalk and gawked.

"Merry Christmas, Olga," Anna called, and waved to her friend before climbing into the plush car. Steve tucked her in, closed her door, tipped his hat at Olga, and got in on his side.

The drive to Nina's seemed much shorter. They talked all the way about a number of things, family and grandchildren, born and unborn, least on the list. Once again she was struck by what an intelligent, interesting man he was.

They arrived at Nina's flushed and full of laughter.

"Mama, I've never seen you look so youthful," Nina cried, pulling her aside.

"How's the turkey?" Anna said, reaching for an apron. She'd forgotten to bring her own. "You don't want to overcook or it'll be dry." Her son-in-law was already leading Steve off toward the den, where the television blared with the noise and hoopla of a playoff game. Steve glanced back toward Anna and shrugged. Anna smiled to herself and hummed as she basted the turkey and went over Nina's menu. Things were surprisingly well organized, and nothing needed her attention. Nina perched on a stool, studying her mother.

"And what is that look all about?" Anna demanded, trying to evade Nina's quivering, barely suppressed curiosity.

"Mama!" she wailed. "If you don't tell me how things are going between you and Steve, I won't tell you my secret."

"Yes, you will," Anna said. "Because you could never keep a secret for very long and because there's nothing going on between Steve Federinko and me. He picked me up today because you asked him to, but I may take a bus home tonight."

"You fibber," Nina cried. "You'll do no such thing, because, for one, we wouldn't let you and, for another, Mr. Federinko wouldn't let you. He's a gentleman. Oh, Mama, tell me you like him the least little bit."

"The least little bit," Anna repeated, making it sound like not at all. But when Nina's expression fell, she relented. "He's a very nice man, but that's all Nina. He's not Papa."

"No, he's not Papa," Nina said. "But Papa's not here and Steve Federinko is."

"Nina, don't start trying to arrange things in my life."

"I just want you to be happy, Mama, as happy as I am with Jerry. I don't like to think of you all alone in that big house. You're still a young woman. You have years and years ahead of you."

"I hope so," Anna said wryly. "When are Susan and Peter coming?"

"Soon. You know what I mean, Mama. I don't want you to live those years alone."

"Alone is not as bad as it sounds," Anna said. "There are worse things. When did Susan and Peter say they'd be here?"

"Soon," Nina said impatiently. "What worse things? Name some."

"Nina, I can't think when you—"

"Just name one thing that's worse than living all alone."

"Having no grandchildren and having children who always try to find a man for you when you don't want one."

Nina was amazingly silent at this answer. Anna swiveled around to look at her. Nina looked like a little girl perched on her stool, her eyes big and tearful, her hands pressed against her mouth as if to hold onto a smile that wavered and threatened to wobble right off her face, given the chance.

"Nina?"

"Oh, Mama, I love you," she whispered through her tears.

"What's wrong, Nina," Anna said. "Something is wrong. I can always tell when something's wrong."

"I think Susan and Peter are here," Nina cried, jumping up.

"Nina, don't run away from me. I'm your mother. If you need someone to talk to, then I'm here."

"Yes, it is Susan and Peter," Nina called with the old gaiety back in her voice. "Good, now we can eat. I'm absolutely famished." She danced away into the safer world of greetings and hugs and hanging up coats, and after that Anna couldn't get her alone, no matter what. Susan seemed to hover always just on the perimeter, ready to spring forward if Anna made the least attempt to talk to Nina. Feeling grumpy and irritated, Anna took her place at the Christmas table.

"Why so glum?" Steve asked at her side.

"I'm not sure. I think the kids are keeping something from me," she answered. "I hope it's nothing serious."

"Trust that they'll tell you when they're ready," he said. She knew he was right. There was nothing else she could do.

The meal progressed in jovial fashion with plenty of laughter and talk. When Anna wasn't worrying over Nina she was noticing how well Steve fit in with her children. Peter and Jerry seemed to hold his opinion in some esteem, and he, in turn, seemed to respect their younger, more aggressive approach to some issues. Dessert was finished, and everyone leaned back to loosen belts and sigh with contentment.

"You men go on in the den, and we'll clear away the dishes," Anna said, starting to rise.

"Not yet," Nina said. "We haven't given you your present yet."

"Nor I yours," Anna said. "Let's go into the living room where we'll be comfortable." She looked around the table at the smiling faces and slowly resumed her seat.

Nina passed a box along the table. "This is from all of us," she said softly.

Looking somewhat skeptical, Anna began to unwrap the solitary box. It was small and flat. She couldn't imagine what it could be: a new expensive wristwatch she didn't need, another necklace of sterling silver or fourteen-carat gold she would never wear. A new silk scarf? At least she wore scarves. The paper fell away and with a final glance around the table at young faces suddenly gone somber, she lifted the lid on the flat white box and looked inside. Everyone around the table was silent. Inside the box was a small book. Anna read the words on the little book, but they didn't register. She read them again, and because they still meant nothing to her, she read them again out loud.

" 'Grandma's Picture Book'!" They'd started to grin again, big lunky, we're-going-to-burst-out-bawling-any-minute grins, look-how-proud-we-are grins, we-love-you-Mama, grins. Her ears were roaring. Steve was chuckling, deep and rich in his chest. They realized she didn't understand, didn't comprehend yet what her present was to be.

"It's true," Nina cried running around the table to throw her arms around Anna. "Jerry and I are going to have a baby in June."

"Oh, Nina." Anna's cry ended high and shrill. She hugged her daughter, rocking her to and fro while tears rained down her cheeks. "A grandchild. I'm going to have a grandchild." She pressed hugs upon Jerry and Nina and Susan and Peter and even upon Stephen Federinko.

"Now you can see why I wanted to start up the old traditions again," Nina said softly. "I want

377

my child to have the kind of memories you gave Peter and me."

Anna wiped at her eyes and looked at Peter. "It will take more than one grandchild," she warned.

Susan's face went pale, and Peter automatically reached for his wife's hand.

"I'm sorry, Susan, if I've spoken out of turn," Anna said, suddenly contrite. She felt so elated, she didn't want anyone else to feel bad.

"Actually, you haven't," Susan said graciously. She nodded to Peter to continue.

"Susan and I have been trying to have a baby for some time, but we haven't had much luck, even with the new medical techniques."

"Oh, Susan, forgive me," Anna cried, leaving her seat to go around the table and hug her daughter-in-law. "I've been so foolish and insensitive. I thought it was your career."

"My career is important to me, Anna, but Peter and I want a child, too." Susan hugged Anna back with surprising warmth. "That's why we began the process of adopting a child several months ago, and now it's just a matter of time. We've been told we'll have a baby by the first of March."

"The first of March!" Anna put both hands over her mouth, but couldn't hold back her gleeful giggles. Weeping and laughing at the same time she hugged Susan and Peter, Nina and Jerry, and then kissed Stephen Federinko.

It took another hour before everyone calmed down enough to think of anything other than the coming babies. By then it was time for Steve and Anna to leave to meet his children.

"This has been the best Christmas of my life." Anna hugged them all a final time. She hated to leave, but Nina looked tired. It had been a big holiday for her, and no doubt they had plans to make once she was gone. Anna didn't feel left out as she might once have.

"I feel . . . euphoric," she cried, holding out her arms as if to embrace the whole city. Steve laughed with her and held open the car door.

"Are you sure you want to leave now?" he asked. "I'd understand if you changed your mind."

"Oh, no," Anna said, getting into the car. "Nina's had enough excitement for one day. Besides, I have to begin to learn how to behave around grandchildren."

"That won't be a problem," he said, starting up the car. "In fact the kids'll show you."

Barbara was a quietly friendly girl with dark hair and dark eyes who must, Anna decided, look like her mother because she didn't resemble her father except in the sudden swift smile that lent her plain features a rare beauty. She took Anna's coat, welcomed her warmly, and offered her refreshments. The dinner dishes had been cleared and desserts and snacks left invitingly on the dining-room table, covered over with bits of plastic wrap. In the living room a television blared out the Christmas day game, toys were scattered hither and yon. A boy of about seven sat near the Christmas tree absorbed in a puzzle. A little girl, three or so, had fallen asleep on the floor, one chubby thumb pressed in her mouth, her other hand clutching a Raggedy Ann. A man dozed in an armchair, a sleeping baby in his arms.

"My crew," Barbara said with mingled pride and amusement. "David, wake up. Daddy's here, and he brought a guest." Anna liked it that she made no pretense of picking up the Christmas clutter.

"Don't bother him on my account," she said quickly, but the dark-haired man called David yawned, scratched his rumpled hair into even greater disarray, and good-naturedly grinned up at them.

"Hello, Dad," he called to Steve. "You won't mind if I don't get up."

"No, of course not, although I'll take away your excuse," Steve said, leaning over to pick up the sleeping baby. Deftly, he tucked the tiny sleepy face next to his chin and ushered Anna to the couch, where toys and new pajamas and sweaters had to be pushed out of the way to make room to sit.

"Where are Bob and Jim and their families?"

"They took the older kids down to the pond to ice-skate for awhile. Everyone was getting edgy. Too much togetherness, too much Christmas and not enough sleep," Barbara explained. "Can't I get you something to drink or eat, Anna?"

"Too much Christmas for me too," she said, shaking her head. "Would you mind if I hold your little one?"

"If you can get him away from Daddy. Be nice and share now, Dad."

They all laughed, and Steve handed over his grandson. Anna enfolded him, drawing in the scent of baby powder, formula and all the other smells of a baby. His warmth and helplessness touched her heart, making her think of the old stray cat she fed off the back porch and the tall, good-looking man who wept over forgotten Christmas tree ornaments. She glanced at him and found his blue-eyed gaze pinned on her.

"Do you want him back?" she asked contritely, and was relieved when he shook his head.

About then a tousled dark head popped up from the floor. Two sleepy eyes peered at them. With a sucking pop a thumb was grudgingly removed from pink cherubic lips.

"Poppy," she cried, throwing out her arms.

"Hey, jelly bean," Steve cried, and scooted off the couch onto the floor where, with a squeal of glee, the diminutive three-year-old flung herself at him.

Pulled from his puzzle by the noise, the little boy joined the fracas which became an out-and-out free-for-all. Anna expected the baby to wake up, but he slept on serenely, obviously used to this noisy home.

Before long there was more noise at the back door and the rest of Steve's children, his children-in-law, and grandchildren entered, their eyes sparkling, their faces rosy from the cold air and exercise. Everyone seemed to be trying to talk at once. No one seemed to listen, yet each one knew what the other had just said, for they carried on a conversation that was responsive and coherent. Anna sat on the couch, in the midst of all the noise and clutter, the baby cuddled to her breasts, and smiled with absurd contentment. Eventually, someone persuaded her to give up the baby, congratulated her on her pending grandmotherhood, and served her tea and carrot cake. By the time she and Steve had redonned their coats and left the house, Anna felt like they'd been shot out of a cannon, launched into quiet and coldness by the very exuberance of the people they'd left behind.

"Whew," Steve said, holding the car door for her. "I hope that wasn't too much for you."

"I loved it," she said.

"You looked like you did," he answered, digging out his keys. "I love it too for a while, but I'm always glad to get back to a slower, quieter pace. God sure knew what he was doing in cutting off the reproductive system after so many years."

Anna laughed. She felt warm and happy. "Christmas will be like that for us next year," she said.

"Not quite that bad," he said. "It takes the little darlings a year or two to really get their voices and get the steam up."

The drive back to her house was pleasant, spent mainly reminiscing over the day's events. When they got to Anna's she glanced at Steve.

"You know, we have all those leftovers my daughter and your daughter sent. Why don't we go inside and I'll warm some of them up and we can watch a little television and—"

"That sounds heavenly," he said quickly. "I was hoping you'd ask and wondering how I could bring it up if you didn't."

They carried all the bowls and boxes of goodies into Anna's kitchen, switched on the small portable television she had in there, then proceeded to ignore it, turning it down a little at a time until only the picture flashed and no sound came. They ate their warmed-over supper and laughed and talked and finally fell silent.

"I have something for you," Steve said, reaching into his coat pocket for a small wrapped box.

"What is this?" she asked.

"A present! For you! Go on, open it," he urged boyishly.

"I can't accept a gift from you. I . . . we hardly know each other."

"I know you better in two days than some people I've known for years," he said, holding out the box.

She wanted to refuse it, to draw her resolve around her, but his eyes were very blue above his ruddy cheeks and his smile was so open and spontaneous. She thought of how generous and giving he'd been all day. How could she say or do anything that would take away his obvious enjoyment of this moment? Slowly, she took the box and looked at it.

"But I have no gift for you," she said hesitantly.

"You've given me the gift of your delightful company. That's more than I'd expected," he said.

"That's how I felt about today," she said slowly. "As if you'd given me a gift of yourself." He gripped her hand.

"Open it!" His grin grew broader, and there was nothing for her to do but open the box. It was a jeweler's box. Surely, he hadn't done something foolish. Inside was a brooch of jet beading and marcasite. Anna didn't know what to say.

"It's kind of old-fashioned," he said in the face of her silence. "My father gave it to my mother when they first arrived in this country. He couldn't afford anything more exotic. Later, when he could, he gave her a diamond brooch, but she always wore this one. I think it was her favorite."

"I can't possibly accept this," Anna said, keeping her head down and blinking her eyes rapidly against the sting of tears.

"I know it's not the kind of gift most women would choose for themselves. You may think it ugly."

"It's not that," she said, raising her head and looking into his kind blue eyes. "It's a lovely brooch. I can see why your mother wore it instead of the diamond one, but I couldn't take something that represented so much love and family and . . ." She faltered to a halt.

"I think of you in that way, Anna," he said softly. "You're a woman who's dedicated her whole life to her family and children. You have a great capacity to give and receive love, like my mother. Please say you'll keep it and wear it once in a while."

"I'll keep it forever, and I'll wear it often," she vowed. He leaned across the table and pinned it on her bodice; then it seemed only natural that his hands went up to cup her face and bring it close to his. She knew before his lips touched hers where it would all end, knew she wouldn't

385

spend the night alone in the big bed she'd once shared with John Storachenko. They stacked the dishes in the sink and turned out the lights and climbed the stairs and stood in the middle of the bedroom, slowly undressing each other, taking their time because they understood they had the time. This moment wouldn't leave them. It might have seemed to some that they'd come to it hastily, but they hadn't. She'd waited five years, he'd waited three. Having waited so long, there was no need to hurry now. She closed her eyes and held her breath as his hands slid across her skin, smoothed away her slip straps, brushed against her ribs, cupped her breasts. With frank admiration, she watched him kick aside his pants, throw off his socks and shorts. He was made well. Tall and broad shouldered still, with taut buttocks and long, muscled legs. There was an elegant fineness to his form, and she found the slight paunch endearing, then erotic as he gathered her close to him.

"Anna," he whispered against her mouth. "You are so beautiful. You're like a dream come true, my very own Christmas angel."

"I don't want to be an angel," she said petulantly. He went dead still for a minute, then threw back his head and laughed.

"Come here," he growled finally, lifting her in his arms and carrying her to the bed. Leaning over her, he gazed into her eyes. "Now show me everything you want to be," he whispered.

There was no hesitation in her movements as she wound her arms around his neck and pulled him down to her. Everything felt so right, the weight of him against her aching body, the tangle of long, hairy legs against her own, the chaff of his jaw against her cheek, the flooding of her senses when his mouth left hers and swooped downward to suckle the dark rosy tips of her breasts, the giving moist womanly part of her that opened to him without resistance. Afterward, when breathing had returned to normal, when their hearts had slowed their wild beating and body temperatures had lowered again and all the nerve endings had relaxed, afterward, when the glory and the wonder had been tasted and its glow still warmed them, it seemed so right to lie clasped in each other's arms and sleep.

"Olga will see the Lincoln," Anna said. The words hung on the chilled morning air over the bed in which she and Steve lay cuddled and warm. Thinking of such problems first thing in the morning made her cranky.

"Maybe she doesn't get up this early," he said hopefully.

"She's up before dawn," Anna said.

They lay quiet, their warm limbs still intertwined, but she could feel that first slackening of muscles about to pull away. She wished she could recall the words, because they would drive them from their warm cocoon of desire and spent passion and lazy abandonment.

The night had been a revelation to her. She'd thought herself an old *baba,* a grandmother without grandchildren, a woman whose passion had been leached from her withered body and soul by the years; but Steve hadn't found her so. He'd said she was beautiful. He'd kissed her body and brushed his hands across it in a frank display of lust, and everywhere he'd touched, he'd smoothed away the rust of years and disuse and left instead a vibrant, responsive body that had surprised and delighted her. She wasn't old, just unused. He'd looked beneath her proper exterior and found a somewhat decadent, generous, and funny woman. She didn't want to lose that even if Olga did see the car. Then reality returned and she realized she couldn't lie here in bed with a strange man and ignore all the other things she was.

As if sensing her inner war, Steve sighed and moved away from her, rolling out of bed and stalking across the room to gather up his pants. Absently, she watched his taut white buttocks until he'd pulled on his shorts and stepped into his trousers. She was glad when he was dressed and she could drag her gaze away from him.

"Do you want to have dinner tonight?" he asked, sitting on the side of the bed to draw on his socks and shoes. Anna closed her eyes and suddenly it wasn't Steve Federinko sitting there, but John Storachenko.

"Anna?" he asked, nudging her knee slightly before reaching for his other shoe. She couldn't answer, so caught up in her dream was she, the sweet dream that John was only an arm's reach away. They'd just spent the night making love, and he was dressing for work, letting her laze in bed because he knew she seldom did so and it pleased him to see her pamper herself a little bit.

"How about if I pick you up at seven and we go somewhere to eat?" John would have said that.

"We have all those leftovers," she would have answered as she did now, her eyes still tightly closed.

"We'll have those another night. I'm getting tired of turkey, aren't you?"

She nodded. "Why don't we go to Dimitri's the way we usually do on Monday nights?" she asked dreamily. There was a long pause. She felt the weight on the side of the bed shift.

"If that's what you'd like," he said, and his voice sounded guarded. His footsteps moved away and her dream faded.

"John!" she cried and sat up, looking at him. Steve Federinko stood at the foot of the bed, staring down at her. "I . . . I'm sorry," she said, putting her face in her hands and grimacing against the pain in knowing that it wasn't John after all.

"For a minute there I thought I was talking to my husband."

"It's all right," Steve said, coming around to sit on the edge of the bed, facing her. "Sometimes our minds play tricks on us."

"It's just that with you there putting on your shoes and socks and talking in such an ordinary way . . . I'm sorry."

"You needn't be. I do understand," he answered. "It will be all right, Anna, if you let it be."

"No, you're wrong. I was wrong," she said, raising her face to his. There were no tears and no pain, only a dull hopelessness, the gray residue of acceptance after the death of a loved one. "I shouldn't have let you stay last night," she hurried on. "I've always known that there could never be another man for me. I'm John Storachenko's wife."

"You're his widow, Anna, and he wouldn't have wanted you to live the rest of your life alone and lonely if it could be helped."

She shook her head. "I'm sorry," she said. "I don't want to see you anymore."

"Anna, you can't mean that. Not after last night. What happened between us was right and good." He took hold of her bare arms and shook her a little. "Don't you see, Anna? It was natural. Two lonely people reaching out to each other."

"No," Anna said. "I can't be someone I'm not. There are old traditions to keep in place, and one of these is that when a woman marries such a man as John Storachenko and has a family and becomes a grandmother, she doesn't act like a—a girl again. I've been a romantic old fool."

"You've been warm and alive, a woman honest enough and brave enough to reach out to take what she needs," Steve said.

"I feel ashamed now that I did this," she said stubbornly.

"You weren't ashamed last night," he said implacably.

"Well, I am today," she said crankily. "What will my neighbors think when they see a man leave my house this early in the morning? There's never been a breath of scandal, never."

"I'll leave, at once," he said, shrugging into his suitcoat, "but I'll be back tonight and we can talk."

"No, don't come back tonight," she ordered. "I need some time to think."

"All right," he said reluctantly. "Then I'll wait for you to call me. But, Anna, we're not young anymore. When we find someone a second time, we shouldn't let anything keep us from the happiness and companionship we both want."

"Please, Steve," Anna said softly. "I'll call you and we'll talk. Right now, Olga is probably just getting up and opening her windows. She'll see your car and know—"

"Good-bye, Anna," he said and turned away. Anna sat in the middle of her bed and listened to his steps disappearing down the stairs. When the front door closed behind him, the house became very quiet and still again. Sighing, Anna rose and made her bed and straightened her room and had her shower. Then she went downstairs to do the dishes they'd left in the sink the night before.

The phone rang, and Anna's hand trembled slightly when she hurried to pick it up. She'd told him she'd call him, but maybe—

"Good morning, Mama," Nina said on the other end.

"Nina," Anna said, feeling her heart flood with happiness at the sound of her daughter's voice. "How are you feeling?"

"Mama, what can I do for morning sickness?" Nina asked with a self-conscious little laugh.

"I always nibbled on dry crackers," Anna said, smiling to herself. This was all she'd wanted, to be consulted by her children about such things as this. It was a dream come true.

"I'll try that," Nina said. "The doctor gave me some pills to take if it gets too bad, but I'd prefer to take as little medication as possible."

"That's a good idea, baby," Anna said, "but listen to your doctor. He'll know what's best for you."

"Not you, Mama?" Nina teased.

"After Mama, he knows what's best for you," Anna said.

"What time did you and Steve get home last night?" Nina asked.

"Late," Anna said.

"How did you like his family?" Nina was not to be put off. This, Anna realized, was the real reason she'd called. She wanted to know all about Anna's day with Steve Federinko.

"They were nice," Anna said noncommittally.

"Oh, Mama!" Nina said with some exasperation. "Are you seeing him again?"

"Neither one of us wants to rush into anything, Nina. I think you shouldn't get your hopes up."

"Well, you could just go out once in a while, for a movie or dinner, without a major commitment," Nina reasoned.

"He didn't ask me out for a movie or dinner," Anna said, thinking that would be the end of Nina's meddling.

"Why don't you call and ask him?" Nina said.

"There's someone at the door, Nina. I have to go," Anna said.

"Maybe's it's Steve," Nina cried. "Call me back if it is."

"Go eat some crackers," Anna ordered and hung up the phone. Of course no one was at the door. Anna had made that up to get rid of her inquisitive daughter. Sighing, she turned back to her tasks.

By ten o'clock, all traces of Steve Federinko had been removed from her little brick house. The cushions sat just so in each corner of the sofa, the line of Duncan Phyfe chairs stood at attention and the old scarred alley cat had been fed and lay in a sunny spot in the back foyer licking his paws. Life was back to normal. Only the tree in the front window reminded her of Christmas and all it had brought. Next year will be very different she thought, happily. Next year there would be grandchildren to cuddle and hold and plan for.

And between now and Christmas? She would baby-sit and knit sweaters and afghans. Her life would be very full. Of course, there would still be the lonely times at the end of the day when no man opened the door and brought the house—and her—to life, there would be no shared late suppers of leftovers, no hasty climbs to the bedroom and long cold winter nights wrapped in the warm presence of a beloved one.

That afternoon, it snowed, a light dusting of white over the gray pre-Christmas slush. Anna put on her galoshes and her coat and went outdoors to sweep away the new fallen flakes. The cold air stung her cheeks and the tip of her nose, making her feel alive. She thought how nice it would be if Steve drove by and stopped and came in for coffee. They could talk and she could tell him what she'd been thinking this morning about the new babies and Nina's morning sickness.

"I see you had company last night," a voice called. Anna steeled herself and looked up at her old friend. Olga Nicolich stood huddled in her dead husband's old coat, a knit hat pulled hastily over her graying hair, beneath the hem of her dress her thin legs encased in thick rumpled stockings. Her sharp features gave her nose a beakish affect, but Anna knew that despite her curiosity, she was a basically kindhearted woman.

"Yes, I had some company," she said noncommittally and continued sweeping her walk.

"A man!" Olga prodded.

"Yes, a man," Anna agreed. She refused to answer Olga's unspoken questions.

"He was very handsome."

"Ummm, I suppose so," Anna commented.

"Very distinguished looking!"

"Ummm."

Olga paused, watching Anna's energetic movements and the flurries of snow she sent up. "Did he have car trouble?"

"Car trouble?" Anna repeated, becoming irritated by the questions. "What's this with the car trouble? There was no trouble."

"I just wondered. I saw his car was still parked here this morning. I thought maybe he had car trouble and went home in a cab."

Olga waited while Anna finished the last block of sidewalk. Anna turned to survey her walk. "He didn't have car trouble," she said and turned up the walk toward her front porch.

"Did you have a good Christmas then, Anna Storachenko?" Olga called after her.

"Yes, Olga. It was a very good Christmas. And did you?"

"Yes, I went to my children's house and played with my grandchildren."

"That's good, Olga." Anna started to swing her door closed.

"Anna," Olga ran up the sidewalk. "Have you got time for a cup of coffee?"

Anna studied her old friend. What would they talk about? she wondered. About Olga's grandchildren. Anna could tell her about Nina and Susan and Peter, but there was time enough to share that good news. What they wouldn't talk about, and what Olga hoped they would talk about, was Steve Federinko. Anna didn't even want to think about him.

"I don't have time for coffee this morning, Olga," she said. "Maybe some other morning. Merry Christmas to you."

"Merry Christmas," Olga answered and turned back down the sidewalk to make her way to her own little brick house. Anna watched her go, watched the slumped shoulders and dragging steps. Why, Olga was growing old. She felt guilty not to have asked her in, not to have shared some of the excitement of Steve Federinko. She didn't know why she hadn't wanted to do that. She and Olga had shared so many things throughout their lives. But now, standing in her living room, watching Olga walk away, Anna found herself less like the slump-shouldered old woman than she did the woman who'd responded throughout the night to Steve Federinko's lovemaking.

There are some things friends can't share, she thought, and went to peer into the hall mirror, searching for signs of age in herself. She didn't look as she had when she'd come to this house as the young bride of John Storachenko, but neither did she look like Olga. She fell somewhere in between. Was that because of Steve Federinko? For a moment she imagined his night of lovemaking had been a fountain of youth.

"You're a fool, Anna Storachenko," she said, and the sound of her voice in the quiet house was oddly, familiarly satisfying. She'd found her way back to the old Anna again.

* * *

For the next few days Anna stayed to herself. She attended church, but didn't pause to chat with her old friends, all widows themselves, all clucking their tongues over their Christmases with their children. Anna saw how they'd allowed themselves to fall into a rut, how their lives were tied up in those of their children. They had no lives of their own. She felt sorry for them, somehow superior, until she recognized that she was one with these women. Soon her body would once again forget the heat of a man's touch. It would grow old and dried up again, and when she walked her skirts would make a sound like that of dried leaves in the autumn winds.

Anna turned away from the window and faced the neat loneliness of her little brick house. For so long she'd been a maiden waiting for her knight in shining armor, a Cinderella awaiting her prince. Frozen in a past time when all laughter and color had come to her through John and her children, in a time that had passed by. People and things had changed, but she'd remained the same Anna Storachenko she'd always been, waiting for life to change back again and return to her what it had taken away.

In a way it has, she thought. There would be babies again and children's laughter and joyous holidays, but in between birthdays and holidays and Sunday afternoons were weeks and days of living, and she must continue to spend those times alone unless she chose to reach out herself. All the changing that was going to happen in life wouldn't occur unless she made it happen. If she wanted more, she must leave her little brick haven and reach out. She hadn't far to reach, she knew. Steve Federinko had made that clear. Where was the risk? Yet Anna knew that each time we turn a corner, we risk not finding our way back again. What she had to decide, what she had to search within herself to learn, was whether she had the courage to let go and turn the next corner without fear, even if it meant never finding her way back.

Standing in the middle of her little house that had forgotten how to echo with cries and laughter, she knew she must be brave because she hadn't the kind of bravery it took to go on living alone. Steve Federinko had made her see that.

Going to the phone, Anna did something she'd never thought she'd do in her life. She called a man to ask him for a date. But Steve didn't answer at the number he'd given her. He must be at work, she thought, and reluctantly hung up. She was afraid she wouldn't find the courage to try again later.

That evening she did try again, but no one answered. In the days that followed she tried his number several times at various times of day in the hope of catching him in. Finally, she called his daughter, Barbara.

"Hello, Mrs. Storachenko," Barbara said. She sounded tired, and in the background a child was singing and keeping time by hitting something metal against metal. "Just a minute, Anna," she said with a little laugh. When she came back things were quieter.

"I was looking for your father," Anna explained. "He gave me a number where he can be reached, but I haven't had any luck."

"He went out of town for a few days," Barbara said. "But he's coming back on New Year's Eve. He has a party to go to. Shall I tell him you called?"

"If you would, please," Anna said and hung up, feeling deflated. Steve had gone away without calling to tell her good-bye, but then she'd been pretty adamant before he'd left. She couldn't blame him for not being there when she finally made up her mind about what she wanted to do.

In the afternoon, Nina called. "Is Steve Federinko picking you up for the party tomorrow night?" she wanted to know.

"Ah, Nina, I'd forgotten you were having a New Year's party. Is Steve coming?"

"I thought he was," Nina exclaimed. "I thought he was bringing you."

"No, we didn't make any plans," Anna said, "and he's out of town."

"Are you coming anyway, Mama?" Nina asked anxiously.

Anna thought of Peter's and Nina's friends, glossy young couples who'd chosen the right careers and stepped effortlessly from graduate school into well-paying positions that insured them an easy life-style. No saving pennies in a sugar bowl or turning coats to wear them a second or third year. No careful hoarding of life's riches. Their confidence in life's continued generosity was alien to her. What would she say to them? If the babies were here, she could sit in the back bedroom and read to them the way Olga Nicolich did. Perhaps it would be best if she didn't go. Yet, Steve might be there.

"I'm not sure," she hedged. "I'll take a bus over if I do come."

"Take a taxi, Mama," Nina said.

"All right, I'll take a taxi," Anna said, smiling at this contemplated extravagance.

She tried once more to reach Steve Federinko. She listened to the phone ringing uninterrupted on the other end and imagined the darkened, empty apartment. It reminded her of her own house, and she shuddered, hung up the phone, and decided to go to Nina's party after all. She thought of wearing her blue dress again. It was safe, noncommittal, then she rummaged at the back of her closet and found a pair of palazzo pants Nina had persuaded her to buy once and black sling-back pumps with a velvet bow on the toe. Finally she came across a beaded and sequined top. She hung the clothes in the bathroom so the steam could freshen them a bit while she showered.

When she'd dressed, she reached for the comb and spray, and brushed her dark short hair high and sleek against her head. When she stood back and surveyed the results, she was startled to find a sophisticated-looking woman who appeared much younger than fifty-one. Was this the way Steve Federinko had seen her? Did she really look so sure about herself and her life?

"Now, we all know that's a lie, don't we, Anna?" she said out loud. She called a cab, checked her evening bag for money, lipstick, comb, and tissues, got her coat, and was waiting when the taxi pulled up in front of her house.

Anna felt rather elegant sitting in the back of the taxi and watching the lights of Detroit flash by. When they reached the condo, the driver's appreciative thank you made her certain she'd over-tipped, but she put the notion out of her mind as she turned toward the elevators and rode up to her daughter's "house." She was trying to adjust, but some things took time. Finding this steel and glass encasement homey was one of those. Just before the elevator slid open to deposit her at her daughter's door, she let herself think of Steve Federinko. Would he be there? Did she want him to be? Why else had she come?

"Mama, you look beautiful," Nina cried with

delight. "Peter, Susan, come see how pretty Mama looks tonight."

They swept her into their party, into the noise and gaiety, into the tinkle of ice in glasses, the shimmer and shine of candlelight on satin dresses and bare shoulders, into the light friendly talk of people who had already guessed, or had yet to learn, the need we have for one another. Their talk was feverish, vivid, profound, silly, all the things it should be on a New Year's Eve when the world holds such promise and we're not alone.

But Anna was alone. In this roomful of well-meaning people, she felt her isolation more poignantly than if she'd stayed in her little brick house. Steve Federinko was not there, and the smiling faces became those of strangers to her. Anna pushed her way through them all and stood at the window, staring down at the frozen river, and felt a bereavement more keen than any she'd known before. She recognized the death of hope, and she trembled with the fear that all of life was so dependent on one person. Was she willing to give away her freedom and independence for so binding a relationship again? Was she willing to let one man's face be the reason for her heart to beat?

A sound made her turn away from the gray-blue world outside the window, back to the color and light and movement of the room. Steve

Federinko had just entered and was shrugging out of his coat. His handsome head nodded slightly to his host, his smile was abstract, his eyes were already searching the room. For her! Anna's heart caught and then began to beat faster. She stepped forward and he saw her. His face lit with a smile, his blue eyes blazed, and he moved through the crowd toward her. Anna smiled and held out her arms to him. Oh yes, things were changing, and Anna was willing to change right along with them. Tradition was fine, but sometimes you had to make room for new traditions and new people in your life. Next year, ah, next year, Christmas would be wonderful.

Peggy Roberts is the author of two TO LOVE AGAINs—*MRS. PERFECT* and *JUST IN TIME*. She lives in Canton, Michigan.

The Eighth Candle
by
Joan Shapiro

Rachel slammed the door behind her and stood in the suddenly alien confines of her own front hall. It seemed somehow different. Damn, everything seemed different. With a harsh abrupt gesture, she scrubbed away the first tear.

Thanksgiving. Just rip the damned day off the calendar, why don't you? Once more, she'd been the "charity" guest, the "poor-thing-she's-all-alone-and-we'll-be-doing-a-*mitzvah*-by-having-her" kind of guest. Well, damn them, these sudden strangers who had only recently been old and dear friends, *damn them and their good deeds:* she'd had it. They weren't going to earn their merit badges from God by way of Rachel Ellis, no sir.

If she'd been smart she'd have seen it last Passover, and certainly by September, with the arrival of the High Holy Days. *That* had been the real eye-opener. And what a beginning for a New Year *that* was. She took a long, deep breath. This

Thanksgiving, though not the first, was, by God, the *last* holiday she'd spend that way. Never again. Not while there was a breath in her body.

She was distracted from her thoughts for a fraction of an instant. *Come on. They were just being what they'd always been—good friends. Friends who were rallying around her and trying as hard as they could to fill the empty spaces.* And she was too mired in self-pity to accept.

Then her eyes were caught by the gleam of the menorah on the sideboard in the dining room, waiting for its complement of colored candles to celebrate the miracle of Hanukkah. Just a couple of weeks away. Well, to hell with it. No one would need to make charitable gestures and condescending invitations again. Because she wouldn't be here. She'd be as far away from Hanukkah and candles and family celebrations and memories as she could get. Nothing and no one to remind her of what had been—and could never be again. She picked up the gleaming brass nine-armed candlestick, heavy and solid, its sense of durability and continuity mocking the inescapable impermanence of life.

Rachel blinked as light glinted off the bright, cool metal. If she tried very hard she could hear the echo of high clear young voices—the children chanting the blessing each night of the holiday—could see them taking their turns lighting the candles and saying the *barucha*, excitedly waiting for their gifts. She and Mort had always given them each one substantial gift, then some small token every other night of the eight days.

"All right, Geri lights the first candle; she's the oldest." "Oh, Mom, she's *always* the oldest!" "Be careful, Kenny, that match is still hot!" "Why can't I be first sometime?" "Stop whining, Molly. Nobody likes a whiner."

Ah, that was Mort, all right, steady and firm, the constant and dependable counterbalance to her own quick temper and equally quick forgiveness. They'd been lucky . . . they'd given their children both. The children! Rachel bit her lips, fingers tightening on the heavy candelabra. It wouldn't have been so bad if they hadn't built up her hopes, led her for so long to expect them home for the holidays.

So Kenny was stuck in California with a broken leg from a recent ski outing, but at least, he'd cheerfully reassured her, Molly and Geri would be here; only, Molly, her husband Eric, and the twins would be in the middle of the Panama Canal, on a cruise they'd won from his company, nondeferrable, of course. And, after all, Molly had reasoned, Mom would be okay—Geri and Kenny would be home for the holiday. Rachel, feeling particularly martyrish that day, hadn't mentioned the leg, the cast, or the long lonely eight days she'd planned to fill with her family. Because Geri and Stan and the children had to

409

go to his parents' home in Chicago . . . his father was scheduled for prostate surgery. What could Rachel have said to that? So, here she stood, alone and . . .

Nobody likes a whiner.

She almost dropped the heavy candlestick. Her head snapped up, she looked around the empty room. No, of course he wasn't . . .

She touched the lifeless metal and drew a deep breath. Right now—pack it away, for good, forever . . . along with all the other reminders of yesterday.

If she never in her life saw another damned palm tree again it would be too soon.

Rachel gritted her teeth, turning abruptly from the balcony of her room in the Curaçao Caribbean, and swore, in a soft and ladylike manner so as not to unduly shock the sun worshippers already gathered on the patio and lawn below. Another perfect day in Paradise.

Shit.

Four days since her plane had landed at Hato Airport and there hadn't been a shred of cloud in the lousy clear blue sky; the sun kept insisting on shimmering up there all day, every day. The laughter from the scattering of chaises longues below only stoked the fire of her anger and resentment. What right had they to laugh? What right had they to happiness and good times? Why them and not her? She'd been asking herself the other side of that question for seven months. Why her and not someone else?

Oh God, what a rotten thing to think! She sank down onto the bright tropical-print pillow of the rattan chair, head back, eyes closed. No, she didn't like what she was turning into—the very thought of it disgusted her. Of course she wouldn't wish her grief on someone else, but there was no way to hide the increasing resentment she'd allowed to corrode every day of her life. Damn you, Mort. We had it all planned; this was *our* time. You finally had all the days and hours you could want for *us*—for *me*, a small voice inside her head taunted. Why did you have to go and die!

She sighed, her sense of self-disgust almost unbearable. "Rachel Ellis, you're one self-centered bitch, you are. Whining about 'why me, poor little me'! But it's *Mort* who's lying in six feet of cold earth in Machpelah Cemetery, *Mort* who won't see his children moving ahead, his grandchildren growing up. *He's* not down here with the sun warming him and the soft Caribbean breeze cooling him . . . he's up there, alone, in the frost of a Michigan winter and you're sitting on your selfish ass in a plush hotel on Curaçao."

But even guilt couldn't quite break through the thick layer of self-pity. It had encrusted her thoughts and feelings since the grim day when

Dr. Gold had put his arms around her and said the words that stole the rest of her life away.

"I'm so sorry, Rae dear. He never regained consciousness . . ."

Sorry. Long ago she'd consigned that hateful word to the same mental garbage heap as those ubiquitous palm trees. Sorry. Sure, they were all sorry. Of course they were, the relatives, the dear friends . . . the children. No, that was awful, and so unfair! They had lives to live, futures ahead of them, and it was right that they get on with living. Had she held on to grief too long, had it become in its own way a comforting substitute for the warmth and companionship of the loving husband she'd lost? Rabbi Lowenstein back home had warned her: excessive grief is just as wrong as no grief at all. And after thirteen months she should have been farther along the road to healing than she was. God didn't want life to end for her because it had ended for Mort.

But how the hell could you turn the faucet off on grief or, perhaps more accurately, loneliness? Easy for him to talk. He was a clergyman—he was supposed to talk that way, in nice comforting platitudes for the survivors. *Again not fair, Rachel. He's been part of our lives for a very long time . . . he was Mort's friend, he really did care, he was truly sorry.* But sorrow, like talk, was cheap. And sorry didn't change one damn thing.

Rachel opened her eyes and willed the tears

away. Tears didn't change anything, either. Too many tears, and she was suddenly sick to death of self-pity and guilt and anger . . . and especially tears.

This is it. I will not spend another day, not another hour, moping alone in this room. She'd come to Curaçao to get away from gloom and doom. As beautiful and light and bright and luxurious as this suite was, like the house back in Southfield it was just another kind of prison, and she'd served enough time! Ah yes, brave words, but . . . She must, at the very least, try to convince herself.

Listlessly, she picked up the large straw shoulder tote, wiped her eyes and put on sunglasses, and prepared to face the relentless sunshine.

"Good morning, ah, it is Mrs. Ellis? You are feeling better today? Such a shame to be ill on a wonderful vacation, no?" The desk clerk beamed with genuine concern and good will, his small black moustache quivering with sincerity, looking for all the world, she almost smiled at the thought, like a Caribbean Hercule Poirot. As she'd noticed even in the limited exchanges they'd shared in the last few days, he seemed to end every sentence with a question mark, as if he were forever unsure of what life had in store for him and did not want to put too much faith in positive answers. *Tell me about it,* Rachel thought.

413

"Yes, thank you, I'm fine." Fine. Oh yes. "Just fine." She actually managed a full-fledged smile. "I was wondering if there's a tour available today. I'd love to see the island. Have you any brochures?"

Lord, would this tour never end? With the windows open and the perpetual seaward breeze, humidity was, fortunately, nonexistent. Still, Rachel was restless, impatient, tired of pasting on a smile and pretending interest in the conversations of the strangers around her.

The voice of the guide interrupted her thoughts. "Now we come to one of the most interesting sights in Willemstad. The Mikve Israel-Emanuel Synagogue is the oldest Jewish congregation in the New World." Amid nodding heads and impressed oohs and aahs, the mini-tour bus ground to a halt. The doors opened and a stiff and straggly group of pale-faced tourists lurched out into the quiet sunlit street, cameras at the ready. Rachel was the last to alight.

"Isn't this a beautiful little place?" the enthusiastic young woman in front of her breathed in appreciation.

"Mmm, yes, beautiful," Rachel agreed. *And just what I wanted to see . . . another synagogue.* Every day, every week, for that first eleven months she'd been a faithful participant in the daily services at home, dutifully reciting *kaddish*, the prayer for a departed loved one. *Departed.* One of those charming euphemisms for "dead." Mort was *dead,* and there weren't synagogues or rabbis or prayers enough to bring him back.

That was progress, of a sort, she thought suddenly. She measured progress greedily these days. And admitting the finality of the word "dead" was progress indeed.

She hung back when the others disappeared through the doorway. She didn't want to go in, and yet, despite her instincts, she followed. The dim interior was cool and welcoming, but it was a few moments before her sun-blinded eyes adapted to the filtered light. She passed through a stone-floored anteroom and entered the main sanctuary of the tiny building.

What a jewel of a room! The bright Curaçaoan day streamed through the high blue-tinted windows spaced symmetrically around all four walls; the room was filled with a lovely glowing light, without the glare of the sun. The rays glinted off the gleaming brass multiarmed chandelier suspended from wood beams squarely above the *bima,* the raised platform where the Torah scrolls were stored. The reading lectern in the center of the congregation was a well-rubbed and polished mahogany, and pews of the same aged wood surrounded the high platform on all sides. As she moved forward Rachel looked down at the floor of the synagogue; it was completely covered in clean white sand.

"The sand on the floor, ladies and gentlemen, is said to be a reminder of the years the Israelites wandered in the desert after the exodus from Egypt. The chandelier is a replica of one in the synagogue in Amsterdam and . . ." His voice drifted away as Rachel tuned out again. She sat down away from the group, in the last row off to one side, shielded from view by a heavy wooden pillar, and after looking carefully around the room one last time leaned back and closed her eyes, the soft drone of the guide's voice blending seamlessly into the background. The present drifted away and she was left to her own thoughts and memories, a strange lassitude settling over her, holding her quiescent in her seat, hands and feet inert, mind leaden and empty of thought . . . She was so damned tired.

When she opened her eyes the room was perceptibly dimmer, surrounding her with a peaceful cool aura of calm and serenity. Rachel sat quietly, looking up at the pale whitewashed walls, breathing in the cool, faintly sweet smell, hearing the silence . . .

The silence. *Oh, good grief, where'd they all go?*

The tour guide and his flock were nowhere in sight, or sound. She rose as quickly as her stiffening joints would allow, looking down at her wristwatch. Damn! The troubled dreams and sleepless nights were taking their toll. She'd been sleeping on that hard wooden bench for more than an hour and a half. An ironic smile turned up her mouth. She'd sure made an impression: no one had even noticed her sleeping there, or that she was missing from the bus. Well, she hadn't made much of an effort to be memorable. In fact, lately she hadn't seemed to make an effort to do much of anything at all. Since the funeral—and that was over a year ago!—the one word to best describe her was "listless." *Or how about apathetic, boring, dull*—quite a lot of dreary adjectives would describe her, Rachel thought in a sudden flash of disgusted honesty, not the least of which was selfish.

There was a footfall behind her, suddenly loud in the utter silence, and she whirled in alarm. A slender elderly man with a small neatly trimmed Van Dyke beard stood in the doorway on the far side of the tiny anteroom cum gift shop cum lobby. He smiled.

"Hello. I'm sorry if I startled you. Is there something I can do for you? I'm Rabbi Geller."

"Oh! I—I was beginning to think I was the only person around. It's so quiet."

"Yes, I sometimes think that's our greatest asset here, that old cliché, *peace and quiet.*" He sighed. " 'Peace' is at a premium lately. There aren't many places anymore where you can find it."

"I'm afraid you're right." Rachel nodded. "The old 'law of supply and demand.'" She turned back to the sanctuary. "Your synagogue is lovely. Is it still in use?"

"Oh yes, of course." He sounded surprised. "If you'd taken a tour the guide would have told you all about it. As the first synagogue in the western hemisphere it's a 'must' on all the tours. That is why I thought you—"

"Actually, I *was* on a tour. I . . . uh, I fell asleep," she admitted sheepishly.

He chuckled, then looked at her, his eyes seeming to take in more than she wished to show. Ill at ease under his gentle scrutiny Rachel smoothed the creased white denim of her jeans, straightened her loose blue chambray shirt over her hips. The outfit had been an obvious choice for a daylong tour in this tropical climate, but a lifetime of tradition made her uneasy at such casual attire inside a synagogue, while talking to a rabbi. *That's dumb. This isn't my synagogue, and he's used to tourists here.* "Uh, is there a phone I could use . . . I need to call a cab to get back to my hotel. My bus seems to have left, minus one."

"You're vacationing alone?"

"Yes, but how did you . . . ?"

He chuckled. "Nothing miraculous, I assure you. If no one came back for you from the bus then . . ."

"Oh, of course. Silly of me. Yes, I'm . . .

alone." The word hung between them, and then Rabbi Geller nodded slowly.

"Come into my office. I have a telephone, if it's working today." He shrugged. "At the very least I can offer you some tea." He gestured behind him, and they walked through the door into a small, cluttered room, books and papers scattered across the battered desk top, a decrepit box sitting on the one and only visitor's chair, the blue and white silk of its contents trailing to the floor. She stared at it, vividly recalling Mort's familiar *tallis*, the prayer shawl he'd worn through so many holiday services back home.

"Sit, sit," Rabbi Geller said as he lit the flame of the small two-burner hot plate on a table near the door. He placed a kettle on top and reached for glasses in silver holders, then a sugar bowl and a dish of lemon slices. At that moment nothing could have seemed more welcome to her than that small homely offering of a *qlez tay* as her grandma used to say. Suddenly Rachel felt the full weight of her fatigue and looked around, eager to follow his direction to, "Sit, sit."

"Where should I put these *talesim*, Rabbi?" She stood uncertainly, the old cardboard box cradled in her hands.

He turned his head. "You are Jewish?" he asked, startled.

Rachel smiled faintly. "Yes, I am." She followed his gesture and deposited the box in the corner,

419

atop an already rickety pile of ragged books, all seeming in urgent need of a recuperative visit to a bindery. With real gratitude she sank heavily onto the straight-backed wooden chair. Rabbi Geller walked around his desk and sat in the cracked brown leather chair, pausing to hand her one of the glasses filled with the steaming dark brew. They both sipped in silence and then he put down his glass.

"Let us see if this is our lucky day." He picked up the receiver and listened for a couple of seconds. Shaking his head, he replaced it and lifted his hands in a gesture of helplessness. "It is not." He studied her face, the unhappiness there barely hidden beneath the first pink tinge of sunburn.

"Rabbi," she asked, frowning, "is there a public bus . . . or a taxi stand within walking distance? Perhaps someone else with a phone . . . ?"

He shook his head slowly; then his eyes widened with a thought and he smiled. "Ah, but I have a car, such as it is," he said apologetically. "And while I cannot drive you myself—I must help my wife get ready for tonight—I will have someone take you."

"Oh no, don't bother, please." Rachel shook off the dismaying inertia and stood. "I'm sure if I can get back to the downtown area I'll find—"

He held up his hand. "No, no, I cannot allow it. Please, don't worry; it will take just a moment. My friend will be here in"—he checked the watch that looked almost too large for his thin wrist—"a couple of minutes. Will that be all right?"

Rachel started to protest, but his expression was so fraught with anxiety over the wish to help her, to make sure she was comfortable, that she sat back down, nodding her head. "Yes, that would be just fine. I really appreciate this."

He smiled again, that soft gentle smile, and took another deep swallow of tea. "When Steven gets here he will take you back. Then I will go and do battle with the potato peeler."

"Potato peeler?"

"Oh, yes." When she didn't seem to respond, he explained further. "It is the beginning of Hanukkah. The children will light the first candle tonight."

"Of course." How could she have been so stupid? Here she'd been trying to forget it and she'd just managed to ensure that he'd remind her. "You'll have to forgive me, Rabbi Geller, but Hanukkah is one of the things I came here to forget."

He studied her in silence for a few moments, then nodded his head.

"So, how long are you visiting our little paradise?" He leaned forward. "Ah, I am sorry. For you it is not a paradise, I see."

Her face must be more expressive than she'd thought, Rachel realized. Have to work on that.

"Paradise is in the eye of the beholder," she answered, a rueful smile on her lips.

"I think . . ." He paused. "Well, perhaps I should not say it, but I think you are a very unhappy lady. I don't wish to pry, but if there is anything I can do . . . ?" He waited, his dark eyes sincere, liquid with concern and understanding and comfort.

Rachel lowered her gaze from that concern, to stare down at the tea glass she gripped. She placed it carefully on the desk top and folded her hands in her lap. "My husband . . . my husband died a little over a year ago, Rabbi. A massive coronary. It was very sudden."

It had been so long since she'd actually spoken it aloud . . . Now, the relief was almost overwhelming—as if a massive weight had been lifted, almost as if the act of breathing had suddenly been restored. Back home everyone went to such pains to avoid the whole subject, as if Mort had never existed. It took her a minute to realize how much better she felt with the release those words gave her.

She shook her head, confused for an instant. "I came down here because it's as different from home as any place I could think of, and because Mort and I were never here, and because"—Rachel bit her lip, swallowed hard—"because I didn't want to be around anyone I knew." That was a hard admission to make, though easier because he was a stranger, a compassionate and concerned stranger.

"It is a long time to grieve. Perhaps you are afraid to show grief any longer in front of people who care about you."

Rachel stared, stunned. "Yes . . . how did you—? That's it, exactly. They're always saying things like 'Time will heal the pain' and 'It's just a matter of time, you'll feel better.' Oh, and my personal favorite, 'In time you'll meet someone else.' " She twisted her hands together. "I don't *want* someone else. I want Mort!"

"But you know you cannot have him any longer; you cannot undo what is. You must accept that." He clasped his hands together in a prayerful position, his voice quiet, thoughtful. "I like to think of life as a path through a forest; now your path has come to a division. You and your companion are parted, and you must go in this new direction, perhaps alone, perhaps not. But you cannot see yet what lies ahead of you on this new path."

He leaned forward earnestly. "My dear, there is a time to grieve and a time to stop grieving . . . I think you know it is that time now. Even grief for a loved one can go too far. It is unseemly. That is why our mourning period ends at the eleventh month, to remind us that despite death God gives us the beauty of life. You must not turn away from life. That would be the real tragedy."

She sat motionless, staring at him, listening, mesmerized by his gentle soft tone and the wisdom of his words. They remained in the cool dim silence for a few moments, then he rose and walked around the desk. "I hope you will forgive my presumption—and my unasked-for advice. My wife tells me, frequently, that I don't know the answers to everyone's problems. But"—he shrugged, his eyes wide and amused—"as you can see, I do not quite believe her."

Rachel looked up at him, a faint smile on her mouth. "No, Rabbi, there's nothing to forgive. My own rabbi, back home, has been trying to tell me the same thing. I guess I wasn't ready to listen. I know you're right, though it's been a long time coming. My husband was a man who thoroughly enjoyed life; we had a wonderful thirty-two years together, and he would hate this . . . this ocean of self-pity I'm drowning myself in. He wasn't a person who wasted time feeling sorry for himself, and he wouldn't want me to do it, either." She reached for the tea glass, slick now with condensed moisture, and sipped the cooled liquid.

"It's funny, but what you said . . . about my knowing now it's time to stop grieving. This afternoon, sitting out there in the sanctuary, I had that same thought myself, at least the beginnings of it." She closed her eyes for a moment, sighed. "Don't turn away from life, you said. Well, that's what I've done for too long, I guess. My life is so . . . so lifeless." She ran her finger slowly around the rim of the glass and shook her head. "I just don't quite know how to start moving again, alone."

"Ah my dear, you needn't be alone if you don't want to be. There are always people whose lives you can touch." All at once he straightened, stared, then smiled broadly. "Do you realize, after all this arrogance on my part, presuming to shower you with unasked-for advice and counsel, I don't even know your name."

She laughed then, a delightful sound in the quiet room, and the slight elderly man smiled back.

"How do you do, Rabbi Geller. My name is Rachel Ellis."

"It is good to know just whose life I am directing today." They both laughed, then turned in unison toward the door as they heard a soft knock. A tall solid man in a dark blue cotton pullover and khaki slacks stood in the open doorway, smiling tentatively at them.

"Ah, Steven, come in, come in. You are just in time. This is my new friend, Mrs. Ellis. I hope that is true, Mrs. Ellis, that you are my friend and that you forgive me?"

"As I said, there's nothing to forgive." She

sighed. "If you're right about something you don't have to defend yourself."

"Good, good. Then I would like to introduce you to another friend, of very many years. Steven Sandler."

Steven had been watching them for a couple of minutes before they noticed him, and now he smiled and took her hand. He marveled in that short moment at how soft and smooth it felt in his, how small, how . . .

Damn, what's your problem? It wasn't as if he'd been living on a mountain top for the past three years. He came into contact with women all the time in his business, often in more intimate settings than this, and he didn't normally make so much of a quick handshake.

"A pleasure to meet you, Mrs. Ellis." He noted the worn gold band on her ring finger.

"How do you do, Mr. Sandler." His hand was large, solid; his handshake firm and steady, like him. Probably in his late fifties, he was an attractive man, "well-preserved" as Kenny would have put it. If Mort had kept himself in this kind of condition perhaps he wouldn't have . . . She blinked away the image.

"I meant to be here a little earlier, Benjamin," he said to the smaller man, "but I fell asleep by the pool and . . ." He shrugged apologetically. "Nobody answered when I knocked, so I dropped the potatoes at your back door. By now you should be in the kitchen helping Devorah peel potatoes. How'd you escape?" His quick grin invited one to share his joy, and the invitation was hard to resist.

Rachel couldn't. The whole room seemed suddenly brighter, and she responded with an answering smile. A lucky man, she thought, to enjoy such contentment with his life and the world around him. Things were good in his world, that smile said, could never be otherwise. *Lucky*.

"Steven, can you possibly do us a favor?"

"Actually," Rachel interposed, "Rabbi Geller means do *me* a favor. My tour bus left me behind, and I need a lift to my hotel. I'm at the Curaçao Caribbean. But I can get a taxi, honestly . . ."

"No, really, it's no trouble at all. You want me to use your car, Benjamin? Is this its day to run?"

"You can't insult my car, Steven. It comes through when it's needed," the rabbi answered benignly.

"Well, then, shall we go, Mrs. Ellis?" Steven suddenly had a great curiosity—was there a *Mr. Ellis?* He shot her a sharp look, and knew there wasn't. The traces of sadness, the faint redness about her eyes, were enough to answer the unasked question. And she'd evidently been on the tour alone.

She turned to the door. "Good-bye, Rabbi Geller, and"—she paused, and almost took his hand, recalling just in time that an observant rabbi was

427

forbidden to touch a woman other than his wife—"thank you so much. I'm more grateful than you can ever know."

"Ah, thank you's are not necessary. I said what you already knew. It was only a matter of time." He looked at her, and they smiled at each other, remembering her earlier remarks about "time." But it was good, he thought, to see how much better she looked already. There was the beginning of acceptance, of interest and pleasure, a sense of *life*.

"Well, perhaps that time will be better spent now." She picked up her purse and sunglasses and walked to the door.

"Steven, here are the keys to the car. By the time you get back we'll have the table set and all you'll have to do is eat." He dropped the small key ring into Steven's palm.

Outside, in the waning afternoon light the three of them walked across a small patio and he pulled open the large wooden double doors of a shabby garage. A shiny blue Ford Escort of indeterminate years sat inside, squeaky clean and gleaming in the beam of sunshine streaming through the opening. Bright and jaunty, despite its age, it might have just rolled off the assembly line.

"She is my one weakness, after Devorah and the children, of course." Rabbi Geller stroked the shiny front fender with a proprietary air. *"Ha-shem* will forgive me, I hope, for this vanity." He looked up as if expecting an answer from the heavens.

"Your carriage awaits, Mrs. Ellis."

"Please . . ." She shook her head. "My name is Rachel."

"Good. I'm Steven," he answered, pleased to have advanced one step.

"Benjamin," another voice called, "what are you doing out there? I need—Oh, I didn't know we had a visitor." A tiny, reed-thin woman, her head covered with a brightly printed scarf, had come out of the door to the small house beside the garage. She held a potato in one hand and a large paring knife in the other. She advanced another step, and her mouth widened in a broad smile. "Steven! I found the potatoes, but why didn't you tell me you were here!" She hurried to the tall man and threw her arms around him. He almost lifted her from the ground with his hug. "Oh, it is good to see you after all this time. When Benjamin said you'd phoned I was so happy!"

She suddenly noticed Rachel standing beside the car. "And who is your pretty lady, Steven? You didn't tell me you were bringing . . ."

Startled, Steven stepped back a pace, suddenly at a loss for words, and Rachel felt her cheeks grow warm.

"No, no, dear, that's not . . . Wait, please." By

now Rabbi Geller was also red-faced and in some distress. "I am sorry I didn't introduce you sooner. Rachel Ellis, this is my wife, Devorah Geller, who jumps too quickly to conclusions." He frowned at his wife. "Mrs. Ellis—Rachel—has been stranded here by her tour bus, and Steven said he would drive her back to her hotel. We came to get the car."

Unperturbed by everyone else's discomfort, Devorah beamed at the small group. "Ah, well, it is very nice to meet you, Mrs. Ellis. Forgive my appearance." She looked down at her worn apron, the potato and knife. "Making latkes is a messy procedure. But," she assured the others, "they'll be ready soon, and we will light the candles."

"I didn't think potato latkes were traditional for Hanukkah down here, too," Rachel observed. "I always heard it was a custom from eastern Europe."

"We still like to observe the traditions we grew up with," Benjamin Geller explained. "We came here after the war, from Poland. And Steven loves them, so it's become our tradition here as well. Steven always arrives with a large bag of potatoes. The customs men all know the 'crazy American.' "

"Well"—Rachel smiled—"God helps those who help themselves, my husband always said. So, I guess if you want latkes, you'd better make sure there are potatoes."

Devorah Geller beamed at her visitor. She'd noted that mention of a husband in the past tense. "Mrs. Ellis—may I also call you Rachel?—if you have no plans for tonight I would be so happy if you'd stay and share our dinner. It is good to be with friends on a joyous occasion." She spoke with such eagerness and sincerity it would have been hard to refuse her, though that was Rachel's first instinct. As it turned out, she wasn't given time to do that.

"That's a terrific idea!" Steven exclaimed. "We can't let you eat in some impersonal hotel dining room when the smell of Devorah's potato pancakes is in the air!"

"Of course, I should have thought of that myself," the rabbi said happily.

"But I—I'm not dressed. I'm so dirty . . . No, I couldn't, really . . ."

Her hesitation caught Steven's ear, and he pounced on it. "Sure you can. Tell you what, I'll drive you to your hotel right now and wait while you freshen up. Then we'll come back and later get a cab to our hotels. Come on, whadaya say?" He felt a quick rush. How could he ignore the lucky chance Devorah had thrown his way, this chance to get to know Rachel a little?

"What a wonderful idea," Devorah agreed happily, and her husband chorused approval.

431

"Well . . . all right," Rachel heard herself say, and was surprised at the words yet glad they'd been spoken. With a sense of anticipation she hadn't felt in months, she opened the car door while Steven got behind the wheel.

"Are the Gellers a family of mind readers?" she murmured dryly, as the car began its slow ascent up the narrow street.

"I've sometimes thought the same thing," Steven chuckled. "What, exactly, made you ask?"

"How'd she know I was alone here? That's why she invited me; she can't ignore stray lambs."

"No, she can't. But it's no mystery. You look . . . oh, not so much lonely as alone."

She turned to stare at him, and he flushed. "Hey, look, I'm sorry. I didn't mean to sound rude. I just meant, well, you look kind of guarded, as if you've shut out the rest of the world. Some part of you is observing but not taking part." He grimaced, hands tightening on the wheel. "I'm not making this better, am I? I only meant, if I saw it you shouldn't be surprised that she did, too. That woman has the most amazing emotional antennae."

He shook his head, smiled. "And I should know!"

"Were you a stray lamb, too?"

He cocked his head, thought for a moment. "Yeah, I guess. It's been a long time since she

432

took me in, though, and I don't think about it much . . . not anymore."

"I'm curious: how long have you known them, and how did you meet them in the first place?"

"Oh, it's got to be eighteen or twenty years, now. You see, I'm with a drug manufacturer, up in Michigan and—"

"*What?* You're from *Michigan?* My God, I can't believe it—so am I!"

"You're kidding! Where from?"

"Detroit—well, really Southfield. You?"

"Kalamazoo." He grinned. "Do you think it's *ba-shert?*"

"Meant to be? Oh, I don't think Fate is taking any particular interest in my affairs," Rachel said tartly.

"Well, then, maybe mine." He smiled at her. "Damn, I can't get over the coincidence. Maybe Benjamin has some kind of mystic tie to Michigan, too. He's gonna make me a believer yet." They laughed together for a moment.

"Anyway, as I was saying, I'm a V.P. now . . . I'm looking ahead to permanent retirement. But when I came to this island for the first time I was a lowly detail man. I was sent down with my boss to discuss the possibility of opening a small manufacturing plant here, in conjunction with one of our European affiliates. It didn't work out, but for me it was the best business deal I ever took part in. At least for personal business." His face was serious for a moment, his gaze looking backward over a twenty-year span. "I met them, the Gellers, and I don't like to think what my life would have been like if it hadn't been for Benjamin and Devorah, and their children. I think Bev loved them almost as much as I did. I know they were very good for her."

"Bev? Is that your wife . . . ?"

"Yes, she was. Died a couple of years ago. You?"

"Mort passed awa—he died just after Thanksgiving last year. It was very sudden. We never had any time to—to plan or get used to it or . . ." She pressed her lips together, fists clenched in her lap.

"No time to suffer, either. No time to watch him waste away, die by inches, lose pieces of him one by one over the years." His voice was dark, hollow, the words almost inaudible over the sound of the car's motor. Rachel stared at him, the white knuckles of his hands clutching the steering wheel.

"What was it?" she asked quietly. "Was she ill very long?" This was, she realized, the first time in a long while she'd actually shown interest in or cared about someone else's troubles. Selfishness, she thought, is an easy habit to acquire.

"Bev had Alzheimer's; it began when she was barely forty." Bitterness crept into his voice, but was gone quickly.

"Forty." God in heaven, she must have been ill almost half their married life. "That must have been terrible for you," Rachel said, almost in a whisper.

He shook his head. "Worse for her. At the end I think it was a lot easier . . . By then she was in her own little world, a world she seemed very content to retreat to. But at the beginning, when she was still aware of what was happening to her, well, even though the progression was slow, we couldn't ever forget what was going on inside . . ." His quiet words trailed off into silence. He sighed. "To know, and know there's absolutely nothing you can do to change it, no treatment, no hope . . ."

She recalled her earlier thought. A lucky man, only good things in his world. Lucky.

She broke off the reflection as he turned into the cactus-lined driveway leading to the imposing Curaçao Caribbean Hotel. Steven passed just beyond the lovely tile-floored lobby that stood open to the fresh air and sunlight and pulled to a stop in the shade of a palm tree. Rachel realized the irony of the fact that this hotel had almost a monopoly on the island's supply of them.

Steven turned off the motor. "Look, I'm sorry I put a damper on the day. I don't usually talk about Bev and . . . all that, not for a long time now. Funny, how I opened up to you."

Yeah, funny.

"You're a good listener, but I apologize." His mouth turned up in a half-smile.

On impulse Rachel put a hand on his arm, the coarse hair that dusted well-defined muscles springy and rough under her fingers, the texture and warmth of his skin causing flares of unexpected excitement to spark through her. It was the first time she'd touched him since their brief handshake, the first time she'd touched any man in a long while; and the feel of his skin was so pleasant, so inviting, so . . . She pulled back abruptly.

"Please don't apologize," she said softly. "Sometimes you have to say the words, maybe to remind yourself that there were good times, too. And that it—death—*did* happen but that life goes on."

She recalled again the peculiar sensation of relief she'd felt in the rabbi's office when she'd spoken of Mort. "Kind of embarrassing to talk about it but . . ." Rachel was suddenly uncomfortable with the intimate level of their conversation. This man was really a stranger to her. And yet Steven Sandler didn't seem like a "stranger" at all, any more than his friend the rabbi.

"And I'm about the last person who should be telling you that," she added ironically. "Rabbi Geller seems to be the specialist in that department."

"As a matter of fact," Steven said quietly,

436

"you're right. He helped me more than I could ever repay. He's more to me than a rabbi, he's a good *friend.*" He looked at her again, saw the residue of pain in her eyes, the uncertainty on her face, and wished he could be the one to erase them.

Rachel glanced away, intent on avoiding his too-perceptive eyes. "Yes, I sensed that in him, the kindness and concern. I don't think you could know him and *not* be his friend."

They were suddenly roused by the harsh blare of the horn from a tour bus that had pulled in just behind them, its parking place blocked by the little car. Steven waved and pulled farther ahead.

"It's getting late," Rachel said. "I'll go change . . . I promise I'll hurry." She smiled and opened the door.

"Yeah, Devorah will have my hide if I ruin dinner. Go on, I'll wait here for you." He watched her walk toward the dim interior of the hotel lobby.

She moved very nicely, he noted, with grace and freedom. It was something most took for granted, but Beverly had been trapped in the prison of her mind for so many years and she had lost it. Steven would never take such freedom for granted.

* * *

"Damn!" Rachel's fingers fumbled with the backing of her small gold earring, and it disappeared into the pile of the carpeting. She spent frantic moments on her knees before the glint of daylight on metal caught her eye. She pushed herself stiffly to her feet and took a deep calming breath. "Ah, Rachel," she said to her reflection in the mirror as she finished putting on the second earring, "you're really losing it. You've been a hermit far too long." It was like a visit to the dentist, except now her whole body felt clumsy and numb, not just her lips.

And there was no reason for this awful jittery feeling, this nervous tension, no reason . . . other than Steven Sandler, she admitted. As implausible as it might be, as unexpected and irrational, it would be foolish to deny the undeniable. Head tilted thoughtfully, she gazed into the mirror. How else could she explain this sudden interest in hair, lipstick, the way her slacks fit a little too snugly across her "mature" hips, the circles under her eyes.

She turned as the sound of soft laughter, the tinkling of ice and glass from the lounge area below where pre-dinner cocktails were being served, intruded through the open balcony door. The memory of her mood the last time she'd been in this room came back. This morning. Just eight hours ago? And a smile touched her mouth. The contrast was so vivid.

Without ever being aware, without thought, she'd begun a transition, weeks, maybe months, ago. Rabbi Geller had spoken of taking a different path, a new direction. She didn't recall when she'd turned down this particular path, but one thing was clear. She was light years away from the woman who'd awakened in that bed this morning.

He was dozing behind the wheel when she returned to the car. In the uncaring limbo of sleep he looked touchingly vulnerable and younger than before. Her watch told her she'd set a personal record—fifteen minutes. Who said miracles don't happen!

He woke at the sound of the door opening. "Wha—? Oh! Boy, I must be more tired than I thought. Either jet lag's getting more intense or I'm getting less so!" He yawned, stretched, and Rachel admired what that did to his chest and shoulder muscles. She quickly busied herself with the door lock and seat belt to avert her face. She could feel the blush right down to her—*My God, Rachel, give it a rest!*

"Well, you are fast, lady," Steven said admiringly. "You deserve some kind of reward for that!" He turned the key and the motor hummed into life.

"Those potato pancakes will be my reward."

Way past time to put the pain behind her. *Too much mourning is as bad as too little.* Where was it written she couldn't enjoy herself with friends celebrating a holiday? And, after all, she owed it to the Gellers not to spoil their celebration. *My, my, how noble we are!* Rachel smiled to herself, unable to hide behind assumed virtue. This wasn't for them—this was for *her.* "Damn the cholesterol, full speed ahead!"

Steven grinned and shifted into gear, heading back to town. He glanced toward the blue sea visible below the drop-off of the low cliffs. "Funny, isn't it, everyone pictures these islands as some kind of lush and fertile tropical paradise, exotic flowers and rain forests all over the place. And it's really one of the driest spots I've ever seen."

Rachel looked out the window, the cool air blowing her short dark hair around her face. "You know, today was my first time away from the hotel," she explained. *First day away from my room.* But she was too embarrassed to mention that. "And I'm afraid the tour was wasted on me. I wasn't paying attention . . . too bogged down with, well, with other things." *Self-pity* wasn't a popular feature on most itineraries, just hers. She inhaled deeply and looked ahead, down the road. *Keep that thought, kiddo—just look ahead!*

"Oh, Steven, I meant to ask you"—she pointed toward the blue line of ocean and the rock-bound

440

shore—"what are those strange-looking trees, over there, by the water."

"They're divi-divis. They get that strange flat kind of shape because of their exposure to the wind. The sea breeze is so constant here that they're permanently bent into that twisted position. Kind of eerie looking, aren't they?"

"Yes, I've never seen anything like them."

"They're all over these islands. You haven't traveled the Caribbean much, have you?"

"Not at all," Rachel answered quietly. "We always meant to . . . when Mort retired and we had the," she almost choked on the word, "the time." She recalled her anger—was it only this morning?—that Mort had dared to die before they'd had a chance to do the things they'd put off all those years. It seemed such a shallow thought now. Strange, the anger—*and Mort*—were now receding, into the past, taking their places in the pantheon of a life's worth of memories, without the harsh immediacy they'd had this last year. She knew she was ready to let them go.

"So, how much longer will you be here?" he asked.

"Just about another week. This was such a last-minute decision, coming down here, that a ten-day charter was all that was available. Otherwise I'd have tried for two weeks." How could he know how comfortable this refuge was, this haven from the well-meaning but unwelcome attentions of friends and relatives back home.

"You said the tour today was wasted on you. I wonder if you would like to take a drive around the island with me tomorrow, see the sights, have lunch, or . . ."

His words drifted away under the soft thrum of the motor, the rush of warm air past the open car windows. For a moment Rachel was flustered, without words. A *man* was asking her to spend the day with him. Was that like a date? *My God, you are such an ass, Rachel. You're not some quivering virgin cornered in a car at the drive-in. He's offering himself as a tour guide, not a Don Juan.* She felt herself blush and rushed to answer before he noticed her hesitation.

"That sounds very nice. Are you sure the rabbi can spare the car?"

"Oh, no," Steven chuckled. "Even I wouldn't push our friendship that far. Uh-uh, I'll get a rental car at my hotel. How about ten tomorrow morning?"

"Sounds good. I should be able to pry my eyes open by then."

"Ah, another night person. The one thing I'm really looking forward to when I retire next month is sleeping past seven A.M. anytime I want."

"That late, hmm?" she said dryly.

He laughed and turned into the narrow drive

between the synagogue and the Gellers' small house. "Mmm, I can smell dinner way out here. Hello, Sara!" he called to the young woman who hurried out to meet them. Steven slammed the door and hugged her, then picked up the little boy, about three years old, whose hand she held. "Well, well, Joshie, you're getting so big *you'll* have to lift *me* up next time!"

Rachel waited quietly beside the car, as a young man, tanned and wearing casual slacks and plaid cotton shirt, followed the girl Steven had called Sara. He put his arm around her, obviously her husband, and clapped Steven on the shoulder with his other hand. "Welcome back, Steve. It's great to see you."

"Same here. I feel the batteries recharging already." He grinned and turned to Rachel. "Rachel Ellis, this is Sara, the Gellers' daughter, and her husband, David Harris. And, of course, Joshua Simon Harris, the *prince!*" They all laughed as he swung the little boy over his head, then set him back beside his parents. "Are Aaron and Angie here?"

"Oh Steve, you really are out of touch," Sara chuckled. "Aaron's doing post-graduate work in Amsterdam, and Angie's spending a few months in Israel, at a kibbutz."

"The Gellers are covering the world."

"Yeah, and if anything could upset my parents, that's it, especially with us living in New York now. You know my mother, she doesn't know how to cook for less than six people at a time." She laughed and leaned against her husband. "There's been a steady stream of 'care' packages between here and New York ever since my brother and sister left. We try to come down whenever we can so Mom and Dad don't get withdrawal symptoms."

They all walked inside, and Rachel found herself in a tiny, cluttered but bright and cheerful living room. Near the open window a cluster of wooden building blocks lay tumbled in disarray, and a soccer ball was wedged between a sofa and an end table. Comfortable, slightly shabby furniture was arranged in a haphazard conversational grouping, and books and assorted table-top picture frames were everywhere; there was more of an air of *mitteleuropa* than of the Caribbean about the room. It invited and welcomed and comforted, and Rachel loved it at once. She wouldn't have wanted to live with all the clutter, yet it was exactly what she needed right now. A sense of home, of family and purpose, of joy.

Devorah hurried in from the kitchen and quickly waved them into the dining room, its table already laden with platters and bowls. On the broad windowsill behind the table stood a large silver and lucite Hanukkah menorah, its stark contemporary lines a startling contrast to the utterly traditional furnishings of the house. The air was redolent with the aroma of freshly fried potato pancakes. Rachel heard her stomach gurgle, and hoped no one else did.

"Come, we will light the candle for the first night. Isn't this a beautiful menorah, Steven? Angie sent it from Israel for our anniversary last month. All right, Joshua." Rabbi Geller beckoned to his grandson. "Here is the service candle." He lifted him in his arms and straightened the skullcap on the boy's head. "First we say the blessings to God, and then we will light the *shammos* and you will use it to light the candle for the first night of the festival." The little boy grinned and hugged his grandfather. After Benjamin Geller recited the Hebrew phrases, Joshua carefully touched the flame from the service candle to the single candle in the menorah. Each successive night one more candle would be lit until, on the last night, all eight would be ablaze.

Rachel's eyes were moist by the time they sat down to eat, yet strangely it was more from a sense of nostalgia than sadness. She looked up and found Steven's eyes on her, his smile telling her he understood exactly what she was feeling. *Well, that's ridiculous. Even I don't know what I'm feeling, how should he, a perfect stranger?*

She knew what Mort would say: Nobody's perfect.

An impulsive bubble of laughter almost escaped her. She suddenly realized how often lately she'd thought of Mort . . . and not felt pain or anger. Just affection and comfort. She looked at Steven again, and wondered if it was just coincidence.

She was relieved that at that moment they all began to busy themselves with dinner. Some thoughts were best left unexamined until a later time, away from the very disturbing presence of Steven Sandler and the perceptive eyes of Geller, Inc. Right now, the inner woman demanded attention. For the next half-hour she got it.

"Mmmm, this is delicious, Mrs. Geller!" Rachel finally had to put down her fork. There wasn't room in her entire body for one more mouthful. It had been a very long time since she'd enjoyed a meal with such uninhibited gusto. "If my son Kenny, the eating machine, ever found his way to Curaçao you'd never get out of the kitchen."

"Please, please, just because I'm married to a rabbi you don't have to be so formal. It's Devorah—please!"

"Well," Steven said, laughing and helping himself to the last of the potato pancakes and a generous dollop of sour cream, "since Kenny can't be here I'll try to take his place. And I'll call you anything you want as long as you cook like this!"

"I'll bet Rachel makes latkes as good as mine. This isn't anything unusual," Devorah answered, smiling innocently.

446

"Mommy," Joshua whispered urgently just at that moment, "when do I get my *present*?"

"What Joshua knows about subtlety could be written on the head of a pin." Sara laughed.

"With enough room left over for his grandmother's knowledge of the same subject," Benjamin interjected dryly.

Rachel tried valiantly to blend into the upholstery. When that didn't seem to work she merely sat quietly and studied her empty plate. Steven, too, sat quietly, studying Rachel.

It was left to Sara and David to banish the awkward silence that had suddenly descended on the little group. "Come on, slugger." David pinched Josh on the ear. "There's a little something in my pocket for somebody, but I don't know who to give it to."

"Me, me! You c'n give it to me, Daddy!" Josh wriggled frantically on his father's lap, and David finally took pity on him. From his shirt pocket he pulled a small net bag filled with foil-wrapped chocolate coins. "Here's some Hanukkah gelt, and save one for your mother." He grinned at his wife, then at the others. "She'd kill for chocolate, and I don't want to spoil this trip."

"Hmmph. On a Dutch island I'm in no danger of doing without chocolate, smart ass. *I* know where to be born!"

"Sara! Such language! I'm surprised at you!"

Her father's reproof tempered Sara's gaiety, slightly.

"Sorry, Daddy. Didn't mean to say that." She laughed, eyes twinkling. "I guess David's wicked ways are corrupting me."

"Don't you blame David," Devorah admonished. "He's a wonderful boy." The "wonderful boy" beamed.

"My mother thinks the center of the universe is in my house, divided evenly between my two men." Sara winked at Rachel. "Me, I'm just the lucky little scullery maid who's fortunate enough to be able to clean up after them." She stuck out her tongue at her laughing husband.

"I know what you mean," Rachel chuckled. "My daughter says I'd probably walk backward across the state of Michigan if my son-in-law asked me to. She says I'm a pushover for him." She reached over and patted David's arm. "She's probably right. She thinks it's 'cause I was so grateful to get rid of her."

Joshua let out a huge yawn from a chocolate-smeared mouth.

"And I think you're going to get rid of us now, folks," David said. He stood up. "The kid's motor has finally run down."

Sara kissed her parents good night. "Great meeting you, Mrs. Ellis." She grinned at Steven and gave him a hug, then looked back at Rachel. "I'm sure we'll be seeing you again."

After they'd gone upstairs to put Josh to bed and Rachel had helped Devorah clean up the dishes, despite loud and repeated protests, Steven called for a cab. "It's getting late, and we've got a full day tomorrow." The Gellers looked at each other, content. Their mutual look said it all: a job well done.

It wasn't lost on either Rachel or Steven. The ride back was strangely silent after all the noise and conversation at the dinner table. The only sound in the dilapidated old taxi was the soft humming of the driver in tune with a song on the radio. At Rachel's hotel Steven got out and walked with her to the lobby.

"Look, I'm—"

"Steven, you don't—"

They laughed awkwardly. "Ladies first," he said, wondering why he was so ill at ease.

"I just wanted to tell you that if you want to forget about tomorrow it's okay. No problem."

No problem. He almost laughed aloud. There was a problem, all right. She was standing right here in front of him and her name was Rachel Ellis. "Unless you tell me you don't want to go I'll be here at ten o'clock tomorrow morning."

His eyes were steady and sure, and Rachel forgot for a moment where she was or what she was doing here. Her key hung on her finger, forgotten, and all she could think of was how good the smell of a man's aftershave could be, how comforting the warmth of his body standing so close. Only not "a man." Steven. Her throat was dry, and she forgot how to swallow, so intense was his gaze. She knew at that moment there was no way on God's green earth she would miss tomorrow's tour. Or the tour guide.

Nothing was worse than second thoughts. Or third. Rachel put the phone down. Again. For the fourth time she didn't call Steven's hotel to cancel their plans for the day. If she had the guts to admit it to herself she was scared shitless. In over thirty years she'd not gone out alone with a man other than Mort. Not ever . . . well, not until yesterday's ride to the hotel. It hadn't been something she'd planned or thought about, it just *was*. If she hadn't been with Mort, or the kids, she'd been with friends, *female* friends. But after the charming and strangely disturbing evening at the Gellers' she was nervous and apprehensive.

What should she wear? What would they talk about? Did she have enough deodorant on? Oh, God! This was worse than her wedding day. What the hell was wrong with her? After all, this wasn't a real *date*. He was being polite, a nice guy making a nice gesture. And she ought to take advantage of the opportunity to see the island with someone who knew it, even if that "someone" was a *man!* When would she have the chance again?

450

It didn't mean she had to think of dipping her toes into the he-and-she world of even numbers and couples again. Oh, sure, everyone was thinking that sometime, way down the line, on some long-distant day, she might start *dating* again. But she wasn't thinking it—not now, not ever.

Never is a long time. Is that really what you want, Rachel my girl? An endless vista of dreary days and lonely nights, tears and old photo albums to keep you from the cold? Is that what Mort would want for you?

She thought of Steven Sandler's warm smile, his hard muscular arm, the heat of his hand, and his firm handshake. Those gentle and persistent gray eyes, the dark fringe of lashes—Good grief! Knock it off, dummy. Just think of Steven Sandler as a tour guide. At the end of the day just say so long, it's been nice! And that will be that.

Her heart lurched when the telephone rang. "Mr. Sandler is here, Mrs. Ellis."

"Yes. I'll be right down, thank you." Frankly, all things being equal, she'd rather climb into bed and sink into a deep senseless sleep—for about a week. Yeah, that sounded wonderful.

No, that sounded like a lie. A coward's way out, safe and unthinking and definitely cowardly.

What had Rabbi Geller said? You can't give up on life. She sighed. Of course he was right. You always had to *try.* It was one of the things she'd admired about Mort, the refusal to give up, give

451

in. He was—he *had been*—a stubborn man, who couldn't—*wouldn't*—quit. That was also one of the things that had exasperated her, she thought wryly.

So, what had she done in the year and the month since Mort's death? Easy answer: she'd done nothing, she'd quit. Gone down with the ship, hadn't fired a shot. Not with a bang but a whimper. God, what an awful memorial for the man Mort Ellis had been. Rachel drew in a deep breath, straightened her shoulders, looked in the mirror. Backhanding away the film of perspiration on her forehead, she winked at herself. *At least the man doesn't bite.* Or does he?

A little bit of wishful thinking, kiddo? She had to laugh at that. This new path was getting to be interesting. Very interesting.

"No iguana today. We couldn't catch any."

Rachel stared at the young waiter, his face deadpan serious. She swallowed and shook her head weakly. Steven laughed and then so did the waiter.

"It's a little joke they have for the tourists," Steven confided, "only I don't think it's really a joke. Oh, and the okra and cactus soup is supposed to be very good. So is the goat-meat stew."

Rachel gave a delicate shudder and opted instead for a prosaic platter of fried fresh fish and potatoes. Steven ordered the same. "No adventure in my soul. And they say goat meat is so low in cholesterol."

"Like I always say: cholesterol be damned." She grinned, thoroughly at ease and enjoying the day immensely. They'd driven westward from Willemstad through the *cunucu*, the countryside which bore a strong resemblance to Arizona, Rachel had observed. Past small thatch-roofed houses in villages where women could be seen pounding cornmeal and fishermen repaired their nets, they had inched their way through a donkey roadblock. "God, they're even more stubborn than I am," Steven had muttered during the seemingly interminable wait for the animals to get out of the way. "No wonder they call them jackasses." Once clear, their first stop had been the Landhuis Jan Kock. The large seventeenth-century estate house had been meticulously restored, and it was impressive; but the view from this small seaside restaurant was the highlight of the day.

Their white cloth-covered table was set in the corner of a narrow terrace overlooking the crowded beach of Westpunt. The place, obviously popular with tourists and Curaçaoans alike, was completely full. The table on their right was occupied by a young couple who seemed sublimely indifferent to anything the waiter could provide. Rachel had the uncomfortable feeling they might at any moment decide to fulfill their fantasies in the middle of the tablecloth.

She glanced to her left. Three women of a certain age, as the French would put it, ignoring the dregs of their iced tea, were casting surreptitious glances at an apparently oblivious Steven. They were beautifully groomed and dressed, with a fastidious concern for the "casual" look, and they were part of a tour group that had stopped at Jaanchie Christiaan's beachfront restaurant. Given the directions of their eyes and their smiles Rachel wasn't dumb or naive enough to think they were seeking a bonding experience with her. She leaned forward to catch Steven's next words.

"I asked you what made you choose Curaçao for a vacation." Whatever the reason, he gave thanks for her choice. He was thoroughly enjoying her company. She was pretty and funny and intelligent, and he liked the way the sunshine glowed on her cheeks, the faint scent of her perfume, the way her tousled dark hair fell in disarray over her forehead. She wasn't forever fixing her hair or worrying about her lipstick—or making him feel she was closing in for the kill.

"Frankly," Rachel answered, "it was the first brochure I saw on my travel agent's desk, and the scenery looked as different from a Michigan winter as anything I could find. I decided on the spur of the moment, and since I didn't need a passport it seemed as good a choice as any." She looked around, then propped her head on her hand and gazed at him over the glass of lemonade in front of her. "I've been wondering if it was such a good choice. Everywhere I look I seem to be surrounded by couples or by groups of single women who would like to *be* part of a couple." He knew behind the sunglasses her eyes sparkled. "He-ing and she-ing is rampant on this island. Do you think it's something in the water?"

He threw back his head and laughed, loud and long, then put his hand over hers and squeezed. She grinned back at him, and knew the rest of the day would be as good as the beginning. The three women all looked slightly sad, slightly envious, and Rachel suddenly hoped that somewhere they, too, would meet someone like Steven, someone who would help them see how lovely the world was, how good life could be, someone who would make them feel glad just to hear his laughter.

Don't be so smug. Maybe those ladies are better off . . . They're discovering that life can be good just because you're ready to enjoy it, that you don't need someone else to make it that way for you. Remember, eight days will go by very fast and if you're not careful good-by will be no laughing matter. No, she mustn't undo the progress she was making. Not for some laughter and a few hours of Steven's companionship. Rachel carefully pulled her hand free.

Steven felt bereft of more than her hand. She

455

had withdrawn in some indefinable, intangible way. He, too, was aware of the ladies. He'd spotted them as soon as they'd spotted him. He recognized them immediately, though they'd certainly never met. Any middle aged man, unattached and reasonably eligible, would be a magnet for their attentions. He didn't flatter himself; they were probably lonely and he was available— they hoped.

He smiled at the irony. They were looking, and he wasn't interested. He was interested in Rachel, but she wasn't looking. Life was too damned perverse for his taste.

"You know, there's nothing wrong with a little he-ing and she-ing." His mouth twitched with a smile. "It sure seems to make life interesting." They both glanced at the young couple who by now were almost in each other's laps. Their sandwiches lay untouched on the plates. "You can almost see 'newlywed' tattooed on their foreheads," Steven whispered indulgently.

"It's been a long time since I felt that kind of enjoyment," Rachel mused. A *very* long time since she'd enjoyed *that*. "As if I couldn't allow myself joy or pleasure. I was angry, all the time, at Mort, at myself. And I think I was afraid to let go of anger because I didn't know what would take its place."

"Yeah," Steven nodded thoughtfully, "I know what you mean. First you hang on to the grief, and that fills the void. Then, the awful loneliness, the *aloneness*. And when that passes you grab hold of anger. But once that's gone . . ." He paused, shrugged, and she picked up his thoughts.

"When that's gone, as my son would say, you have to 'get a life.' And that's terrifying." She looked out at the surf-lashed shoreline. "What if I can't? What if there isn't one to get?"

Steven took her hand again, this time holding it tightly between his. "After Bev died it took me a while, but I finally found that if I just let myself get caught up in living, if I didn't work so hard at resisting—and believe me, that wasn't as simple as it sounds"—his voice was laced with irony—"it turned out to be much easier than if I'd held on to my resentment."

Rachel gripped his hand hard, stared at him. "Resentment. Funny, you're the first person to understand that. That's *exactly* what I felt. That's *all* I could feel for a long time, whenever I thought of Mort's . . . dying." She grimaced. "The ever-dreaded 'D' word."

"Yes, we avoid it as much as we can, don't we?" That had a nice sound to it—*we*. "Come on! Let's go for a walk." He gestured to the beach below. "I need to work off those French fries." He needed to keep moving, have something besides her face to look at, to think about . . . until later. Later he'd have to do a lot of thinking about her.

Within moments they were picking their way along the rocky shore. "Not much sand, but the coral is beautiful!" Rachel exclaimed, bending to pick up an oddly shaped chunk of brain coral. "I'll take this home for a souvenir."

"With all that duty-free shopping in town you want this? I don't believe it!"

"Now, Steven, you don't believe all that propaganda about women and shopping. I'm disappointed in you." She laughed up at him. "Actually, I hate to shop. Mort was the buyer in our family. He loved to go shopping with me for clothes or to poke around in shops and flea markets when we were on vacation. Me, I'm lazy, I'd rather lie in the shade with a book."

"Okay, okay, I apologize," he said, laughing. "Too bad, all those shops going bankrupt because you prefer the great outdoors."

"Well, don't feel too bad. My daughters don't share my sentiments. I'll have to bring them back something from all those 'poor bankrupt shops,' which always seem to be filled with people carrying overstuffed shopping bags. I think the shopowners are very good at stalking the 'great white cruise ships'!"

He grinned and asked her, "How many daughters do you have? I thought you only had a son."

"Lord, don't let the girls hear that. They think I treat him like a king already. Kenny's the youngest. Geri is the oldest, and then there's

Molly-in-the-middle. And of course the next generation. I'm a proud grandmother, but I don't tote pictures to the beach. I can show you some later if you want."

"Yeah," he said softly, "I want." He looked at her sun-pinked face, the round cheeks and chin, velvet soft, her hair tossed carelessly by the offshore trade winds. She'd turned toward the sea for a moment, head thrown back, inhaling deeply of the fresh salt air, her shirt molded to her attractive woman's body by the incessant splash of ocean spray, utterly unaware of the lovely picture she made. *Yes,* Steven admitted to himself in that moment, *I'm beginning to want her, badly.*

The thought was disturbing. It had been an awfully long time since such a thought had crossed his mind, and he wasn't really prepared for it, for all the possibilities it raised, all the questions. "Tell you what, why don't we start back toward town and I'll pick you up this evening. We'll go to dinner. Have you ever had rijsttafel?"

"I don't know. Is it anything like goat stew?" she asked, a wry smile on her lovely mouth.

He tore his gaze from that mouth. "My God, don't even mention goat stew in the same breath. Rijsttafel isn't just a meal, it's an experience. Come on, we'll head back to the car, and I'll drop you at your hotel. I've a couple of calls to make, so I'll come by about seven-thirty. Okay?"

"Okay!" Funny, all of a sudden her seclusion and solitude were full of Steven Sandler. And she thought that wasn't such a bad thing. At that moment she felt an overpowering urge, a need to call home, speak to her children, touch base with the old Rachel, refresh her memory as to who and what she was. Because the old Rachel was blossoming into something brand new.

Yes, a few minutes of conversation with Geri and Molly, and maybe a call to Kenny, would get her perspective in order. She hoped. Her sense of loyalty was suddenly in need of attention. *Oh boy, that's all I need now, an attack of Jewish guilt.* But, she realized suddenly, she really didn't need to talk to them. She had to rely on her own instincts and judgment, then hope they'd agree and understand. It wasn't their future, it was up to her to figure out where she was now on this new path.

And wherever that was, it didn't shed any light on where she was going.

Rachel groped for Steven's hand and he took hold of hers. A moment later they walked up the path to the car, smiling at each other.

"Either they'll have to roll me off this island or it'll sink under my weight." Rachel sat back in the deep chair and pushed her plate away. It was almost completely clean. "That was maybe the best meal I've ever eaten. It's just not my idea of Dutch food."

"That's because it isn't," Steven said. "It's Indonesian. The Dutch merely adopted it from their colonies."

"I don't blame them; they're very smart people. My God, a twenty-course buffet! They've discovered the perfect food . . . one meal can last a lifetime. I don't think I'll ever eat again."

"Oh, yeah. Well, tomorrow we can test that theory. Curaçao may be small but we haven't finished yet," he said, the corners of his eyes crinkling with good humor. "How about ten o'clock again? You game?"

"You bet. Lay on, MacDuff. If today was a sample, you've missed your calling. You're a terrific guide."

"No." He shook his head, studying her face. "Maybe you were just ready for the tour."

She stared at him for a long moment. Then her mouth began to turn up, and the gentle smile glowed in her eyes. "You know what they say: in life, timing is everything. I guess our timing was right." In a sudden moment of clarity she heard her own words and wished she could have ripped out her tongue before she'd let them loose. Boy, if *that* didn't sound like a come-on!

"Well . . . it's really late, Steven. I think I'd better get back to my hotel." She tried to inject a modicum of coolness between them. Polite and

461

friendly, but not too friendly. God, it was tough walking that thin line between acting poised and acting predatory. The single life was exhausting. "Ten A.M. it is, then. I'll be ready and waiting, that is, if anything I brought with me still fits." Good God, everything, inside and out, is changing shape on me!

The next morning, and all the mornings for the rest of the week, dawned clear and beautiful, and exciting. That last, Mother Nature could take no credit for. Steven Sandler was responsible for the spice in her island stew. The week slipped past with the speed of light. Each day, whether spent at the Curaçao Seaquarium or wandering the charming old-world streets of Willemstad in search of gifts to bring home or just vegetating beside the pool, there was a sense of discovery, and rediscovery. Discovering the things that made Steven the kind and intense and stubborn man he was, a man who could comfort and console or buck impossible odds and make her laugh, make her begin to want, and dream about "what if ..." She was rediscovering the woman she had once been, one who could strike out on her own if she wished, not needing to seek approval from anyone but herself; who could look beyond the narrow confines of the life she'd once made and see what lay over the next hill. Who wasn't afraid to take that first step.

But she couldn't deny that more and more she felt that step would be more exciting with Steven beside her.

Toward the end of the week he tried to convince her to go with him on a scuba-diving trip. "You can't imagine how magnificent it is down there. Another world!"

"I have enough trouble right now in coping with *this* world, thank you very much." Rachel settled herself more firmly on the brightly striped chaise longue and adjusted her sunglasses. "I'll wait here while you go." She grinned up at him. "It'll be the first peace and quiet I've had all week, you pest. I'll finally get past chapter two of this book."

He leaned back on his elbows and shrugged, smiling. "I'm still not sure whether you're lazy or chicken."

"Bawk, bawk," she chirped from behind her book. "Why can't I be both?"

He chuckled and tickled the bottoms of her feet. "I'll show you what a pest I can be. And next time we're here, you are going diving with me." He lay back on his lounger, eyes closed, one hand resting on her shoulder.

Next time. She slanted a glance toward him behind her dark, concealing lenses. Did he really mean . . . ? Rachel made herself stay still, but slowly, casually, she put one hand on top of his.

Next time.

* * *

"Despite all that number thirty-five sun block, I know I'll look like a pair of old shoes by the time I go home. But the sun is too glorious to waste." Rachel sat up, stretched, and began to gather up her towel and beach bag. She patted her stomach. "A *large, out-of-shape* pair of old shoes. I have consumed more calories these last seven days than anyone since Diamond Jim Brady or maybe Godzilla." She shook her head and grimaced. "I'll never make fun of the eating machine again. I know now where Kenny gets those genes. Yuck! Me!"

"Well, I've only seen pictures of Ken but he doesn't look as if your genes have done him any harm." Steven gazed up at her from his lounge chair, admiring all over again this lovely woman who'd turned his life inside out in the short space of seven days.

Seven days. She'd leave and . . . and what? *Will you let her go, just like that? You've been a hardass all your life; you fought for jobs, promotions, new accounts, against Bev's illness, against despair and grief, and pity, against every obstacle you ever encountered. What the hell happened to your spine? When did you lose your balls?*

At that he smiled to himself. He knew exactly where *they* were. The time he spent with Rachel

464

was proving to be a painful reminder. He shifted uncomfortably, pulling the towel over his thighs.

"You know, tomorrow is the last night of Hanukkah—"

"And my last night here," she interjected slowly.

"Yes." They stared at each other for a heartbeat. "Well, the Gellers asked if we'd like to come over and spend the evening. I didn't know if you . . ."

"Of course! I want to see them again. I haven't had much of a chance this week, but I feel very close to them," Rachel said. She owed them both a lot. She wasn't sure yet just how much. But more than she could ever repay, whatever happened.

"Okay, I'll tell them. But that means tonight is our"—he didn't even want to say the words—"our last night. So, let's make it a special evening."

"Where are we going?"

"Don't be so nosy. It's a secret."

"I'm not nosy, I'm curious. And, for God's sake, don't mention the cat. If you start speaking in clichés I'll be disappointed in you." She smiled. "Come on, give. Tell me where."

" 'Tell me where, Daddy,' " he whined, then grinned at her.

"You hardly remind me of my daddy, Steven." *Hardly!*

"Well, you can put bamboo shoots under my

465

nails and I'll never tell! The only way is to go along."

Rachel made a face. "Then I'll go along. I'd never waste perfectly good bamboo shoots on you. I'll be ready at seven."

"Dancing! Oh, Steven, I haven't been dancing in—God, I can't even remember when. It has to be twenty Bar Mitzvahs ago! Mort never really liked to dance. He'd get out on the floor for the slow ones, if he'd had a couple of drinks first. After a while I took pity on him and gave up." She looked longingly out at the couples on the crowded floor. "But I used to love it!"

"Well, let's get to our table first, and then . . . then we'll see how much punishment your toes can take. It's been quite a few years for me, too." Steven held out her chair while she sat down, smoothing the flaring skirt of the silk dress over her thighs. He knew, without knowing how he knew, what the silk and her hot, sun-bronzed skin would feel like if he slid his hand where hers had been . . .

He quickly sat down opposite her at the small table covered with white linen, silver, and crystal. The fresh hibiscus was a bit paler than the color in her cheeks. Her eyes were glittering in the flickering candlelight, and shadows were pooling in the hollow of her neck, the valley between her breasts.

The cynical old joke flashed through his head: in the dark they're all the same. Bullshit. Somehow he knew nothing and no one would ever be the same as Rachel. His mind knew it, his body knew it. His heart knew it. There, it was finally out in the open, the one thought he'd feared, kept submerged, until now. But he couldn't say anything. She'd turn and run all the way back to Michigan if he told her what he was thinking. If *he* was having trouble with the idea, what the hell would it do to her?

They ordered dinner, and when the small combo began to play "Where or When" Steven took Rachel's hand and drew her out onto the dance floor, into his arms. She felt perfect there. *This is where I belong.* The thought crackled through her mind, and she stiffened in his arms. But his hand on her back, his fingers gentling her nervousness, the solid strength of his shoulder beneath her hand—all melted away her apprehension. She knew what it was, what it had to be. It was just so long since she'd danced . . . *so long since she'd been held.* She closed her eyes and let the lovely flow of melody and rhythm take over. Let the movement of his body direct her, the pressure of his hand . . . against the length of him, her body melting into his, dipping and swaying and so close each could sense the

467

other's intent before a move was made . . . as one.

But she'd spent almost all of her adult years as half of "one." One pair. One couple. Could she turn her back on those years as if they'd never been? Was she so fickle? Or was she so horny!

The attempt to shock herself didn't work. She was still in Steven's arms and had no desire to be anywhere else. This wasn't something she'd sought. She hadn't dressed to the nines and gone for the kill, looking for eligible men. She and Steven had just found each other. That was something it wasn't possible to ignore, or forget. Or turn away from.

"You're a wonderful dancer, Rachel. You feel," he sighed, "so good in my arms." He hadn't meant to say that. But she didn't pull away. He tightened his hold, pulled her closer, and he could smell the perfume of her hair, the sunshine and 'musk and spice that were Rachel. Always Rachel. He held her tightly, and they swayed together in the midst of the other dancers, hardly moving, hardly speaking. Not needing words.

The music ended, and both felt regret and relief. Too quick. Too intense. Too sudden.

Back at the table they sat quietly, watching the dancers, watching each other. "You must have enjoyed dancing a lot when you were married." She knew it was a perverse desire to dissipate the strange mood she was in, deliberately bringing his wife to share their table. It was a desperate gambit, made in self-defense, and she was ashamed of herself for using it. But she waited to hear his answer.

Steven's look was direct, steady. He almost seemed to read her thoughts. "Yes, a very long time ago. Bev was ill for so long, and then in a wheelchair, well, dancing was a pleasure we gave up a lifetime ago." Sadness and regret lay beneath the quiet words. She realized all over again what patience and fortitude he'd needed all those years. His life, and Bev's, had been taken, ravaged. If anyone was entitled to self-pity, it was Steven. But he had handled his despair and broken dreams with a courage and strength that she hadn't ever found in herself in the days after Mort's death.

She had a vivid recollection of Steven the first time she'd seen him, standing at the door of the rabbi's office, silhouetted against the light of the sanctuary windows behind him. And then of his smile, full of joy and eagerness. Funny, how suddenly the tour guide's words sounded louder now in her mind than they had the day they'd put her to sleep. . . . *the Israelites wandered in the desert.* That was what her life had become in the past thirteen months—a desert. She'd been stumbling through it, weighted down with a burden of self-pity, and while she knew she'd slowly begun to find her way out of it, it had taken this man, this dear, good, caring man, to show her what she could find on this new path—if she dared to look.

"I think I'd like to dance one more," Rachel said clearly, and this time it was she who led him to the floor, she who nestled close and turned into his embrace, who held him tightly and told him with her body, so unused to this sensual language of music and motion, all the things he wanted to hear. All the things they were ready to tell each other.

"Are you sure about this, Rachel?"

"Nope, not at all." They stood close, facing each other in the bedroom of his suite at the hotel. "I'm fifty-three years old, a zaftig middle-aged housewife who not only hasn't been around the block, she doesn't even know where the block is or what direction to take if she ever got to it." She shrugged, a mischievous smile on her mouth. "But you're such a great tour guide, Steven, I figured you'd show me around."

She smiled joyously, suddenly very calm. It was almost as if she'd rehearsed this scene in her mind countless times. And maybe she had. Who knew what she'd been dreaming all week: she never remembered the next morning, but this felt very . . . well, damn, it actually felt comfortable.

She walked to the dresser and watched herself in the mirror as she took off her earrings and laid them on the uncluttered surface. "I didn't realize how neat you are. I guess there's a lot I don't know about you." She took off her bracelet . . . and slipped the wedding band from her left hand. "But I want to find out."

Steven stood where she'd left him, watching her, sensing this new air of decisiveness. He liked it, he decided, but he wondered where she was heading.

She proceeded to show him. She came toward him, seeming to sway slightly in the dimly lit room. One by one, the buttons of his shirt were undone, and she slipped it from his shoulders with a fluid feathery motion. When she ran her fingers up and down his arms he suddenly came to life.

"That's enough," he whispered hoarsely. "It's about time we started where we left off." He held her face between his hands and bent to kiss her.

It was all the things she'd dreamed his kiss could be, had known it would be. It was gentle and sweet, demanding and eager. It sent coils of sensation spiraling downward through her body, delicious tremors across her skin. Flushed with a heat no sun could ever bring, she wished she could give up breathing forever just so she wouldn't have to part from him. Nothing had ever tasted as sweet as his mouth.

When at last they did part it was to stare at each other without speaking or breaking the magic of the moment. Then, with a quiet sigh, Rachel went into his arms again, stood there holding him, savoring his scent, the hard strength of him, the gentle caress of his hands on her body. His fingers slowly inched the zipper down the back of her dress, and the fan-cooled air sent shivers down her spine. Or was it the air? She smiled. She wasn't that stupid!

"Steven, please . . . turn off the light."

"Why, Rachel? I want to look at you, when we—"

"I think I'd rather leave some things to your imagination, my dear. Much more satisfying, believe me!"

"You're wrong. But if you'll feel better, off it goes." He reached behind her and pressed the switch on the table lamp. The room disappeared into a hazy blur of silvery moonlight, and dappled reflections from the mirror lay in stripes across the ceiling. The only sound for a moment was the hum of the ceiling fan and their uneven breathing. Then he took her hand and they walked together to the bed.

"I don't need to see you to know how beautiful you are right now. I think I've known that from the first time I heard you laugh that day in the synagogue. You're face was sad, yet your laugh was delightful. As if you wanted to enjoy happiness but had forgotten how." He slipped the

472

dress down over her hips, sliding her slip down with it. When she shivered he held her close to keep her warm.

In a few moments they were lying beneath the cool sheets, and he leaned over her to kiss her again. The gentleness became a fierce, deep wanting, a hunger he hadn't realized was within him, waiting until this moment, this woman.

"Ah, Steven, it's been so long . . ."

"For me too." He kissed her throat, her shoulders; and when he took her heavy breast into his mouth, his tongue suckling the pebbled crest, they arched together as if an electric current had passed between them. His hands moved over her hot skin with an urgency he wanted to control, and could not.

When his fingers pushed through the thick curls between her thighs and caressed the moist heat of her, Rachel gasped and twisted restlessly, incoherent words caught in her throat. Prickles of heat flared, raced across her skin, and when at last Steven filled her, became part of her, it was as if, after so long a time, her body and her heart had finally come back to life.

Later, much later, they slipped away from conscious thought and slept, the deep dreamless sleep of contentment and fulfillment, wrapped in each other's arms. As she held him to her Rachel's eyes filled with tears of gratitude. They'd been so lucky, finding each other, discovering this joyous renewal of life and of all the things life can be, should be. So lucky.

"So, do you respect me in the morning?" He was propped on one elbow, lying on his side, watching her wake up to the new day.

"Mm-hm," Rachel murmured, then yawned. "After all, you didn't go all the way on the *first* date. I could see right away you're not that kind of guy."

"See, I knew there were depths of wisdom and understanding in you. I'm glad I got to, uh, explore your depths."

She swatted him on the side of the head. "Smart ass. I'll give you 'depths'!"

"There's *more?* No, wait, I'm just kidding!" He laughed, and hugged her with the exuberance of a young boy. "I swear, I feel like a kid. Ah, Rachel, you are . . . wonderful!" His expression was ineffably tender and his smoky dark eyes made love to her all over again.

"Please, Steven," she said, flustered and suddenly shy. She pulled the sheet higher over her chest. "You don't have to say all those—"

He sat up abruptly. "I know I don't *have* to—I want to. I think you're wonderful and exciting and—well, do I have to sit down and make a list?"

"I—I'm nothing special," she stammered. "My kids are always telling me my clothes just fade into the woodwork. My hair is the same as it's been for God knows how many years, I could certainly stand to lose more than a few pounds, and . . . and I bite my nails!''

He laughed and hugged her; then he grew serious again. "Look, do you remember those ladies at lunch the other day, at the beach? Well, I didn't notice their nails, but they *were* beautifully dressed; their hair was, even to my ignorant eyes, obviously styled within an inch of its life; and they were *skinny*." He made a face. "Scrawny is more like it." He took her hands, held them firmly. "And you're wrong, you know, Rachel Ellis. You are a very, very special lady. I think your husband must have known it, known how lucky he was. I know it too. How come you don't know it?"

She turned her head away from him, but he saw the tears gathered beneath her lashes. He cocked his head, then touched her cheek with one finger, wiping away the tears. So soft, smooth. Sure, the lines were there, you couldn't mistake her skin for a twenty-five-year-old girl's. And that was just fine with him. His heart beat a little faster, his hormones flowed a lot swifter, because of a *woman*, a woman who'd experienced life, been tempered by it, and knew what was important and lasting.

"A special lady," he repeated. "Look, Rachel honey, I know this is happening too fast, but I don't want us to waste any more time: the minutes become days and years. We both know life can play some dirty tricks on you, and often you don't get any choice. But this we *can* choose. I know what I feel, and I know it will only grow stronger. If you aren't sure, well, I can wait."

"It's so hard to believe this can be happening. I've always *known* where I was, and where I'd *be*. I never wanted to improvise. My life was *set*. And then everything changed. Now I've changed. But I don't know if I can change that fast—or that much."

Steven held her close; she could feel his heart thudding against her own.

"Rachel, I think I love you. No, I'm sure I do, and "love" is a word I don't take lightly. I want to be with you. Maybe we can change together, grow together." She heard the smile in his voice. "We're going to take a lesson from Mother Nature and her divi-divis—they bend with the prevailing wind. They bend so they won't break."

Rachel swung around and reached for him, slipping her arms around his neck. "Steven . . . you talk too much. Why don't you just shut up and kiss me?"

"What a dirty trick. That's a very underhanded way to win an argument." He slid down beneath the sheet and tossed it aside. She wouldn't need it anymore; his body covered hers, and she was quite warm enough.

* * *

The compact car headed down the two-lane blacktop toward Willemstad. "I wasn't looking forward to this day, not until now," Rachel murmured, moving her hand up and down Steven's thigh as he expertly shifted gears.

"Watch it, or we'll have a divi-divi for a memorial. No, no, you don't have to *stop*, just exercise some restraint." He reached over and ruffled her hair, gently touching her cheek before he put his hand back on the wheel. "It's just as well I won't be flying home until next week. I know you'll need some time to talk to your children. Do you think there'll be a problem? Are you sure you don't want me there with you?"

Rachel leaned over and kissed his cheek. "No dear, I don't think there'll be any trouble. Oh, they'll probably want to check your credentials, make sure their dotty old mother hasn't handed the family jewels to a nefarious fortune hunter or a white slaver. 'Poor innocent old Mom.' Boy, I can hear them now!"

Steven's chuckle was wicked. "I could tell them a few things about 'poor innocent old Mom'!"

She put her head on his shoulder, her hand still touching his leg. "They're really pretty good kids—most of the time. Spoiled, I suppose. And selfish, the way the young always are. Not able to even imagine what their parents are thinking or feeling, just slotting us into their convenient little pigeonholes. But I think you'll like them. I *know* they'll like you!" They have to. Dear God, please . . . But in the end she knew it wouldn't matter; they had their own lives and futures to take care of. She and Steven would take care of each other.

"I'll feel bad, saying good-by to the Gellers. I don't know if this—us—would have happened without them. They've done so much for me."

"For us," Steven corrected her. He sat back, hands resting loosely on the steering wheel. "I was so bitter, and angry and *scared,* when Bev first got sick. We both were, but"—he gave her a wry smile—"it's impossible to stay that way when you're with the Gellers any length of time. Still, there were things I couldn't say even to my oldest friends. They were Bev's friends, too, and it would have seemed like a betrayal. I was always trying so hard to keep her spirits up. With Benjamin, at least I could take off the mask. Later, of course, she got worse, and he was my rock. So, when she died, it was just natural to come down here after the week of *shiva.*"

"I came here to hide, but they just wouldn't let me." He smiled again, and the cheerful optimism reappeared. "Don't let them fool you, those two gentle souls are the stubbornest pair on the face of the earth."

"I believe it. I have a feeling I wouldn't have gotten off this island if you and I hadn't, uh, if we hadn't . . ." She blushed, "Well, you know."

478

"Yeah, I know. And so will everyone else if you look like that." He leaned over and kissed her quickly on a reddened cheek. "And so what? They'll be as happy for us as we are. Nobody can be more of a realist than a rabbi. Over the years he's seen and heard more than we could begin to realize. I don't think anything would shock Benjamin. But he helps, he doesn't judge. So," he grinned at her, "blush away!"

The small group of people stood once more before the menorah, but this night all its branches held candles ready to catch the flame in Joshua's small hand. His grandfather grasped him with one arm, and in his other hand was a glass of wine.

"The joy of life is like this flame; it warms us, and it can light the way ahead. And like the miracle we celebrate on this festival of light, that joy has no limit. It is the same as that first miracle. Even though there did not seem to be enough oil to last, each day the flame continued to burn, in defiance of the pessimists and what they thought was truth. The miracle of Hanukkah promises renewal, and the light does not die. Each day it regenerates itself, even as we kindle new flames each night to banish the darkness." He and Devorah both looked down the table at Rachel and Steven, and smiled.

"But God's miracle requires our participation.

It is we who must take that first step, we who must strike the flame to light the candles. And, despite pessimism and pain, we continue to strike that match, draw that flame. Perhaps *that* is the miracle. We do not give up on life." He smiled brilliantly at the happy group around the crowded table and raised his glass.

Rachel and Steven looked at each other, and for that moment no one else in the room existed for either of them. Their eyes promised each other love and life, and looked into a future they would share together. Rachel marveled at the miraculous change that had overtaken her in this short eight days span, and at the beautiful loving man beside her who had brought her to this moment . . . and at all the moments that lay before them. She could hardly wait until they were alone, until she could put her arms around him, feel his strength and heat, kiss him and tell him in all ways of the love she felt for him. But for now she put her hand over his, and together which was holding a wine glass, and they sipped from the glass together as Rabbi Geller made his toast.

"To Rachel, to Steven . . . to life!"

Joan Shapiro, who lives in Bloomfield Hills, Michigan, is the author of *HELLO, LOVE*—a spring 1993 TO LOVE AGAIN. Look for her new novel in July of 1994. Write her c/o Zebra.